THE EIGHTH GUARDIAN

ANNUM GUARD 1

MEREDITH McCARDLE

SKYSCAPE

SKYSCAPE

Published by Skyscape, New York

www.apub.com

Amazon, the Amazon logo, and Skyscape are trademarks of Amazon.com, Inc., or its affiliates.

ISBN-13: 9781477847138 (hardcover)
ISBN-10: 1477847138 (hardcover)
ISBN-13: 9781477847664 (paperback)
ISBN-10: 1477847669 (paperback)

Book design by Susan Gerber and Katrina Damkoehler

Printed in the United States of America

For Scott, for always

CHAPTER 1

The man in the green tie has been watching me all day. It's weird. Both the tie and the watching. His tie is green—not the crimson or navy that seems to be the uniform color for these guys, but green. And he has no business watching me like this. I'm tired. Sweaty. My body has been through hell, and it's not over yet.

I failed the first challenge. The man should have stopped watching me then.

They hung me by my ankles and plunged me headfirst into a swimming pool chilled to a hypothermic forty degrees. The lock on the chain around my ankles had a code. An alphanumeric code that they flashed in Morse code with the pool light. I had fifteen seconds under the water to figure it out before they'd bring me up for a ten-second break, then dunk me right back under.

But the water was cold, too cold, and every vein in my body exploded when I hit it. Water rushed up my nose, and I sputtered and choked. I whipped my head around and couldn't even find the pool light. They brought me up, and the ten seconds passed before I could process it. They plunged me back down, and water filled my throat. I coughed and choked and breathed in more, feeling the vomit rise.

I tapped out as soon as they brought me up.

The men and women evaluating me shook their heads. Most of them packed up and said they'd seen enough. But the man in the green tie kept watching me as I stood there, soaked to the bone, shivering under a towel, collapsing under the weight of my failure. His eyes only left me once, when he pulled out a small, worn Moleskine notebook and scribbled something.

His eyes should have left me earlier. I failed.

He was the only one who showed up for my second challenge. Two men grabbed me from behind. They were shouting at me in a foreign language. I think it might have been Yoruba, but I'm not sure. They threw me into a metal chair in a windowless detention room and left. The door locked behind them.

I didn't think, didn't breathe. I hopped up on the chair, pulled the emergency sprinkler, and ripped down the plastic halogen light fixture. An alarm blared as cold jets of water rained down on me in the dark room. But I didn't let it faze me. I waited by the door, and the second it opened, I looped the electrical wiring around my captor's neck. He submitted, and I trotted out of there in under thirty seconds.

Green Tie nodded his head, made a note in his notebook, and walked away.

Now I'm standing on a wooden platform twenty feet in the air. I'm blindfolded.

"Turn around," a voice commands.

I obey, and the blindfold disappears from my face. I'm looking over the hills of western Massachusetts. The leaves are orange and yellow and red, creating swirling patterns of color that make my eyes dance. I have no idea what time it is. None. It's light out, but the gray sky is blanketed with clouds, so I can't make out the sun's position. It could be seven in the morning. It could be three in the afternoon. I've been awake for at least twenty-four hours now.

"Look down."

I do. There's a plywood maze below me. It goes in and out of focus, the twists and turns fusing together into one giant mess of veneer. I close my eyes to give them a precious second's rest. When my eyes open, the maze stands still. It's probably fifty yards by fifty yards. Massive. I locate the entrance. I locate the exit.

"Five more seconds," the man standing next to me says.

My eyes scan the maze, darting from entrance to exit, back over all the turns. There are lefts and rights and a series of rectangular spirals inside the maze. It's easy. Too easy.

"Done," the man says, and I've got it. A left. Three rights. Two lefts, then two rights. Three lefts. One right to the exit.

But there's a sinking feeling in my stomach. This is way too simple.

I jog down the steps and over to the woman holding a stopwatch at the start of the maze. She looks at the clipboard she's holding, marks a notch, then looks up at me.

"Ready?" she asks in a flat voice. No compassion. Typical.

"Yes," I tell her as I tighten my ponytail. Even though that's not really true. I just want this to be over with; that's the truth.

I take a breath and notice that a crowd has formed to watch.

Looks like everyone who gave up on me after the first challenge is back. They're so fickle. It almost makes me want to smile, but then I glance over and see that man in the green tie staring at me again with those same intense eyes. I'm being scrutinized, evaluated like a real candidate. My stomach flips over.

"Go," the woman says, pressing down on the stopwatch. I take a breath and run forward into the maze.

A few steps and I dart left. All the way to the end, then a right. There are two turns I could take before that, but I run past both of them. They're dead ends. I hit the last right and take it, then keep running.

There's nothing in my way. No obstacles. This can't be right. There has to be something. I make the next right and—

I gasp as a man dressed from head to toe in black jumps in front of me. His left hand grabs the collar of my shirt, and his right hand presses the tip of a knife blade up to my chin.

"Gotcha," he says.

I don't make eye contact. You never make eye contact. I stare into his sternum and look at his hand position. Then I lean back before he has a chance to react. My left hand grabs his right wrist, and I loop my elbow through his, forcing him to swing the knife down. I step back with my left foot, pivot, and grab the knife out of his hand.

That took all of about two seconds.

"Sorry, what were you saying?" I ask.

The man raises his eyebrows, then lifts his hands in submission and jogs toward the start of the maze. Away from me.

Only then do I breathe. I look down at my own hand. It's shaking.

I take the knife with me as I make my third right, then a quick left. I need to make another left here somewhere, I think. I repeat the rest of the pattern in my head.

Two lefts, then two rights. Three lefts. One right to the exit.

I need to make a left, but when? There are so many. There's one right in front of me, but it feels wrong. I think I'm supposed to go to the next left. Or the one after that? I can't get lost in this thing. I can't. *Focus!*

I close my eyes and let the maze appear in my head. I'm supposed to take the second left. I think.

I turn. The path leads me down a long plywood corridor, and this has to be correct. Yes, it has to. One right, then another quick right. I keep the knife held high, protecting my face. I must be more than halfway through the maze. I have to run into someone else soon. I have to—

Click.

I round to the left, and there's a gun in my face. A woman is holding it. She's about my height and all muscle. She looks younger than me, but I know she has to be at least eighteen.

"Drop the knife," she tells me.

"Or what? You're going to shoot me?"

"Yep," she says.

I look at the gun. It's a black assault rifle, standard issue. Just like the ones they make us shoot here, but with a key difference.

"That's a paintball gun," I say.

The woman doesn't blink. "Ever been shot with one of these at close range?"

I have. It stings like a bitch and leaves a purple welt that doesn't fade for at least two weeks.

"Plus," the woman says, "I shoot you, you fail. Now drop the knife."

I grunt in disgust as I toss the knife behind me. It clatters as the handle hits the plywood floor. And then I stand there with my hands at my sides, waiting. Waiting for the cue.

"Hands up," the woman says.

And there it is.

I raise my hands and go right for the gun. I jerk it up, then twist it down so it's hanging by the woman's side. Disarming is a really simple skill. You redirect the assailant, control the weapon down, attack the assailant, then finally take away the weapon, which usually involves broken fingers. I did steps one and two, but I really don't think I'm supposed to punch this woman in the face or break any bones. So I go for an easy elbow strike and let the woman deflect it.

She drops the gun into my hands, steps back, and raises her hands. "Well done," she says. She nods toward the exit of the maze.

I fling the gun over my shoulder and run. Adrenaline courses through my veins. I round to the left. I'm almost there. I take the last left I can into a long corridor. There are a number of lefts in this corridor, but I race past all of them.

Right. The way out is a right.

I see it ahead. I sprint down the corridor. My footsteps pound against the wood, making a slapping sound. I'm almost there. One more right, and I'm—

My arms fly out to the sides, and I skid to a halt. The floor is different. The grain of the wood. The height. There's a large square section that was cut from a different sheet of plywood and is about a quarter inch higher. I peer around the corner. The exit is right there around the bend, but this section is so big and in such a tricky spot that I can't jump over it. I drop down to all fours to look at it. I bet it's one final obstacle. A bomb.

It is. It's a simple pressure-plate bomb. You step on it, you're done.

I take a breath of relief. I'm good at pressure-plate bombs. Most women are. There are two hooks on the side, and all you have to do is unlatch them; but you can't move the plate more than a quarter of an inch or it'll trip. Men usually use too much force. Macho BS or something that blows up in their faces. Literally.

I slip off the first hook, then shimmy myself backward to get the second. And then my hands start shaking. The exit is right there. I can see it. I want this to be over so badly. My hands jump so much that my teeth start chattering. I breathe and clench and unclench my fingers. I'm close. I can do this.

I suck in my breath and steady my hands as much as I can. My fingers grab the metal hook, and I let out my breath one second at a time as I press down on the hook.

It sticks.

No! I release it, and it snaps back up. My body shakes from my teeth to my knees. Why won't this day end? I blow out whatever air is still in my lungs. *Pull it together.* I press down on the hook, just barely, then wiggle it to the side. It gives way, and the plates are disarmed.

I think.

I stand up and take three jumps to get the blood pumping. So close. And there's only one way out. I leap onto the bomb.

Nothing happens.

I exhale. *I did it!* Not that they'd actually blow me up or anything, but I'm sure there would be consequences of some sort if I didn't diffuse it correctly.

The exit is only a few feet in front of me; and I hurl myself forward, out of the maze, and onto the ground. A gong sounds.

I'm lying in the dirt, panting and trembling, when the woman with the stopwatch appears over me. "Seven minutes, four point three-eight seconds," she says.

I push myself to a seated position. I have no idea whether that's a good time or the worst time ever recorded. My gallery is there. Most of them have already turned away and are walking back toward campus. A few stragglers are hunched over clipboards. But that man is staring at me. Again. Making a note in his Moleskine.

I look away and get to my feet. Every muscle in my body protests. I would kill for a hot bath and my bed right now.

"You'll be escorted back to campus," the woman with the stopwatch says. Like all of the other test proctors who showed up on campus yesterday—or is it two days ago now?—I've never seen her before in my life. But in this moment I hate her.

I can't believe I have to do this again next year.

My escort arrives. I know her. Katia Britanova. She's a sophomore who lives in my dorm, on the floor below. She has an impossibly large array of Hello Kitty crap, although that pales in comparison to her Bowie knife collection.

"How was it?" Katia whispers as we start the long walk back to campus.

I shake my head at her. My left foot makes contact with the pavement, and soreness races up my body. My right leg makes contact with the pavement and wobbles. Katia hooks her arm under my armpit and steadies me.

"Is he done?" I ask her.

"I'm not really allowed to talk about—"

"Katia, come on. Is he done?"

Katia nods her head. "Finished about an hour ago."

We trudge on in silence. Testing Day is over for me. Until next year. Dear God, help me. I have to do this again.

I really shouldn't complain. I've known this was coming since I was fourteen, ever since I got a letter congratulating me on my acceptance to the Peel Academy, which was surprising considering I'd never applied. Or had even heard of it.

But my mom had. After the letter arrived, she locked herself in the bathroom and cried for three days straight. That's not an exaggeration. She's been known to do that. Plates of food pile up at the door. The phone rings for hours. Begging is pointless. Bargaining goes unanswered. Worry turns to anger, sours to contempt.

When a trustee of the school showed up a week later, dressed in a red skirt suit with an American flag pinned to her lapel, she whispered two magical words that made the decision easy for me: legal emancipation. I didn't care who she was or what the school taught at that point. All that mattered was that it was my ticket out of Vermont. And then the woman told me that the school was run by the government and was by invitation only for a select group of students whose bloodlines looked promising, and I *knew*.

I was chosen because of my dad.

Katia and I pass through the iron gates leading to the main part of campus. She walks me past the building that houses science labs, past one of the dorms, past the administration building, and into the dining hall. Another sophomore, Blake Sikorski, stands guard at the door. He checks my name off a list pinned to a clipboard and nods his head toward the hall. Katia gives my shoulder a squeeze and trots down the stairs.

The dining hall is littered with sleeping bodies. Juniors and seniors lie around the room like fallen dominoes, their bodies twisted and broken into sleeping positions that can't be comfortable at all. But when you've been awake for as long as we have and been through what we have, comfort is an afterthought.

I spot Abe in the back corner, sitting with his back against the wall. He's awake but staring straight ahead like a zombie. My heart flutters. He didn't have to stay awake for me. But of course he did.

He doesn't hear me until I'm a few feet in front of him. His head turns, recognition dawns, and his mouth twitches upward.

"I'd get up, but—"

"Don't bother," I say as my legs buckle, and I fall to the floor beside him. "Holy cornflakes, that sucked."

Abe chuckles. "What, no expletives?"

"I'm too tired." I fold my hands over my chest and close my eyes. Abe hates swearing. Always has. He says it's a sign of a small vocabulary. But I grew up in a house where four-letter words were pretty much standard protocol, so Abe's used to hearing them from me.

Except now. I'm not kidding about the too-tired thing.

I crack open one eye and glance at the clock on the wall. A few minutes until four in the afternoon. So that makes thirty-four hours that I've been awake.

Peel's graduation works a bit differently from most other schools. We don't have caps and gowns; we don't have long ceremonies and boring speeches. No, we have Testing Day. Once a year, a group of proctors arrives at the school without any warning whatsoever. It could be in September or it could be in May. Testing Day always starts at night, after a long, hard day of work, when you're tired and ready to unwind. Then—surprise!—the fun begins.

The first part is a twelve-hour written test that stretches through the wee hours of the morning. You're quizzed on physics, biology, history, geography, calculus, computer programming—you name it. There are also ethics questions. Stuff like: You're locked in a room with a known terrorist who has planted a bomb somewhere in Washington DC that is set to explode in thirty minutes. You have a drill, a pair of needle-nose pliers, and a gallon-size bucket of water. What do you do? (Here's a hint: The correct answer involves none of those things.)

After that come the physical challenges. They're never the same, no matter how many years you go back. Every junior and senior at Peel is tested, although I don't know why they bother to test the juniors. No one has graduated as a junior in more than thirty years.

Still, I can't ignore the sinking feeling in my stomach as I think of the man in the green tie who watched me so intently today. His piercing eyes flood my memory and make me shudder.

"I couldn't finish the first challenge," I confess as I slide my head into that nook of Abe's arm, an old, familiar spot.

"That's fine," he assures me. "This is just a warm-up, remember? We get to do this again next year."

"I don't think there's going to be a next year for me."

Abe's eyes are closed, but he opens one and gives me the side-eye with it. "Of course there is. We're juniors."

"There was this man," I say. "He was watching me all day."

Abe opens the other eye. "There were a bunch of people watching us."

"Not like this. This man was . . . intense. Creepy, even."

"Then he's probably CIA," Abe says. "They're all like that."

I don't say anything. I want to believe him. I mean, probably ninety percent of us go on to join the CIA. We're drafted at eighteen, and I have to admit, it's a pretty sweet deal. They move us to Langley, and we go to Georgetown on their dime. But weekends aren't spent binge drinking at frat parties or cramming for finals at the library. Weekends are spent in Mumbai or Mosul or Manila, breaking into banks or climbing into bedroom windows. Well, after six brutal months of additional training and next to no sleep, that is.

We all assume that's our future. Abe and I have always assumed it. We've been together for more than two years now, ever since the first week of freshman year, and we've been planning our next steps together for probably that long, too. Abe's sure he's going to be a technical intelligence officer in the science and technology arm (I'm dating a computer-engineering-stuff-that-makes-my-head-hurt genius), while I'll be an operations officer in clandestine services. It'll mean a lot of time apart, since he'll be based in DC and I'll be all over the world, but Abe's even gone so far as to scout out the best areas in the capital for us to get an apartment to serve as our home base. You know, someday. (I'm also dating a poster boy for type-A personalities.)

"Hey," he whispers, gently turning my head to look at him. "Stop worrying. You're not graduating."

"But—"

"One word," Abe interrupts. "Tyler Fertig."

"That's two words."

"Tyler. Fertig," Abe repeats. "If he didn't graduate as a junior, you're not going to."

I nod my head. He's right. Of course he's right. Two years ago, Tyler Fertig was a junior when we were freshmen. Pardon my French, Abe, but Tyler Fertig rocked the shit out of Testing Day like no one ever had before. He only missed one question on the written test—*one*—and outscored every single senior during the physical challenges. And yet at the banquet that night, where the names of the graduating students are called and blissful boys and girls trot to the stage to be handed an envelope containing an assignment, Tyler's name was skipped. He was sitting at the next table over from me, and I can still picture his reaction. Shock, denial, then anger. He got up, pushed his plate across the table, and stormed out of the room. I never understood why he was so angry, but I guess I get it now. Testing Day sucks. He must have thought that for sure he wouldn't have to do it again.

Abe's right. I'm not graduating.

Tonight I'm going to sleep in my own bed, and tomorrow we'll have Professor Kopelman's International Relations class waiting for us. The fall is creeping to a close, and the holidays will be here before we know it. We'll do Thanksgiving with my mom, Hanukkah with Abe's family, then put in another quick appearance with my mom at Christmas. Just like last year. Just like next year.

I nestle into Abe's arm a little more, and he rolls to the side and envelops me.

"I missed you today. I kept wishing you were there with me," he whispers in my ear before he kisses my earlobe.

"I have to smell like a dead cat."

He laughs and kisses my neck.

"We're not alone," I whisper, though I wriggle myself closer to him.

"We're in a room full of hibernating bears."

"I kinda wish I was one of them right now."

Abe's fingers interlace through mine. "I could get behind that plan." He goes still and gets very quiet. But then a few moments later, in a voice barely more than a whisper, he says, "Love you, Mandy Girl."

I close my eyes. "I love you too, Abey Baby."

And then I'm out.

CHAPTER 2

I'm woken by a high-pitched whistle screaming into my ears. I open the corner of one eye, and it protests in pain as light rushes in. I immediately close it. I haven't slept long; that much is clear. Beside me, Abe grumbles.

"You have to be kidding, right?" He slowly pushes himself up. "Ugh, six o'clock?"

"A.m. or p.m.?" I ask. My body already knows the answer.

"P.m.," Abe confirms.

"Juniors and seniors!" a voice booms. I force myself to open my eyes and sit up, then lean into Abe for support. Headmaster Vaughn stands at the front of the dining hall, hands on his hips. "Testing Day is at an end, and decisions have been made. You all have one hour to shower, change, and get back here for the banquet."

People groan and grunt as they stand up. Abe stands first, then puts out his hands to help pull me up.

"I wish we didn't have to go to this stupid banquet." Abe holds open the door for me. A gush of crisp fall air cuts right through me, and I hunch my shoulders and shiver.

"Don't you want to see who goes where?" I ask. We take the shortcut past the science building to the quad.

"What's the point? I think I could tell you where every senior is going. Look there"—he points to Regina Browne as she pulls open the door to her dorm hall—"CIA. And there"—Steven DiFazio, entering another hall—"CIA. Oh, and look over there"—Becca Stein, Jacob Wu, and Maria Bazan—"CIA, CIA, CIA."

"And what about this girl?" I point to myself.

"CIA," Abe says with a smile. "But not for another year." We've stopped in front of Archer Hall, my dorm.

"Are you sure?"

Abe raises an eyebrow. "Do you remember what Samuels said our very first day of Practical Studies ever?"

I do. We had been lined up against the wall, and Professor Samuels had gone up and down the line, critiquing our appearances—the way we looked—and making judgments based on them. That would not fly at any other school except for Peel.

Samuels got to me, and his face had lit up in a smile. "You, my dear," he'd said, "are what I like to call ethnically ambiguous. The CIA will snap you right up in four years for sure." And then he'd moved down the line.

I was confused at first—and a little insulted, if I'm being honest—but the more time I spent doing mock missions in class, the more I realized that maybe there was some truth to what Samuels had said. I inherited most of my features from my mother, who is Romanian and Moroccan by way of Spain (and then Brooklyn). I have her thick, wavy, deep-brown hair, her thin nose, her strong cheekbones, and her medium skin tone. I was surprised to discover that with the right clothing and a little bit of makeup, I could pass for a number of different ethnicities.

I guess what Professor Samuels said all those years ago is true. The CIA is my future.

But I'm not asking Abe whether he thinks I'm CIA. I'm asking if he's sure it will be next year. I don't press him for another answer. But the green tie lingers in my mind.

Abe bends down and plants a kiss on my forehead, then stands up. "You do kind of stink."

I playfully push him away. "Yeah, well, you're no Abercrombie store yourself." He flashes me another smile, then trots off toward Mace Hall, his dorm on the opposite side of the quad. I watch him jog for a few seconds before I push open the door. Someone's got a fire going in the common room. It crackles and pops, and a couple of junior girls have collapsed into the armchairs in front of it. I don't blame them. It's so warm and inviting in the common room. But I also don't want to be the one still stuck in line for the shower when the hot water runs out.

I start up the stairs, looking at my mud-stained sneakers, and I don't realize someone's coming down until we've collided.

"Gah! Sorry!" I say, looking up. It's Katia.

"Oh, hey," she says, then immediately looks away, ducks her shoulders, and pushes past me.

I grab on to her arm. Something's wrong. Something's very wrong. Katia's no shrinking violet. She's gorgeous, with this (dyed) platinum-blond hair that hangs to her waist and legs that are four miles long. She's one of the best students at Peel when it comes to hand-to-hand combat. No one is quicker with a knife. And she totally knows it. Katia doesn't walk anywhere. She *struts*. She's always the life of the party, always the friendly ear. She's not the girl who ducks her head and tries to stay hidden. Not by a mile.

"What's going on?" I ask her.

"Nothing," she says. I know it's a lie because she doesn't try to loosen my grip on her arm. And she could. She could probably flip me over the banister this second.

"Katia, what's going on?"

She lets out the softest sigh. "I don't know." I give her my toughest, I-haven't-slept-in-forever-so-just-tell-me-already face. "Honestly. I don't. I do know that there was a man who followed Headmaster Vaughn back to his office after Testing Day ended. I was in the administration building helping sort files. He said your name twice, but I couldn't hear what they were talking about. Then they shut the door."

"And you don't know anything else?"

"No. Now can you let go of my arm so I don't have to break your fingers?"

I drop Katia's arm. I hadn't realized I'd been holding on to her so tightly. There are four red, finger-size welts on her bicep. "Sorry," I mumble.

Katia's halfway across the hall.

"Katia!" I call.

She turns her head.

"What color was his tie?"

Katia scrunches her nose. "Vaughn's?"

I have to restrain myself from groaning. "No, the other man."

"Oh." She thinks. "I'm not sure."

"Please try to remember. I mean, it's not like they teach us superspecial skills of observation here or anything."

Katia cracks the smallest smile and closes her eyes. She opens them a few moments later. "Green. I'm almost positive it was green."

An invisible fist punches me in the gut. "Thanks," I mutter. My heart sinks lower with each step I take up the stairs. As I stand in the shower and let the warm water spill over me, I think about what Abe said. And I think about Tyler Fertig. They're not going to pick me tonight. They're not.

But the sinking feeling doesn't wash away with the dirt and grime.

I find Abe in the dining hall, sitting at our usual table. He tilts his head at the seat he's saved me, and as I glide over to it, I look at Abe. *Really* look at him. He's not what you would call conventionally handsome, with deep-set eyes, crooked teeth, and a nose that's been broken so many times the doctors have given up. But to me he's the most beautiful guy in the world.

I slip into my seat just as Headmaster Vaughn takes the stage. Salads are already on the tables.

Vaughn clears his throat and straightens his tie. His silver hair doesn't budge as he leans toward the microphone. "A very talented, highly gifted group of individuals is going to graduate tonight."

Individuals. He said individuals. Not seniors. I rack my brain, trying to remember if he said *individuals* or *seniors* last year.

"There were some choices made this year that surprised even me."

Surprises? Like . . . a junior being chosen? Oh no. Oh no oh no oh no. I push the salad away and turn to Abe.

"I love you," I whisper.

He tilts his head to me but doesn't turn it. "Yeah, I love you, too."

Headmaster Vaughn continues. "But before we get to the specific assignments made this year, I invite you all to feast." He opens his arms, and the kitchen staff carries out trays of silver-domed plates.

"Will you wait for me?" My words are barely audible.

Abe turns his head this time. "What are you talking about? Wait for you for what?"

A waiter lifts the dome off a plate of pot roast and sets it before me, but I push it back. It clinks into my untouched salad plate.

"If I graduate tonight. Will you wait for me?"

Abe shakes his head. "Tyler Fertig," he reminds me.

"Abey, I've got this really funny feeling. It's unnerving."

Abe puts down his fork and squeezes my hand. "Hey," he says in the calm, reassuring voice I know so well, "it's Testing Day. It's meant to unnerve you. But I guarantee you that this banquet is going to be over in an hour, and you'll be sleeping in your own bed tonight."

I raise an eyebrow at him. "You guarantee it?"

"Yep." He looks so sure, so confident. I don't have the heart to tell him his pep talk did nothing to settle my nerves. So instead I smile.

Abe pulls back his hand and stabs a potato with his fork before shoving it into his mouth. Then he turns to Aaron Zimmer on his left and jumps into a conversation about the water challenge this morning.

I stare at my plate of food. I'm not hungry. I haven't eaten since dinner the night before, but I can't stomach the idea of food. I try to nibble on a carrot, then set it down. I'm going to throw up.

Headmaster Vaughn takes the stage again after the dinner plates have been cleared and coffee and cheesecake are being set on the tables.

"Congratulations to you all. Those of you graduating tonight have seen the ceremony before."

I press my legs together and start bouncing on my toes. His words are careful. He's deliberately not saying *seniors*.

"Assignments are strictly confidential"—though it's pretty easy to guess—"so when I call your name, I will hand you an envelope, which you will read once you have proceeded to the back room. Look around, students, and say your good-byes now, because this is the last time many of you will be in this room."

Look around, *students*. I bend over and rest my elbows on my thighs. My legs bounce higher.

Abe puts his hand on my back, then leans over next to me. "Are you all right?" There's genuine concern in his voice.

I shake my head.

"Matthew Alder," the headmaster calls. A boy from a few tables over gets up and walks to the stage as the crowd applauds.

"Hey," Abe whispers, "it's fine. I promise."

It's not fine.

Headmaster Vaughn goes through rest of the *A*s, then the

*B*s. Our school isn't that big, so he's flying through the alphabet. Once he gets to the *M*s, I can't breathe.

"Alyssa Morrison." I hear a chair scrape back somewhere but can't look.

"Portia Nichols." Closer. We're getting closer.

"Samita Nori." And my heart stands still. Time slows to a halt. I suck in my breath. Here it goes. I have to be next. *Please,* I beg, *please no.* I'm not ready to say good-bye to Abe. Not yet. Not today.

I look at Vaughn, willing him to skip to the *P*s. Vaughn's face goes very still, and he places two hands on the podium.

He's pausing.

And then he opens his mouth.

"Amanda Obermann."

No one claps. But just about everyone gasps. I feel every head in the room turn to look at me. The plates on the table swirl together in front of me, a mess of coffee and cheesecake. How is this happening? *Why* is this happening? I failed the water challenge. I must have finished in the middle of the pack. Why why WHY?

Headmaster Vaughn clears his throat into the microphone. I don't make eye contact with him, but I don't have to. I can feel him staring at me. I look over at Abe. His mouth has fallen open, and his eyes are moist. He reaches over and squeezes my left hand.

"Amanda Obermann," the headmaster repeats with firmness.

I push back my chair and stand. The sound of the chair scraping against the floor echoes throughout the stunned room.

"I'll wait for you," Abe gasps. "And you wait for me. It's just a year. Just a year."

I squeeze his hand back. "Just a year," I whisper. Then I pull away and walk toward the stage. My legs trudge up the five steps and over to Headmaster Vaughn. His lips are pressed together in a smile as he hands me a plain white envelope with my name typed in the center. I take it and look out over my fellow classmates. They're all wearing the same expression of shocked silence. I have to look away.

Logic tells me I should be happy. I'm the youngest student to graduate in a generation. This is an honor. A privilege. But my heart wants to be back at the table next to Abe. Where I belong.

The headmaster gestures offstage to the door leading into a meeting room. The dining hall is spinning. I stare at the American flag pin the headmaster wears on his left lapel to find my bearings, then at the bald eagle pin on his right—although I'm so dizzy it looks more like a hawk with a bad perm right now. My legs move again, taking one step, then another, on their own because my head's not there. I glance back at Abe once more before I open the door. This is the last look I'm going to get for a year. He has his hand clenched into a fist over his heart, as if he's fighting to keep it inside his chest. I make the same gesture and open the door.

The room is empty save for one person. A man. *The* man who was watching me so intently before. His green tie stares at me.

"Who are you?" I ask.

The man draws himself up to his full height. He's tall and trim and intimidating as hell. He looks as if he could be a hit man or something. His light-brown hair is shaved down, though it's not short enough to hide the receding hairline creeping across his scalp. And even though he's wearing a suit, it's obvious that he's pretty ripped—not as bulky as a body builder, but enough to where you'd be stupid to try to pick a bar fight with him. I have no doubt he's trained in some sort of martial arts. I try to guess how old he is and decide he's probably around the age my dad would be if he was still alive.

For one brief second my heart pangs at the thought of my dad. I wish he was here with me. I could use a father at this moment.

"Open the envelope," the man says.

I look down at my name, then flip over the envelope to the back. It's sealed with red wax. There's a symbol in the wax, and I bring the envelope closer to my face to inspect it. It's an owl. But not a cartoony-looking owl. A scary owl. A hold-you-down-and-peck-your-eyes-out owl. I look up. The last time I checked, the CIA didn't use an owl as its symbol.

"Go on," the man says.

I slide my finger under the flap and break the seal. There's a single, folded sheet of paper inside. I flick it open, and my head pops back. It doesn't say Central Intelligence Agency. Not even Federal Bureau of Investigation. No, there in the middle, in fancy script that looks as if it was scratched on with an old-fashioned quill, it reads,

Annum Guard

"What the hell is Annum Guard?" I look up at him.

And then I gasp. The man is standing only a few inches in front of me now. He's holding a black cloth bag in his hands, and

I know what's about to happen. I drop the letter and raise my hands to fight, but I'm too slow. The bag goes over my head, and I inhale a faint, sweet smell with obvious chemical overtones.

Chloroform.

I kick.

I scream.

"No!"

I can't breathe.

I can't. . . .

CHAPTER 3

I open my eyes. Light swirls in front of me. Foggy shapes become clearer the more I stare. I'm lying down. There are fluorescent tubes lining the ceiling, each set to the maximum wattage. I drop my chin to my chest and squint. My mouth is dry. My head is pounding.

Where am I?

I try to lift my arms, but they won't budge. I'm strapped down. I turn my head to the side. There's a needle stuck in my arm, pumping blood into or out of me—I don't know which.

I gasp. I thrash on the gurney. This is wrong. This is all wrong. No government organization would do this to me, would it? I've been kidnapped. I've been taken by someone. I have to get out of here.

A man appears over me. He's changed his tie. It's red now.

"Hello, Iris," he says.

I go still. "My name is—"

"Iris," he repeats. "At least it is now."

"Who are you?"

"You can call me Alpha."

"Where am I?" I swear I can hear my heart thumping in my chest cavity.

"A room."

"Why?"

He clears his throat. "Routine physical."

Not likely. "Why did you take me?"

"You graduated, remember?" His voice is low, flat. "You're no longer a student, Iris. You work for the government now. You work for me."

The government. The piece of paper Headmaster Vaughn handed me. What did it say? My head is a helium balloon. I can't concentrate. I can barely see straight. But then it comes back to me.

"Annum Guard," I whisper.

"Exactly."

"I've never heard of it."

"That's because we're a secret."

A door opens behind me. I turn my head to look, but I can't turn far enough. All I see is the side wall.

"It's almost ready," a female voice says.

What's almost ready?

"Here," she says.

Here? What's here?

The door shuts, and the man who called himself Alpha

appears over me again. "I'm sorry for the restraints. They're for your own protection. You lost some blood, and we're replenishing it for you."

Lost some blood? How did I lose some blood? My heart flies into my throat, and I think I might throw up. My training is failing me. I'm supposed to be able to handle this. They taught us to keep our cool. But I can't. In this moment I can't.

Breathe, Amanda. Breathe.

"Tell me what's going on." My voice is raspy.

"I told you," the man says. "You're the newest member of Annum Guard." He's holding something in his hand. Something thin and metallic, like a pen, but I know it can't be a pen. He holds it to my right forearm, right below where the needle is pumping blood into my veins. "This might hurt."

I don't have time to brace myself or even voice a protest. The man punches it down, and pain erupts through the entire right side of my body. I scream. My body bucks up, fighting the leather straps holding down my arms and legs.

"Sorry," the man says as he pulls away.

"Let me out!" I scream. "Untie me! You can't keep me here!"

"I believe I can, and I'm going to. You belong to me now, remember?"

"No, I don't remember. I don't know anything."

"Annum Guard," the man says.

"I've never heard of it."

"No, I don't think you would have. Not many people outside of Annum Guard have, short of the president and the secretary of defense. We're a secret, Iris. We're the guardians of time."

The guardians of time?

The man takes a minute. His eyes flick to the wall, then back to me. "We have the ability of Chronometric Augmentation."

What the hell is he talking about? I thrash and kick against my bindings, but then he's above me again.

"You see, we project back in time and tweak the past to improve the present."

"That's ridiculous," I practically spit. "No one can travel—project—whatever the hell you call it—back in time. It's physically impossible."

"Oh, but it's not. You'll see."

I suck in my breath. "I'm going to give you ten seconds to let me out of here or else—"

"What?" the man interrupts. "Just what do you plan to do? Scream? Go ahead. But I think I've already proven that you're stuck here until I let you out." His fingers wrap around one of the leather straps holding down my ankles, and he tugs it for good measure.

"Who are you?" I hear my voice starting to crack. Not good. I need to pull it together.

"I've already told you that. You can call me Alpha. I run Annum Guard. We project back in time to—"

"Stop lying to me! How did you get me out of the school? There are cameras and gates everywhere. You couldn't have just drugged me and carried me out."

"Unless I had the express permission of your headmaster," Alpha says. "Which I received the second I told him I had chosen you to graduate and join Annum Guard. Then you became mine."

"What did you put in my arm?"

"A tracker. I need to know your location at all times."

A tracker. There is a tracker in my arm. My head spins as I try to process this, but then the door opens again. I don't bother to turn this time. I can't see behind me.

"It's ready," the same female voice says.

What's ready? My heart is pounding.

Alpha clears his throat. "Thank you." A few seconds later he appears over me, holding something. He opens his hand and brings a round bronze pendant of some sort toward my face. I don't flinch. But then the pendant stops, an inch or so above my nose, and I can finally see it. It's a pendant on a chain. A necklace. As it swings back and forth in front of my face, I focus on it. It has an owl etched into it. The same owl that was on the wax seal back at school.

"What is that?" It comes out as a whisper.

"This is what gives us the ability to project back in time."

"It's a necklace."

"Very good. No one can ever say you lack intelligence." Is he mocking me?

"Are you telling me that a necklace gives human beings the ability to travel back in time?"

Alpha nods.

"And you expect me to believe that?"

"I do. But not just any human beings, Iris, only those who have been chosen. And you have been chosen."

"Why?"

"Does it matter?"

"Yes." I don't believe him. He's insane. People can't travel back in time. That's a physical impossibility. I mean, I'm not a physics genius or anything, but *you can't do that*. This man has stolen me for some reason, and I need to figure out why.

"Because I recognized qualities you exhibited during Testing Day, qualities that will make you a good fit with Annum Guard."

"I don't understand," I say. "I didn't finish the water challenge."

"That doesn't matter to me."

He's giving me nothing to go on here. Absolutely nothing.

"And what about the other challenges?" I ask.

"You showed intelligence in the detention challenge. Most of your classmates sat there until the men came back and then tried to overpower them. You didn't even consider that as an option. You were proactive. I didn't care about the final challenge after that."

His tone hasn't wavered once, and his answer is intentionally vague. Damn, he's good. He isn't giving anything away.

"Are you ready for me to prove to you that time travel exists?" he asks.

I don't respond for a few seconds. Things are changing. He's going to untie me. I know the door is behind me and that he's the only person in this room. Alpha's bigger than me, but I'll have the element of surprise. I can do this. One step at a time. First I get out of this room. Then out of the building. Then back to Peel. Back to Abe.

"Sure," I say, my voice slow.

Alpha nods his head once. He unties my hands, and I leave them by my side. No use wasting energy when my legs are still tied to the table. He fiddles with the left strap, then the right. Here we go.

I spring off the table and launch myself at Alpha, ready to attack, but he's quicker. He anticipated this. Shit. I don't have time to respond. All I know is that my hands are behind my back, and Alpha has slammed me to the floor. The side of my face rests against the cool concrete. Alpha's knee is pressing into my back, between my shoulder blades. I can't move.

"Honestly now," he says. "You didn't think that move was a little obvious? That's disappointing. I thought we were going to be able to do this the easy way, but I guess not." There's a metal *click-click* as a pair of handcuffs are slapped onto my wrists.

Alpha pulls me up. He marches me forward, out through the doorway and into a blindingly white hallway. I have to squint because the fluorescent bulbs overhead make my eyes water. The walls are white and the floor is white, which only magnifies the light. I feel as if I'm stumbling around inside a solar flare.

Alpha leads me to the end of the hallway. There's a door straight ahead and a girl standing outside of it. She can't be much older than me. She has straight hair that falls to her shoulders in a bob. And it's purple. Bright purple. It really pops against her light-brown skin. There's a gold-plated plaque hanging above the door. It reads:

ENHANCEMENT, NOT ALTERATION

"Here." The girl holds out a plain black knapsack to Alpha. He takes it. I recognize her voice as the one from the room before. I think back to my training. *See everything.* I try to take in her voice, the smell of this hallway, the lighting, *Enhancement, Not Alteration.* My eyes scan the walls for identifying marks. But there are none. And it's all happening too fast.

THE EIGHTH GUARDIAN

Alpha lets go of me with one hand and slips the necklace around my neck. The owl pendant falls to my chest with a thump. My heart rate picks up. This is not good. Something is about to happen here. I need to make a break for it now.

But before I can move, Alpha is back on me. His elbow loops around my neck, and he's got me in a choke hold. He's had some serious combat training. I can't move. My heart is thumping so loudly that the two of them have to hear it.

"Why did you choose to attend Peel?" Alpha whispers behind me.

I'm starting to get dizzy. "What?"

"Why did you choose to attend Peel?" His voice is rougher. Firm.

I repeat Peel's mantra for him. "To learn the tools necessary to someday serve my country to the best of my ability." And that's true. But it's only half of it.

"Well, then." Alpha unlocks my handcuffs. "That day has come. Go forth and serve. Listen carefully, because I'm only going to tell you your mission once."

The girl with the purple hair flings open the door to reveal blackness. How is that possible? This hallway is so bright that I should be able to see something in there. But I can't see anything.

What is this place?

Alpha shoves the knapsack into my chest, and my fingers claw at it.

"There's only one rule," he says. "No communication. Do not talk, do not gesture, do not interact with anyone."

"What?" Don't interact with whom? What is he talking about?

Alpha comes around to the front of me and fiddles with the

necklace. I glance down as he pushes on a knob on the top. The owl pops open, revealing a watch face. It's a pocket watch. The necklace is a pocket watch. Alpha spins a dial to the right of the face, then fastens the watch shut. He takes hold of my chin and jerks it up.

"Your mission is simple. Get back. Leave from the place where you started."

"I don't understand," I say, but Alpha turns me around and pushes me through the doorway. I hear the door shut behind me, and suddenly the room is spinning so fast I don't know if I'm up or down. But I do know I'm going to vomit. My brain is crushing against my skull, flattening and trying to seep out through my ear canals. My hands fly to my ears, and I'm pretty sure I scream.

I'm falling.

Down.

Down.

Down.

I land. Hard, right on my backside, with a thud. My wrist braces my fall, and I cry out. I cradle my wrist in my hand, carefully moving it side to side. It hurts, but it's not broken.

I groan as I look up and take in my surroundings. And then my jaw drops open. I'm in . . . a closet? It's dark, but there's enough light coming under a door behind me to make it out. I grab the door handle and jiggle it, but it doesn't budge. It's locked. I shake it and yell, then pound on the door and throw myself against it. Nothing.

I turn around and lean my back on it, and that's when I see the other door. There's another door.

I grab the handle and turn it. The door swings open, revealing a cobblestone street lined with redbrick buildings. I step out into the empty street, and the door closes behind me.

"No!" I yell. Because the handle on this side doesn't turn. I'm locked out. Or in. I don't really know.

"Pardon me, are you all right?"

I look up. There's a young man stopped on the street, maybe twenty feet away. He's staring at me. He's insanely good-looking. Movie star good-looking. Big, bright eyes, a strong jawline, and chiseled cheekbones.

But I can barely even process that. Because he's wearing a tuxedo and a top hat. And he's sitting in the back of a horse-drawn carriage.

CHAPTER 4

This has to be a joke.

I open my mouth to say something, but then Alpha's voice is ringing in my ears. Not his actual voice—his warning.

Do not interact with anyone!

I have no idea what's going on, but one of the first rules they teach at Peel is never to act before you know your location. Have an exit strategy. I can't start breaking Alpha's artificial rules—or try to get away—until I at least know where I am. And so I turn and run as fast as I can down the alleyway, far away from the runway model in the carriage.

"Oy!" he yells after me. "I must ask that you stop! You're bleeding. Allow me to fetch a doctor."

I run faster. I'm dizzy. My elbow bangs into the side of a brick building. I'm sure that's bleeding now, too, but I keep going. I zip to the left at the first intersection and throw my back against a wall. I didn't run that far, but I can't catch my breath.

I bend forward and clutch at my chest, willing the air to stay in my lungs. I feel like a balloon stuck with a pin. All the air has exploded out of me.

I'm dizzy. I've slept for—what is it?—one hour in the past thirty-six? Maybe two? I have no idea what time it is now or how long I was out before I woke up strapped to the table. But none of that matters. I have to figure out where I am.

I straighten up. I'm in a sea of redbrick brownstones with black shutters and black wrought iron railings. They're to the left. They're to the right. They're on both sides of the street.

It's . . . charming. The sort of place I like to imagine myself living someday. For one brief second I picture myself clutching the metal railing and floating up the staircase, laughing at Abe as he follows behind me.

Stop it.

Stop thinking about Abe. That won't help.

And then one of the doors opens. The door to the corner house. A girl about my age steps out. She has an impossibly small waist, and her mauve dress with ivory lace trim sweeps across the floor as she turns to let an older man pass. Her father. Must be. He takes her hand, and she shrugs her shoulders to keep her shawl from falling. Her head whips back toward the door, as if she hears something, and her tendrils of light-brown spiral curls follow. Now she's laughing, turning back around, and—

She sees me.

I freeze.

But that doesn't change the fact that she sees me. She reaches out and points.

"What's that?" she asks her father. "That boy with the long hair. What is he wearing?"

I bristle at being called a boy, but only for a second. I push off the wall and run as fast as my legs will carry me back down the street I came from. I stop halfway and sink down so that I'm sitting with my back against a black door in the middle of a red-brick wall.

What the hell is going on? Seriously. I look down into my lap. That girl back in the courtyard thought I was a boy. It wouldn't be the first time. I have a boyish frame—no hips, no chest—and I put on muscle really easily. But my hair is long right now. I never get mistaken for a boy when I have long hair. It has to be because of my clothes. I'm wearing my old Peel uniform: a white shirt, a navy blazer, and a pair of khaki pants I chose over a skirt because it was a little chilly.

Pants.

That girl thinks I'm a boy because I'm wearing pants.

Who the hell mistakes a girl for a boy just because she's wearing pants? *What is this, the nineteenth century?*

A pit forms in my stomach. Of course not. That's a ridiculous thought. But I can't help letting myself think the obvious. That what Alpha said before was true. That he gave me the ability to travel back in time, and now I'm here—wherever this is—trapped in a different era.

Your mission is simple, Alpha's voice echoes in my head. *Get back. Leave from the place where you started.*

Could it be possible? Could I actually be in a different time?

No. No way. I'm being messed with. Alpha is trying to wear me down for some reason I haven't figured out yet. He wants something from me. This is an elaborate setup with a bunch of people in period costume meant to throw me off guard.

Well, that's not going to happen. All I have to do is determine where I am, and I'll be out of here so fast Alpha won't know what hit him.

I stand up, take a breath, and walk to the other end of the alleyway, to where the guy in the horse-drawn carriage was. Another horse clomps down the street in front of me, but I shake my head and ignore it. *Elaborate setup,* I repeat in my head.

I step out of the alley and immediately know where I am.

Boston.

I grew up in Vermont, but my mom would take me to the city to go shopping several times a year. Always in August to hit up Filene's Basement right before school started. Always in December to buy Christmas gifts and ice-skate in the Common. And always one Saturday in the spring, at the first kiss of warmer weather. My mom would want to ride the swan boats in the Public Garden, though she'd never say anything as we drifted across the water. She'd close her eyes and inhale and do that thing she does where she purses her lips together really tight because she's trying not to cry. And then I'd turn away and pretend to be looking at daffodils because my mom does that a lot and it never gets any easier to watch.

I can see the lake in the Public Garden from where I'm standing. It's to the right and down the hill. Boston Common is directly in front of me, and the huge dome of the Massachusetts State House is looming over me. But it's not gold like it usually is. It's only partly gold but mostly this dismal leaden-gray color. It almost looks like they're in the middle of gilding it.

That doesn't make any sense. It doesn't need to be regilded. At least I don't think it does.

There's a *clomp-clomp-clomp* sound getting louder. I look down the street and jump away as yet another horse-drawn carriage rides past. A small boy hangs out of the back.

"Mummy," he says. "Look at that boy in the funny pants. Why is his hair so long?"

A young mother gasps from inside the carriage and smacks her son's hand down.

"James, you're being impolite!" she scolds as the carriage rides away.

Every hair on my arm stands on end as I follow their carriage out of sight. Because there are more carriages. Dozens of them. And there are men and women walking by, giving me strange looks. The men have on top hats and suits, the women long, sweeping dresses. A man passes by me with a torch, lighting the streetlamps.

I blink.

This is real.

There is no way you can fake this. You can't fake the entire city of Boston.

My eyes fly back to the Public Garden. To the pond. It's dusk, but there's enough light that I can see as clear as day that there aren't any swan boats on that lake. I have to be stuck in a different time, a time before there were any swan boats.

A young man bumps his shoulder into mine and immediately jumps back.

"Oy!" he yells. "Watch where you're going." He looks me up and down, and I do the same. This guy is probably about my age, but that's where the similarity ends. His clothes are dirty and torn, and his hair is unwashed. A layer of grime coats his skin, although even that doesn't conceal the acne covering nearly every inch of his face. And then he takes a step toward me. I have at least four inches on him.

"Give me your money," he demands.

I don't think so. This little punk is not going to rob me—not like I have any money on me anyway.

"No," I tell the pint-size thug.

He reaches into his pocket, and I see a flash of metal. I grab his arm, twist it around, and force the knife out of his hand. It clatters to the cobblestone street. That makes two knife attacks I've deflected in one day.

A woman screams a few yards away, and there's a scuffling of footsteps as people try to get away. Two policemen wearing tall domed hats and carrying nightsticks push through the crowd to get to us.

Do not interact with anyone. Alpha's warning rings in my ears once again. But this time I ignore it.

I've already talked to this boy. I can't let these cops catch me. Best-case scenario, they'll want to talk. Worst-case, they'll pitch me into a jail cell.

I push the punk kid to the ground and take off down the same street as before. I round the corner to the street lined with brownstones, then look back. The cops aren't following me. I pause and wait, just to make sure, but no one comes. Dodged a bullet there. But I've got to get out of these clothes. They're killing me.

My hand starts tingling. The knapsack. I'd forgotten about it, even though I'm clutching it so hard the pattern of the cloth's weaving is embedded in my skin. I kneel down and drop it into my lap. I fiddle with the tie until it opens, then I upend it. A mess of black fabric and a black, metal, twisted skeleton key fall into my lap. I set the key aside and unfurl the fabric. It's a dress. It's full-length with long sleeves, and that's about all there is to it. I've never done more than sew a button on to a shirt, but I bet I could make this thing myself.

Still, it beats khaki pants in terms of blending in, so I glance both ways to make sure no one's coming. The entire street is deserted. I slip my blazer and shirt over my head. For one quick second I look down at the red lump on my forearm. Where there's now a tracker. A *tracker*.

I yank on the ugly dress and grunt as I try to wriggle it down my body. I kick off my shoes, slip off my pants, and hop up, swishing my hips side to side as I try to pull down the dress. It barely makes it. And I mean *barely* makes it. The seams are stretched so tight I see them straining, as if they're about to give up and split open.

Please don't split open, I tell them.

I can barely move, so bending over is out of the question. I catch the strap of the knapsack with my toe and kick it up in the air. My fingers snatch it, and I shove my hand in to pull out the shoes . . . only there are no shoes. The sack is empty.

Of course it is.

I shove my feet back into my Peel-issued oxfords, and without thinking, I bend down to help my heels in.

R-I-I-I-I-I-I-I-I-I-I-I-I-I-I-I-I-I-P!

Someone is laughing. Someone else is here. My head whips up to see a guy and a girl about my age, arm in arm, standing in front of a brownstone several yards away. The guy is average height but very thin, like a marathon runner, with sandy hair and a relaxed face. The girl is miniature sized. If her driver's license says she's five feet tall, it's a lie. Both avert their gaze and turn onto the next street. Something feels off.

I grab my pants, jacket, and shirt and shove them into the knapsack, then toss the skeleton key on top. In one quick movement, I tie my navy-and-crimson Peel tie around my waist. It does nothing to hide the fact that there's a huge tear along the side seam. My charm bracelet slides down on my wrist until it's exposed. It's very out of place for wherever—*whenever*—I am, so I fiddle with the clasp; but it sticks and it won't budge and that couple is getting away. I don't know why, but I need to follow them. So I tuck the bracelet under my sleeve, grab the knapsack, and run.

The couple is almost to the end of the street, back onto Beacon Street. I chase after them, but as soon as I make it to the street, I've lost them. I scan left and right, but they're nowhere to be seen. The cops are still there, one of them holding the arm of the kid who tried to rob me. He's begging and pleading, and . . . whatever. *Punk. You deserve it.* I turn my head toward the Public Garden.

Forget the couple for now. I need to figure out where I am.
When I am.

I draw in my breath. Can it be possible? Could I really have traveled back in time? What was that fancy term Alpha used? Something Augmentation?

I jump back as a horse-drawn cart barrels down Charles Street, then fall in line next to a man with a thin mustache wearing a shopkeeper's apron and cross into the Garden. Every year the swan boat drivers would talk about the history of the boats and when they first started, and I can't remember what they said. Why hadn't I paid better attention all those years? And the dome! In middle school we'd taken an American history class field trip to Boston and toured the state house, and I know they told us when the dome had been gilded, but I can't remember that either.

I close my eyes and breathe. I imagine my Practical Studies professor's voice in my head, telling me to slow down and focus and let the answer come to me. But then I hear the *clomp-clomp-clomp* of another horse and the dress starts itching and I sway to the side as a high-pitched wail brought on by extreme sleep deprivation erupts in my eardrums, and I can't do it. I can't focus. I open my eyes.

I hate myself in this moment. I wish I could just whip out my phone, open the browser, and look it up.

Well, why can't I, exactly? Maybe I'm in some sort of weird universe where I have a network connection.

It sounds weak even as I think it, but still I dig around in the knapsack until I find the back pocket of my pants. My fingers tighten around the phone, and I pull it out, trying to be as inconspicuous as I can. I look down to unlock it and . . . nothing. The screen is dark. I hit the power button, but nothing happens. It's fried.

There's laughing again. My head whips up, and the same couple I saw before, standing on the bridge. The guy bites his lip and turns his head when he sees me, but his head bobs as if he's chuckling. But not the girl. She looks at me with eyes that spit fire before she raises a bony hand and tucks a stray white-blond hair behind her ear.

And then I see it. Because even though that girl is dressed in a long, green-striped gown with a corseted waist and several pickups on the skirt, and even though her hair is half pinned up and tucked underneath a flat hat that matches the dress, that bitch is wearing a sparkly pink plastic running watch.

This couple reports to Alpha, I'm sure of it. They're Annum Guard, too.

Annum Guard. The words float around in my head. Can it be true? Can there really be a secret government organization that travels back in time? The answer is staring me in the face, screaming at me.

YES.

But how can people time travel? Like, my brain cannot even begin to process this. I need to get back. Back to my time. Then I'll get some answers.

I turn away from the couple and stare straight at the dome up on the hill. A man and a woman approach me, he in a suit that looks like something from a really pretentious wedding and she in a light-gray pinstriped dress that's collected about three inches of dust on the hem. I step out of their way. I'm sure I still look pretty ridiculous in a torn dress with a silk tie wrapped around my waist, and let's not forget about the shoes; but the couple don't even blink as they saunter past.

I close my eyes and take a breath. I know the swan boat drivers said the boats dated back to eighteen something. Same thing with the gilding of the dome. *Think think think think think.* I take a breath and close my eyes. *Please focus.* And then I remember that the tour guide said something about how they wanted to gild it earlier on, but then the Civil War broke out and they had to spend the money on that until the war ended.

The Civil War ended in 1865, thank you very much, every American history class I've ever taken. So we're somewhere between 1865 and 1899.

Back to the swan boats. *Focus. Focus.* My mom and I haven't ridden in the boats since I moved away to go to school. The last time we went, I was in the eighth grade. It wasn't a huge anniversary for the boats, like the hundredth or two hundredth; but the number ended with a zero, so everyone was acting as if it was the biggest deal in the world, which I remember thinking was pretty lame. *What was it?*

And then, like magic, the number floats into my head. I can see the sign hanging behind the ticket counter with fireworks and balloons, proclaiming the anniversary.

So subtract that from the year, and I get that the swan boats were started in 1877, which means, Hallelujah, praise Jesus, I am a freaking genius! I am sometime between 1865 and 1876.

Except that now I'm totally stuck.

I drop my head into my hands and rub my eyes. My nose is all sniffly. That always happens when I'm so tired I can barely keep my head up. I can't process anything. Just as soon as a thought enters my head, it's out. *Time travel is real. I'm hallucinating. I'm going to wake up from a bad dream in my dorm room at Peel.*

The thoughts all swirl together. I need to keep moving. Moving will help me stay focused.

I look both ways to make sure a horse isn't about to mow me down again and walk into Boston Common. There has to be a trash can around, right? Maybe someone will toss in a newspaper and I'll find it, like Michael J. Fox did in *Back to the Future*. Mom and I watched that movie a lot. On her good days.

I'm halfway across the Common when it hits me. The smell. I was so worked up before that I didn't pay attention, but the scent is there, sure as day. It's a musty, sweet smell blown in on the wind. I've lived in New England my entire life, so I know that smell. It's fall.

One glance up confirms it. It's dark out, but there's enough light to notice the yellow and orange leaves looming over me. The dead ones, long tossed from their branches, crunch beneath my feet. So I left during the fall in the present, and now I'm in the fall in the past. Somehow this is comforting.

I stop. I can't remember what I was doing. I sniffle again. Oh. Right. Trash cans. I blink. Did I really just center a plan around a plot point in an '80s movie and think that was a good idea? What is wrong with me? I've been trained better than this. I *am* better than this.

But still, I glance around to see if I can spot any trash cans, because you never know. I don't see a single one. I sigh and walk toward the state house. Maybe someone is selling an evening edition of the newspaper?

I have no plan. This is awful. If this was another Testing Day challenge, I'd fail.

I stop in my tracks and gasp. What if this *is* another Testing

Day challenge? Oh my God, why didn't I think of this before? There's a Testing Day that's legendary around Peel's campus. Testing Day: 1995, also known as the Testing Day That Would Not End.

There was the twelve-hour written test, followed by the three challenges, followed by the banquet. But then armed guards wearing all black and night vision goggles cut the electricity, stormed the place, captured all the juniors and seniors, and took them to a remote location off-campus for more testing. One kid died. A junior. There was never an official cause of death, but if there was a box for "Testing Day from Hell" on the coroner's report, you can bet it would have been checked.

What if this is like 1995 all over again? I'm not done! I haven't graduated yet. I'm still a student. I have to work my way back to the present, and then Testing Day will finally be over. Holy crap, this could all be a drill!

Suddenly, the idea of a secret government organization that has the ability to time travel doesn't sound so far-fetched to me. I mean, you would be surprised at all the stuff the government can do, and I only know about a small sliver of it. I can imagine how shocked I'll be when I get full clearance.

Full clearance. I blow out my breath. Time to get serious. What was the plan? Oh, right, newsboys. That is a *stupid* plan, and not just because there aren't any newsboys at the state house.

Focus.

There's a shuffling of footsteps behind me, and I turn just as two men wander up to look at the dome. The guy and the girl who are tailing me are half a block away, and the guy leans in to the girl and whispers something in her ear when he sees me looking at him. For a split second I think about waving, but I'm sure that would violate the no-interaction rule. And I'm not about to blow this now.

So instead I fiddle with my collar and pull out the owl necklace. I press the knob up top by the feather, the way Alpha did, and the lid covering the watch face pops open. The face itself is white, and there are black numbers in a fancy, swirly font I've never seen before. ANNUM is stamped below the point where the two hands lie on top of each other. The whole face is enclosed in a brass circle, and there are tiny knobs on the right side of the circle. And I mean *tiny*. There's . . . something inscribed on each of the knobs, but I can't see what it is. I fiddle with the one on the bottom, but it doesn't budge. Neither does the one in the middle. But the knob on top moves. I spin it to the right. The minute hand moves, too, and—

Click.

Click.

That doesn't sound good. No, worse than that. That sounds bad. *Really* bad. As if I've just messed with a bunch of wires, and a bomb is about to go off. I turn the knob back two clicks to the left, back to where I started, and hold my breath.

"Already exceeded two thousand dollars?" a voice next to me yells.

I don't want to be obvious, so I make only a little quarter turn and shift my eyes to the side. It's the two men who walked up before. They're still looking at the dome.

I stare back at the watch. I bring it closer to my face and

squint, trying to make out the inscriptions on the knobs. They're letters! The top knob has a *Y*, the middle an *M*, and the bottom a *D. YMD*.

"If they exceed the budget any further," the same man says, "they'd better not levy a single tax to pay for it. At the first sight of a tax collector, I'm grabbing the missus and the boy and heading west. We'll become border ruffians."

The other man laughs and claps his friend on the back.

"Bully for you, Morrison!"

Man, people sure talk funny back . . . whenever I am. *YMD*. This seems as if it should be easy, but I'm so tired right now I don't think I could spell my name correctly on the first try. *YMD*. Yeapons of Mass Destruction?

"Mark my words," the first man says, "the Centennial will dawn, the dome will be half completed, and the cost to us all will be five thousand dollars."

The other man laughs again. "The Centennial! Morrison, you're mad! Simply mad. That's a year and a half away. The remainder of autumn, perhaps, but it will be gilded by new year."

The owl necklace slips from my fingers and thumps into my chest. The Centennial is a year and a half away. Even a first grader could tell you the country was founded in 1776, so that means the Centennial is in 1876. Which then means I'm in 1874. It's fall 1874. I want to leap on both of these men and kiss them, but instead I turn away and start walking back toward the alley.

I'm close. So close. I know the year, and I know the season; but I still need to figure out the month and the day.

I stop in my tracks.

YMD. Of course! *Year Month Day*.

I'm already turning the knobs on the watch before I'm the whole way back. Today in the present is October 21, and I'm willing to bet anything that today in the past is October 21, too. That's why the month and day buttons won't budge. The mission was to get back. And that means only figuring out the year.

I turn the Y knob, and the big hand flies around the clock, clucking like a chicken. One whole turn. I bet that's sixty years. Another turn. And that's a buck twenty. I slow down and count each tick after that. I can't screw this up.

And then I remember Alpha's instruction. Leave from the place you started. That alley? The broom closet? But I'm locked out, and I don't have—a key!

I shove my hand in the knapsack as I run down Beacon Street. I zip to the right at the first street and find the door. Sure enough, there's a lock on the outside, and the key slides right in.

"Yes!" I shout to no one. But then there are footsteps. I turn to find the guy and the girl coming toward me. The girl has that look on her face again, like she's about to pull out a dagger and knife me. What the hell is her problem?

Guess I'll figure it out later. I open the door, jump into the tiny closet, and snap the lid of the watch face shut. Here goes nothing.

CHAPTER 5

There's a ride at Six Flags New England. Scream. You're strapped into your seat at ground level, and then with no warning at all you're shot straight up, twenty stories in the air at sixty miles an hour.

This is what's happening to me now. My empty stomach soars and lodges itself into my esophagus, and I don't have time to scream as my hair is plastered to my face, my arms fly to my sides, and I'm shot up.

Up.

Up.

Up.

How much longer?

And then I stop, midflight. There's a *ziiiiiiiip* sound from below, and I crumple to the ground. My elbow slams into a metal grate on the floor, and I groan.

"Welcome back," a voice says from above. It's Alpha. He

reaches down a hand, then immediately draws it away when I reach for it.

"I don't want you to get hurt," he says. "Which I assure you is a statistical certainty should you try to escape from me again. So tell me, are we past all that?"

I don't answer the question. Instead I decide to call his bluff. Here. Now.

"I don't know. Is Testing Day over now?"

Alpha's honey-brown eyes narrow into a look of pure puzzlement. "Testing Day has been over for hours. You graduated. Did you not believe me?"

I don't say anything. I don't know what to say. His tone is one of finality; his eyes seal my fate. In this instant I know. This is real. And now I'm drowning in an ocean of disappointment, pulled under by a rogue wave of reality. I'm really done at Peel. I can feel it. And that means I'm really done with Abe.

I start to push myself up, but Alpha grabs both of my shoulders and pushes me back to the floor. "Uh-uh. First you have to promise me that you're past trying to run away."

I'm Annum Guard now. Annum Guard. An organization I've never heard of. I have to come to grips with the fact that time travel might be possible. I think. Ugh, I don't know what to think. But one thing I do know is that Alpha is stronger than me and clearly has more combat training, so I'd be foolish to try to take him in a fight again.

"We're past it," I say.

Alpha's hand reaches down again, and this time I take it. He pulls me to my feet. "Glad to hear it. Now you need to project again."

My head snaps back. "I need to . . . what?"

Alpha takes hold of the watch hanging around my neck. "You're not in the present."

I blink. "How . . . I don't . . ."

"When you go back in time, you lose time in the present day. If you go back twenty-five years, two minutes pass in the present for every one minute you're gone. The further back you go, the more time passes. Ever heard of a Fibonacci sequence? It works like that."

I try to process what he's telling me. I don't even know if I believe him.

"For instance," Alpha continues, "you go back four hundred years, and every minute you spend there passes nearly two days in the present."

My mouth drops open. I don't mean for it to. It's betraying nearly everything I was taught in Practical Studies about keeping my cool.

Alpha clears his throat and presses on the top knob of the watch. The lid pops open, and Alpha presses the top knob again. The dials fly around the watch six times.

"For future reference," Alpha says, "whenever you need to get back to the present, just press on the top knob when the lid is open. It will automatically take you to the present. You're about six hours behind, in case you were wondering."

"What—"

Before I can finish the thought, Alpha pushes me backward into the black room and shuts the watch face lid. I'm sucked up again, and I choke from the shock. But only a second later I land in a heap on the same metal railing.

Alpha's hand extends in front of my face. "We still past it?" he asks.

I think I'm going to throw up. The grate below me starts to swirl. "Past it," I say.

Alpha yanks me up, and I follow him back into the too-bright hallway. He stops outside a door at the other end and enters a code, then turns the handle and cracks open the door an inch. He looks back at me.

"Are you ready to serve your country in a way you never thought possible?"

When he says that, the hair on my arms stands on end. I don't know if it's the fact that I'm more exhausted than I have ever been, or that it's only about sixty degrees in this hallway, or that, maybe deep down, there's a tiny little part of me hoping Annum Guard is for real. That there's a secret government organization with the ability to time travel. And that they want me.

I nod my head.

Alpha opens the door and gestures me inside. The first thing I notice is the green-striped dress. That bitch who was tailing me is here. She's taken off the hat and let down her hair. She has pale-blond locks that spiral in curls around her face, and she might actually be pretty if not for the look on her face. It's the look you might get if someone was holding a bag of dog crap under your nose. I don't like this chick. I don't know anything about her, but a girl just has an intuition about these things. She's not going to like me, and I'm not going to like her. End of story.

She's standing off to the side of the room whispering with the guy who was tailing me before. He's smiling at me, but it doesn't annoy me like it did back in 1874. The smile is . . . friendly. Relaxed. But still I don't return it. Not yet.

There's a long table at the front of the room with two people seated behind it and an empty seat in the middle. One chair is set front and center before the table, and another row of chairs sits behind it. Seven, I count. Seven chairs. Five of them are occupied by guys and girls who have their backs to me. It's like everyone is waiting for me.

Alpha pushes me forward, and I walk past the row of chairs on my way to the seat that I assume is for me. I pass by the girl with the purple hair, but I don't look down the row. I'm staring straight ahead, at the people sitting behind the table. It's clear they're in charge. Alpha takes the empty seat, pulls out the same worn notebook he had on Testing Day, and jots down something. There's a woman to Alpha's left, and I know I shouldn't stare, but I can't help myself. She's in a wheelchair, and her arms and legs are bent at unnatural angles and are as thin as twigs. There's despair on her face, and it makes me think of my mom.

I look away, to the man on Alpha's right. He's in much better condition. Like Alpha, he's probably around the age my dad would be today. He doesn't have that tough, gritty look that Alpha does—if I'm being honest, he was probably a bit of a pretty boy when he was younger. He has dark-brown hair flecked with slivers of gray, an angular jaw, and aquamarine eyes staring at me from under eyelashes that most girls would kill for. But still, behind the exterior, there's something about the way he carries himself that's really intimidating. That's one thing he has in common with Alpha. He has to be military or former military, too.

"Sit," Alpha commands. I do. "You passed the test. Welcome to Annum Guard. From this moment on, your code name will be Iris. You will go by this name until the day you die. Understand?"

I don't move. Don't blink.

Alpha stares right at me. "Annum Guard was founded by seven men in 1965," he says. "These seven men were given the ability of Chronometric Augmentation, to project through time and tweak past events to improve present consequences. They are our founders—our forefathers, if you will. They created the organization and the rules we abide by to this day, including the use of code names. These seven men used numbers as their codes: One through Seven." Alpha gestures to the people sitting at the table. "My colleagues and I are the second generation of Annum Guard. You already know me. To my left is Epsilon, to my right, Zeta. We are all that remain of the second generation."

I rack my brain, trying to remember the Greek alphabet. Alpha Beta Gamma Delta Epsilon . . . what?

"The people seated behind you are third generation. Your generation." I crane my neck, but I can only see the guy seated all the way on the left. He has dark hair, olive skin, and cheekbones like a movie star's, and is wearing a white button-down shirt and a pair of navy pants.

"Red!" Alpha says, and the guy I'm staring at jumps up. "Introduce your team."

He nods his head once. "Sir." I turn all the way around in my seat to look at him. If he was going to give a presentation, you'd think they would have come up with a better seating arrangement beforehand, one that wouldn't require me to sit backward in a chair.

"I am Red," the guy says, even though Alpha made that clear. "The leader of Annum Guard Three. Our code names are colors.

"This is my team," he continues, "*your* team. Orange!" The

guy next to him stands up. He does, in fact, have orange hair. That's unfortunate. "Yellow!" The bitch in the striped dress stands. "Green!" My gazes follows down the line to a short guy with long brown hair. "Blue!" I stare at a tan, blond guy who has his head down, staring at his feet. But at the very last second he looks up and makes eye contact with me. My heart lurches, and I let out a sputtered choke.

It's Tyler Fertig.

I barely hear Red introduce the guy who was tailing me as Indigo and the girl with the purple hair as Violet. Because Tyler Fertig is Annum Guard. Tyler Fertig, superstar of Peel who didn't get selected to graduate as a junior. Tyler Fertig, who looked angry enough to punch a wall during that graduation. Tyler Fertig. He's here.

This does more to solidify Annum Guard in my mind than that little stunt back in Boston. If Tyler Fertig is a member, it has to be legit.

Tyler and I lock eyes, and I know he recognizes me. He knows who I am. But then he breaks his gaze and sits down with the others.

Alpha clears his throat, but I hesitate before I turn back around to look at him. I can feel Tyler—Blue—whatever his name is—staring at the back of my head, boring a hole through my skull.

"And you are Iris," Alpha says.

"Which isn't a color," I point out.

"It's not," he admits as the man to his right—Zeta, I think?—raises his eyebrows, as if he's shocked that I just spoke to Alpha that way. "And that's because you are here on a trial basis." He clears his throat. "Before we get to that, I think we'd all like to hear a report of how you performed on your first mission. Indigo, we'll start with you."

Indigo makes his way to the front of the room. He's standing off to the side, in between me and the table.

He clasps his hands together in front of his body. "Iris did an admirable job. She used powers of deduction to determine the precise year, and she figured out how to use the Annum watch in record time. I think she'll make a fine addition to Annum Guard."

I like Indigo. Not how I like Abe, of course, but I'll get along with Indigo.

Behind me, someone clears a throat.

"Yellow?" It's the man on the right. "You disagree?"

I hear her get up behind me. Her dress swishes against the floor as she walks over and stands next to Indigo.

"I absolutely disagree, sir. Iris committed a number of infractions." She tosses her head back to get the hair off her shoulder and shoots me a dirty look as she does it. "First, she was seen in civilian clothing by several of the historical subjects. Second"— she pauses, and I'm sure it's for dramatic effect—"she tried to use a *cell phone*. In 1874."

Behind me, there's a soft ripple of laughter.

"I don't blame her for trying," Indigo says. "She had no idea where she was, and for all she knew, it might have worked."

Yellow holds up a hand to silence him. "Third, she made vocal contact with an historical subject." I want to tell her that I'd like to see her not react when someone tries to rob her, but she's talking so fast I can't get a word in. "Finally, she nearly blew the mission by walking around in a torn dress with a modern-day school tie wrapped around her waist."

I open my mouth to tell her that no one seemed to notice my tie and that I did the best I could with a dress that was clearly too small, but then she's looking straight at me, one eyebrow raised and a sneer on her face.

She looks me up and down, her gaze lingering on the torn waistline of the dress, and says, "You're going to need to lose some weight."

"And you're going to need to kiss my ass." The words tumble out of my mouth before my brain can process them. Everyone behind me gasps, but I don't blink. I jump to my feet, and Yellow crouches down like a trained combatant. *So she wants to fight? Well, okay then.*

Alpha jumps up and bangs his hand on the table so hard I'm surprised he doesn't break it. "Everyone, sit down!"

I don't take my eyes off Yellow as she slinks away and slides back into her seat between Orange and Green. It's only then that I turn forward, to Alpha's angry eyes waiting for me.

"I told you to sit!" he barks at me, and I do. "Do you not remember me telling you that you were here on a *trial* basis?"

"Well, maybe someone should have asked me if I wanted to be here before they plucked me out of school in my junior year, strapped me to a table, implanted a goddamned *tracker* in my arm, and forced me to join an organization I've never heard of." I'm so angry I don't care if I'm breaching protocol.

Alpha leans forward. His eyes are furious, and I expect him to leap across the table and slam me to the ground again. I brace myself. Instead he leans back, grabs a file, flips it open, and starts rifling through a bunch of papers. He pulls one out, walks over to me, and slaps it into my chest. "Remember this?"

He lets go, and I glance at it. The Peel Academy seal is emblazoned at the top, and I immediately know what it is. It's the commitment letter I signed my freshman year.

"Read it," Alpha says.

"I know what it says."

"Read it," he repeats. "Out loud."

Anger courses through my veins and seeps out my pores. But I take a breath, fan the paper in front of me, and start reading in a calm voice.

"I, Amanda Jean Obermann, hereby give the United States government the authority to assign me to any given organization they deem necessary of my service, at any time such service is deemed necessary." My signature is at the bottom.

I drop my arm. "I've never heard of Annum Guard." There's still an edge to my voice.

Alpha breathes a sigh. I can't tell if it's one of frustration or one of relief. "Well, there are certain things you're going to have to take at face value, this included. So you have two options. Stay here, on a trial basis, or leave."

I straighten. "Leaving is an option?" Abe's face flashes in my mind. I could see him tomorrow.

Behind me, I hear someone say no in a hushed, angry whisper.

"Of course it is," Alpha says. "But probably not in the way you're thinking. You're done with school. You've graduated and moved on. Iris is a pupil no longer. And Annum Guard happens to be among the most secret government organizations in existence. You're one of a handful of people who know about it, so I'm afraid we wouldn't be able just to turn you loose. If you choose to leave, you will be . . . detained."

My mouth goes dry, and I feel little pricks of electricity in my shoulders. Alpha's voice got low. Scary. Ominous, even.

"Detained how?"

Alpha's mouth presses into a thin line, and he pauses, as if he's trying to figure out how to word his response. "You'll be taken to a secure facility where your actions and interactions will be monitored on a full-time basis in the name of national security."

My vision clouds as I read between the lines.

"You don't mean detained," I say. "You mean *contained.*"

Alpha's lips curl up into the smallest smile, but he doesn't answer me.

"Where?" I demand.

"Most likely Carswell."

I jump out of my seat with such force that the chair falls over. I know what Carswell is. It's a women's federal prison in Texas. And now I fully understand what *detained* means.

Solitary confinement.

We studied solitary at Peel. It's a form of psychological torture. Humans are social creatures by nature, and you can't change that. Cut off from contact, isolated prisoners slowly go mad. Years and years of untreated madness. And I already know what that's like.

My only thought is escape. I have to get out of here. Now. But before I take even one step, hands are on me from behind. Lots of them. My supposed teammates. Someone picks the chair back up, and I'm lowered down into it. I kick and fight, but it's no use. It's like ten on one.

"You're really going to have to learn to control your temper," Alpha says in a flat, almost bored voice. "Now, do you choose to stay or to go?"

"Do I really have a choice?" I spit.

"Yes. You can choose to stay or go."

"So no," I say. "I don't have a choice. Of course I choose to stay."

Alpha nods his head. "On a trial basis," he repeats. "You see, our numbers are set. Teams have always been made up of seven. The government is thinking of expanding us, but they're not sure yet. You're the trial. If you succeed, you're in, and we're open for business. If you fail, well . . . you're out. And I've already explained what that entails."

I try to jump out of the chair, but several pairs of strong hands hold me down.

"Why are you doing this to me?" My voice is bordering on wailing. "I did everything right. Everything. I've always played by the rules." My voice cracks. "All I ever wanted was to—"

I cut myself off before I say too much. No one here needs to know about my dad, although chances are they already do. They seem to know everything.

"Was to what?" Alpha says. "Gain clearance levels? What makes you think you can't do that here?"

And there it is. Alpha knows. I've never told anyone my true motives in choosing Peel—the realization I had as soon as I found out what the school really was—not even Abe, but somehow Alpha knows.

His words replay in my mind. I could have clearance. It's the one thing I've wanted since I was seven years old and figured out that asking my mom about my dad was getting nowhere. I could finally—*finally*—discover what happened to him. Why he died. What his mission was. I wouldn't have to speculate, to build an explanation in my mind around a sole pair of U.S. Navy dog tags I found hidden deep in a shoe box at the back of my mom's closet. My mind wouldn't go back and forth between thinking my dad was a fighter pilot who got shot down in a covert mission in Somalia or a Navy SEAL who was taken hostage and killed in North Korea. I could know the truth.

An image of my mom from this past summer flashes in my mind. It was the week before school began, and she hadn't left her room in days. I went in to check on her and discovered gashes all over her forearms. Some were scabbed over, but others were fresh. I recoiled in horror—self-harm was a new one for her. Dried blood caked her fingernails, and she twisted her fingers in the air as she looked up at me. Stared at me. Like this was my fault.

Guilt washes over me. Because I left. Left the room. Left the house. Left the state. I couldn't deal. But maybe I could go back to her if I knew what happened to my dad—and then maybe, just maybe, my mom could get closure and seek out the treatment she so desperately needs.

I hold up my hands in submission, and my teammates behind me slowly walk away.

"I'm sorry," I say. I don't know how much of that apology is true, but it's a start. If it's going to get me to the truth about my dad, it's the only start I have.

Alpha sits back down, and the man to his right—Zeta, I think—slowly nods his head, as if he knows something I don't.

"Violet!" Alpha announces. I hear someone stand up behind me. "Show Iris to her room. I think we're done for the night."

Violet is suddenly by my side. "Come on," she whispers.

I stand, but no one else in the room moves. I follow behind Violet, glancing down the row of chairs as I pass. I'm staring right at Tyler—Blue—but he won't make eye contact with me. I have to talk to him. Tomorrow, I guess.

We're back in the too-bright hallway, and I squint and raise my hand to shield my eyes.

"You get used to it," Violet says as she makes her way to a door all the way down at the opposite end of the corridor.

She punches in a code and opens the door, which leads to a concrete stairwell like you'd find in any hotel or office building. Gray walls, metal railings. We walk up one flight of stairs, where there's another door ahead. Violet places her hand on a metal scanner outside the room, then enters another code, and the door clicks unlocked.

She opens it to reveal the most gorgeous room I've ever seen in my life. There's plush sage-green carpeting with ivory swirls and a round marble table directly in the middle of the room. The table must be five feet wide, and nearly every inch of it is covered with flowers. All white flowers in a bunch of clear vases. There are roses and lilies and hydrangeas and a number of flowers I've never seen before and have probably never even heard of.

My eyes are drawn up to a massive crystal chandelier hanging over the table, then to a wooden staircase that curves up to the right. This place can only be described as a mansion, and I'm pretty sure my jaw has dropped open at this point.

"What is this place?" I ask.

Violet's beside me now. "Annum Hall. This is where we live. Come on, I'll show you to your room."

CHAPTER 6

Violet starts up the stairs, but my feet are cemented to the floor. There's a pair of French doors off to the right leading into a dining room. Inside is the longest table I've ever seen, and chairs are lined up uniformly around it. The table is set with china and crystal, and even though I'm too far to really see the place settings, I'd bet you anything that's real sterling silver.

Holy crap.

This place is out of control. I grew up in a two-bedroom Cape with unreliable plumbing and a measly nine hundred square feet. When I first went away to school, I was impressed with the fact that it had a heating system that actually worked, rooms with polished wood floors, and tables that weren't duct taped together. I thought that was the big-time.

I see now that's like bragging about your used Chevy to someone who just rolled up in a Bugatti.

We get to the second floor and keep going up the staircase to the third. There's one massive window and seven closed doors making a U around it on this floor. Four doors to the left of the window, three to the right. I memorize this detail.

Violet stops in front of the first door on the left. She pulls a key out of her pocket and hands it to me.

"Welcome home," she says. There's an air of sarcasm in her voice.

The key is plain silver, like the ones you can get copies of in any big-box hardware store. I'm a little disappointed that it's not another old-fashioned skeleton key.

I stick the key in the lock and open the door. The room is small, but it has the same plush carpeting as downstairs. I immediately notice there's no window—no sunlight, no means of escape—and a momentary sense of panic washes over me. I breathe it out. Fear isn't going to change the situation, only make it worse.

There's a single four-poster bed centered on the wall straight ahead, a dresser on the left wall, and a desk and hutch on the wall with the door. There's a closet and another closed door on the right wall. A white duvet clothes the bed, which looks soft and fluffy and more luxurious than anything I've ever owned. It sure beats the cheap, poly-blend comforter in my room back home in Vermont or the Peel-issued thick, navy blanket that itches when you lie on top of it.

"This is all mine?" I ask, which—dammit, I totally sound impressed. I don't want to sound impressed.

Violet clears her throat. "All yours." She steps in and opens the door on the right. "This is all yours, too."

It's a bathroom. It's painted a very pale lilac and has black-and-white tile, a pedestal sink, and a claw-foot tub. The entire place is sparkling. It's like the "after" bathroom on a home makeover show.

"I kept it really clean," Violet says behind me. Her voice is clipped, angry even. "Use it well."

I turn to look at her. "This room was yours?"

She nods. "Everything here works on a hierarchy. This room belongs to the most junior Guardian. I moved into Indigo's room, and so on. Red moved downstairs. I know Indigo probably tried to keep his room clean, but he's still a boy. There's a boy smell in my new bathroom." She says it like it's my fault.

I step back into the room and open the top door to the dresser. It's full of socks and underwear; and, holy crap, unless they'd managed to go out and find the same hot-pink underwear with tiny black skulls I'd bought like two years ago, I'm going to guess this is all my stuff, which means someone was *rifling through my underwear.* I slam the drawer shut.

"So this is your room," Violet says in a tone that makes it clear that she just wants to get out of here already. She has one foot outside.

"Violet?"

Her neck cranes back around. I know I shouldn't ask. It's showing them my number one weakness, giving them something with which to manipulate me. I should keep my head down, follow orders, and climb the ranks. It's what my dad deserves. But another part of my heart won't listen.

"I had—have—a boyfriend."

"Abraham," she interrupts. "Yeah, I know. I read your file. What about it?"

Her tone rubs me the wrong way. It's combative and off-putting, and it doesn't look as if I'm going to be making friends with any of the girls here. Strike that. Considering my only other option is Yellow, I think it's safe to say I'm *definitely* not going to be making any female friends here.

And then Violet confirms this fact. She reaches up and tucks a purple hair behind her ear. "What are you, one of those girls? The ones who think the world revolves around them because they have a boyfriend?"

My head snaps back. "That's not at all what I just said. And I'm not one of those girls."

"Good to know." Violet narrows her dark-brown eyes. "Because you really need to forget about that boyfriend of yours. That's in the past. You're Annum Guard. Well, for now, at least."

The implication is obvious. She wants me to fail. She doesn't want me to be in the Guard.

Well, screw her. Screw Yellow. I forget my dad for a second and take a step closer to her.

"Do you feel threatened by me?"

"Why would I?" She laughs, although I can tell it's a nervous laugh. *Good.* "You don't belong here. You're an outsider."

I raise my eyebrows. "Outsider?"

Violet's face falls. She's said something she shouldn't have. I'm an outsider. What does that mean? I'm getting the feeling from Violet that this organization is very . . . cult-like.

"Stay in your room," Violet tells me, and I laugh. She's sending me to my room? But then she points to a camera hanging over the stairwell and to another one in the corner by the massive window in the hallway, and I can't believe I didn't notice them before. "They'll know it if you don't."

I shrug, like, I'll think about it, even though I'd be foolish to try to leave. I step back into my new bedroom. "Thanks for your warning. I'm sure it comes from a place of love and concern." And then I shut the door.

A quick glance at the clock tells me it's four in the morning. Ugh. I can feel the physical exhaustion straining my limbs, even though my brain feels as if it's been shot with adrenaline. I yawn.

I flop down onto the bed but almost immediately sit up. I want to look around before I pass out. For kicks I open the rest of the dresser drawers. Shirts, jeans, sweats—they're all there. My old, dingy workout pants are hanging on the left side of the closet, which makes no sense—who hangs up yoga pants?—while the right side is full of a bunch of clothes I've never seen in my life. There's a lot of pastel, a long tweed skirt that looks like it would make me itch for days, and a bunch of fabric that doesn't seem very breathable. Maybe that's Violet's leftover stuff. Whatever. I'll burn it as soon as they give me match privileges.

I wander into the bathroom and sit on the edge of the tub. I turn the knobs on the tap and let the warm water spill down over my fingers. There's a faint smell of lavender in the room.

I rip off the Peel tie that's still hanging around my waist and pull the torn dress over my head. I slip off my shoes and socks and kick them and the tie into the bedroom. The dress gets stuffed into the trash can under the sink.

The water is bordering on being too hot, so I turn the cold water knob a little more as I sink down into the tub. I'm probably still in Boston, unless I somehow passed through a vortex in the stairwell that unknowingly whisked me to, I don't know— Utah? But I bet I'm in one of those brownstones on Beacon Street, probably one of the few that hasn't been converted to condos or apartments. This place must have cost a pretty penny.

It's good to know where I am, to have a handle on my location in case I want or need to escape. And I know Boston. I could disappear here in a second. Of course, not with this tracker in my arm.

I look down at my right forearm. There's a puffy lump just below my elbow. I touch it, then immediately wish I hadn't as pain spirals down the entire right side of my body. Dear God. *There's a tracker in my arm.* For the rest of my life, someone is going to know my location at every second of the day. I plunge my head under the water and let my mind wander to Abe as I come up.

Maybe I should put him out of my mind. Maybe that would make this easier. Let me focus. But I can't. Abe is a part of me, just as I'm a part of him.

Abe and I got off to a bit of a rocky start. We met the first day of freshman year, in the auditorium. Classes were pretty standard fare—we were all put in the same math, government, computer, and science classes, and we'd already been to Practical Studies (which is just a fancy word for a class that teaches you how to spy on people, shoot sniper rifles, and dismantle bombs); but when it came to combat training, we got to choose. I'd scanned the options and picked Krav Maga. I'd never heard of it, but the subtitle of "Israeli hand-to-hand combat" sold me. The Israelis are pretty badass.

After I'd circled my selection, I'd leaned over to the guy next me, who happened to be Abe, and seen that he'd circled karate.

"Karate?" I'd laughed. "What are you, seven? Going to work on your orange belt?"

Abe had stood and stormed off, clearly upset; and then his roommate, Paul Andress, had taken his place.

"Way to be an asshole," Paul had said. "He's a second-degree black belt already, and his sensei just died."

I'd swallowed a lump in my throat, but then Paul put the icing on his cake. "His grandmother was his sensei."

So yeah, my first interaction with Abe was to make fun of his dead grandmother. That's one for the scrapbook.

I apologized the next day, and Abe forgave me because he's the most wonderful person in the world. And that was that. Abe and I became an "us." I went home with him for holidays. His family opened their arms and invited me in. They became my family because my real family is the definition of dysfunctional.

I shake my head, like my brain is some sort of Etch A Sketch, like it will rid the image of my mom that's flooding my mind. But there she is. And right behind her is the guilt.

My mom was a pretty crap mother by any standard, but for some reason I'm the one who feels guilty. As if it's my fault. I breathe and squeeze my eyes shut. *Here we go.* Anger, bitterness.

Anger because "not sacrificing her art" is more important than getting better for me. Bitterness because I've known proper lithium dosage levels since I was seven. Anger because all the good memories from my childhood have faded away into fuzzy nothingness, to the point where now I can't remember if they really happened or if my mind invented them as a coping mechanism. Bitterness because while most kids my age were memorizing multiplication tables, I was taking it upon myself to scour the Internet and learn the brand names for drugs such as valproate, lamotrigine, and fluoxetine.

And mostly anger because my mom refuses to get off the damned roller coaster. Because every time I get my hopes up and think my mom will finally stick to a treatment plan, she calls it quits in less than two weeks.

I ball up my hands into fists, then grab both edges of the tub and stand. *Abe. Think about Abe.* He's waiting for me. And I'll find a way back to him. Somehow.

There are fresh towels hanging on the bar. Big, fluffy, white towels that smell like fabric softener. I wrap one around my wet hair, pull on purple fleece pants and a T-shirt, and tumble into bed. *Abe. Think about Abe.* But an image of Tyler Fertig flashes in my mind right before I close my eyes, and then my body shuts down.

Bang! Bang! Bang!

I gasp and bolt up in bed. Someone's knocking on the door. I push out of bed, and my palm lands on the towel.

Dammit, did I fall asleep with wet hair?

I pull open the door. Yellow stands before me. Of course she does. She's wearing a cardigan, a miniskirt, tights, and boots. Huge diamond studs hang from her earlobes. Her blond hair is perfectly coiffed again, pulled back with a wide headband. And I'm wearing pajamas and have a major case of bedhead.

Yellow wrinkles her nose when she sees me and shoves a folded note into my hand. "Breakfast is at seven sharp. Alpha doesn't like it if anyone is late. It completely slipped my mind until now that I was supposed to tell you that. Oops."

I glance at the clock on the dresser. 6:58. Seriously? Doesn't anyone believe in a good night's sleep?

I slam the door in her face and throw open my dresser drawers. The note gets plunked on top of the dresser unopened. I grab the first sweater and pair of jeans I see, then spend all of ten seconds brushing my teeth with such force I'm surprised my gums don't start bleeding. I shove my feet into my sneakers, stepping on the backs rather than taking the extra second required to slip my heels into them.

I pull my still-damp hair into a messy bun as I fly down the stairs. I'm pretty sure it's 7:00 on the dot, but I'm the last person to arrive in the dining room. Everyone else is seated, and a man dressed like a waiter is pouring coffee at all the place settings while a woman follows behind him with orange juice.

It's clear there's a hierarchy here at the table, too. Alpha sits at the head, and then it trickles down from there. Epsilon is absent, but Zeta sits on Alpha's right, and Red is on his left. Then it crisscrosses from there, from Orange to Yellow, all the way down to the one empty seat at the very end of the table.

But the weird part—and I mean *bizarre*—is that half the table look like they're waiting backstage before a community theater production. Zeta has on a brown coat, white tights, and a pair of short pants that puff out just after his knees. There's a powdered wig sitting next to him on the table, which just seems unsanitary.

Violet is wearing an electric-blue minidress with jelly shoes and a bunch of bangle bracelets. Her purple hair is teased so high it stands at least six inches above her head. Tyler—aka Blue—has on a suit with high-waisted pants and serious pinstriping. And Indigo is wearing drab gray pants with a vest and dress shoes, and these funny-looking black-and-white shoes. My mouth falls open as I scan the room.

"Yellow," Alpha says with a serious voice as he pours a dab of cream into his coffee. "I thought I asked you to make sure Iris knew how to dress this morning."

Yellow sits up straight in her chair. "I did, sir. I wrote her dress assignment on a piece of paper and hand delivered it this morning. I guess she ignored it."

I blink. That folded note Yellow shoved into my hand is sitting untouched on my dresser.

"I was rushed for time this morning," I say, then wince. I hate excuses. Detest them. If you make a mistake, own up, accept the consequences, and move on. Yet here I am, whining like a second grader. I wait for Alpha to call me out.

"You can change after breakfast," he says. "Please sit."

Is he mad? I can't tell. I slide into the empty seat next to Indigo but keep my eyes trained on Tyler. He's staring at his empty plate, but he has to feel me staring at him. *Come on, Tyler, look up.* I need to talk to him. I haven't even fully scooted my chair in when the man with the coffee appears at my side. It smells like hazelnut. Gross. I hate flavored coffee. And not just because my mom loves it.

"No, thank you, I don't really like . . . okay, never mind," I say as he fills the cup all the way to the top. The woman with the orange juice pitcher pauses before the crystal goblet as if asking me whether I'd like some. It's a nice gesture. "Yes, please."

I pick up the juice and take a sip when I notice Yellow staring at me, a smug look on her face. She turns to Tyler on her left. "It's shocking how much sugar is in orange juice, don't you think?" she says. Her crystal goblet is empty.

Tyler shrugs and tosses his napkin into his lap.

I turn to Indigo. "This orange juice is a little tart. Would you kindly pass me the sugar?"

Indigo squeezes his lips shut as if he's trying not to laugh and hands me the crystal sugar dish. I take the little sterling teaspoon and drop three spoonfuls into the juice. I take a sip.

"Well, that's better," I say.

It's not better. It's disgusting. But I make myself suck it down like it's a chocolate milk shake.

Alpha clears his throat at the head of the table, and every neck in the room cranes toward him.

"You all have your assignments for the day, I take it?"

Every head in the room nods, with the exception of mine.

"Excellent," he says. "Iris. You'll be with Zeta, just as soon as you've changed into something a tad more appropriate."

With those words the waiters bring out silver trays in batches and set them in the middle of the table. There are scrambled eggs on one platter and bacon on another. There's also toast and potatoes and some sort of vegetable-looking thing that gets set right next to Alpha.

I'm freaking starving. I can't remember the last time I ate anything of substance, so I load my plate with everything that's passed around. There isn't an inch of my plate that isn't covered with food. I glance up to see Yellow staring at me in horror, then stab a potato with my fork and pop it into my mouth. I chew slowly while I stare right at her, savoring every bite.

When the waiters are taking away the plates, Alpha clears his throat. "Yellow, go help Iris get ready."

Yellow and I both protest at the same time.

"What?" she says.

"I don't need help," I say.

Alpha holds up a hand. "It seems I can't trust either of you to complete a simple task, so you do it together. Both of you, go. Ten minutes."

"Ten minutes! I'm not a miracle worker," Yellow says with a laugh. Then her face flushes, and she gets bug eyes, as if she can't believe she just said that. "I mean, I'll do my best."

"Ten minutes," Alpha repeats.

Yellow yanks me out of my chair and up the stairs. I pull my hand away because there is no way in hell I'm letting her hold it. I trudge up the stairs behind her. Yellow stops in front of my door.

"Key!" she demands, opening and closing the fingers of her outstretched hand in rapid succession.

I hand it over, and Yellow barges in. She doesn't look around the room, doesn't make a single comment about how messy it is, but bounds straight to the closet. She takes out all the clothes on the right-hand side—the stuff I thought was Violet's leftovers—and tosses them on the bed.

"Where's the note?" she asks.

I point to the dresser, and she raises her eyebrows.

"What, you don't know how to read?"

I have a good six, seven inches and like fifty pounds on this girl. I could snap her in half easily, even if she does have some combat training. I let that image play in my mind for a second, then walk over to the dresser and unfold the note. It says,

NUMBER FOUR

"Number four," I tell her. "Don't you already know what it says? I thought you handwrote it yourself." I try to match the brownnosy, singsongy voice she used with Alpha.

Yellow narrows her eyes at me and starts rifling through the clothes. As items go flying, I see that every hanger is numbered. One, Two, and Three get tossed on the floor, and Yellow holds up a scoop-neck dress made from yards upon yards of brocade fabric.

"There's no way this is going to fit." She eyes the small dress, then looks at my midsection.

I snatch the dress from her hands and throw it onto the bed.

"Shut up," I spit at her. "I'm athletic and I'm muscular and I'm strong. Stop trying to make me feel self-conscious."

Yellow's eyebrows shoot up, and she gives me a look of genuine shock. She actually raises her arms in defense.

"Hey," she says. "I wasn't trying to do that. Just pointing out that all your clothes were tailored based on measurements we received ahead of time; and since the black dress clearly didn't fit, none of these will either. They'll fix them; but for today, I'll just pull the corset tighter."

She seems genuinely sorry. Maybe I overreacted just a tad. But then Yellow holds up a different hanger, one that contains an ivory, whalebone torture device.

"I'm not wearing a corset," I tell her.

"Yes, you are. We're wasting time. I need a blow dryer and a curling iron. Do you have those?"

"I have a blow dryer." I point to the one I've had since sixth grade, which is dangling on the side of the pedestal sink.

Yellow glances into my bathroom and gives me a disgusted look. "Mine's better. Hang on."

She's out the door in a flash. I touch the corset. It's stiff and unbreathable, and there's no way in hell I'm wearing it. Women rebelled against corsets for a reason, and then gave birth to girls who wore pants, who then gave birth to girls who burned their bras. I would personally be undoing hundreds of years of progress by wearing that thing.

Yellow's back only a few seconds later. She's holding a blow dryer, a curling iron, and the biggest makeup bag I've ever seen.

"Sit," she commands as she plugs the curling iron into an outlet by the bed. "We only have seven minutes." She yanks out my bun, runs her fingers through my damp, wavy hair, and flicks on the dryer. She turns it off after only a few seconds.

"You have thick hair," she spits, as if it's something I can control. She shoves the dryer into my hands. "Here, you dry while I start on makeup. Try not to move too much."

I hold the blow dryer above my head and wave it around while Yellow attacks me with black eyeliner. She throws powder at me, swishes blush on my cheeks, smears ruby-red lipstick on my lips, then grabs the blow dryer from me.

She switches it off. "You're too slow." She takes the curling iron and touches it lightly with her fingers to make sure it's hot. Then she grabs big sections of my still-damp hair and winds them around the rod. My hair sizzles as it touches the heat. She pins it up around my face as she goes.

Finally Yellow sets down the curling iron, rips the plug out of the wall, and walks over to the bed. I catch a glimpse of myself in the bathroom mirror.

Holy crap!

Yellow made me into a white-faced, time-traveling hooker. I don't wear much makeup as it is, so this is complete overkill. The eyeliner is so thick I look like a raccoon, and my cheeks are bright pink. And my face. My face is white, like I'm about to perform Kabuki.

I blink. "Yeah," I say, "I'm pretty sure they didn't wear makeup like this . . . wherever I'm going."

Yellow drops the corset to her side and shoots me a look of pure contempt. "You don't know anything, do you?"

"Excuse me?"

"That dress is Italian silk, and it's very clearly colonial style. Therefore you're dressing as a well-heeled, upper-class colonial woman, in which case you absolutely would be mimicking the fashion and beauty styles of late-eighteenth-century Europe, which, yes, means I did your makeup perfectly."

"I . . ." I don't know what to say. How did Yellow know all that?

"Stand up!" she commands. She's holding the corset.

"Not wearing it," I say.

"Fine." She tosses it onto the bed. "You can explain that to Alpha and Zeta then. You want to fail? You want them to toss you out before you even begin?"

I bristle as the thought of solitary confinement crosses my

mind. An image forms of me pacing an eight-by-ten cell for the rest of my life, and I shudder.

"Okay," I mumble. I slip out of my shirt and let Yellow pull the corset over my head. It settles in around my waist, and I brace myself, knowing full well that this is going to suck.

"Inhale," Yellow commands, and when I do, she grabs the ribbons and pulls with such ferocity that I gasp. Before I can recover, she yanks again, and I think my ribs break. I take short, panting breaths, but that only makes my lungs hurt.

"Can't. Breathe."

"You get used to it," Yellow says. She grabs the brocade dress and slips it over my head. I wish I hadn't eaten so much for breakfast. This corset is squeezing it all back up my digestive tract.

"Where do you keep jewelry?" Yellow asks.

I point to the jewelry box on the dresser while I gasp in short breaths, trying to figure out how to breathe. The jewelry box is the same one I've had since I was four. It was a Christmas gift from a grandmother I'd never met. It plays music and has a little ballerina that spins around. Yellow rolls her eyes as she rifles through it.

"You don't have any pearls?" she asks.

"Sorry, I must have left them at the last Junior League meeting." I put my hands on my hips and take a slow, easy breath.

Yellow ignores me and takes out my charm bracelet. She holds it up and flicks the little birdcage with her finger.

"That was a gift," I say, in case she was thinking of tossing it aside. My mind goes back to Abe, to the first Hanukkah I spent with his family—the first Hanukkah I celebrated ever—and the plain, small, black box tied with a silver ribbon and a note welcoming me to the family from Abe's grandfather. I wasn't much of a jewelry person, but I wore that bracelet every day. Still do. Well, except for this morning because I was too rushed.

Yellow drops it back into the box and shuts the lid. "You have nothing period appropriate. Where's your Annum watch?"

I point to the bathroom, where the necklace is resting on the edge of the pedestal sink.

"Yeah," Yellow says. "You might want to be a little more careful with a piece of government property that cost like twenty million dollars. Try explaining that to Alpha. Oops, sorry, I dropped a wormhole down my bathroom sink."

My ears perk up. "Wormhole? That's how the necklaces work?"

"Of course it is." Yellow hands me the necklace, and I drop it over my head. "You have, like, thirty seconds. You'd better run."

I can barely walk, but somehow I manage to make it down the stairs without falling on my face. I feel ridiculous. Completely ridiculous.

Zeta is waiting for me in the lounge, near the table with all the flowers. "Are you ready for your first mission?"

"I thought last night was my first mission."

Zeta doesn't smile. "That was your admission test. This is your first *real* mission. Your first Chronometric Augmentation."

"And I'm ready," I tell him, even though I don't think this is true. Shouldn't I be brushing up on my history or learning the mechanics of time travel? I mean, even a quick briefing would be nice. But I don't want Zeta to think I'm weak, so I say nothing.

I crane my head toward the dining room, hoping to catch a glimpse of Tyler, but the room is now empty.

Yellow skips down the stairs and waves to Zeta, who smiles

and nods at her. His face is relaxed, as if he genuinely seems to like her. That's bizarre. I can't imagine how anyone could possibly like Yellow.

She opens a pair of heavy, dark wood French doors across the hall from the dining room and slips inside. But not before I scan every inch of that room I can from where I'm standing. Tall bookshelves line the walls from floor to ceiling, and I even catch sight of one of those ladders on wheels. There are a number of desks in the middle of the room. A library. They have their own library. Of course they do.

Zeta clears his throat. "You ready to go?"

And then I get nervous. A bunch of little butterflies start flittering around in my stomach, which is weird because nerves are one thing I normally can control. But something about going back in time—projecting—Chronometric Augmentation, whatever— scares the crap out of me.

"Where are we going?" I ask.

"1770," Zeta says matter-of-factly. "We're going to change the Boston Massacre."

CHAPTER 7

"Excuse me?" I say. I blink as I try to remember my last American history class. The Boston Massacre was one of the driving forces behind the Declaration of Independence. If we change the massacre, wouldn't that mean the colonies would never declare independence? Would we *still* be colonies? Am I going to look out the window and see the Union Jack flying over the Massachusetts State House? Holy shit, will there even *be* a state house?

"Annum Guard has three rules," Zeta says as he trudges down the stairs. "Three very important rules. Break even one of them and you're out, so you'd do best to remember them."

I'm still thinking about the state house.

"Is it really a good idea to mess with the Boston Massacre?" I ask.

"Rule number one. We do not project in front of anyone who is not an Annum Guard member, meaning we do not project in front of the public. Ever. Rule number two—are you listening?"

I clomp down the stairs and nod.

"Rule number two. No second chances. You only get one mission to change the past. If you bungle it, it stays bungled. If you manage to get yourself killed, you stay dead. Got it?"

I'm stunned into silence. There's a chance of dying on these missions? I mean, I know I was trained for high-pressure situations at Peel, but I guess I never thought too hard about the risks I'd actually face one day. And why can't we go back to fix mistakes? That makes no sense.

"Rule number three," Zeta says. "Absolutely no personal missions. If you think you can make a quick buck by going back in time and betting on last year's Super Bowl, think again. That's part of the reason for the tracker. You go on an unauthorized mission, you'll find yourself sitting in a jail cell."

Zeta opens the door for me, and I step out into the too-bright hallway. "Do you understand these three rules?"

"Why can't we go back and fix any mistakes?"

Zeta looms in front of me. He's not nearly as tall as Alpha—Zeta only has a few inches on me—but it feels as if he's towering over me. If he's trying to make me feel intimidated, it's kinda working. "Wormhole restrictions." His tone makes it clear that the questions are over. "Now, do you understand these three rules?"

I nod.

"Good," he says. "Because it's the only time I'm going to tell them to you." We walk down the hall to the door I went through yesterday. Zeta points up at the gold-plated plaque that hangs above it.

"Enhancement, not alteration," he says. "That is what we do. We enhance the past; we do not alter it."

It seems like a funny line to me—where enhancement ends and alteration begins—but before I can say this, Zeta punches in a code, and the door opens. Overwhelming, all-encompassing blackness is waiting on the other side.

"What is this?" I ask, pointing.

"A door."

Thanks.

"What's in there?" I ask.

"It's a gravity chamber." Zeta's voice is bored, as if it's obvious. I back away from the door, but Zeta grabs my arm and squeezes, and once again it's clear to me that I don't have control over this situation. I look down the hallway, up in the corners and crevices; and, sure enough, there are cameras everywhere, stalking my every move. "This room is a recent addition. Gravity helps ease the physical effects on the body that Chronometric Augmentation can wreak. It slows us down. Less stress on the bones and joints."

My mind can't help flashing to Epsilon, the woman in the wheelchair. Her body has been broken beyond repair. Is it because of Chronometric Augmentation? Is that why the other members of Annum Guard are all dead? Their bodies couldn't handle the physical trauma?

Now I'm not so sure I want to do this, even though my options are either climbing the ranks to find out the one thing I've always wanted to know or life imprisonment.

Zeta pushes me toward the door. "You first." He takes hold of my watch and presses the top button so the lid pops open. Then he hands it back. "Program it. We're going to March 5, 1770."

I hesitate before taking it. But I have to do this. I owe this to my dad. To his memory. And to my mom. I failed her once. I can't do it again.

I spin the dial. Year first. We're going back to before the American Revolution. That's a lot of spins around the watch. Next is month. It's October here and March there, so I guess that's seven spins back. Then the day. Seventeen spins backward. Zeta is standing next to me, staring at me. Like he wants me to hurry up. And now I've lost count. *Was that seventeen spins or only sixteen?*

"Ready?" he asks.

I have no idea. Seventeen or sixteen? Why didn't I focus? I hate myself in this moment. I spin the day dial back one more click and nod my head at Zeta.

"Go," he says.

I take a cautious step forward, then inhale. Let's do this.

"Go," I repeat. I leap into the room and snap the lid of the watch face shut.

It's as if the floor is there one moment, and the next it's whisked from under me. I fall, and my heart flies into the back of my throat, and I choke on it. I open my mouth to scream, but nothing comes out. I fall and fall and fall, as if I'm on an endless roller coaster.

And then my knees slam into the floor of the broom closet. I gasp and slap my palms to the ground. This is what makes Chronometric Augmentation easier? What the hell was it like before?

I push up. The closet is completely empty. There's not a whole lot of room in this closet, so maybe I'm supposed to wait outside.

Or maybe I'm supposed to wait right here and Zeta will be pissed if I leave. He doesn't strike me as a warm-and-fuzzy kind of guy.

Time passes. Several minutes. Too much time. Enough time to make it clear that I'm not supposed to wait here in the closet. I turn the door handle and brace myself to find an angry Zeta waiting for me on the other side, but all I see when I open the door is a field. What the—?

But then there's a loud *swoooosh!* It's coming from above. I look up, and Zeta appears beside me, out of nowhere. He pulls me back and slams the door shut, trapping us in this little broom closet.

Zeta turns on me with angry eyes. "Tell me, did you fail second-grade math?"

My heart skips a beat. "I . . . what?"

"You're in March 4, 1770, not March 5. Can you really not handle a simple task like counting backward? Do you need me to program your watch for you like you're a toddler?"

I bristle because I'm still tired, so my fuse is short; but I also shrink inside myself at the same time. This is partly my fault for not paying better attention when setting the watch. I hate messing up. Hate hate hate when I do things wrong.

"I'm sorry," I mutter.

"I had to project to March 5, realize you weren't there, then project back to the present, trudge upstairs, activate your tracker, and figure out where you were. You're wasting my time."

"I said I was sorry."

"Don't apologize. Get it right the first time. Reset your watch. One day forward. Do you think you can handle that?"

I don't respond. Instead I pull out my watch, turn the day

knob once, and shut it. I brace for the fall, but it doesn't come. Instead I'm pulled up like someone tosses me in the air, and less than a second later I'm on my knees in the same broom closet. Zeta lands on his feet next to me.

"Ready now?" He straightens his powdered wig and stomps his buckled shoes. He doesn't wait for a reply but instead opens the door and walks out.

I linger behind and try to figure out the sensations of projecting. Why did I feel as if I was being sucked up that time and not falling? It happened before, when I left 1874 to go back to the present and—oh. I get it. You fall into the past. You're whisked up to the future.

Zeta clears his throat, and I shake my head and jump out of the closet. And then I stop in my tracks as colonial Boston spreads out before me. And I do mean spreads out. I'm not looking into an alleyway. I'm staring at open land. There are cows where the Public Garden will be one day. There's no Back Bay. There's . . . water. It's an actual bay. I look out over Boston Common. There's no looming state house with a giant dome. There are no skyscrapers, no downtown shopping district. Instead, in the distance I see the Old State House. That's where the Boston Massacre took place. It's right there, unobstructed from view.

There isn't a row of brownstones either. Just this one house, set here on what will one day become Beacon Street, one of the most densely populated streets in Boston. I mean, the cheesy Cheers replica will be going in right down the street, a tourist trap for the unwary. The house we're standing in front of is tall and wide, with brown, stone walls and a balcony off the front.

"What is this?" I ask. "Where's the brownstone?"

Zeta doesn't blink. "The brownstones are still about a hundred years away. This is Hancock Manor. And that"—he points across the Common to the Old State House—"is our destination. You are to listen to me and do exactly as I tell you, understand?"

"Do we have some sort of plan?"

"*I* do," Zeta says. He yanks on his sleeves to tighten them and doesn't look at me. But his implication is clear. I'm on a need-to-know basis, and Zeta doesn't think I need to know *anything* at this point.

Just then church bells ring in the distance.

"Come on!" he shouts. "It's starting!"

Zeta zips down a Beacon Street that looks more like a cow pasture than the crowded road I know. He makes a right, and I have to run to catch up. I can't breathe in this damned dress! We make a left, where the state house sits in front of us. A crowd has already gathered. I head for the action, but Zeta pulls me back.

"Uh-uh," he says. "We watch from afar." He whips me around so that I'm facing him. His hands are pressed into my forearms so hard I'm going to have bruises. It's a display of strength. A way of telling me not to bolt for it because he's stronger and faster than I am. Yeah, I get it. Let's not forget the fact that I also have a *tracker* in my arm.

"What's our motto?" Zeta asks.

"Enhancement, not alteration."

In the background, dozens of men rush toward the Old State House. They're cursing and shouting about taxes, and a chill runs down my body. People are going to die. Soon. The crowd is yelling at the soldiers, pelting them with sticks and clubs. The soldiers'

THE EIGHTH GUARDIAN

faces are white with terror, a polar contrast to their gleaming red coats. They're young. So young. They could be me.

The whole scene is chaos. Frantic chaos. It reminds me of one of my mom's paintings. Whirls of competing colors racing around on canvas, so frenetic that your eye doesn't know which way to look. Her paintings display madness, and that's all I see here. A red coat here, a flash of white there. A woman screams, a baby cries, a man behind me barks an evil laugh as he launches a rock over my head. It misses a soldier by several feet.

"Tell me how you'd alter the past," Zeta shouts over the crowd. "Tell me how you'd alter history here, right this second."

"What?" I yell.

I look at the crowd and try to focus. Their numbers are swelling, and the British soldiers have called for backup. Panic screams in all directions from their eyes. This crowd is about to pummel them. One man yells to string them up, and I gasp. This is not at all how I remember the Boston Massacre from my history textbooks. Where are the soldiers firing on helpless, unarmed civilians? These colonists are a mob, and this is mob mentality. There's no stopping this.

"I can't!" I shout to Zeta. "There are too many people!"

A light-skinned black man bumps into me as he rushes to the front of the crowd. He looks back for a split second, as if he's sorry, but then turns and runs toward a white man standing in the center shouting the loudest. The white man seems to be a leader of the group. He's shouting cries, which the crowd echoes.

"That's Crispus Attucks," Zeta says, pointing to the black man. "And that"—he points to the white man leading the crowd—"is the rope maker Samuel Gray. Both of these men are going to die today. Do you want to know who else?"

My mouth falls open as I watch two of the soldiers shout at the men to back up and keep order. One man throws a stick that hits a soldier straight in the jaw, and the crowd cheers at the crunch.

Zeta grabs my arm and points to two boys pushing their way to the front of the crowd. "James Caldwell and Samuel Maverick. Victims three and four."

One of the boys turns to the other. "Is there a fire?" he shouts. "We have to help!"

He doesn't know. Neither of them does. They're about my age. Sixteen. Seventeen at most. They shouldn't die like this. I try to break away from Zeta to run to them, to try to pull them back, pull all of them back, but Zeta holds on to me tight.

"There's number five." He points to a man standing on the edge. "Patrick Carr."

I stop breathing when I look at Patrick Carr. He knows what's about to happen. It's written all over his face. But that's not what gets me. It's the young boy standing next to him. Patrick Carr is a father.

"Go home," he says to his son.

"But—" the boy says.

"Now. You go home now."

His son turns and runs away, as fast as his little legs will carry him.

The crowd throws more sticks. Rocks. Whatever they can find. A big, burly man launches toward a soldier. "You sons of bitches to fire! You can't kill us all! Fire! Why don't you fire? You dare not fire!" he shouts. I gasp.

"And there's who we're helping." Zeta points to a man across the crowd. "Christopher Monk. He is going to be shot today but will not die for nearly ten years, during which time the city of Boston will pay an exorbitant sum to see to his care. We're going to ensure the money gets put to a better use."

I barely notice the guy Zeta's pointing at, a guy about my age holding something that looks like a small baseball bat and shouting at the soldiers. I'm still staring at Patrick Carr. The crowd swells forward toward the soldiers.

"When I give you the signal, you are to run to Monk and pull him to the ground," Zeta yells over the roar of the crowd.

A shot rings out, and I duck my head, then look toward the soldiers. One of them has his rifle raised in the air.

"What?" I yell to Zeta.

"No!" Samuel Gray shouts in the middle of the crowd. "God damn you, don't fire!"

But it's too late. Shots ring out, and the crowd screams as Samuel Gray falls. I squat down, but Zeta jerks me back up. "Hang on! Almost!"

I can't think. Men zip this way and that, ducking their heads and screaming. Soldiers are still firing. Patrick Carr waves to someone across the street and motions the person away, then steps out to cross.

No! He can't! His little boy is going to have to grow up without a father. I know what that's like. And I can't let him feel that pain. I twist away from Zeta and run just as the crowd reaches us.

"Iris!" Zeta shouts. "Don't do anything!"

I block him out. I head right toward Patrick Carr. I'll take him down. I'll tackle him to the ground, and then he'll miss the bullet that was meant for him. He's close. And my eye flashes to a glint of red a few feet away. A soldier takes aim at Carr. I scream and rear back to launch myself forward.

But then I'm on the ground as a shot rings out. A few feet away, Patrick Carr goes down, and only then does he make a sound. His mouth opens, and an anguished moan bursts from his lips. I scream, too, as Zeta pins my arms to the ground, not letting me move. Blood seeps out of Carr's hip, and I cry. I don't care who sees me. I cry. I think of my dad, dying somewhere, and now I will forever have the image of a fatal rifle shot to the side entrenched in my mind. This will be how my dad dies in my dreams.

Zeta yanks me up. Carr writhes on the ground, and I kick at Zeta. I have to help Carr. Maybe if I can stop the bleeding, he'll live. But Zeta pulls me away, down the street. We step over a bloody, still Christopher Monk on the ground and round a corner, away from the crowd. It's only then that Zeta drops his hands and pushes me backward. I trip over my feet.

"Godammit, what the hell is the matter with you?" he roars. "What were you thinking?"

The tears are still falling down my face. "I was saving him! I was enhancing the past to save him."

Zeta's eyebrows shoot up. "Enhancing? You think that's what I mean when I say enhancing? Do you have any idea what you could have done? Patrick Carr was not the mission."

"I could have given his little boy a father to watch him grow up!"

Zeta's bright-blue eyes grow wide as the moon and fire erupt behind them. "Whatever happened to you in the past is in the past. *This* is your job now, and you do not let emotion take over. Let me tell you a little something about Patrick Carr. He's going to die nine days from now—a slow, painful, agonizing death—but he single-handedly is going to change the course of American history. What did you see back there?"

"I saw a bunch of people die," I say as the realization sinks in. I saw people die. *Die.* In front of me. It's a first. I've seen photos of dead bodies and have watched plenty of violent movies, but I've never seen the real thing. It's awful. This whole scene is awful. No amount of training could've prepared me for the screams of anguish, the fallen bodies, the finality of death lingering in their open eyes.

"Why did they die?" he asks me.

Do I tell the truth? What I really think? I have to.

"Because they provoked the British soldiers, and the soldiers shot at them in self-defense."

Zeta nods. "A little different from the history they taught you in school, right? And the truth could be buried forever if not for the heroics of Patrick Carr. He's going to out the truth on his deathbed. He's going to tell his doctor that the soldiers were greatly abused by the crowd, that the soldiers would have been hurt or killed had they not fired. He's going to confirm that it was self-defense. And because of the bravery and honesty of Patrick Carr, those soldiers are going to be acquitted at trial.

"Had Carr not been honest, those soldiers would have been martyred, the British would have retaliated, and the American Revolution could have started five years before we were ready to fight it. We could have lost the Revolution had you tackled Patrick Carr to the ground like you were about to."

Zeta pauses, and I let his words sink in. America could have lost its fight for independence because of me. Because of *me*.

"Enhancement, not alteration," he repeats. "You were about to alter history in a pretty big way."

"I don't understand what the difference is," I say.

"Clearly."

I bristle. And I can't help but feel this isn't my fault completely. "Well, maybe you should have explained it a little better before you just plunked me down in the middle of the Boston Massacre."

I probably shouldn't have said that. No, I *definitely* shouldn't have said that. Zeta's eyes narrow, and he stands up really tall. Yep, he has military training. He looks as if he wants to break me, and I don't doubt for a second that he could.

"Or maybe," he says in a quiet, dangerous voice, "you should learn to exercise better impulse control. You're now the seventh recruit I've trained, and not one has had a single problem obeying orders in the field. Not one. But if you want to do this the old-fashioned way, we can. You won't learn in the field. You can learn in the library. You can write me so many essays on the difference between altering and enhancing that your hand will want to fall off. You'll never gain access to more of our secrets, and you probably won't survive this probationary period. Is that what you want?"

My stomach sinks. I'm better than this; I know I am.

"I'm sorry," I say.

"Save it. We're going back." He turns and starts walking toward Beacon Hill. Well, the empty tract of land that will one day become Beacon Hill, I guess.

Zeta doesn't say a word to me. He watches me press the knob that automatically sets the watch to the present—as if he thinks I could screw up something that simple—and doesn't speak as he pulls out a special key that unlocks a hidden door in the side of Hancock Manor. The only communication I get is when he jerks his head toward our broom closet, indicating that I should go first.

Alpha is waiting for us upstairs when we get back.

"How did it go?" His smile is wide.

I bite my lower lip as Zeta saunters up next to me, shaking his head. "How would you like it if we were still under British rule? Because that's what your star recruit here almost did." There's sarcasm dripping from every syllable. "Oh, and we failed with Monk."

Alpha's face gets very still.

"I'm not taking her out into the field again until she can prove she understands the difference between enhancing and altering and demonstrates a better sense of self-control."

Zeta whips off his wig and stalks toward the stairs, leaving me alone with Alpha in the living room. Alpha doesn't move for a few seconds. When he finally does, he takes out his old Moleskine notebook from his inside jacket pocket and makes a note with a heavy sigh. Then he tucks the notebook back inside and turns to me.

"So, all in all, not such a great first day?"

"I'm sorry," I say. It's, like, my tenth apology of the morning.

Alpha looks at me. There's a flash of anger in his eyes, but then something changes as he stares at me. He softens, and I'm confused.

"Eh, you win some, you lose some." But he winces when he says it.

I've failed. I know I've failed. I feel like I've disappointed Alpha, and it dawns on me that I feel guilty. Guilty. Like I should feel bad for letting Alpha down. The man who ripped me away from Peel as a junior. Ripped me from Abe.

I do feel bad. Why is that?

His lips press into a grim line. "Do better tomorrow." And then he leaves.

But his implication hangs there. *Do better tomorrow*, because there might not be another chance after that.

CHAPTER 8

The next morning there's a note slid under my door. It's from Zeta. He wants me to write an essay on any historical event of my choosing. I have to explain the difference between enhancing and altering, then bring the essay to his office when I'm done.

Great. An essay.

I ball up the note, whip around, and send it sailing through the air. It bounces off the back wall and lands on the bed. Essays are not going to help me gain clearance. I'm angry. Partly at myself, but mostly at Zeta. No organization sends its operatives on a mission without a thorough briefing beforehand. Learning in the field can get you killed. Everyone knows that. Well, everyone except Zeta, I guess.

I decide to skip breakfast so I don't have to face Zeta or the rest of them. I bet Yellow's heard about my failure, and I can't trust myself not to hurl a fork at her when she smirks at me. Instead, I take a nice, long shower and let the hot water rain down on me. I wish it would wash all of this away. I wish for a second I could step out of the shower and into my old dorm room at Peel, that I could throw on my uniform and dash across the quad to the dining hall, that I could slide in next to Abe and he'd kiss me on the cheek. Like normal. Like how it used to be. Like how it never will be again.

If I'm going to be stuck in the library all day, I'm dressing for comfort. The corset and eighteenth-century dress still lie in a crumpled heap in the bottom of my closet. I opt for a pair of black, stretchy pants and Abe's old sweatshirt. Traces of his cologne linger on the neckline, and I inhale as I slip it over my head. My fingers grasp the neck, and I close my eyes.

I remember the last time he wore this sweatshirt. We were on our way back from a brutal TRX session at the Peel gym. I shivered in the night air, and Abe took off the sweatshirt and tossed it to me without hesitation, without asking. I never got around to giving it back.

I miss him. Is he really planning to wait for me, like he promised? He's going to be waiting a long time, because I'm never getting out of Annum Guard.

He has to move on.

I rip off the sweatshirt and throw it on top of the corset. I sink down to the ground as it lands and place both hands on top of my heart. My chest aches as if my heart is really breaking. I always thought that was just an expression, but now I know it's not. I want to scream, cry, throw things; but I won't. I refuse to let myself sink into a deep, cavernous well of depression because, God knows, mental illness runs in my family, and I will not be her. I won't.

An image of my mom sitting curled up in a chair, motionless for hours, floats into my head, immediately followed by one of her rushing around the house, throwing paint at canvas and singing at the top of her lungs to the radio, not concerned that she hasn't slept in two days.

I grimace. This day sucks. This whole week sucks. I push myself up, grab a hoodie from the drawer, and stomp down the stairs.

Breakfast is over, and there isn't a soul in sight. Good. I don't feel like seeing anyone today. I take a breath before I open the doors to the library, praying it's empty.

It is. Floor-to-ceiling bookshelves line the perimeter of three of the walls, but I head straight to the computer on the fourth wall. It's set out of the way, behind two oversize red velvet arm-chairs, as if they don't want us to know it's there. I guess that makes sense, what with the living history and all. Computers are a reminder that we actually live in the present.

I turn on the computer, and a box pops up asking for my user name and password. I type *IRIS* as my user name and then hesitate. What are the chances my password is going to be something simple that I already know? I shrug and type *IRIS* into the password box, then hit ENTER.

The screen goes black and ACCESS DENIED pops up on the screen in huge white letters. And then the computer beeps. Over and over and over again.

I scramble and nearly fall out of the chair as I bend down to shut it off. The beeping stops, but I hold my breath, waiting for someone to barge into the room and yell at me.

But the room stays still. I exhale.

Books it is. I tuck the chair into the desk and walk the room, scanning the titles of the books as I go. History books. They're all history books. *The History of the Decline and Fall of the Roman*

Empire. Great Britain and Her Queen. A People's History of the United States. There are a few that look like they might be fun to flip through for the pictures. *A Brief History of Italian Renaissance Architecture. Early Colonial Costume.* Okay, strike what I said about pictures. I know what early colonial costume looks like, and it's terrible. Constricting and terrible.

I grab a book on the Civil War and flip through a few pages. It's talking about Lincoln's Emancipation Proclamation. *Whatever.* That'll do.

According to the book, the Emancipation Proclamation didn't actually free a single slave since the South had already seceded from the Union, so the Union technically didn't govern the South at the time the proclamation was issued. The whole thing was just one giant political move. Huh. One more thing they didn't exactly teach us in school. I distinctly remember learning in the eighth grade that the Emancipation Proclamation freed all the slaves, and, hallelujah, ain't Lincoln great? First the Boston Massacre, now the Emancipation Proclamation. What else is a lie?

Hell if I know how I'd alter this or enhance it.

I decide I'll focus on the timing. Let Lincoln actually free the slaves by issuing the proclamation before the South secedes. I pick up a pen and start scratching on the paper. I write that I'd alter the past if I went back in time, broke into the White House, held a gun to Lincoln's head, and made him issue the proclamation before the South seceded. Then I write that I'd enhance the past if I sent an anonymous letter warning Lincoln that the South was about to secede and that maybe he'd want to issue a proclamation or something freeing all the slaves.

I set down my pen and look over what I wrote. I squint and

hope it's at least legible. Dainty, neat handwriting has never been my strong suit.

Now to find Zeta. It would have been nice for someone to tell me where Zeta's office is. Hell, it would have been nice for someone to tell me Zeta had an office.

Indigo's in the living room. He's sitting on the brocade velvet sofa wearing a gray uniform of some sort. Two heavy black boots are propped up on the coffee table. There's a rifle resting on the floor. Indigo's popped off the bayonet and is polishing it with a rag. He stops and looks up at me.

"Hey," he says, as if it's totally natural that he's sitting there in a uniform that belongs in a museum, polishing a rifle.

"What are you, headed out for a Civil War reenactment?"

Indigo flashes a coy smile. "Minus the reenactment part, yes. Where are you off to?"

I hold up my essay and wave it around for show. "I have to drop this off at Zeta's office, but I have no idea where that is."

Indigo smiles wider and turns his neck around. He points the bayonet toward the hallway just past the staircase. "Through there. Second door on the right. Don't go in the first. That's a bathroom." He winks at me, and I stand up straight as a flutter of electricity jolts down my body. Really? Just because an attractive boy winks at me doesn't mean my body needs to respond.

And then I feel a pang of guilt as the image of Abe clutching his chest at the graduation banquet fills my mind.

"Good luck," Indigo says. "With Zeta, I mean."

I scowl and pick at one of the calluses on my hand. "That guy's a dick."

Indigo rears back his head and laughs. Hard. Genuinely. He

sighs with an amused grin and plops the bayonet onto the sofa next to him. "Boy, they sure haven't told you a whole lot about how this place runs, have they?"

Somewhere deep inside of me a little rumbling of anger erupts, but I keep my face neutral. Just like they taught us at Peel. Never show emotion when in stressful situations. Emotions are a road map to your weaknesses.

"Nope, they sure haven't," I say.

Indigo drops his feet from the edge of the coffee table and stands up. He's not that much taller than me. "No worries, kid." He squeezes my shoulder. "I'm sure they'll tell you eventually, just as soon as they make you a permanent operative." Indigo leans down so that his mouth rests right beside my ear. I feel his breath on my skin, and no amount of willpower in the world can stop the chills from racing up my arms.

"And don't worry," he whispers. "When you do have it all figured out, I won't hold it against you."

Huh? Hold what against me?

Indigo stands up, grabs his rifle, and hooks the bayonet to the front. He slides the gun over his shoulder, gives me a salute, and heads toward the underground stairs.

What in the world was *that* about? I shake my head and amble down the hallway. First door. Bathroom. Second door. The door is shut, but there's a bronze plaque just to the right of it that reads ZETA. Right below the plaque is a keypad. I look across the hall-way, where there's a plaque that reads ALPHA, along with another keypad. There's another office to the right of Alpha's door with a plaque that says RED. Red has his own office? Does everyone have an office but me?

Well, here goes nothing. I raise a hand and rap my knuckles on the door.

"Come in," a voice calls from the other side.

I take a breath and turn the knob. The office is small. Maybe ten-by-ten. There's a desk set in the middle of the room, and Zeta sits behind it. He sets down the file he'd been reading. He's wearing normal clothing today: a pair of tan pants and a navy sweater with the sleeves pushed up past his elbows. Even though all that's peeking out are his forearms, my guesses about him the day before are confirmed. Zeta works out. A lot. His forearms are freaking sculpted.

He holds out a hand. "You have an essay for me?" I hand it over, and he points at one of the two chairs in front of the desk. "Sit. Please."

The "please" was a total afterthought, but I look past it and sit anyway. Zeta plunks the essay onto the desk and picks up a red pen. He reads the essay quietly, then flips it over, as if hoping there's something more on the back. That's not a good sign. He sighs and hands it back. "Do it again. You're not even close."

"But I don't know where to start. No one's even tried to explain the difference between enhancing and altering to me."

"And whose fault is that?" Zeta's eyebrows arch up. "Figure it out. I trust you're a smart girl. Alpha wouldn't have picked you otherwise." There's something funny in his voice. A little inflection that I can't quite decipher.

I make a fist, crumbling the corners of the paper with my fingers as I leave his office. I want to slam the door behind me, but that would be childish. So I close it softly as if nothing's wrong. *No emotion,* I tell myself.

Alpha's door is right in front of me, and, without thinking, I knock.

"Enter," Alpha says on the other side.

I open the door to find that his office is a mirror image of Zeta's. Alpha has his back turned and is typing something on a computer screen. It's a memo of some sort. I squint my eyes and read it. I make out the words *Iris* and *Boston Massacre* in the first sentence and sigh. Alpha turns, sees me, and flips off the screen.

"Hello." He swivels the chair around to face me. The black notebook is sitting on the desk, and Alpha scoops it up and tosses it toward the computer.

"Level with me," I say. "What are my chances of being promoted to a full operative?"

Alpha leans back in his chair. "Do you want to sit?"

"No." I feel more in control when I stand.

"Do you want me to be blunt?"

"Yes." I think I do.

"Your chances aren't up to me. I don't get to make that call. But if it was up to me, I'd have some serious doubts at this point."

Ouch. It takes every ounce of my being not to recoil. Instead I stand up straighter. "That's hardly fair. No one explained to me the difference between altering and enhancing. I thought I was enhancing."

Alpha raises an eyebrow. "We've never explained to recruits beforehand the difference between enhancing and altering. Your task is to figure it out for yourself in the field. And I do believe you were given very specific instructions not to do anything without first running it past your superior. So if you're going to make excuses for yourself, you'll have to do better than that."

Dammit. I am making excuses again. So I simply say, "Point taken. May I be excused?"

"No. Let me see the essay."

I hesitate a second before handing it over. I wish I'd just gone back to the library and kept quiet. Alpha scans my essay and hands it back.

"I'm not going to spell it out for you," Alpha says, "but I will say this. The key to understanding the difference between enhancing and altering isn't to look at the effect. It's to look at the *cause*. If you want a man to be late to work, are you going to blow up his house, or are you going to let the air out of his car tires? When in doubt, be subtle. Understand?"

I nod my head.

"Now you may be excused." He swivels around in his chair, flips on the computer monitor, and starts typing.

I wander back toward the library. Look at the cause, not the effect. That makes sense. I'm already thinking about how I can crib what Alpha just told me and change it enough so that Zeta will think it's my own idea.

The library isn't empty anymore. Tyler Fertig is standing to the side, a book in his hand. My heart leaps, and I shut the door behind me.

"Tyler," I call.

He drops the book to the floor and whips around with a shocked look on his face. But then his eyes narrow when he sees me, and he flies across the room, so fast I barely know what's coming. He grabs me by the shoulders and slams me back into a bookshelf. It rattles, and several books fall to the floor.

"It's Blue!" he spits. "*Blue!* Don't ever call me by that name again. Tyler is dead. Do you understand me?"

He's holding me all wrong. He has the front of my shoulders pinned and nothing else, so I could easily drop down, punch him where the sun don't shine, and spin away before he falls. But instead I nod my head.

Blue gives me one last push into the bookshelf, then unhands me. I stare at him. Long and hard. I look right into his eyes, and he stares back at me with a hollow glare. And then it hits me. It's so obvious, I can't believe I didn't see it before. Blue is sad.

I don't mean sadness in the sense that your dog just died or your girlfriend dumped you. I mean sadness that never ends. Sadness that wraps over you like a blanket, consuming you with its darkness. Sadness that holds you tight and won't let you go. I know it well. It's the sadness that I've watched overtake my mom, watched battle with the manic episodes for control. I see her depression in Blue's eyes, looking back at me, pleading with me, begging me not to go; and I look away.

"You don't belong here," Blue whispers. "This place is going to kill you just like it does everyone else, and you don't have to be here."

An image of Blue as Tyler pops into my head. Tyler strutting into the dining hall at Peel two years ago, months before Testing Day. He was smiling and laughing, and his arm was thrown around Deanna Verster. Heads turned to watch him walk, because you had no choice but to admire his confidence. And then I think of him the following year, when he was a senior. He kept his head down, never said much. I watched his friends move to the other side of the table, then find a new table. Deanna Verster started hanging out with someone else. Tyler sat with freshmen but stared at his food the entire time and never talked. To anyone. It was like he knew what was coming after graduation. He knew about Annum Guard. But how?

"What happened on Testing Day, Blue?" I whisper. "Junior year. What happened?"

Blue stares past me to the bookshelf. Then he whispers, "They lied to me."

"Who lied to you, Blue? About what?"

"They told me if I did well enough, I could go someplace else. I wouldn't have to follow the path. I could be free. They lied."

"Who's they?"

"Vaughn. All of them."

The headmaster? Headmaster Vaughn knows about Annum Guard? I guess that shouldn't surprise me. It seemed like Vaughn knew about me, too.

I shake my head. "I still don't understand. What path are you talking about, Ty—"

Shit.

I cut myself off, praying he won't notice, but Blue's enraged eyes are back. I hold up my hands. "I'm sorry. Please. I'm sorry."

Blue pushes past me, heading toward the door. But he turns back to me at the last second. "You should start praying at night that they don't let you in. You'll be better off in solitary than you will be in here. It wasn't right for them to take you like they did. You don't belong here."

He opens the door.

"Blue!" I call, but it doesn't matter. He's already gone. In more ways than one.

CHAPTER 9

Blue doesn't show up for dinner. I stare at the empty chair between Yellow and Violet. I'm glad Zeta sits on the same side of the table as I do, but all the way down by Alpha. It means Zeta is completely hidden from view, and I don't have to see his face and remember how he nodded his head at me when I handed in my second essay. I basically just copied what Alpha told me word for word, and Zeta looked pleased, which of course made me feel like crap, because technically I was cheating. And really, I still have no idea how altering differs from enhancing. You can slap whatever label you want on it, but tweaking the past is still changing it in my book.

I don't know what I should do. A sour taste lingers on my tongue following my run-in with Blue. I've known that they weren't telling me much, but now I can see that the truth is much more than that. There are things that they intentionally *aren't* telling me.

I glance around the table and try to find the weakest link, the person who will tell me what I need to know. Alpha and Zeta are out, obviously. And I'll just go ahead and count Red out, too. He's a member of the office club, and I don't trust anyone who has an office. Next is Orange. I don't really know anything about Orange, except that he looks to be way older than everyone else, like Red. Midtwenties, maybe. He's also never spoken to me, and I get the feeling that he resents my presence here. Yellow is a definite no. Green presents the same problem as Orange; while he's about my age, I don't know where to start. That leaves Indigo and Violet.

That leaves Indigo.

After dinner everyone piles out of the dining room except Green and Indigo, who are deep in a conversation about some battle Indigo fought in today in the Civil War. I pretend I have to tie my shoe, even though I've been slipping my feet into these sneakers for so long that I couldn't untie the laces with a pair of pliers.

Finally Green and Indigo wrap up, and Green leaves. Indigo turns to me. "Something I can help you with?"

I sit up. "No. Why would you say that?"

"Um, because it's very clear you've been sitting here waiting for me to finish my conversation. So unless you'd just like to gaze longingly into my eyes"—he bats his baby blues at me—"I'm going to assume you want me for something."

No on the eyes thing. Although he is right. I *do* want something. I want the full story. But I'm not going to be dumb about it and come out and ask. These things take time; I know that from reconnaissance lessons. First you have to track the subject and learn his every move. Human beings are creatures of habit.

Once you learn those habits, you know the weaknesses. Same thing here. I have to learn Indigo's weaknesses by watching him, by befriending him. Get him to let down his guard and trust me.

I just hope I have enough time.

"Fine," I say. "I do want you for something."

Indigo raises an eyebrow and grins.

"I was hoping you could help me with this essay I'm working on for Zeta."

Indigo smiles. "That guy's a dick."

I clear my throat. "I'm still having a few problems understanding the difference between altering and enhancing, and I was hoping—"

"I'm not really supposed to," Indigo interrupts. "You have to figure it out on your own. That's what they told us."

"Who told you that?"

"Alpha. Zeta. Red. You'll figure it out."

Everyone seems so sure of that except for me. I sigh and push my chair back to stand. I hate being shot down. It makes me feel like such an ass for asking in the first place.

"Hey." Indigo puts his hand on my back, and for one brief second I'm surprised to discover that I don't want him to move it. "I can imagine this is very frustrating for you."

I crane my head left to look at him.

"And I really can't tell you about the difference between enhancing and altering. Zeta specifically told us not to. But—" He looks out the door into the living room, then back at me. "I can tell you some other things if you'd like." He pulls his hand away, and I scoot the chair back in.

My brain tells me to slow down and go for the important

questions first. But my mouth has other plans. I start vomiting out questions faster than I can think of them. "So how were you all chosen for this? Is there some sort of path you're following? Why is Alpha in charge? What happened to the rest of Annum Guard Two? Or Annum Guard One for that matter? Why the hell does Red have an office? And—"

Indigo holds up both hands. "Whoa. Simmer down there. I said I could tell you some things; I didn't say I could tell you everything I've ever learned in my entire life."

My mouth snaps shut, and deep within the bowels of my imagination, my brain locks my tongue in a basement and starts beating it with a baseball bat. Way to blow it, genius.

Indigo looks at the door one more time. "I can tell you this. Chronometric Augmentation—all the projecting—is really, really hard on the body. The first generation didn't last very long. At all. There's only one member left. Seven. And he's only around because he didn't project that often. He sort of ran the missions."

"Where is he now?"

Indigo shrugs. "I guess technically he's still 'in charge of the Guard' since he's the most senior living member." I ignore that Indigo just used finger quotes. "But he doesn't really want much to do with us anymore. He rarely comes around. I don't think I've seen him in at least a year. Alpha's in charge now. Has been for a really, really long time. Like, since before we were born."

"How come Zeta's still alive?"

"Wow, you really don't like him, huh?" Indigo says with a laugh.

"I didn't mean *that*. I mean, how come he doesn't seem to be fazed by the projecting?"

"The gravity chamber," Indigo says. "Zeta invented it. Look, I know you don't like him, but he's really smart. He figured out that gravity lets us project without all the physical trauma. He used himself as a guinea pig while he was testing the chamber, and it turned out to be a really good call. Everyone else is dead or . . . on their way out."

I think of Epsilon in the wheelchair. Talk about dying for your country in the slowest, most agonizing way possible. But thinking about death makes me think about my dad, which makes clearance codes flash before my eyes. I turn back to Indigo. I stare him right in the eye as if daring him not to answer my next question.

"So why were you all chosen for this? Huh? Why am I considered an outsider?"

Indigo's eyes drop to his lap, and he deliberately ignores the question. "Red has an office because Alpha is grooming him to take over leadership someday. The end." He scoots his chair back and stands.

Dammit. This isn't the first time I've come on too strong. And it won't be the last time it all blows up in my face either, I'm sure.

"That's really all I can tell you, Iris. I hope it helped clear up a few things." His voice is distant, reserved. Time to backpedal.

I pat his hand for one quick half second. "It did." Even though he didn't answer the questions I wanted to know the most. "Thank you. Can I ask you one more?"

Indigo looks pained. "Um, okay?"

I lob him a softball to get him back on my good side. "Who came up with the term 'Chronometric Augmentation' anyway? Didn't they realize that sounds like we're giving time a boob job?"

Indigo's head falls to his chin and he laughs. Really laughs. Then he pushes in his chair and squeezes my shoulder as he walks past me and out the doorway.

No one speaks to me much over the next few days. They sure as hell don't take me on any missions. I spend my days in the library, reading book after book on American history, taking enough notes to fill an entire three-ring binder. Essays. All essays for Zeta. Each time, I pick an event and only make one minor little change. I still have no idea what the difference between enhancing and altering is, but I have to do something to win back his trust.

I'm in the library, hunched over a desk writing, when Alpha walks in. I look up, and he shuts the door behind him.

"Hello," he says. He's a very tall man standing over me, looking down as I sit at my desk. It makes me feel small and powerless.

"Hi." I drag out the word. Alpha has a troubled look in his eyes. It's unsettling.

"What are you working on?"

I hold up my essay. Zeta wasn't kidding when he said he'd make me write so many essays it would feel as if my hand is about to fall off. My right hand is numb, and I'm not entirely sure I can straighten out my fingers.

"May I see?"

I hand Alpha my essay. It's on Prohibition. I argued that I would alter the past if I'd tossed a bomb onto the Congressional floor and stopped the vote that would kick-start the whole thing. I'd enhance the past if I prevented a whole bunch of Congressmen from making it to the vote.

Alpha sighs and puts down the paper. "Really? This is the same damned example I gave you four days ago, and it's not even right. What else do you have?"

I look down at the myriad of papers strewn about my desk and pick up one I started on Pearl Harbor.

Alpha holds out his hand. "Let me see it."

I hand it over. It only takes him a few seconds to scan it. I don't have that much written. Just a background paragraph explaining how the Japanese launched an attack on Pearl Harbor on December 7, 1941, which killed more than twenty-four hundred people and led directly to the United States's entry into World War II. And then the essay stops because I have no idea whether I'm supposed to try to stop the bombing and save all those people or let it happen so that the US enters the war. Alpha hands back the essay.

"Pick up your pen," he orders.

I do.

"I want you to copy this down exactly."

I put the pen to the paper.

"An Annum Guardian would engage in alteration if he infiltrated the naval headquarters at Pearl Harbor and warned the commanding officers of the impending attack. However, if that Guardian were to arrange for the battleship *USS Arizona* to remain moored at the quays along Ford Island rather than move it to Pearl Harbor on December 6, 1941, thereby saving the lives of more than a thousand men and ensuring the *Arizona* could be used in the Battle of Wake Island, that Guardian would engage in enhancement."

I'm scribbling furiously, even though there is no way that Zeta is going to think I wrote this myself. It's leaps and bounds above anything I've given him before.

"Did you get all of that?" Alpha asks after I stop and set down the pen.

I nod.

He holds out his hand again, and I hesitate. Because, really, if I was to change the past so that the USS *Arizona* could help America win a victory at Wake Island, how is that *not* altering the past?

Maybe I really don't belong here. Maybe I'm not nearly as bright as I always thought I was.

I pass the paper over. Alpha scans it, then reaches and takes my pen. He marks a big A+ on top of the essay and gives it back.

"Congratulations. You demonstrate sufficient knowledge of the difference between enhancing and altering, and I think we can skip the rest of these essays and throw you back into the field. I trust you've learned to utilize some better self-control?"

I sit up straight. *Back into the field? No more essays? Finally!*

"Of course," I say.

"You will follow orders exactly and not make a move until told to do so?"

"Yes."

"And you will not question what it is you're asked to do but rather accept your mission and perform it to the best of your abilities?"

"Yes," I say without hesitation, even though a little warning bell is going off inside my head. Why would I question a mission? What exactly are they going to ask me to do?

"I will trust your word," Alpha says. "And I will give you this." He reaches into a pocket on the inside of his suit jacket and pulls out a folded piece of paper. He hands it to me, and I turn it over. There's another red wax seal holding it closed. The scary-looking owl stares up at me, and my heart skips a beat as I remember that day at Peel. It feels like a lifetime ago. I can't believe it's been just over a week.

It dawns on me that I haven't really thought about Abe at all today. I know I told myself I had to forget about him, but I didn't think my mind would obey quite so quickly. . . .

"What's this?" I ask.

"Open it."

I hesitate for a second before sliding my index finger under the crease and breaking the seal. I unfold the paper and read.

$$874ZEPHYR\%0\%$$

"Memorize it," Alpha says.

I look at it again. *Zephyr.* That's easy to remember. *%0%.* So's that. It's the numbers to worry about. I repeat *874* in my head a few times—*874 874 874 874*—and look up. "Okay, I did, but—"

Alpha holds out his hand. "Give it back."

I fold the paper over and hand it to him, repeating the code in my head once more. This is it. My security clearance password. It has to be.

"I passed along the progress report I filled out on you to the folks in Washington," Alpha says. "They sent that."

"So I have a new clearance level."

Alpha purses his lips together and doesn't respond, probably because I just stated the obvious.

I feel weightless for the first time since Headmaster Vaughn dimmed the lights at dinner and announced it was Testing Day.

"You and I got off to a rocky start, Iris. But I have your back in this. I want you to stay."

He stands and heads toward the door but then turns around again. He tilts his head toward the computer on the far wall.

"Use it wisely."

As soon as the door shuts, I spring up and race to the computer. I start it up, and the log-in screen appears. I type in *Iris* as my user name and enter the password that Alpha just gave me. For a second I worry that I remembered the number wrong and that I'll get the black screen of death, but then a plain white screen appears with the United States seal in the top left corner. There's a search box; and I click on it, type in my father's name, and hit ENTER. I hold my breath as the screen flashes.

This could be it. I realize I'm not breathing and exhale.

The search results are up, and there it is. A file in an unspecified personnel directory.

Obermann, Mitchell Thomas

I stop breathing again as the mouse hovers over my father's name. Am I ready for this? Ready to know the truth? There's only one way to find out. I click on it.

The screen flashes away, and a new one pops up.

Mitchell Thomas Obermann. Born Natick, Massachusetts. Died [XXXXXXXX]

I'm not aware of my sharp intake of breath until my lungs burn. Eight *X*s. I count all of them twice. They're the computer equivalent of taking a big black marker to a piece of paper and scrawling the word *redacted* on top. A truth I don't get to know.

I rest my head in my hands before I look back at the screen. My dad's date of birth is listed, too, as well as his date of death. Dates I already know. *Information I already freaking know.* My breath chokes inside my throat, and I look away. This page isn't going to tell me anything. Just like the dog tags.

A surge of anger shoots through my body. Anger at the injustice of the whole thing. Anger at how helpless I feel. I've worked so hard to make sure I'd never have to feel helpless again, but in this game of life, the house always wins. Screw the house.

Still, a small part of me hopes there's even one useful nugget of information. I look back and keep reading.

Educational Background
Johnson School, Natick, Massachusetts.
Coolidge Junior High School, Natick, Massachusetts.
The Peel Academy, Upton, Massachusetts.
United States Naval Academy, Annapolis, Maryland.

And now I sit up straight. My dad did go to Peel. I mean, I always suspected he did, despite the dog tags—because how else would I get in?—but you never know. Peel doesn't exactly keep public records of its students. You won't find any old yearbooks in the library. No photos of past valedictorians hanging on the walls.

I guess my dad was in the ten percent who didn't go CIA. That happens. Some go FBI, some go NSA, some don't go government at all. Like Abe's dad, who went private sector after Peel.

According to this, my dad went on to the navy. So he graduated from the Naval Academy and then . . . Wait. I stare at the dates I skimmed past the first time. That doesn't make sense. My dad only spent three years at the Naval Academy. He didn't graduate.

Something isn't adding up here. I scroll down the page, but there's no employment information. Nothing to tell me what my dad did from the time he left the academy until he died. Not even an [XXXXXXXX]. That means it's really classified.

I scan the Personal Information section. There's a bunch of information on my grandparents—my dad's parents—both of whom are long dead. Walter and Dorothy Obermann. I never knew them. Although—I stare at their birth and death dates—my grandfather died young. I never knew that. That must have been hard on my dad.

My mom's name is there. I stare at it—

Spouse – Joy Crina Obermann (nee Amar). Born Brooklyn, New York.

I wonder how's she's doing today. Is it a manic day? A depressed day? Has she maybe started having normal days again since I left?

I shake my head and move down to the next line.

Child(ren) – Amanda Jean Obermann.* Born Jericho, Vermont.

I blink. Over and over again, but it doesn't do a thing to get rid of that star next to my name. I'd scroll farther, but I'm already at the bottom of the page. I look at the entire page, but just like I thought, the star isn't explained anywhere. It's a stray star hanging there, taunting me.

Which just means that I'll have to work harder to weasel the next level of clearance away from them.

Screw you, house. I *will* beat you.

CHAPTER 10

I find a note under my door the next morning, and I yawn as I bend to pick it up.

NUMBER EIGHT

My neck snaps up. When Alpha said I was back to training missions, I didn't realize he meant the next day. I race to my closet and push all the hangers holding my things to the side, eager to get to my historical wardrobe. I find the hanger marked with an 8 and pull it down.

It's a knee-length baby-blue dress with a wide skirt and a white Peter Pan collar. There's a matching purse. I wrinkle my nose. That collar looks like something I would have worn on a jumper when I was four. But then I remember the star next to my name and tell myself it's time to get serious.

I take a quick shower and zip up the dress. It looks even

more ridiculous on me than it did on the hanger. With a pair of white wrist gloves and some sensible heels, I'd be ready for bridge club in the church fellowship hall. I have no idea what to do with my hair, so I throw it back into a low ponytail. I add a thin layer of black eyeliner and a smidge of a shimmery brown eye shadow, then I swipe a few dabs of mascara onto my eyelashes—only because I'm afraid Alpha would put me through another Yellow makeover if I don't. I take one quick look in the mirror, and the mascara tube clatters to the floor.

I look so much like my mom with the makeup. The old pictures of her. The ones from before her diagnosis or from shortly after, when she was still medicating. The ones when she was young and happy, full of life. Her eyes are green and wide, while mine are brown and close set—my dad's eyes; but everything else is my mom. In this mirror, I am her.

I hope and pray every single night that looks are the only thing I inherited from her. She wasn't that much older than I am now when she got the diagnosis. There could be a ticking time bomb lying dormant inside of me, waiting for the right moment to explode its mania and desperation all over the normal life I'm trying so hard to build. I chew my bottom lip for a few seconds, then I'm out the door.

There isn't. I'm not.

I slide into my place next to Indigo and try to delete my mom from my mind. Indigo leans over and lifts one of the flaps of my collar. "Cute."

I bat his hand away but then notice he's ditched the Civil War getup today. Instead he's wearing a pair of high-waisted, pleated pants and a charcoal tweed skinny tie over a short-sleeved white button-down. His hair is slicked back with probably an entire bottle of gel. It's not the best look for him.

"Iris," Alpha says. "We were just discussing you."

I look at the clock on the wall. It's seven on the dot. I'm not late, am I?

"This morning you'll be going on your second training mission."

"Great!" I say. "You and me? Where are we going?"

A few people at the table exchange worried looks, which is not lost on me. *What did I say?* Alpha takes in a breath through his nose and closes his eyes for a short second.

"Ah. No. Zeta handles all training missions."

Ugh. Awesome.

"And Indigo will be accompanying the two of you," Alpha continues.

I look at Indigo. That would explain the hair. He leans over and jostles his shoulder into mine. "We're a team, kid."

I'm not sure why, but I bristle when Indigo calls me "kid."

Alpha pours a dab of cream into his coffee and gives it a quick swirl with a sterling spoon. "The car will be here in ten, so eat quickly."

Car? What car? But I don't have time to think about it, because trays of food are set in front of us. I try to inhale it, but I've only managed a piece of toast and a few bites of a scrambled egg when Zeta stands up and announces it's time to go.

Zeta punches in a code to disengage the alarm before we go out the front door, and once I'm outside it dawns on me that I've never been out this way. Just through that little door on the side street, and even then, only in another time.

And now here we are, standing on the sidewalk in modern-day Boston, watching the cars go whizzing down Beacon Street. A group of schoolkids passes us on their way to school, and Zeta gives them a quick nod of his head. On the other side of the street, a young mother speed walks down the steps into Boston Common, hoisting a small toddler to her hip while balancing a Styrofoam cup of coffee in one hand and holding a cell phone up to her ear with the other. She doesn't even pay us a second glance. These people are our neighbors. They go about their lives every day and have no clue that there's a group of time travelers living next door with a freaking *gravity* chamber in the basement.

I turn back around to look at the house. There's a small bronze sign tacked to the door that reads THE CLAREMONT SCHOOL.

Must be our cover.

A black Lincoln Town Car pulls onto the street and stops in front of Annum Hall. The driver hops out, but Zeta waves him off and opens the back door for Indigo and me. Indigo slides all the way over, then I get in after him. Zeta sits in the front.

"Logan," he tells the driver.

"We're going to the airport?" I ask.

"Affirmative." Zeta reaches into his suit pocket and pulls out two envelopes. He hands one to me and one to Indigo. Indigo and I look at each other before opening them. A driver's license bearing my picture and the name Kelly Hodges tumbles into my lap, as well as a ticket to Washington DC's Reagan National Airport and several bills and coins. I look over at Indigo, who's also holding a ticket, ID, and money.

"Hold on to them carefully," Zeta says. "Otherwise you're going to be hitchhiking your way home."

The three of us get through the security line in record time. The plane is boarding as we walk up, and it's not until we're on the plane that I realize we're sitting in first class. I stop in my tracks in front of Row 2. Indigo comes up behind me and leans down so close that I can feel his breath blow on my neck. It sends shivers down my arms.

"Aisle or window?" he asks.

"Window," I say.

"Then get in there and quit holding up the line." He's smiling at me, so I playfully punch him in the arm and climb in. Zeta takes the seat across the aisle and instantly pulls out his phone and starts typing an e-mail. Or maybe he's changing national security codes. I have no idea really.

"I've never flown first class," I say, settling into the roomy leather seat. I could get used to this.

"We always fly first class," Indigo says. "Although don't get too excited. This flight is barely more than an hour, and you're not going to be happy when we land."

I'm about to ask him what he means when a man comes around and offers us bottles of water. I reach up to the seat in front of me to unhook the tray table, but there isn't one.

Indigo chuckles behind me and taps the armrest of my seat. "It's in here."

I stare out the window as we take off, then close my eyes and lean the seat back. I'm starting to think I was too quick to judge Annum Guard before. I'd always thought I'd live a high-pressure life where I was constantly all over the world, putting my life in danger almost daily, never having a permanent address. But now I imagine myself jetting across the country, maybe even the world, traveling back in time and *enhancing* our history, then making it home all in time for dinner.

Of course, there is no Abe in my future with Annum Guard.

Before I know it, the pilot announces our initial descent. I straighten my chair and fold up the tray before tucking it back into the armrest.

When we deplane, there's a driver dressed in a black suit outside the airport, holding a handwritten sign that says SMITH. Zeta walks up to him and shakes his hand, then we all pile into another black Town Car and head into the city. No one says a word the entire trip, which only takes about twenty minutes. The driver drops us off on the corner of Potomac and N Street. We're in a residential zone, and there are a bunch of brownstones lining the street.

Zeta stops us at a house on the corner as a college-age guy wearing black plastic glasses and a yellow-and-green plaid shirt tucked into black skinny jeans slows to a halt in front of us. He turns to Indigo. "Cool tie, bro. Urban Outfitters?"

I bite my tongue to keep from laughing as Indigo flashes a coy smile. "It's vintage."

"Going for legit cred. I like it." And then he nods his head and keeps walking. I look at Indigo and can't help but smile.

"Can we focus, please?" Zeta asks in a clipped voice. I wipe the smile off my face and turn to see him gesturing toward a brick three-story with a bright-red front door and a little herb garden planted out front. "This is it," he says.

"Annum Guard headquarters?" I guess. It makes sense that a government organization would have its headquarters in the nation's capital, but Zeta shakes his head.

"You live in Annum Guard headquarters. We don't have an official presence in DC. They don't mention our name in public, our funding is hidden in miscellaneous Title 10 projects, and only those persons with the highest level of clearance know about our existence. Anonymity keeps us safe, Iris."

I don't know what it is about Zeta, but he has a way of making me feel as if I'm being scolded every time he speaks to me.

He clears his throat. "Training mission number Iris-Two," he says as he points to the house we're standing in front of. "In the fall of 1960, this brownstone was home to one Eugene McCarthy, a Democratic senator out of Minnesota. Do you know anything about Senator McCarthy?"

Senator McCarthy. That name sounds familiar. And then it hits me.

"Communism!" I practically shout. "Senate hearings to determine whether there were any communists living in America. He organized it. Led to a lot of Hollywood people being blacklisted."

Zeta shakes his head. "Wrong McCarthy. You're about ten years too late. And that was Joseph McCarthy. We're dealing with Eugene McCarthy."

"Oh," I say. "Then I know nothing about Senator McCarthy."

"Nor do you need to. Your mission is a simple one. At precisely 8:53, Senator McCarthy is going to walk down those steps, hail a cab, and head to the Capitol building just in time for an important vote, which takes place at 9:08. You are going to make him miss that cab and miss that vote, thereby freeing up funds that your modern-day commerce secretary has decided would have been better spent on . . . other projects. Understand?"

This is just like Alpha's first example to me. The smallest

feeling of disappointment creeps in. Making someone miss a cab? Ho-hum. But I nod my head.

"You get one try," Zeta says in a hushed whisper as he walks a few yards down Potomac and stops in front of a black gate leading into the backyard. He takes a black leather pouch from his inside suit pocket, jiggles the padlock on the gate, and pulls a tension wrench and hook lock pick from the pouch. The lock clicks open in about three seconds. "If you fail, you fail. No going back in time again to correct your mistakes. We can project back here without being seen. Now set your watch. October 25, 1960."

I look over at Indigo, who's already turning the knobs on his watch as he steps through the gate into someone's backyard. I do the same. I start to shut the lid, but Zeta reaches out and grabs my hand before I can.

"One word of caution. This is your first time projecting outside of Annum Hall. The gravity chamber spares us some of the stresses that projection can wreak on our bodies." Beside him, Indigo nods his head with his lips pursed. "Traveling this way is rough, I won't lie to you. Most times we opt to travel from Annum Hall and commute to our location in the past. Sometimes this is impractical, say if I needed to get from Boston to San Francisco in 1849. Much easier to hop a flight to San Francisco in present day than to travel three thousand miles in a covered wagon."

"They had air travel in 1960," I point out. At least I think they did.

"I know. But I wanted you to experience this. To know how it used to be for all of us."

"So this is like hazing?" I clutch the watch in my hand and squeeze.

Zeta doesn't respond. He turns to Indigo. "Are you ready?"

Indigo swallows what I can only assume is the lump in his throat and gives one quick nod of the head. "Ready, sir."

And then Zeta looks down at me. "Iris?"

"I'm as ready as I'll ever be." It's the truth.

Zeta stares straight ahead. "Watches shut, on the count of three. One . . . two . . . three!"

I slam my watch face lid shut, and instantly I know something is wrong. I'm falling too fast. My body can't keep up. My limbs are straining, stretching, and I can't breathe. Can't talk. My eyes are bulging out of their sockets as wind whips through them, threatening to yank them free. My limbs are being stretched too far. They're going to pop off. Every muscle in my body shrieks in pain. I try to scream but make no sound. I want this to stop. I want this to stop now.

And just like that I slam hard into the ground. I gasp for breath and look up. I'm on my hands and knees in Senator McCarthy's backyard.

Indigo and Zeta stand over me, and Indigo bends a knee and comes down to the ground. "Are you all right?"

I nod my head, but it's a lie.

It's no big secret that had I been recruited by the CIA, I would have gone through some serious Survival, Evasion, Resistance, Escape (SERE) training, where they would subject me to Abu Ghraib–type shit. I think this might have been worse. Indigo grabs my hand and pulls me up, and my legs protest. I'm unsteady on my feet. I sway back and forth a few times, trying not to fall over.

Zeta looks amused. Of course he does. He swings open the gate, which apparently doesn't have a lock in 1960, and I follow him to the corner. He points to the brownstone, and my eyes follow. The front door is black, not red, and there's no herb garden; other than that, the house is the same.

Nothing else is. Not at all. Huge cars that look more like submarines line the streets. Men hustle down the sidewalk wearing hats. Fedoras. The women all wear dresses and gloves, and one walks past me wearing cat's-eye glasses.

"Time check," Zeta says.

I look down at my watch. 8:52. The second hand is ticking past forty seconds on its way to the top. Whoa. Talk about not giving me much lead time. I haven't even caught my breath yet. A big yellow boat of a cab turns onto N Street a block away.

That has to be the cab.

Behind me, the front door of the brownstone opens, and a very proper-looking man with dark hair and a serious face trots down the steps. He plops a hat on his head, spots the cab, and raises his arm. The car slows, and I forget how much pain I'm in. It all disappears. I have to get to that cab.

"Go," Zeta hisses behind me, pushing me forward.

I don't hesitate, don't think. I sprint across the street, throwing myself in front of Senator McCarthy as he's reaching for the handle. I open the door and fling myself into the backseat. The senator looks at me with wide, angry eyes.

"Sorry," I mumble. "Medical emergency. Driver, I need a hospital immediately."

Senator McCarthy blinks a few times with disbelieving eyes, but then he nods at the driver and shuts the cab door. I breathe a sigh of relief and sink down in the seat as the driver steps on the gas. I did it. I prevented him from getting the cab. That was so simple. Too simple.

I pivot around to see if I can spot Zeta or Indigo. But all I see is Senator McCarthy climbing into the backseat of a cab that must have pulled up ten seconds later.

Son of a—

"On second thought, I'm feeling better," I snap at the driver. "Let me out here, please!"

The driver slams on the brakes, which sends me flying into the back of the front seat. He pivots around, a cigarette dangling from his lips. "What the hell do you mean, let you out here? We've gone half a block."

"I'm very sorry." I open the door. "What do I owe you?"

The driver lets out a noise of disgust. "Thirty-five cents."

I fish out two quarters from the purse and shove them into the front seat. "Keep the change." I slam the door shut and take off running back down the block. I need to get Senator McCarthy out of that cab!

It's coming close. What do I do? What do I do? There's only one thing I can think of. The cab's not going that fast. I can do this. I draw in my breath and lean back. Here it comes. Just another couple seconds—

"Iris!" Zeta shouts from down the block. He runs toward me. "Stop! No!"

But I've already launched myself up in the air. My shoulder lands hard on the windshield, and I cry out in pain. The cab slams on its brakes and swerves to the right, and I go flying off the hood onto the hard, unforgiving pavement of N Street.

I groan as I hear two cab doors open and slam shut, and Senator McCarthy crouches down beside me.

"She jumped in front of me!" I hear the old cab driver yell. "This crazy broad jumped in front of me!"

"Quiet!" the senator barks. "Are you all right? Are you hurt?"

"Yeah, in the head," the cabbie says.

I turn my head to the side and see Zeta and Indigo, standing across the street half a block down or so. They've stopped running, and Zeta has his arm out, holding Indigo back. I'm on my own with this one.

"Are you all right?" the senator repeats, his voice firm.

Am I all right? No. Clearly not. My body has already been through hell this morning, and then I got hit by a moving vehicle. A snaking line of purple bruises is already starting to dot my right arm and shoulder. My left arm is scraped and bleeding. But I don't think anything is broken.

"I think so," I say. But then I glance at the senator's wrist-watch. It's only 8:55. There's still plenty of time to get to the Capitol for the vote. I have to stall him. He pushes off his hands to stand.

"Wait, no!" I yell. "My leg, I think it's broken!"

Senator McCarthy looks down at his own watch. He sighs. "I'm sorry, but I can't tend to you now."

But then the cops show up, in their long, flat, black-and-white cars with domed flashing lights; and I know this mission is over. No way a cop is going to let an eyewitness leave an accident scene. Sure enough, the cops survey the scene and make every-one stay for questioning. I ditch my purse in a nearby bush, then tell the cops I realized I'd left it back at the house and had run to get it and didn't see the cab. No one gets ticketed or arrested, but the cops take almost half an hour. I've done it. I've made the senator miss the vote.

The senator and the driver get back into the cab to head off to the Capitol, I assume, and I smile. Every muscle in my body is protesting; and as I see Indigo and Zeta walking toward me, I get a sinking feeling in my stomach, too.

"Damn!" Indigo calls as he gets close. "That was so badass! That's dedication right there, huh, Z?"

Zeta doesn't say anything as he comes up next to me. Instead he stares at me with cool, hard eyes. "That's . . . something," he finally says. "Tell me; did you forget that the laws of physics have always existed? Or did you think that hurling your body in front of a moving vehicle wouldn't hurt you in the 1960s?"

"I just thought—"

Zeta makes a buzzer sound. "Eh. Wrong. You clearly weren't thinking about anything. Had you been thinking, you would not have jumped in front of a car."

"Okay, fine!" I say. "I wasn't *thinking*. I just knew that I had to stop the senator from getting to the Capitol, and I did the first thing that popped into my head. But it worked, I'd like to point out."

Zeta takes a slow breath. "Indeed it did," he admits. "You successfully completed your mission, and my report will reflect that." Yes! *Finally*. I've finally done something right. "However, I told you before that whatever happens on a mission stays a permanent part of history. Had you died, it would have been nice knowing you. So I will also make sure your reckless behavior is included in the report. Now are we ready to go back?"

I get that uneasy feeling my stomach has come to know and love. And now we have to go back. My body will be put through hell again. The voice in my head cries out in protest. Throws itself on the floor, kicking and screaming like a toddler who's been told to do something she doesn't want to do. But I whip out my watch and punch the top knob like it's as easy as climbing a flight of stairs. *Never show weakness.*

"I'm ready, sir," I say as I march myself toward the senator's backyard.

Zeta lifts an eyebrow and looks over to check that my watch is set correctly. "All right. Then go."

I snap the watch face lid shut before I have time to reconsider. My body is shot up so fast that my arms are plastered to my side. It's as if I've been stuffed into a cannon. A real one, not a circus one. All the pressure is on my shoulders. They're pulling down and away from my body. They're going to be ripped off. My head is pulled up, as if someone is trying to twist it off. Pressure. So much pressure. My neck muscles strain and scream, and the pain travels down to my arms, already bruised and black from the cab. It feels as if someone is taking a rubber mallet and swinging away at the bruises. I would scream if I could.

And then I land, back in present-day Washington. I hear two pops as Indigo and Zeta appear. I'm still on the ground, the wet morning grass staining my dress. *Never show weakness*, I remind myself. But I can't get up. I can't move.

Indigo drops to my side, and I lower my chin. Everything hurts, and I want to cry. I can't believe that this is how they used to travel all the time. That this was routine. It's no wonder nearly all of them are dead or disfigured. Time travel—projecting—is hell.

Indigo reaches out a hand and gently guides my chin up. I should push him away. I should fight him off. But I don't. I stare into his eyes, unable to hide what I'm feeling. His hand is still on my chin, and he lifts a finger to tap my nose.

"It's okay," he whispers, and I choke. Because that's something Abe would have done.

I jerk my head to the side and push up. I wobble, and Indigo hops up to help me. I try to shake him off, but he puts an arm around my shoulder. I miss Abe. He's going to be here next year, almost right where I'm standing. Georgetown. And I'm not going to be with him. Ever again.

I lean into Indigo. It hurts so much. More than that time I broke my arm when I was eight, and it took four tries to reset the bone. More than when I took a roundhouse kick to the groin during combat training at Peel. Physical pain subsides. Emotional pain never will. I know that all too well.

Zeta has already called for the car, and it pulls up only a few minutes later. Zeta gets in front, and Indigo and I climb into the back. We sit on opposite sides of the seat, not even remotely close to touching, and I stare out the window at the yellow and orange trees the whole ride.

I just projected back in time. I have the ability to time travel. *Chronometric Augmentation,* my mind says in a superserious government voice. I'm one of only a handful of people in the world who can do it.

So why aren't I happier?

Zeta hands us first-class tickets again. The plane takes off, and I recline my seat and shut my eyes.

"Can I get you something to drink?" I hear the flight attendant ask.

I shake my head without opening my eyes, but then I hear Zeta say across the aisle, "Three glasses of champagne," and my eyes pop open. Champagne? I've never had it before. I don't drink. Ever. When you grow up with a mom who counts alcoholism among her many problems, you don't really have a desire to drink.

The flight attendant gives Indigo and me the once-over. "I'm sorry; I'm going to have to ask for some identification."

"It's okay," I say. "I don't want—" But then Indigo elbows me in the rib. My right rib, which is so sore and tender that I cringe.

"I'm so sorry," he gasps.

"It's fine." I reach into my pocket and pull out the ID Zeta gave me that morning. I glance at it and, holy crap. It says I'm twenty-one. My boss got me a fake ID. I hand it to the flight attendant, who examines it and hands it back.

"Three glasses of champagne, coming right up."

She brings them, and Zeta tips his glass to me across the aisle. "All in all, a very successful day." My head whips over to look at him. Did he just use the words *very* and *successful* in the same sentence, directed at me? "You still have to work on your impulse control, but I would be honored to teach you further." He takes a sip while my hands shake.

Then Indigo practically shoves his glass in my face. "Cheers." He taps his glass into my mine. It makes a soft *clink!*

"Cheers," I tell him before taking the smallest sip. The champagne is sweet and bubbly and goes down way too easily, so I set it back on the tray.

"Not thirsty?" Indigo downs his glass.

"Not really."

He smiles. "You fascinate me, you know."

"I . . . what do you mean?"

"I mean—" Indigo reaches for my glass. "You gonna drink that?" I shake my head, so Indigo picks it up. "That I can't quite figure you out."

"Who says I want you to figure me out?"

Indigo chuckles and empties the other glass. "That's part of what fascinates me." He sets the glass on the tray, leans his seat back, and closes his eyes. I can't help but stare at him for a little while. I try not to think at all.

CHAPTER 11

Throwing myself in front of a cab turns out to be the way to Zeta's heart. The very next day, he takes me on another mission. And then another after that. And three more the following week. I experience Harlem in the 1920s and Philadelphia in the 1790s. October blinks into November, and I turn seventeen without a hint of celebration. Before I know it, Thanksgiving is looming over me like a dark cloud.

Thanksgiving. Abe and I were supposed to spend it with my mom. I always go back to her for the holidays. It was never the same between us, not after I'd chosen a school I'd never heard of over her; I would put on a brave face anyway. Having Abe with me always helped. Abe can talk to anyone, anywhere, anytime—about anything. His warmth and humor is contagious. One time he was even able to get my mom to crack the smallest smile during one of her lows. That was the moment I realized I loved him.

But now I'm not going to see either of them. Ever again.

I'm in the library poring over a book on early-twentieth-century American politics, something Zeta has assigned me in preparation for a mission that may or may not happen. Who knows?

I don't have the room to myself today. Indigo is sitting at the desk next to me, and Blue has plopped himself in one of the armchairs in front of the fireplace. Violet sits in the other, her nose in an ancient-looking book with a peeling cherry-red leather cover.

I'm reading a section on Teddy Roosevelt's early presidency when a note flies on top of my desk. I set down the book and look at Indigo. He jerks his head toward the note, as if it's not completely obvious who threw it. I pick it up.

Looking forward to Thanksgiving?

Dammit. One more reminder of what will never be. An image of our dog, Dos, jumping up on me and licking me while doing a whiny little cry because he's so excited to see me again pops into my mind. Then my mom's face. I haven't allowed myself to wonder whether she'd be so happy to see me that she won't have slept in two days and will have baked seven different pies because she doesn't know which one I'll want, or whether she'd be in one of her moods where it wouldn't even matter that I'm there. I wonder what will happen for real when I don't show up this year.

And Abe. Abe will spend the holiday alone with his family. Unless he's met another girl by now. Will another girl be sitting next to him at his grandfather's worn oak table, laughing at his jokes and mentally planning to take him home to meet her family?

I pick up my pen and scribble a response.

No.

I sail the note back, but it lands on my desk a few seconds later.

Why? :(WE PUT ON A good show hERE; you'll SEE.

My eyes scrunch closed. A frowny face? Did Indigo seriously just draw a frowny face? I scrawl another quick note and pass it back.

I'm just not. Don't really want to talk about it.

I watch Indigo read the note out of the corner of my eye and hope that will be the end of it. He drops the note onto his desk and turns to me.

"Hey," he whispers. "What's wrong?"

"I said I don't want to talk about it," I whisper back. I pick up the book and pretend to read.

"Hey," he whispers again, this time louder and with more force. "I didn't mean to upset you. Sorry." He looks dejected, like a lost puppy.

I snap the book shut. "Stop being so offended. I just don't like loaded questions." My voice is louder, and Violet looks up at me and narrows her eyes. I ignore it.

"Are you looking forward to Thanksgiving? How is that a loaded question? You don't need to snap at me."

I wrinkle my nose. "Are you serious? I didn't snap at you. I told you I wasn't looking forward to Thanksgiving and that I don't really want to talk about it."

He starts to roll his eyes but stops himself. "Dude, it was a simple question."

"Fine, hotshot," I say. "You want to know why I'm not looking forward to Thanksgiving? Because I always spent it with my boyfriend. My ex-boyfriend, thanks to Annum Guard. We always went to my mom's house in Vermont, which was nice because I had my boyfriend there as a buffer. My mom's bipolar and refuses to medicate, you see, so I never know if I'm going to get happy Joy or miserable Joy. Yeah, that's my mom's name. Joy. Ain't life fuckin' ironic sometimes?"

Indigo holds up his hands. "I didn't mean—"

"And my dad's been dead for sixteen years, so my mom has no one now. *No one.* Because I selfishly abandoned her two years ago when my Peel letter arrived. It's really great for someone with severe mental issues to be all alone. I'll probably be an orphan soon, and it's going to be all my fault."

A book slams shut by the fireplace. I look over as Blue throws the book to the floor and stands. "Are we supposed to feel sorry for you?"

"This doesn't concern you," I say.

"Of course it does. You think you're the only person in this room missing a parent? I haven't had a mother in more than three years. Violet hasn't had—"

Violet jumps to her feet. "Leave me out of this!"

Blue jerks his head toward Indigo. "Poster boy over there has two healthy, functioning parents, but he's the exception. This place kills you. At least you didn't have to grow up watching it eat away at the people you love. You didn't have to watch your mother's mangled body slowly give up on her."

"Blue!" Violet snaps. "Shut up!"

But Blue can't take back what he's said. Bits and pieces of information float together in my mind, and then suddenly the truth slaps me across the cheek.

"Your parents were all Annum Guard." And now I can't believe I didn't figure this out sooner. That was Blue's path. The path of his parents. Blue's mother died like Epsilon is now dying. Slowly. Painfully. One of Violet's parents was the same. Indigo's parents are still alive. Which means. Oh my God. Of course.

I whip around to Indigo. "Your dad is Zeta." He doesn't deny it, and his face admits it. "You were all born into this."

"Chronometric Augmentation is genetic," Blue says.

"Blue, shut up!" Violet says again. "She can't know this!" She launches herself at Blue, but he pushes her aside.

"No!" he yells. "Why shouldn't she know the truth? If she's going to be one of us, she has a right to know."

"No, she doesn't." She jumps toward Blue again. "She doesn't even belong here. She's not one of us."

"She does belong here," Indigo says, pushing himself between Blue and Violet. "Alpha chose her. It's not right that they're still keeping her in the dark like this."

Everyone breathes heavy, and we all exchange glances, as if we're daring one another to make a move.

Indigo blinks first. He grabs my hand and spins me to look at him. "Our grandfathers started Annum Guard. Their children took their place. And now it falls to us. That's how it's always been. Until you."

He glances at the door, and Blue and Violet do the same.

"She's not supposed to know any of this," Violet says.

"Violet, hush," Indigo says. But now he looks nervous. Like he's about to change his mind.

I cross my arms over my chest. "Why until me?"

Blue jerks his head to me and juts his chin up in the air. "You're the first outsider. You weren't born into this like we were. The government is using you to decide whether they want to expand us to a host of outsiders."

Outsider. He's now said it twice. They *all* view me as an outsider. But I already know this.

"How is it that I'm able to project then?" I ask.

"Alpha took your DNA," Indigo says, and just like that I'm snapped back to waking up in a cold, sterile room, strapped to a gurney with a needle in my arm. I never bought the "routine physical" line, obviously, but it's nice to finally know the truth. "He took it, and they injected it into one of the Annum watches. Ergo, you can now project."

My head is swimming. They stole me from school, from Abe, from my mom, from every truth I've ever known. They stole from my body. They used me. It's too much. It's all just too much.

I bolt out of the library, then out the front door. An alarm sounds as I go, but I don't slow down. I have to get away from here. The cars are barreling down Beacon Street, but I fly into the road. A big black SUV slams on its brakes, missing me by inches, and I bang my fists on its hood before darting past it.

"Iris!" a voice behind me yells.

I'm across the street now. I turn back to see Indigo shouting to me. "Iris, come back!"

I tear down the steps into Boston Common. The Frog Pond is to my right, Park Street to my left. I run straight, as fast as my legs will carry me.

"Iris!"

Indigo isn't far behind me, I can tell. He's faster than I am. He's going to catch me at this pace. I bend down and sprint toward the other side of the park, toward Tremont Street. It's close. There's a bustling downtown shopping district on the other side. If I can make it across the street, I can lose Indigo no problem.

There's a pizza shop on the other side of the street. It's all I'm looking at. That's my target. I'm at the street, still running full steam. I take a breath and leap out onto Tremont when a strong arm grabs me and yanks me back.

A bus barrels through the intersection.

I gasp.

A bus.

I look into the eyes of a very shaken young businessman. He releases his grip on me, and his mouth pops open as his briefcase clunks to the sidewalk. I stare back at him, panting hard. And then another hand grabs my shoulder from behind. I don't have to turn.

"Iris!" Indigo pants. "What the hell is wrong with you?"

"You're a liar!" I try to push his arm off me, but he just holds on tighter. "All of you! You lied to me!"

I ignore the group of Asian tourists gaping at me outside the Boston Common Visitor Information Center. A tour guide dressed as a colonist—powdered wig and all—tries to divert their attention to the Park Street Church just a block away.

"Nobody lied to you," Indigo shouts. "They withheld the truth. There's a difference."

"There's no difference." I duck down and dart left, then grab Indigo's shoulder and flip him onto his back. "A lie told is no different than a truth omitted."

Indigo's eyes pop open in shock, but he doesn't try to get up. "I'm sorry," he whispers.

"Iris!"

It's a different voice this time. A louder voice. An angrier voice. I already recognize it.

I look up to see Alpha running toward us. That's when I also notice the crowd of people gawking at us from both sides of Tremont Street. It's not just the tourists. It's everyone within a two-block radius. Can I turn and run? Doubtful. But there is something I can do. I have *time* at my disposal. I pull the Annum watch out from under my sweater.

"Don't even think about it," Alpha growls as I pop open the lid. He's closing in on me. Only a few steps away.

I spin the top knob a few times. I don't even know what I'm doing. I don't want to project—that would be stupid—but I don't want to be here right now.

"I'll track you," Alpha says. "I'll track you, and I'll find you, and I'll strip you of that watch and ship you off to Carswell so fast your head will spin."

Carswell again. Prison. Texas. That's far away from Massachusetts, from Vermont, from everyone I know and love. And I have a tracker in my arm. Even if I did run, I'd never make it.

I drop the watch and it plunks against my chest. Indigo pushes himself off the ground and stares at me with worried eyes.

Alpha grabs on to my shoulder, spins me around, and marches me back toward Beacon Street. His grip is strong. "Explain yourself." He's whispering, but it's low and dangerous.

"You explain yourself," I spit, and Alpha yanks on my shoulder to let me know I'm out of line. But I don't care. "Chronometric Augmentation is genetic? And I'm your guinea pig?"

"I told you all of that before."

"No, you didn't!"

Alpha stops halfway across Boston Common and whips me around so fast I stumble over my feet. "I told you that membership in Annum Guard has been set since it started and that the government wants to experiment with adding new members. So tell me, what exactly did I lie to you about?" Indigo comes to a halt a few feet away and looks at the ground.

"It's what you didn't tell me," I say.

"I didn't tell you that Chronometric Augmentation was genetic. Fine. Now you tell me. Why is that such a big deal? Why are you acting like such a child over this?"

"I'm not acting like a child," I say, knowing full well that it makes me sound like a whiny kid. "Your parents were Annum Guard, too. You're all a part of this secret society, and I'm the outsider."

Alpha stares at me, long and hard. One second passes. Two seconds. Five. Six. Way longer than necessary. Then he jerks his head toward Beacon. "Walk."

We cross the Common without saying another word. Indigo

follows behind us. I'm dreading reaching Annum Hall. Hall of Lies.

I wonder if this is it. If they're going to throw me out and lock me up. I never found out about my dad.

My feet feel heavy on the stairs leading to the stoop, and Alpha unlocks the front door. He holds it open for Indigo, then pushes me through.

"I trust you have an assignment to keep yourself busy?" he asks Indigo.

Indigo nods and then shoots me the same look as before. Concern. Genuine concern. Dammit. Why does Indigo have to be so nice all the time? I give him a stone-faced stare in return, and his brow creases and his face crumples. He walks into the library and shuts the door behind him.

"Follow me," Alpha orders.

I do. I have no choice. We cross the living room to the hallway by the stairs. We're going to his office. Dread washes over me, threatening to suffocate me.

Alpha stops in front of his office and raises his hand. He angles his back to me but not enough to fully block my view. I pretend to look at my feet but train my eyes up and over to the keypad, just like they taught us at Peel. Never stare at someone when they enter a code. But never miss what they type either.

Alpha enters *940211*, and I've already got it broken down and memorized as the door clicks open. *940*. That's an area code in Texas. It covers Wichita Falls, where my freshman year roommate at Peel was from. The area code would pop up on her phone all the time. *211*. That's the community service phone number in Vermont. They play it on commercials. *940211*. Got it.

Alpha turns the handle and gestures me inside. I'm not sure whether I'm supposed to sit or stand, so I stay on my feet. Alpha crosses around the desk and sits. "I should report this."

I don't know what to say, so I don't say anything. Pleading is a sign of weakness.

"Give me one reason why I shouldn't."

Alpha wants a reason? I could give him one. I could call him out. But I don't. Not yet, at least. "Because nothing happened. I went for a stroll across Boston Common, and that's it."

"That's not it, and you know it."

"I was upset because I found out you've all been lying, and—"

Alpha slams his hand down onto the desk so hard the entire thing shakes. For a second I wonder if it's going to crack in two.

"If you say that word one more time, you're done. I am your superior. They taught you this at Peel, no? Listen to your commanding officer; do what you're told. CIA, FBI, it's all the same, Iris. It amazes me that someone with such an authority problem made it this far." Alpha pauses for a few seconds and then continues. "The information I choose to disclose to you is based on security concerns and is done on a need-to-know basis. So stop acting like I'm your father."

The hair on the back of my neck stands up. *Father.* I don't have one of those. But when I look at Alpha, his light-brown eyes, buzzed haircut, and five-o'clock shadow fizzle away, and I can't help but picture my dad's face on Alpha's body.

The image is fuzzy. All I've seen of my dad are two old photos in my mom's house, but the image is there. What is it like to have a dad who cares enough to yell at you when you mess up? God, do I have daddy issues or what?

I shake the image from my mind and look back at Alpha. "I never—"

"Save it. You've been trained better than this, and I don't want to hear it anymore. Just remember what I told you the first day we met. There's no running from me. I'll find you. Wherever, whenever you go, I'll find you. You almost made a very, very foolish decision today. Don't repeat it. Now go."

Alpha points to the door. I can barely remember how to walk. But I put one foot in front of the other and leave the office. I trudge over to the stairs and start climbing. Holy Jesus. That was . . . scary.

I shut the door to my bedroom behind me and think about what Alpha said. I clench and unclench my fists, but that doesn't release my tension, so I do what I always do when I have excess energy. I drop down and start doing pushups. I only get through twelve when I sit up and cradle my head in my hands. Is it really that big a deal that they haven't told me about the genetic thing before? Why am I so upset over this?

I don't know the answer to either of these questions.

CHAPTER 12

Alpha doesn't mention my jaunt through the Common the next day at breakfast. He just hands out assignments as if nothing's wrong.

"Orange, solo mission that we have previously discussed," he says.

Orange nods his head, and his mop of orange hair falls in his face.

Alpha looks back down at his notepad. "Green and Blue, historical prep today."

Green nods his head, but Blue doesn't. Instead he stares at me from across the table. He's been doing that since I sat down this morning. Staring. It's kind of creepy.

"Indigo—where's Indigo?" Alpha asks. It's like he's just noticed that there's an empty chair beside me. Funny. It's the first thing I noticed this morning.

"I'm not sure, sir," Red says. "He didn't tell me he'd be absent this morning."

"He's not feeling well today," Zeta says as he clears his throat.

"Nepotism at its finest," Blue mumbles under his breath. Most people in the room gasp and turn to look at me. Only Alpha, Zeta, and Violet don't flinch. But that's because they already know that I know the truth.

"Oh, shut up, all of you," Blue says. "She knows."

Alpha folds his napkin and sets it down on the table. Then he straightens his tie and stands. "Blue, a word." He jerks his head toward the door. "The rest of you have your assignments."

I guess breakfast is now over, even though I have no idea what my assignment is. No one's assigned me anything in days, except "study the early-twentieth century." I guess I'll do more of that today. I scoot my chair back and stand along with everyone else. But Green backs away from me, as if I'm a lion in a cage and everyone just figured out the door is open. Orange makes eye contact and quickly looks away.

Okay, guys, I get it. I'm an outsider here. I'm not one of you because none of your time-traveling mothers expelled me out of her uterus.

I turn to head toward the library.

"Iris," Zeta says. "Where are you going?"

"Library," I mutter, not bothering to turn around.

Zeta sidesteps in front of me. "Uh-uh. It's mission day. Your first real one."

I whip around. Real one? As in nontraining? "No one told me about this."

"I know," Zeta says. "Alpha only decided you were ready last night."

Weird. Did he make that decision before or after gave me that good verbal spanking?

Zeta whips his head over to the door. "Yellow and Violet, you're going, too."

Yellow clucks her tongue in disgust while Violet gives me an icy stare. I stare right back. If she thinks I'm going to blink first, she's got another thing coming.

"Come with me." Zeta walks toward the back staircase that leads to the basement. Yellow turns on her heel and prances toward the staircase, while Violet stomps behind her. Stomps. Like a toddler.

"I hate fire missions," Violet mutters to Yellow on the stairs, and I have no idea what she's talking about.

Zeta holds the door open for us and gestures to the classroom on the right. We all file in. There's a projector and a screen set up in the front of the room. I slide into one of the dozen or so desks, each of which has a yellow legal pad and a sharpened number 2 pencil set atop it. Violet leaves a desk between us, and Yellow sits on the other side of her, away from me.

"Ladies," Zeta greets us, then he looks right at me. "Iris. I believe in trial by fire. You're not going to learn until you're thrown into the flames and made to find your own water. All first missions are designed to be high pressure, high stakes, high risk. The chance of failure is great, the chance of violence even greater. It's, quite literally, do or die. You ready?"

My heart is thumping against my chest. This is what I've been trained for. It's what Peel excels at: training its students for missions such as this. I've been on dozens of high-stress simulations but never anything real. Ever. I always got the jitters before, but I'm shaking now. I feel weightless.

"I'm ready," I say.

But inside I'm crumbling. Because this is just great. I'm about to go on a high-pressure mission with an excellent chance of violence, and my team members don't even want to sit next to me.

Zeta flicks the light switch and snaps on the projector. The screen becomes awash in a glow of white light before there's a *click* and an image pops up. It's a painting. There's a woman sitting at a piano and another woman standing behind it, her arm raised slightly and her mouth open as if she's singing. A man sits with his back turned. It's pretty. So pretty. I squint my eyes and examine the detail on the singer's dress.

"*The Concert*," Zeta says. "Painted by Johannes Vermeer around 1660, stolen from the Isabella Stewart Gardner Museum on March 18, 1990, along with twelve other pieces of art. *The Concert* alone is valued at two hundred million dollars." My mouth drops open. "The total value of all art stolen that night is about five hundred million. None of the stolen works has been recovered.

"And, ladies, tonight the president himself has authorized us to prevent that burglary from ever happening in the first place."

I sit up straight in my chair and lean my elbows on the desk. I glance over and see that Yellow and Violet have done the same. My heart is beating faster, but now there's excitement mixed with nerves. This is what I'm talking about. Forget causing someone to miss a cab. *This* is what I want to be doing.

Zeta clicks the remote again, and a cross-section of the

museum pops up on-screen. He grabs a pointer and aims it at a corner of the first floor.

"At precisely 1:24 a.m. on the morning of March 18, 1990, two thieves disguised as uniformed police officers knocked on the museum's service entrance door. They told the guard—a young, poorly trained college student—that they had been alerted to a disturbance at the museum related to the St. Patrick's Day revelry that was still taking place on the streets of Boston. The guard buzzed them through the door.

"The two thieves then told the guard that he looked familiar and that they both had seen a warrant issued for his arrest. The guard stepped out from behind the desk, leaving the only panic button that would have alerted the real police force. The thieves then forced the guard to summon the other guard, and when he arrived, both were handcuffed and led to the basement. The thieves then wrapped the guards' hands, feet, and heads in duct tape, and secured them to posts forty yards apart."

Yellow and Violet are just sitting there listening, but I'm scribbling notes like crazy.

Zeta continues. "At approximately 1:48 a.m., the two thieves made their way up the main staircase into the Dutch Room on the second floor." Zeta moves the pointer to the top right corner of the second floor. "For the next forty minutes the thieves tripped alarms as they traveled between the rooms on this floor. From the Dutch Room, they stole three Rembrandts, a Flinck, *The Concert*, and a nearly three-thousand-year-old Chinese bronze beaker. Across the floor in the Short Gallery"—the pointer whisks to a room on the left—"they stole five Degas drawings and a bronze finial that sat atop a pole holding a Napoleonic flag. At some point, a Manet was stolen from the Blue Room on the first floor as well"—the pointer falls on a room on the first floor that looks to be almost directly below the Short Gallery—"but investigators have not been able to determine the precise time it was stolen.

"The thieves exited the museum at 2:45 a.m., making off with half a billion dollars' worth of art that has not been recovered. And after too many decades of false leads and no breakthroughs, the FBI director has decided that the loss to the art world is too great and the windfall to the thieves is too high. So he went to the president, and here we are."

Zeta sets down the pointer and clasps his hands together in front of his body. I remember to take a breath.

"You get one shot to stop this thing. The thieves are very likely armed, and there is a chance that they'll try to use their weapons. Iris—"

Zeta turns directly to me, and Yellow and Violet do the same.

"This mission is designed to play to your strengths," Zeta says. "You're the leader of this one. I want the three of you to spend the day at the museum. Get to know its ins and outs. Prepare yourself. Meet back here at five p.m. to get changed and ready."

We catch the Green Line at Park Street and take the E to the MFA stop. Neither Violet nor Yellow say a word to me the entire train ride, and I don't know if it's the fact that they really don't like me or if it's bitterness that Zeta named me the leader. I snort. *Leader.* Right. A woman can't lead without people willing to follow her.

"All right," I say as the three of us stand in front of the museum, gazing up at its boxy brick exterior. The outside of the building is completely underwhelming. It could be a condo complex or even an old factory. "I think we should split up and—"

"Yeah, I got this," Yellow says. "This is my fourth fire mission. I'll wander around and make notes of the scene, and then I'll devise a plan of action from there."

I wrinkle my nose. "Maybe you didn't hear Zeta, but I'm the leader of this mission."

Yellow raises a perfectly plucked eyebrow. "He can name you whatever he wants, but I'm going to lead this mission."

"Says who?" I ask.

"Violet?" Yellow turns to face her. "Who are you going to follow on this mission?"

"Duh," she says. "Let's go inside."

Yellow gives me a smug look and brushes the hair off her shoulder. Then she and Violet walk toward the main entrance. I let them go. Idiots. They're not even going to check out the service entrance? As soon as they're inside, I make a left onto Palace Road. About half a block down, there it is. The service entrance. It's a green door sticking out of what looks like a concrete addition. A guy and girl only a few years older than me stroll by, deep in a conversation about some party last weekend, and I bet they have no idea that half a billion dollars walked through this door years ago.

But we're going to change all that tonight.

I double back to the front door and pay my admission fee. I have no idea where Yellow and Violet scampered off to, nor do I care. Screw them. I can do this myself.

I've never been to the Gardner before, and the courtyard takes my breath away. Sunlight beams down on grasses and plants, and it's so pretty. Like being in a tropical garden. But I'm not here to gawk. I'm here to prevent a burglary.

I go up the main staircase. I'm standing in a long hallway with high arched windows overlooking the courtyard. I check the map they gave me downstairs again. This floor is laid out in a big rectangle with the courtyard in the middle. To my left is the Early Italian Room, which sits in a corner. If you round it, you hit the Raphael Room and the Short Gallery. That's where all of the Degas drawings were taken from. To my right is the Dutch Room. That's the money room. Three Rembrandts, a Flinck, the Chinese beaker, and the Vermeer. I start in there.

I imagine I'm one of the thieves. No doubt they'd visited the museum numerous times before the heist. The museum still has empty frames hanging where some of the pictures once were—a reminder of what was stolen. I walk past each of them and try to think like a criminal. Hands down, I would go for the Vermeer first. Get the most valuable one in case you have to abandon the rest and bolt. I walk the entire room, noting the empty frames, then double back past the hallway and through the Early Italian and Raphael Rooms into the Short Gallery.

This is a no-brainer. You have one person steal the pictures from the Dutch Room while the other is taking down all the Degases in the Short Gallery. Then you grab the Manet on the first floor on the way out.

So how do we prevent this? The easiest thing to do would be to stop the guards from even opening the door in the first place. We take down the fake cops on the street and then we don't have to go into the museum at all.

But a little voice nags me that this plan won't work in the long run. The thieves will just come back another night. No, the only way to truly end this thing is to end it in the museum. To stop the burglary while it's in process. I'm suddenly conscious of my heart beating away inside my chest, and I don't know if it's nerves or excitement. Probably both.

I find Yellow and Violet downstairs in the courtyard.

"There you are," Violet snaps. "We've been ready to go for like twenty minutes."

I check my watch. It's eleven thirty. "We have until five to get back."

The two of them stare at me, blank faced.

I shake my head. "I thought it would be best if we made a plan of attack. I figure we put one person in the Dutch Room and one by the Short Gallery upstairs, then we have one of us act as backup down in the Blue Room where the Manet is. That way if—"

Yellow holds up a hand, cutting me off. "Why are you talking? We've already got it figured out. We're going to wait outside and call the police to report two suspicious individuals loitering around. That way they never have to enter the museum. We save the art and spare the guards the trauma of thinking they're going to be dragged to the basement and shot in the head. Win-win."

"Yeah, and what happens when they come back the next night?" I ask. "You're going to leave that to chance? Uh-uh. We need to find a way inside the museum so that we can be there when the break-in happens. Then we apprehend the perps, tie them up, and bolt back to the present before we're seen by the cops. We'll be nameless, faceless heroes."

"No," Yellow says. "This mission is to prevent the burglary from happening. We're going to do it the quick, easy way."

"That's not going to work!"

"Violet, are you ready?" Yellow asks. Violet nods, and the two of them turn and head toward the front door.

"Listen to me!" I shout after them, but they're already gone.

I ball up my hands into fists. I want to punch something. Or *someone*. I'm not going to let her blow the entire mission. I'll do this myself. I head back up the stairs. I'm about to learn every square inch of this museum. And I'm going to be here on March 18, 1990, at 1:24 a.m.

CHAPTER 13

I rifle through the clothes hanging in my closet. 1990. What was popular in 1990? I think of all the old sitcom reruns my mom liked to watch back when she was still having normal phases—before she started rapid cycling—and pull out a pair of black jeans. I slip them on and roll up the bottoms, then grab a plain black sweater. I shove my feet into black sneakers and hope this is close enough. Before I leave, I pull my dark hair back into a pony-tail. Simple. And then I grab my bag. Can't do anything without the stuff in this bag.

Yellow and Violet are already standing with Zeta in the main room. Zeta's still wearing khakis and a sweater, so I guess he's not joining us. I won't lie—I wish that he was. I mean, I get the whole trial-by-fire thing, but not having him on this mission seems more like trial-by-volcanic-eruption-spewing-lava-onto-the-unprepared-people-of-Pompeii. Annum Guard has a warped way of doing things, that's for sure.

Zeta has a serious expression on his face—I'm starting to wonder whether he *has* any other expression—and the flecks of gray at his temples seem to have multiplied since this morning, and he's clasping his hands together so tightly his veins are bulging out of his forearms. At least someone else recognizes the importance of this mission.

Speaking of my oh-so-competent teammates, Yellow has on skin-tight, high-waisted black jeans with a leather motorcycle jacket. Her hair is teased and frizzed and piled half on top of her head in a ponytail that resembles an ostrich plume. The whole look is not at all fashionable today, but somehow Yellow pulls it off. I hate to admit it, but she does. Violet's wearing black leggings with a black miniskirt and a black off-the-shoulder sweater. She's ditched the purple wig, and her real hair is cut supershort, like a pixie. I sort of look like the homeless cousin next to them, and both of them stare at me when I walk in. But I don't care. I'm going to stop a burglary tonight. The two of them can do whatever they want.

"One shot," Zeta tells us. "That's all you get to stop this."

"I still don't understand why we only get one shot," I say.

Zeta turns to me with patient eyes. Polar opposite from the Boston Massacre, the last time I asked this question. "It's not our doing; it's the wormhole. Once you open it to a specific date, your watch can't go back there again."

"What about someone else's?"

Zeta tilts his head to the side an inch. "It's possible, but then you'd run the risk of injuring your fellow team members on a mission you bungled in the first place. Too many cooks in the kitchen, so to speak. Does that make sense?"

I guess? Not really.

"Plus it gives you a false sense of security," Zeta says. "No do-overs. It's a better motto. Now are you ready?"

We all set our watches for midnight on March 18. That will give us almost an hour and a half to get to the museum before the thieves knock on the door dressed like cops. I spent four hours after Violet and Yellow left, trying to figure out a way to break into the museum beforehand, but I failed. It's just impossible. There are too many alarms and too many cameras. Going to have to go in after the thieves. It's the only way.

Yellow enters the gravity chamber first. Zeta shuts the door behind her, waits a few seconds, and opens it for Violet. And then it's my turn. Zeta puts out his arm to stop me.

"You can do this," he tells me.

"I know," I say. I'm staring straight ahead at the door, bouncing back and forth between my heels. I'm a bundle of nervous energy, and I just want to go already.

"I believe in you, Iris." Zeta's voice sounds different than it ever has. It's softer. There's no intensity in it. He really wants me to succeed. It's as if he knows I'm the only one who can. I turn to look at him.

"I won't fail," I tell him. Zeta nods his head and opens the door, and as I hurl myself through it, all I can think is that I hope I'm right.

I land in the broom closet. It's dark, and I can't make out my hand five inches in front of me, but I don't sense anyone else.

"Yellow?" I whisper. "Violet?"

Nothing. I fumble around, tripping over something long and wooden, until I find the handle that leads into the alleyway.

Yellow and Violet are already turning onto Beacon Street when I step out.

"Hey!" I call to them. "What the hell?"

"Keep up," Yellow tosses over her shoulder. Neither of them slows down.

I want to slam the door, but that will only attract attention, so I shut it as softly as I can. And then I punch the air.

St. Patrick's Day festivities are in full swing as I step onto Beacon Street, even though there's a cold, light rain falling. A group of drunken college girls wearing green, oversize shirts tucked into light-wash, high-waisted jeans stumble past me. One of the girls has on a glittery shamrock headband that bounces as she ambles by.

"Hurry up!" I hear Yellow say. I look past the girls to a cab. Violet's already in the backseat, and Yellow is holding open the door. "The T doesn't run anymore. Let's go."

"Actually, it does; it's just totally unreliable this late," I mutter under my breath as I jog over to the cab. Yellow squeezes into the middle seat, and I slide in next to her.

"Where to?" the cab driver asks as he resets the meter.

Yellow touches the front seat. "The Isabella—"

"Simmons College!" I interrupt her. "We're heading back to the dorms." And then I shoot Yellow a look that lets her know I think she's a complete moron. Why would anyone need to go to a museum at midnight when it's closed? Idiot. And Simmons is practically next door.

The driver lets us out in front of the dorms, and we wait until he's rounded the corner before we walk toward the museum. There are a bunch of college kids hanging around, either coming home from a night of St. Paddy's Day drinking or still in the middle of it.

"Now what?" Violet asks.

Yellow comes to a stop in front of the museum. "Now we keep an eye out for two men dressed as cops." She's standing right in front of the main door, and I sigh.

"Where did you go to school?" I ask her. "Before you joined Annum Guard. Where did you go? Did you even complete kindergarten, or do you really have no idea how to stake a lookout?"

Yellow wrinkles her nose. "I went to Andover. Maybe you've heard of it. It's—"

"Not the kind of school where they teach you anything you need to know in the field," I say. "Or else you'd know not to stand in front of the building like a big 'Hey, thieves, look at me!' sign. And besides, they come in the service entrance, not the front door." I point back at Palace Road.

"This is my fourth fire mission," Yellow snaps. "I've been doing this for almost a year and a half."

"Congratulations. Did you mess up the first three missions just as badly as you're about to blow this one? Now, if you don't mind, I'm going to stop a burglary." I keep walking and turn onto the street that lines the other side of the museum, one street up from Palace.

"Where is she going?" I hear Violet ask.

"Quiet!" Yellow hisses. But then I hear them follow behind me. I walk to the end of the block and make a right on Tetlow Street to head back to Palace. There's a dingy golden-brick apartment building on the corner, so I plant myself on the crumbling concrete stoop, underneath two very out-of-place, very large, black, winged griffins hanging on either side of the front door. I wait for Yellow and Violet to catch up.

"Now what?" Violet asks as she glances up at one of the griffins and shudders.

"We wait," I say as I look at the other one. Those things are really creepy. They're not calming my nerves.

We do. For a long time, nothing happens. We hear kids shouting from the streets and ambulance sirens wailing toward Beth Israel, dropping off the people who partied a little too hard downtown. But we don't see anything.

Then at a little before one, a small hatchback creeps its way down Palace Road with the lights turned off. I drop to the ground and press myself against the building's glass front door. Yellow and Violet at least have the common sense to do the same. I peek my head out and stare at the car as it drives past, and every hair on my arm stands on end. There are two uniformed police officers sitting inside of it. One has light-brown hair and is wearing gold, wire-rimmed glasses. The other has dark hair and a mustache. They park the car a few yards away from the service entrance.

"There they are," I whisper.

Yellow springs up behind me. "Okay, now we just have to call the real cops, and we can go home."

"No." I stand up. "Calling the cops will ruin everything. They'll just come back later when we won't be able to stop it, I told you."

"It's the safest way for the guards inside," Violet says.

"And who's to say they won't decide to put two bullets in

the guards' heads next time? We have to stop this inside, in the museum. Tonight. It's the only way. We wait until they go in and then we follow."

"No." Yellow narrows her eyes at me. "I'm going to go find a phone somewhere and call the cops."

I grab her arm as she takes a step. "You're going to go find a phone *somewhere*? Your plan all along was to call the cops, and you didn't even figure out where the nearest phone was? You're more incompetent than I thought."

Yellow yanks her arm away. "At least I'm smart enough to realize a cell phone won't work in the past. And we'll see who's incompetent after I stop this thing."

"Yellow, don't call the cops," I say through gritted teeth. "You'll ruin everything."

Yellow turns on her heel, and before I realize she's about to attack, she kicks me hard in the right shin. I choke back a yell and grab on to the steel railing while Yellow hops down the two steps and takes off running back toward Simmons with Violet right behind her. I throw my hands up and slam my palms onto the top of the railing.

Fine. Whatever. Let them go. I check my watch again. It's three minutes after one. That gives them twenty-one minutes to find a phone, call the authorities, and have the cops show up. I'm going to guess "possibly suspicious-looking car" isn't going to be top on their list of priorities on the night of St. Patrick's Day. Maybe Yellow and Violet won't even be able to find a phone. I'm going to wait right here.

They're back five minutes later.

Yellow flashes a smug smile. "Done. Called and reported two

men dressed as police officers sitting in a hatchback outside the Gardner. The dispatcher said there was a car in the area she'd send to check it out. Consider this mission over."

I could punch her. Instead I pray the cops don't come until after 1:24. But sure enough, a cop car turns onto Palace Road at 1:19 and heads toward the hatchback. I drop to the ground and flatten myself against the building again. My breath catches in my throat. This is not good. Not good at all.

When the car is past, I tiptoe down the steps, making sure to stay low, and peer around the corner as the cop car slows in front of the hatchback. And then I gasp. The hatchback looks empty from here. Where did the thieves go? The cop gets out of the driver's seat and walks over to the hatchback. He shines a flashlight through the hatchback's windows and makes a complete lap around the car. And then he shuts off the flashlight, gets back in his car, and drives away.

I'm still crouched down, but I pivot behind me to look at Yellow. Her mouth has dropped open, and her eyes stare straight ahead in disbelief.

"Brilliant plan," I say.

"Where did they go?" Yellow whispers as if she can't believe it didn't work.

I take a breath and steady my hands. "We have to go in. It's the only way. Like I've been telling you all along. Maybe you'll listen now."

Violet gasps and points down Palace Road. Yellow and I both whip our heads to follow her finger. The two thieves, still dressed as cops, are walking down the street toward their car. One of them pops the hatchback, rifles around in the back, then shuts it quietly. The two men turn to each other, nod, and head toward the service entrance. They ring the buzzer, and a few seconds later they disappear inside.

"Go time," I say. I tiptoe around the corner, and Yellow follows me after a moment's hesitation. But Violet doesn't budge.

"I don't want to go in," she whispers. "I'm scared. We don't have a plan."

I make a disgusted noise and turn to look at Yellow. There's fear written all over her face, but she nods her head. "Why don't we just call the cops again and say that we saw someone breaking in?"

"Yeah, the cop plan worked out so well the last time, didn't it? Listen, the *president* gave us a mission to stop this. Us. Not the cops. You can be a weak little chicken shit if you want and stay here, but I'm going to complete the mission." I look right at Violet. "And for the record, I do have a plan. I always have a plan."

Yellow slowly nods. "No, you're right. We're going in. We're *all* going in."

I reach into the pocket on the front of my bag and pull out an index card.

"What's that?" Yellow asks.

"My cheat sheet," I tell her. "I made it this afternoon in the library. There's tons of information out there on the burglary in addition to what Zeta told us. I was able to re-create a timeline of what happens inside. At 1:24, the thieves enter the building. That's already happened. They spend twenty-four minutes tying up the guards and sticking them in the basement, and then they head upstairs at 1:48. When they're in the basement, that's our only shot to get into the building after them."

"What time do they go into the basement?" Violet's voice quivers.

"I don't know," I say. "Probably closer to 1:48 than 1:24, but I don't know exactly."

Violet's eyes pop open, and she bites her bottom lip.

"1:40," Yellow says. "I think that's our best shot. That gives them sixteen minutes to round up the guards and handcuff them, then get them to the basement. That sounds about right to me."

I nod my head in agreement. "Once we get inside, one of us should stake out the Blue Room. Violet, that will be your post. Yellow and I will head upstairs. I'll go into the Dutch Room; and, Yellow, you hide out in the Raphael Room. It's just before the Short Gallery, and there are more places to conceal yourself. The Short Gallery is too small. At some point the thieves split up. If we're one-on-one, we'll have a better shot. Can you do that?" I look right at Yellow.

"Listen, I know you think I'm some prissy little wunderbitch who hates to break a nail, but I've been doing Tae Kwon Do since I was six. I can take one of them."

Tae Kwon Do? That does surprise me. But I'm oddly relieved.

"Okay," I say. "Chances are you and I will be able to over-power the two of them." I reach into my bag and pull out a bundle of zip-tie handcuffs, bungee cords, a few rags, a small bottle, and three pairs of black gloves. I hand some of the supplies to Yellow, who raises her eyebrows. "I'm prepared," I say, waving her off. "Once you have the thief down, knock him out with the chloro-form, secure his hands and feet, and hog-tie him with the bungee cord. I'll take care of the other one, then we'll grab the security tapes and get out."

"What about me?" Violet says. She's probably trying to hide her fear, but her voice shakes and betrays her.

"Have you been trained to fight?" I ask.

"Of course she has," Yellow says. "We all have. Violet, pull yourself together and stop acting like a baby."

I give Violet handcuffs and a bungee cord. "Take these just in case. No one knows what time the thieves enter the Blue Room. It's either first or last, but I'm willing to bet it's last. The most valuable stuff is upstairs. If they do hit it first, just hide. Yellow and I will take care of them when they come upstairs. But"—I swallow a lump in my throat—"if for some reason we fail, it's on you. It has to be. Can you do that?"

Violet stares straight ahead and bites her bottom lip. Then Yellow shoves her shoulder into Violet, and Violet snaps to attention.

"Yes," Violet says. "I can do that."

"All right." I check my watch. 1:35. "Gloves on. Let's do this."

CHAPTER 14

The three of us slink toward the service entrance while looking over our shoulders to make sure the cop doesn't come back. The real cop, I mean. We stop in front and look up at the camera.

"Hopefully one of them isn't keeping a lookout right now," Violet says.

"Hopefully." I pull the last item out of my bag. "If both of them aren't in the basement, they're certainly going to hear this." I hold up my crowbar and examine the hollow metal, green service door again. I take a breath. This won't be easy. A hollow metal door requires a lot of force, and I may be strong, but I'm not a six-foot-eight, 350-pound linebacker.

"I think this is going to take all of us," I say. "I'll work on the crowbar, and the two of you kick like hell. Got it? We have to do this as quickly as we can."

Yellow nods. "I can kick," she says. She lifts her right knee and takes a practice thrust kick.

I nod back. That had some force to it. We might be all right. I jimmy the crowbar into the lock and take a breath. "On three," I say. "One . . . two . . . three!"

I yank at the crowbar with all the strength I can muster; at the same time Yellow kicks right below the doorknob, at the weakest part of the door. She spins away, and Violet swoops in with another thrust kick that lands on the same spot. That does it. The side splinters, and the door swings open. Yellow squeaks in delight and jumps up and down.

"Shh!" I say. "We have to be careful." I turn to look at Yellow and Violet. "Look, I know you don't like me, and truth be told, I don't like either of you; but we *have* to put that aside and be a team in there. Otherwise all three of us could wind up dead." As soon as the words escape my lips, the full truth of them becomes evident. This is real. Not a drill. And we could die. Very easily. Fear creeps into my skin and overtakes me. Suddenly I don't want to go in. I want to call the cops and be done with it.

Yellow puts her hand in the middle. "A team." I look at her and put my hand on top, then Violet does the same. This comforts me a little. We can do this—we have to.

"Watch out for the alarms," I say. "They're everywhere. Trip one, and the thieves will know they're not alone. And then they'll come looking for us. So please tell me you both know how to bend around laser alarms."

Violet nods, but Yellow shakes her head. "I'll figure it out," she says.

I guess that will have to do.

Yellow enters first, and I go in after her. Violet brings up the rear. I raise my hand for them to wait for a second, then duck into the security office and synchronize my watch with the security system so I'll know my cheat sheet will be right. It's 1:40 exactly. We have eight minutes until the thieves head up the main staircase to the second floor. I stash my bag by the entrance. Then we tiptoe quietly through the maze of doorways that leads to the main staircase. We're standing in front of the courtyard, which is dark and spooky, and I'm not liking this one bit.

And then I stop because I can't see a thing. At least, not a thing I'm looking for. There are no green lasers crisscrossing the floors and walls, showing us where the alarms are.

"I thought you said there were lasers," Yellow whispers to me.

I wave her off. I thought there were. My eyes scan the courtyard and stairs, and then I spot something. A small white cube hanging in the corner. An electric eye. Dammit. I should have anticipated that the museum would have a much more primitive security system in 1990. *Dammit.* I can't keep making mistakes like this.

I point to the cube. "Electric eye."

"Violet." I'm whispering so softly I'm practically just mouthing the words, but Yellow and Violet hear me and turn their heads. "We just have to look out for them."

I look at Violet and nod my head in the direction of the Blue Room, and she nods back. There's another electric eye in the corner by the Macknight Room, and I hold my breath as Violet flattens herself against the wall. I don't know whether the eye is hooked up to any sort of audible alarm, and I really don't want to find out the hard way.

Violet rounds the corner, and the museum stays silent. But still, I don't exhale. Not yet. This is like a game of limbo. Life or death limbo.

I look down at my watch. 1:42. Six minutes to go.

There aren't any eyes on the stairs, but when Yellow and I get to the top, we find three of them. Yellow points to each, and I see her calculating how to avoid them. I'm thinking the same. A modern, high-tech security system would be so much easier. At least I could see what I need to watch out for. Electric eyes work by sending an invisible, infrared light beam that detects when a person is around because the beam is broken. But I can't see the damned beam!

Think!

And then I get an idea. The eyes are trained to detect people walking *through* the museum.

I turn to Yellow and point at the floor. "Crawl."

I have no idea if this will work, but it's worth a shot. Yellow looks at the floor and nods. It's time for us to part ways. The Dutch Room is to the right, and the Short Gallery is to the left and around the corner. Yellow and I make eye contact. She's terrified, and I am, too. I'm not even going to try to hide it. But we both drop to the floor and scoot away from each other on our stomachs.

I low-crawl like they teach in the military—like they taught me at Peel—until my shoulders scream in pain, but I know it's only a minute or two tops. And I ignore them because the hall stays silent. I get to the Dutch Room and stand. Watch check.

1:47.

My stomach lurches. I only have a minute before the thieves come upstairs.

I scan the location of the electric eyes in the room. If I stick to the perimeter, I should be safe. So I hop up and find myself staring at *The Concert*. It's not hanging on the wall. It's attached to a small board and placed on a table alongside the window. There's a chair in front of it, as if you're supposed to sit and stare at it. It's so pretty in person; it almost gives me chills.

I'm wasting time! I'm here to save the damned thing, not gawk at it. I throw myself against the wall and scoot along it toward the back of the room.

The second hand on my watch clicks to 1:48.

I'm too exposed. There's nothing to hide behind. I'm wearing black and my hair is dark, but the security lights are bright enough that anyone would see me in a heartbeat. I have to get out of here. Now. It's quiet. Too quiet. A total absence of sound.

Except not.

Footsteps.

Quiet. Barely audible.

Footsteps on the stairs.

I have to move! I scoot around the other door, which leads into an elevator lobby. I could probably stay here, but I keep going into the Tapestry Room. There's an eye in the corner, and I don't know if it will catch me, so I throw myself down and crawl into the Tapestry Room just as I hear footsteps in the Dutch Room.

They're here.

I tuck myself into the southwest corner of the dim, cavernous room, behind a table that a sign tells me is from the mid-eighteenth century. I pull out my cheat sheet again. My hands tremble so much I can barely read it. There are two men not even twenty feet from me. Very bad men here to do very bad things. And then I jump as there's a rip and a crack in the next room. I breathe and tell myself it's the thieves taking a painting down from the wall. I look at the paper in my hands.

1:51. One of the thieves leaves and trips an alarm in the stairway. That thief then goes through the Early Italian Room, through the Raphael Room, and into the Short Gallery.

Where Yellow is waiting.

1:53. That thief comes back into the Dutch Room and trips the alarm.

1:56. One or both thieves come into the Tapestry Room and trip the alarm.

My Tapestry Room.

I'm breathing so hard I swear they have to hear me. *1:56*, I tell myself. I'm okay until 1:56. And at 1:51 I'll know for sure whether there are audible alarms or not.

I look down at my watch to check the time, but I don't have to. An alarm blares on the other side of the floor, and I jump so high I drop my cheat sheet. I curl into a ball on the floor. My breathing is short and shallow, and my hands are shaking in full vibrations as I pick up the note card. The thief's in the stairway. Oh God, he's heading for Yellow.

A few seconds later another alarm blares. Its ringing isn't the loudest alarm I've ever heard—not even close—but still it pierces my eardrums and makes me jump even higher. He's in the Raphael Room. *Please, Yellow.* Please take care of him now, while the alarm is still going off, so no one can hear the scuffle.

The alarm in the hallway goes silent, but the one in the Raphael Room is still going. It shuts off a few seconds later, and then there's total silence. I stop. I try not to even breathe. I listen. For anything. Any sort of sound to let me know who won. But there's only silence.

I guess that means either Yellow got him or she hid from him. If he'd found her, there would be shouting and chaos. I look at my watch. 1:52. Back to the cheat sheet. In another minute I'll know for sure whether Yellow got him. If an alarm sounds in the Dutch Room, he's still free. If not, we only have one to go.

I watch every second tick by on my watch. It's 1:53 now, but I'm not breathing until it's 1:54. Ten seconds go by. Oh God, please. Please let Yellow have knocked the other one out with the chloroform. Another ten seconds. If she didn't, I'm not sure what I'll do. Twenty seconds. I can't take out both of them at once. Thirty seconds. And I don't think Yellow can get here fast enough.

1:54.

The museum is silent. She did it! Yellow did it! Now it's my turn.

I crouch lower and slide myself out from behind the table so I'll be able to strike. The other thief is going to enter at 1:56, and I'm going to jump on him, choke him into unconsciousness, and get out. I hope.

Suddenly an alarm rings on the other side of the floor.

I slap my palms to the wall behind me. *What the hell is that?*

It's 1:55. I look down at my cheat sheet again. There are no alarms at 1:55. This is new. Who is that? Is it Yellow? The other thief?

There are footsteps in the elevator lobby. What do I do? Do I still try to take out this guy? What if the other thief is free? What if he tripped the alarm and is on his way back here? What if Yellow is dead? What if I'm next?

I don't have time to think. The alarm rings in the Tapestry Room as the thief enters. It's the bigger guy, the one with the dark hair and the mustache. He looks around the room, then turns to go.

And then he sees me, and I switch into autopilot.

He jumps back. I jump forward and throw myself at him. I deliver an elbow strike right to the jaw, and he stumbles backward. I rear back to kick; but in a quick second he's on me, staring at me with wide, murderous eyes. He grabs hold of my arm and twists, but I spin away. This guy has no formal training, but he's still way bigger than me.

And he's got a gun.

I launch myself at him, grab the gun, and twist. I feel his fingers break, so I jerk the gun to free it, and it's in my hand. I raise it and slam it into the side of his head, then I throw it across the room and jump on his back. I hook my elbow around his neck, grab my other arm, and yank like hell. The thief chokes and swings, trying to get me off him, but I wrap my legs around his waist and squeeze.

He slams his back into the wall, trying to break free of me, but I can see he's getting weaker. He's swaying from side to side. He's almost gone. I squeeze my hands into his throat a little harder, and he crumples to the floor face-first just as the alarm goes off.

I keep choking for a few seconds before I roll off and check him for good measure. He's out but still breathing. I don't even bother with the chloroform. I reach into my pocket and cuff him, then loop the bungee cord tight and tie his hands and feet together. My hands tremble so much it takes me three tries. But I get it.

I'm dizzy as I stand up to look around. The room is otherwise empty. I need to figure out who tripped that other alarm. I drop to the floor and crawl into the elevator lobby again, then tip my head into the Dutch Room. No one. I flatten my back against the wall and work the perimeter.

All of the stolen paintings are hanging in their frames except for the Vermeer, which is lying on the floor beside the table. Just as I thought. Go for the most valuable first. I bend down to look at it for just a second when a hand grabs my shoulder.

I whip up, grab the arm, and slam Yellow to the ground.

"It's me," Yellow groans, her mouth smashed between my hand and the floor.

"Oh God!" I say. "Sorry!" I lift my hand.

"I got the first guy. He's out in the Raphael Room." She hops up as if nothing happened. "Did you get the other one?"

"Yep, he's in the Tapestry Room."

Yellow gasps and grabs my hand, then jumps up and down. "We did it!"

"We have to get Violet and get out of here!"

Yellow nods and ducks to the floor, but I pull her up. "Screw that. Let's just go."

We race through the hallway, and the alarms ring immediately. But we don't stop. We tear down the steps to the first floor.

"Violet!" Yellow screams. "Let's go!" She runs into an alarm just in front of the main staircase, and it goes off. "Violet!"

"She can't hear us over this," I shout.

Yellow takes off down the West Cloister and rounds the corner into the North. I follow after her. Another alarm goes off, but we don't slow. Yellow jumps into the Blue Room and triggers another alarm.

The Blue Room is empty.

"Where's Violet?" Yellow shouts. I shrug my shoulders. Not good. Not good at all. We have to get out of here now. With this many alarms going off, you might be able to hear them from the outside.

We run out of the Blue Room and round into the East Cloister. It's empty, and another alarm rings. Where is she?

"We have to go!" I shout.

"We can't leave her!" Yellow shouts back. She runs into the Spanish Cloister next door, and another alarm goes off.

"Yellow, we have to get out of here!" My heart is pounding. Sweat is pouring down my face and stinging my eyes. "We're going to get caught!"

Yellow looks down the hall and screams in frustration. "You're right! Let's go! Hopefully she got scared and bolted."

We run down the North Cloister and then the West. We pass the main staircase, and the alarm that had fallen silent screams at us once more. We're close. Just the maze of doors leading to the service entrance.

And then Violet steps out into our path.

Yellow and I grind to a halt.

"Where the hell were you?" Yellow shouts over the alarm.

Violet holds up a VHS tape. "Grabbing the security tape. Let's go!"

The three of us run out the doorway and onto Palace Road. I grab my bag just before the door closes, and we don't slow down until we're a block away at a pay phone. Yellow fishes a quarter out of her pocket and dials 9-1-1.

"Yes," she gasps into the receiver. "I think there's something going on at the Isabella Stewart Gardner Museum. I hear a bunch of alarms going off, and it looks like the service entrance door has been busted."

And then she slams down the receiver, and the three of us run like hell. We duck into the Fens so that the trees will hide us. Three people dressed all in black running down the road at two in the morning are bound to attract some attention. We reach Boylston Street and make a right, then finally slow down when we hit the Berklee College of Music. Good enough. Students are still roaming around, and most of them look like we do. It's safe.

My heart is racing as we try to hail a cab.

"Oh my God," Violet whispers.

"Oh my God," I agree.

"That was the fire mission to end all fire missions," Yellow says.

"Who tripped the alarm at 1:55?" I ask.

"Me," Yellow says. "It was an accident. I backed into the Early Italian Room."

I nod my head as the cab pulls up in front of us, and I hold the door open for Yellow and Violet. None of us says a single word the entire ride back. I'm so shot full of adrenaline that I'm dizzy. Headlights of oncoming cars blur into balls of dancing light, so I close my eyes and try not to think about what just happened. It's still too new, too real.

Zeta is waiting for us when we get back to Annum Hall. "So?"

"Success," I say. "Nothing was stolen from the museum."

Zeta smiles and leads us into Annum Hall. "I'm sure you're exhausted. Yellow and Violet, go upstairs to bed. Iris, wait here."

Neither Yellow nor Violet turns to look at me as they head up the stairs, and I'm a little hurt. I don't know why. What was I expecting, that we'd all get matching BFF tattoos after this?

I turn to Zeta. "Yes?"

"Excellent job." He's smiling. Actually, genuinely smiling. "I'm very proud of you. I know I've been hard on you, but it's because I see leadership in you. I'm going to be making my full recommendation to the DOD tomorrow that you be promoted to full and permanent Annum Guard member. I know Alpha is doing the same." He holds out his hand. "Welcome to the Guard, ma'am."

I shake his hand and don't try to hide the smile that spreads across my face. "Thank you."

A full and permanent member of Annum Guard. Maybe it's the adrenaline, but I like this. I actually *like* this. I feel pride beaming from my chest. This feels right. So right.

I let go of Zeta's hand and head toward the stairs.

"Hang on," Zeta says. "You're skipping the best part."

I turn my head back to look at him. "Which is?"

He points to the library. "Don't you want to see what history has to say about you?"

My mouth drops open. I didn't even think about that. I run into the library, open a search engine, and type in ISABELLA STEWART GARDNER MUSEUM BURGLARY.

I click on the first link, which takes me to an encyclopedia

entry on the attempted burglary of the museum. My heart skips a
beat when I read the word *attempted*.

In the wee morning hours of March 18, 1990, two thieves
dressed as uniformed police officers knocked on the service
entrance door to the Isabella Stewart Gardner Museum
and were let through the door by one of the security
guards. A second guard came downstairs, and the thieves
overpowered the men and locked them in the basement.

At just after 2 a.m., the Boston Police Department
received an anonymous phone call from a female a block
away from the museum that tipped them off to a possible
burglary occurring inside the museum. When police
arrived on the scene, they found two men handcuffed and
unconscious in the museum. *The Concert*, a painting by
Johannes Vermeer valued at over $200 million, was found
lying on the floor of the museum's Dutch Room, but no other
artwork had been taken.

Police believe a third person was involved in the heist,
despite the fact that the security guards testified that they
only let two men through the door. The police reached their
conclusion after discovering that the service door had
been pried open, probably by use of a crowbar. In addition,
numerous alarms were tripped in close succession minutes
before the phone call to police. A popular theory holds
that a third person who was well known to the thieves
betrayed them the night of the heist. Both men apprehended
adamantly denied this theory, and police were unable to
follow any additional leads.

Perhaps the most puzzling piece of evidence left behind is a note that appears to be a detailed timeline of how the thieves planned the burglary. The note details when certain alarms should be tripped and when the thieves should appear in each room. The police have not been able to make sense of the note, and both men charged with the crime deny having written the note or having seen it before.

I gasp and jump up, then plunge my hands into my pockets. And that's when it hits me. I don't have my cheat sheet. I must have dropped it in the scuffle.

CHAPTER 15

No one says anything to me about the missing cheat sheet, so I guess either it's not a big deal or no one knows. Neither Yellow nor Violet say a word to me. Not one. It's like no matter how hard you try to bend them, the rules of physics are set. We'll all go back to the place we were meant to be. And that place has me as the outsider.

Indigo shows up for breakfast the next morning. I slide in next to him, remembering that our last interaction involved me body slamming him to the ground and muttering several choice words.

"Hey," he greets me. He doesn't even make eye contact.

"Hey," I say back.

I'm sorry, I say in my head. Before I can get the words to my lips, Indigo plops a heap of potatoes onto his plate and turns so that he's facing Green, not me. Point taken.

But then Alpha clears his throat to start making announcements, and I forget Indigo for a second and sit up straight. Here it comes. He's going to say something about the museum heist. I'm beaming with pride. Maybe people will start to see me as an equal around here for once. And then maybe I'll get my clearance codes.

"Big announcement this morning," Alpha says, and I bite my bottom lip in anticipation. "Our funding has come through, and it looks as if we're going to be adding a second gravity chamber in Los Angeles. And there are plans to add a third in Chicago, hopefully within the next five years."

There are cheers and hoots and hollers, and I guess that's okay. A second gravity chamber is big news, but I can't help but feel a little disappointed. Come on. I completed my first mission last night. They're going to make me a full member of the Guard.

"Second big announcement of the morning," Alpha says, and I scoot around in my chair. Here we go. "Red has been promoted to senior team leader. He's going to start designing some of the missions."

Okay, I guess that's pretty important news, too. We'll get to me next.

"And those are the announcements for this morning," Alpha says. "You will all be meeting with Zeta and Red for the remainder of the day to discuss a very important matter." And then Alpha's looking right at me. "Except for you, Iris. You'll be with me."

Alpha's voice sounds reserved. He doesn't make eye contact with me. Suddenly it hits me. *They know about the cheat sheet.* If it was important enough to make that stupid encyclopedia site, it's important enough for me to have a face-to-face conference about it with my boss. Shit. I mean, crap. No, I do mean *shit*.

THE EIGHTH GUARDIAN

Breakfast ends, and everyone piles out of the dining room except for Alpha and me. He takes a long time folding over his napkin and setting it next to his plate. Then he stands and pushes his chair into the table before finally turning and facing me.

"We need to talk," he says.

"Is this about the Gardner mission?" I hold my breath, waiting for him to bring up the cheat sheet.

Alpha takes a long inhale through his nose and lets it out just as slowly. "Yes and no." He pauses a second. "I'm afraid I have good news and bad news. Which do you want first?"

"The bad." Always get the bad news first. It's like ripping off a Band-Aid. You just have to do it.

Alpha shakes his head and hands me a piece of paper that's been folded over and sealed with wax. "Good news first."

I take the paper and look down at the wax owl. "Then why did you pretend to give me a choice?"

"To see which you would choose. I'm a bad-news-first kind of person, too. Go on and open that."

I slide my finger under the crease and break the seal.

GREEN
67^CAPITOL8*8

My breath catches in my throat. "Is this . . . Green's log-in and password? Why are you giving this to me?"

Alpha takes a second before responding. "Because I think you deserve it. Don't tell anyone." He nods his head toward the library. "Go. You have five minutes. I'll be in my office. Meet me there when you're done."

He walks toward his office, leaving me alone in the dining

room. I don't hesitate. I bolt into the library and pull out the chair in front of one of the computers. I flick the mouse from side to side to get the screen to turn on. Then I enter Green's log-in and password.

Green. Green's? What does this have to do with the Gardner museum? Anything? As soon as the US emblem hits the page, I type my dad's name into the search box and wait for the page to load. *There it is.* I click on it and hold my breath.

A new page pops up, and my face falls. I only scan it, but it's the same thing as before. Just a long, boring family tree. What is Alpha doing? Am I supposed to be looking for something else? Maybe something on the Gardner museum, something I don't have clearance for? I move the mouse up to the search function and start typing. I've gotten as far as ISABELLA STEWART GAR when I notice something. This page is different. I stare at it, and my mouth drops open.

His dates of birth and death are there, but that's not all.

Mitchell Thomas Obermann. Born Natick, Massachusetts. Died Dallas, Texas.

Dallas, Texas. My dad died in Dallas. In the United States. That doesn't make any sense at all. He was in the navy. I always assumed he died a hero, saving our country in some foreign locale. But not in *Texas.* Why would my dad be in Texas?

I stare at the screen for several minutes, waiting for an answer that will never materialize. I glance at the clock. I'm supposed to meet Alpha in a minute and a half. I close the government window and launch the Web browser, then quickly type DALLAS, TEXAS and the date he died into the search engine.

I scan the results. There was a Hole concert. That's probably not why he was there. A meeting of the Dallas city council. Maybe? We'll come back to that. A mixer of the Texas Iron Spikes, whatever that is. A wire fraud case. Gah! No. To all of these. I glance at the clock again. Thirty seconds. I click on the city council meeting, which takes me to a PDF. I scan it. Economic studies, housing reports, legal BS. A bunch of boring nothing.

I close the browser and slide the mouse across the table. I don't get it. Did Alpha know I wanted to look up my dad? He had to have known. I push back the chair and head to his office. The door is open when I get there.

"Did you find what you were looking for?" Alpha asks.

"No," I say.

His face doesn't give away anything. He gestures to the chair on the other side of the desk. "Ah. Will you sit?"

"I'd rather stand."

Alpha nods his head, very slowly. "The bad news."

"The bad news," I repeat.

"Well, there's no reason to beat around the bush or try to build you up with platitudes. Late last night we received word from the DOD that the experiment is over."

I blink. "What does that mean?"

"It means . . ." He takes a slow breath. "They've decided to keep Annum Guard as it is. No new members."

I gasp. "I'm out?"

"You're out," Alpha says.

I scramble backward. My back hits the door, while my brain flies in a billion different directions at once. I'm out. The word bounces around in my mind. *Out. Out. Out. Solitary. I have to get away from here. Now. They're coming for me.* I reach behind me to the door handle as the other hand reaches up to the Annum watch.

"Iris, wait!" Alpha says. "I think I have another solution!"

I keep my hands where they are and stop. "What other solution? Why?"

"Because I don't want you to go. Neither does Zeta. We protested the decision, pointed out how well you'd done on the Gardner mission, but this goes higher than either of us. So much higher. It's not our decision. But I think I know how to fix this. Will you listen?"

I still don't move as Alpha's words replay in my mind.

"You're going to have to trust me." His eyes travel to my hands, and I let go of the handle and watch. "And I know your past. This is going to be really difficult for you. But I think it's your only shot. Are you with me?"

My past. Something that involves my past. My bipolar mother? Peel? Small-town Vermont? Or maybe—

My dad. A jolt of electricity shocks my system.

"I'm with you," I say. It's barely a whisper.

"You're going to have to leave now. One last mission before the suits from DC show up for you. You're going to have to go back in time and meet the man who invented the Annum watches. And you're going to have to convince him not to add the genetic link. That way everyone will be able to project, and the government won't care that you're an outsider. Do you understand?"

I nod my head, but I don't really understand. Alpha turns around and starts rifling through a filing cabinet. My dad invented the Annum watches? No, he couldn't have. Annum Guard was started in the 1960s, when my dad was a baby.

Alpha finds a file and picks it up, then shuts the drawer. "This is your only shot," he tells me. "You have to convince this man to change his entire design."

"I understand," I say.

Alpha pauses for a second, then flips over the file and plunks it down on the desk. My breath catches in my throat as a picture of someone I know very well stares back up at me. It's not my dad. It's Abe's grandfather.

CHAPTER 16

The first day of combat training at Peel, I got paired up with a girl named Jordan Magnus. It was the first Krav Maga class either of us had taken, but it turned out that Jordan was already something of a jujitsu maven. I learned this the hard way when I took a roundhouse kick square to the gut. It knocked the wind out of me and left me writhing on the ground, gasping and choking and sure I was going to die.

That's how I feel at this moment.

"Dr. Ariel Stender," Alpha says. I stare at the photo. I don't breathe. I can't breathe. I know who he is. Of course I know who he is. Alpha starts talking about his background, and I nod and nod and nod. I don't know what else to do.

Alpha keeps saying the name. Dr. Stender. Dr. Stender. Dr. Stender. Over and over and over again. Stender. Ariel Stender. Abe Stender. And I'd be lying if I said that there wasn't a notebook lying around somewhere from freshman year with a bunch of hearts and the name Mrs. Amanda Obermann-Stender scribbled in it.

I stare at the picture in the folder. Ariel looks so much like Abe it's scary—it was always a big joke at the Stender dinner table. They have the same protruding brow, the same intense, heavy eyes.

According to Abe, it's bad luck in the Jewish religion to name a baby after a living relative, so many times parents choose a name starting with the same letter as a deceased relative. Abe technically was named after a distant second cousin named Adam, but everyone kind of understands that—wink, wink, nudge, nudge—he's named in honor of Ariel.

Alpha is still talking about Ariel's background. Why? I already know it. He has to know that I know it. Ariel received a bachelor's degree in engineering physics from Harvard, then a PhD in aeronautics from MIT. I'm sure it goes without saying, but the man's wicked smart. He was in the running for a Nobel one year, although he was edged out by some guy who studied liquid crystals and polymers. He lectures all over the world and has even been on a first-name basis with the last three presidents.

Although, honestly, you'd never know that Ariel has all these amazing credentials. There aren't any diplomas hanging in his study, no awards littering the hallways. You won't find any of the dozens of books he's authored shoved into his bookcases. He lives in the same modest house in Cambridge that he grew up in as a child, and he drives a Toyota that's older than I am.

"Ariel invented time travel?" I ask.

Alpha stops midsentence. He was saying something, but I'm not sure what. I haven't taken my eyes off the picture.

His shoulders drop, and he lets out a quick breath. "No. He invented the Annum watches."

"Ariel," I repeat. "Ariel Stender. He's involved with Annum Guard?"

"He invented the Annum watches," Alpha repeats. "I warned you that this was going to be difficult for you, but you have to focus now. It's our only chance."

I can't focus. I feel as if I've been handcuffed and blindfolded and pitched into the deep end of a swimming pool.

"You know about Abe and me?" I ask. It's a stupid question. Of course he does. He doesn't even respond to it. I drop my head to look at the picture again.

Alpha gently guides my head back up with his hand. His eyes are soft. "Can you do this? I need you to look me in the eyes right this second and tell me you can do this. You're only going to have one shot. I've been given orders to detain you in Annum Hall until this evening, when the proper authorities will arrive to take you and dispose of you."

I recoil. *Dispose* of me. Like I'm trash.

Last night I was the happiest I've been in a really long time. Maybe the happiest I've ever been. What a difference a few hours can make.

"Iris," Alpha says.

"I can do this," I tell him, looking him right in the eyes.

It's a lie. Maybe. I don't know. My head is a foggy mess. I can't think right now. Abe's grandfather invented the Annum watches. I knew he was smart, but how else is he involved? Does he know about Annum Guard? He has to. Does *Abe* know about Annum Guard? My heart skips a beat. If Abe knows about it, then there's a chance he'll come looking for me when he realizes I haven't gone CIA.

Unless he's moved on, found another girlfriend, and doesn't care about me anymore.

I don't have time to think. Alpha bends down and inserts a key into a lock on his desk drawer. He pulls out a silver case, and I immediately know what it is.

"I'm not going to need a gun," I tell him.

Alpha hands it over anyway. "Take it for protection."

I hesitate. What does he think I'm going to do, shoot Ariel if he won't change his design? And then I look in Alpha's eyes, and I understand. That's exactly what he wants me to do.

I drop the gun on the desk.

"Never mind," I say.

But then an image of myself as an old lady pacing an eight-by-ten cell fills my head. There are track marks crisscrossing the floor. I weigh about eighty pounds. I'm hunched over with long, wiry hair and crazy eyes. I scream at the guards. I tell everyone who will hear me about Annum Guard. But no one believes me. After all, I've been telling the same story for the last seventy years.

I pick the gun back up.

I head upstairs to change into something period appropriate. I barely even notice what I choose but somehow wind up in black pants with a light-pink sweater. So not my color. And then I'm downstairs, with a gun holster strapped to my ankle, and Alpha is walking me toward the gravity chamber.

"One shot," he says. "This is all up to you."

I nod my head.

"Set your watch to go back to March 30, 1962. Stender has

invented the watches but hasn't yet added the genetic controls. He's on the faculty at MIT. That's where you'll find him. You can do this."

I don't say anything. I just keep nodding my head like a deranged seal. And then Alpha opens the door and pushes me through it.

I fall into familiar blackness but barely feel the sensations today. The ache and confusion in my heart have blocked out everything. I land in the broom closet and hesitate. Will this be the last time I'm here? The door opens into the street. The last time I see the sun?

I shake the thought from my head and jog toward the Red Line. Charles Street is only a few blocks away, and MIT is right across the river. The gun feels heavy as I run. It's weighing me down. I should stop and get rid of it. I'm not going to need it. But I don't.

The Charles Street station is there, but there's no sign directing me to the Red Line. Instead it's telling me I've found a Boston Elevated stop. Whatever. There's no time to think about it. There's a rumbling and a screeching above that can only mean the train is approaching. Massachusetts General Hospital looms in front of me as I race up the steps. Sure enough, a train is pulling in just as I get there, and I push myself in between the mass of morning commuters squeezing themselves through the doors. The train is jam-packed, mostly with men wearing business suits and hats, holding a handle with one hand and a briefcase with the other. A lot of them have the *Globe* tucked under their arms, including the man next to me, the one I'm currently pressed right up against as the final wave of passengers boards the train. I glance at his paper.

Friday, March 30, 1962

I strain a little harder to read the headline.

VOLPE GETS HUB POLICE BILL; POWERS DARES HIM TO VETO IT

I have no idea what that means. I don't care either. The doors slide shut behind me. I grab a handle just as the train starts rocking and swaying its way across the salt-and-pepper bridge. I don't know what the real name of this bridge is. I've just always called it that because the statues on top look like salt and pepper shakers.

Will this be the last time I see this bridge? The full enormity of the situation starts to sink in. If I fail—if I don't convince Ariel to change the design—they're going to take me away. Part of me screams that they can't do that. It's unconstitutional. It's inhumane. But another part of me knows that the rules are different here. The Constitution doesn't apply to people like me. I'm a part of the government but outside its laws and protections. They can do whatever they want with me. After all, I've already given them permission to do it.

The train ducks underground and stops at Kendall station a few minutes later. I push my way through the crowd and trudge up the steps. MIT is across the street, so I hang back as a big black submarine of a car rolls through the intersection, then join a throng of students shuffling to class.

I sidle up to a young man wearing dark pants, a white shirt, and a skinny black tie. "Excuse me."

He turns to look at me, his big blue eyes hidden behind horn-rimmed glasses. He could be a modern-day hipster.

"Where's the physics building?" I figure that's where I'm going to find Ariel.

The guy's brow creases, and he pushes his glasses up on to the bridge of his nose. "Which physics building?" he asks. "There are a number of them."

Oh. Right. Of course there are.

"Are you looking for a specific professor?" he asks.

"Stender. Dr. Ariel Stender."

The guy nods as if he's heard of Ariel. "Oh, okay. I had Stender for eight oh four." And I nod as if I understood that. "His office is in Building Twenty-six."

Wow. That's lucky. I thank him and jog across campus, although I have to ask two more people to point me in the right direction. This campus is confusing. Finally I find a five-story rectangle with louvered windows and an orange sign telling me I've found Building 26.

I step into a long hallway with white linoleum floors and overhead fluorescent lights. It would be nice if there was a directory, but at least the first person I ask—a girl in a gray tweed suit with a pillbox hat—knows Ariel's office is on the fifth floor.

I thank her, then take a deep breath and follow behind a cluster of guys heading for the stairs. His office is right off the landing. PROF. A. STENDER is stenciled on the door in big black letters I can't miss. The door is shut, so I knock. My heart is hammering in my chest, and I place my hand over it like it will escape if I don't. I think I'm more nervous than I was for the Gardner mission. There's so much riding on this, and I'm about to plunge back into my past. And what I always hoped would be my future.

I hear footsteps inside the office, and I hold my breath. The door swings open, and a young, petite female wearing a plain, long-sleeved olive-green dress opens it. She's holding a sandwich in her hand and is standing in stocking-clad feet. She looks vaguely familiar, but that can't be right.

"Yes?" She holds the sandwich out to the side. "Can I help you?"

"I'm looking for Dr. Stender."

"He's not here."

I look past her into the cramped office. Its shelved walls are about to burst with books piled haphazardly on top of one another. That's so very like Ariel. Cluttered chaos. Yet he always knows exactly where everything is.

"Where can I find him?" I tap my foot against the floor. Nervous tic.

"That depends on what you need him for." She shoots me a raised eyebrow. I'm not sure who this girl is, but she's clearly no-nonsense. I kind of admire that. But I don't have time to make friends. I have to find Ariel, convince him to change the design, and then get the hell out of here. Now.

"I'm here about—" And then I stop talking. What do I say? I'm a visitor from the future here to convince him to change something about his time machine? "His funding," I decide on. "I'm here about his funding."

The girl's eyes get wide. "Oh shoot." She drops the sandwich onto a plate set on the messy desk and wipes her hands on her dress. "Are you from the Kershul Group?" But then she stops and looks me up and down. "You look so young."

"I'm older than I look."

The girl offers a meek smile. "I'm so sorry if I sounded cross before. I'm trying to finish these calculations for Dr. Stender, and I'm a little frazzled right now."

I hold up a hand. "It's perfectly all right. My name is . . . Peggy Hart." That name sounds as if it's from the sixties, I think. "And yes, I'm from the . . ." Dammit all, what did she say the name of that group was?

"You're from Kershul." The girl slips her feet into black heels. "We got your telegram yesterday. You're early. We weren't expecting you until next week."

"Oh, well, I was in the neighborhood," I lie. I'm just going to go with it.

"From San Francisco?" the girl asks as she grabs her pocketbook and pulls the door shut behind her. She sounds confused, but she smiles at me as if she's not. "Dr. Stender is in Building Twenty. I'll take you there."

"I had other business to attend to on the East Coast." We start down the stairs. I really need to stop talking now. The best lies are the simplest. They taught us that at Peel. I'm making mine far too complicated. They're going to see through it.

The girl stops in the lobby and looks at me. "Not at Harvard?" There's an edge to her voice now.

I clear my throat. "Where's Building Twenty?"

The girl laughs and pushes open the door, then holds it for me. "You're funny. Building Twenty. You know where it is. It's where the Rad Lab used to be. Kershul helped fund it."

I nod my head even though I don't understand a word she's saying. "Of course." Dammit. I'm blowing this. *Keep it simple.* "What did you say your name was?"

"I didn't." The girl stops and holds out her hand. "I'm Mona. Mona Hirsch. I'm Dr. Stender's research assistant." She reaches into her purse, pulls out a pack of cigarettes, sticks one in her mouth, and lights it. "This way."

I can't walk. My feet won't move. Because she's Mona. *The* Mona. Ariel's future wife. Abe's future grandmother. And she's going to be a karate sensei someday.

Without thinking, I leap over to Mona and tear the cigarette from her lips. I throw it to the ground and stomp on it.

Mona looks at me with horrified eyes. "What'd you do that for?"

How am I supposed to answer her? I can't very well tell Mona that she's going to die of lung cancer in a few decades, caused solely by her pack-a-day habit. And I certainly can't tell her that the love of her life, who I guess is currently her professor, is going to be completely heartbroken over her death.

"Cigarettes cause cancer," I mutter.

Mona shrugs. "I'm nineteen. I don't need to worry about that."

"Yes, you do." I've never met this woman, but I know the void her death will cause many years from now. "Besides, I don't think Dr. Stender likes girls who smoke." This part is true at least. Ariel used to rage whenever someone would light up in front of him. I don't know whether he's always been that way, but it's worth a shot.

"He doesn't?" Mona asks, and I hear it in her voice. She already has a thing for Ariel. I knew the two of them had met at

MIT, but the way I'd always heard it, Mona was a grad student, not a nineteen-year-old undergrad. Maybe that's why I'd never heard about it. Or maybe they don't get together for another few years. "How do you know that?"

"It came up in conversation," I say.

Mona raises an eyebrow at me, just enough for me to wish I hadn't opened my big mouth, but then she points to a huge, ugly building that stretches forever. It's white concrete with plain, square windows. "There's Building Twenty."

We enter a dingy, dark corridor, and Mona leads me to the B wing. The floors creak, and most of the windows have mold growing in the corners. I rub my hands over my arms. This place is creepy.

We stay on the ground floor and head down another dirty corridor until we're at the last door. Mona holds it open, and as she does, a short, thin man looks up from behind a very odd-looking machine. Ariel. I stop in my tracks. It's like looking at a slightly older version of my boyfriend.

"Dr. Stender," Mona calls over the whir of a machine, "this is Miss Hart. She's here from the Kershul Group."

"Is she now?" Ariel switches off the machine he's working on. It's small, with two discs on either side connected by a thin copper wire. There's a thin silver switch on the base of the machine. "I was expecting Jack Briggs from Kershul. He's who I've been communicating with. But he's not due to arrive until next week."

Ariel is young. *So young.* I'm used to the man with silver hair and age spots dotting his hands, not this trim, fit, slightly older version of Abe that stands before me. My heart is hammering away inside my chest. I miss Abe. I've been trying my best to leave him behind and go about my business, but now he's standing here before me and I want to run to him and throw myself into his arms.

It's not Abe, I tell myself. Not Abe. Ariel. And I have to focus.

"He couldn't make it. I came in his place. From San Francisco." My voice is wavering.

"Hart, you said?" Ariel's voice is skeptical. I'm being naive if I thought such a weak, poorly thought-out cover story was going to fly. "Ah yes, we've spoken before, have we not?"

I choke back my shock. What's Ariel playing at? Either there really is a Miss Hart he's actually spoken to somewhere at the Kershul Group—whatever that is—or he knows something's up. It has to be the latter. After all, how many teenage representatives are hired by huge funding groups? I'm dead in the water.

"We have." I extend my hand. "But I'm short on time today. Can you show me what you're working on?"

"Oh, did Jack not give you the designs I sent?" Ariel starts rifling through a stack of papers on a nearby table.

"No," I say.

"Where did I put those?" Ariel wonders out loud. Mona comes to his side and helps him look, then pulls out a plain brown expansion folder.

"Is this it?" she asks in a tone that says she already knows it is.

Ariel takes it from her. "Thank you, Mona," he says without looking at her. Her face falls just the slightest bit, and I know they're not a couple yet. He barely even sees her. "You can leave us." Her expression goes still.

Ariel's already flipping through the papers in the file as Mona walks out. He doesn't say good-bye or even turn to watch her go. I hurt for her. I feel like I'm being shunned by Abe. And I know I'm not supposed to interfere with the past or alter things, especially for my own personal gain, but what does it matter? If I fail, no one is ever going to see me again.

"She's very pretty," I tell Ariel.

"Huh?" Ariel grabs several pieces of paper and pulls them out of the folder, then looks at the door. "Who, Mona? Yes, I suppose. Here"—he shoves the papers at me—"these are the final designs for this beauty." He taps the machine he was tinkering with when I first got here, the machine with the two discs and the copper wiring.

I look down at the designs. There's a picture of the machine, then arrows labeling all the parts on the first page. I flip to the second page and am hit with page after page of complicated mathematical calculations. I have no idea what any of it means, and I don't see anything that talks about a genetic link. Does this machine even have anything to do with the Annum watches? I glance at the clock on the wall. An hour has passed since I arrived in 1962. That means almost three hours have elapsed in the present. This is not good.

I flip the papers closed. "Walk me through it."

Ariel nods and heads over to the machine. He spins the discs on either side of it. "This is just the prototype, of course. The actual device is larger. *Much* larger." He chuckles like he just made a joke, and I give a weak smile. "When it's turned on, these discs start spinning faster than the speed of light." He points to the copper wire in between the discs. "And this tunnels exotic matter, which creates a wormhole between the two points. I've figured out a way to load the wormhole into a small, everyday object that would allow time travel."

Ariel switches off the machine and turns to me.

"We're limiting it," he tells me. "We're loading the genetic makeup of seven men, hand-picked because of their strength, acumen, physical prowess, and intellectual capacity. The time travel devices will only work for those seven men."

"Why?" I ask.

"This is an experiment. The fewer people who can travel through time, the better." He drops his voice. "It's never a good thing to go messing with time unnecessarily. Time is a powerful and dangerous tool."

A chill races up my back.

"I have folks at the Department of Defense interested in this project," Ariel continues. "They're the ones who've asked us to limit it."

"Have they given you money?"

"No," Ariel says. "Not yet. They promise they will if the proto-type is to their liking, but until that day, I need the help of the Kershul Group."

Yeah, Kershul Group, whatever. "And what if someday you want to expand it past those seven individuals? How do you do that?"

"Well, their children would be able to time travel, obviously—"

"I'm talking broader than that," I interrupt.

Ariel takes the papers from me and flips open to the fifth page. He points to a calculation. "That's this. A later addition to the machine down the line. It's only in the design phase. The machine was specifically designed to reflect only the genetic makeup of the chosen seven. Adding another person would require complicated and *expensive* changes to the design. We're not there yet. We don't have the funding."

I ignore the push about funding because, oh my God, this is my solution. I don't have to ask Ariel to scrap the genetic thing and let anyone time travel. I just have to make sure he doesn't ever change the machine to add other travelers. This is even better. This way I'll never be recruited into Annum Guard in the first place. I'll leave 1962 and go back to Peel. Go back to Abe.

Or will I be stuck in 1962 forever? If I'm suddenly incapable of projecting, how am I going to get back?

I look at Ariel. I know this man. I love this man. He doesn't know me yet, but he's going to come to love me just like a grand-daughter. Maybe I should trust him with my secret. Tell him that I've come from the future and beg him to help me.

Or do I trust Alpha? He says he really wants to help me, and part of me wants to believe him. Ariel or Alpha? Ariel or Alpha? Who's to say I can really trust this Ariel from the past? I don't know him. People change so much over the years. Maybe young Ariel is greedy and ambitious and out to prove his name no matter what. That's so different from the generous, caring, genuine Ariel I know; but it's definitely possible.

I don't want to spend the rest of my life locked in an eight-by-ten cell with a small, slatted window. Or maybe no window at all.

I decide to trust Alpha. To complete the mission he gave me.

"I'll give you the funding on one condition," I say.

Ariel's eyebrows pop up. "What's that?"

"Change the design. Get rid of the genetic link. Make it so that anyone with one of your watches can time travel."

Ariel blinks. Then he scowls. "I never said anything about a watch."

My heart skips a beat. "I—uh—" I flip through the papers Ariel gave me while my heart beats wildly. "Um—" I flip past a page of calculations, another page of calculations. Oh, please please please let there be a visual in here somewhere. "I mean—" And then I gasp. "Here!"

I shove the page in Ariel's face. It's a drawing of the machine, and in the bottom left corner there's a rendering of a watch. I'm not religious, but thank-you to anyone or anything that might be looking out for me right now.

"Ah," Ariel says. "Of course. You've seen this before." But there's something funny in his tone. I'm blowing this big-time.

"So you'll get rid of the genetic link then?"

"What?" Ariel shakes his head. "No."

I blow out a breath from my lips. "No?"

"No," he repeats. "The DOD wants the genetic limitations. It's always been my intention to partner with them on this, to let them use the power of Chronometric Augmentation—that's what I've been calling it—to improve our lives. I'm unwilling to risk this machine falling into the wrong hands."

"Then I'm not funding you." My voice cracks and wavers. I can't lose it. Although, what's the point? The real Kershul Group representative is going to show up next week and probably provide the funding anyway.

Ariel sticks out his hand. "Sorry to hear it. It would have been a good fit for your interests. I'll start looking elsewhere."

I hesitate before taking Ariel's hand in my own. My heart puddles onto the floor. Is this the last time I'm going to have physical contact with another human being? I blink back tears. I have to get out of here. I have to go *now*.

I turn on my heel and race toward the door, then down the stairs and onto campus, and I don't stop until I've reached Massachusetts Avenue. I drop onto a bench. This can't be happening. I can't believe this is happening. I've failed.

Good-bye, Abe. I hope you know how much I love you. Be happy. Good-bye, Mom. I'm so sorry your life turned out the way it did and that I wasn't there for you. I hope you find the help you need someday. I'm never going to see either of you again. I'm done.

Except that I'm not. The thought flies into my brain and yanks my breath away.

Ariel hasn't finished the prototype. The machine doesn't have the genetic link yet. And I have a gun strapped to my ankle. I could take care of this now and go back a free woman.

But I can't do that. I *won't* do that.

Or will I?

I don't leave the bench. An hour ticks by, which means I've lost three more hours in the present. Maybe I'll just stay here forever. Except that they'll track me. They'll win.

My watch clicks to noon, and campus bustles with lunchtime activity. Students and professors dart this way and that, but I see Ariel straight ahead. He waits for traffic to die down, then jogs across Mass Ave.

I spring up off the bench and follow him. His house is only a few blocks from campus. I know it well. I hang back half a block and follow him to the wooden-shingled Cape-style home stuck plumb in the middle of the block. There's a long, flat, baby-blue

Chrysler out front; but apart from that, the house looks exactly the same. Same white eyelet curtains in the windows. Same wrought iron bench on the stoop. I can't see that well from where I am, but I bet you anything there's a twisted metal S nailed above the doorbell and a mezuzah on the frame. I stop walking and watch Ariel enter the house.

The gun on my ankle feels so heavy.

I park myself on the stoop across the street and sit, staring at the house. The light in the living room is off. I wonder if Ariel is in the kitchen, which is next to the living room. Maybe he's pulling leftovers out of the fridge and sitting at the kitchen table eating his lunch. The house doesn't have a formal dining room, just a little space right off the kitchen. It's tiny, but somehow we always managed to squeeze eight or even ten people around the table at holidays. I was there a couple months ago when Abe invited me to celebrate Rosh Hashanah with his family.

Ariel wanders into the living room and opens the window. I don't try to duck, don't try to hide. My hand travels down to my ankle, and I unhook the gun from its holster. I raise it, just to see if he's in my line of fire. He is.

I wonder if past-Ariel knows how lucky he's about to become. He's going to get married and have a son, then his son is going to get married and have a boy of his own, a boy who's going to have his grandfather's physics genius and his father's athleticism. I wonder if past-Ariel has any idea he's going to fall in love with his research assistant and marry her. I wonder if past-Ariel can possibly know the pain and sadness her death is going to cause him. I wonder if he'll know that his grandson's girlfriend will stare longingly at the picture of Mona hanging at the top of the stairs and hope and pray that her boyfriend loves her even a tenth as much as Ariel loved Mona.

I want to run across the street. I want to bang on the door and beg Ariel to let me in. I want to wander the house I've become so familiar with, calling out for Abe. I want to find him sitting on the old yellow plaid couch in the basement, playing video games on an ancient, thirteen-inch TV because Ariel refuses to have a set in the living room. I want to cuddle next to Abe and sink my head into that warm crook in his neck. I want Abe to set down the video game controller and kiss me. Kiss me everywhere. Not to stop kissing me until we hear the creak of the old, rotted stairs and look up to see Ariel holding a laundry basket and hiding a smile.

I drop the gun on the step. Even if I can't ever be with Abe again, even if I can't ever *see* Abe again, I'll never do this. Abe deserves a chance to live. A chance to be happy. A chance to have a family. I can't take that away. I won't.

I pick up the gun and toss it into a trash can on the sidewalk.

I've failed. My life is done.

So be it.

CHAPTER 17

It's seven at night when I land back in the present day. I step out of the gravity chamber, expecting to find at least two men in suits waiting, a pair of metal handcuffs dangling from one of their fists. I expect Alpha to hang back, mostly as an observer but also as backup if necessary. He's a company man through and through, after all. I wonder if any of my teammates will be there to bear witness or if they're going about their business, as usual.

But no one's there waiting for me. Not my teammates, not Alpha, not any government suits. Maybe they're upstairs.

If I'm going to do this—turn myself in—I need to do it now, before I lose my resolve. I trudge up the stairs with my head held high. I should be proud of myself. I did the right thing. I refused to take a life just for my own gain.

But really, all I feel is fear. Overwhelming, swallowing fear.

The living room is empty. So is the dining room. And the library. I glance at the clock to make sure it's really seven p.m.

People are always loitering about this time of night. Dinner even runs long sometimes.

I head down the long hallway off the staircase. Alpha's office is right there on the left. I reach up my hand and lightly rap my knuckles as I turn the handle. But the door is locked. The handle doesn't budge.

Where is everyone? Did I come back on the right day? If not, they'll find me, that much is certain.

I stare at Alpha's locked door. I wonder if his computer is on behind that door. It's been on and logged in every time I've been in that office. Why not now? If I could only use Alpha's clearance, I could find out what happened to my dad once and for all. It wouldn't torment me for the rest of my life. I look at the metal keypad staring at me from above the handle.

940211.

That's the combination Alpha used before. It jumps right back into my mind. Texas area code, Vermont community service number.

What the hell? What are they going to do if they catch me, tack ten more years onto my life sentence? I type in *940211*, and the door clicks unlocked. I glance behind me, then quietly slip through the doorway and shut the door as softly as I can.

I sit down at Alpha's desk and swivel around to face the computer. I flick the mouse around on the pad, but the screen stays dark. It's off. I power it up, then lean back in the chair. I don't know what I think I'm going to accomplish here. Watching him type in the door combination was one thing, but I wouldn't even know where to start with Alpha's computer password.

This doesn't feel real. My thoughts are clouded. This is a dream. Or a movie. And I can't even begin to imagine how it ends.

Except . . . I do know the ending.

I should go. Find Alpha. Try pleading.

But then I notice that the top file cabinet drawer is slightly ajar. I slide it out and stare down at a number of plain, unassuming files. They're alphabetized, and each one has a different name typed on the tab.

Julian Ellis

I don't know who that is.

Tyler Fertig

Oh, but I do know who that is. These are files on us. On Annum Guard members. Am I in there, or have they already taken me out, burned my contents, and tossed the empty file?

I flip past Jeremy Greer, followed by four Masters, which is weird. How can there be four? Intermarriage? There are three McKays next in line, and then, there it is.

Amanda Obermann. I'm still here. I pluck the file out of the cabinet, and my heart skips a beat.

Literally.

Skips a beat.

There's another file behind mine.

Mitchell Obermann

My dad.

My hands shake as I lift the file from the cabinet. But there's another one behind it. Walter Obermann. This can't be real. This can't be happening.

I lay all three files on the desk, pushing Alpha's Moleskine notebook out of the way. I don't breathe as I flip open Walter Obermann's file. And then I do. Because the first thing I see is that Walter Obermann was Four. A founding member of Annum Guard. That means—

I flip open my dad's file. DELTA screams from the page. My father was second-generation Annum Guard. There's a picture paper-clipped to the front page. My dad stares up at me. He can't be more than twenty-one. So young. So handsome. He's smiling at me, and I smile back.

"Dad," I whisper. I touch the photograph. Then I grab my photograph—I recognize the shot as the one Peel snapped of me my first day of freshman year—and compare them. Our eyes are identical.

I was born into this, too. I have the genetic makeup. The full force of the situation hits me. There is no secret government trial going on. No one took my DNA and inserted it into the machine. There's no solitary. No Feds waiting to arrest me. I've been able to project since the day I was born. Alpha lied to me. They all lied to me. Zeta, Blue, Indigo, all of them.

They knew.

And they lied.

Why?

There are footsteps outside the door.

I scramble as the code is being entered into the door. My picture falls to the floor, and I don't have time to grab it as the door swings open. Alpha's eyes pop out when he sees me.

"Iris!" His tone is one of shock.

I narrow my eyes. "You lied to me."

His eyes dart between the file cabinet and the open folders on his desk and then fly to the notebook I pushed out of the way. His face is panicked. He knows I've caught him.

"I didn't lie to you," he says calmly.

"My father was Delta? My grandfather was Four? There is no government program, is there? And there aren't any agents coming for me."

Alpha holds up both of his hands. "You don't understand."

"I understand perfectly. And I'm getting the hell out of here. Away from you, away from everyone."

Alpha backs toward the door. "No, you're not. You're not going anywhere." He glances at the notebook again. "Let me explain it to you."

"I'm not going to believe a word you say!" I yell. "Ever! You basically ordered me to assassinate an innocent man. You're using me because of my connection to the Stenders. Why?"

"Because—"

"Don't answer!" I swipe my hand through the air to bat him away, even though he hasn't reached for me. "I don't care what you have to say. I told you I'm leaving, and I'm going. Now."

Alpha stands up straight and grits his teeth. "And I told you that you're not going anywhere." He stares at me with cold, hard eyes, as if daring me to try to get past him.

But I don't have to try to get past him. In one motion, I grab the three files off the desk as well as Alpha's Moleskine notebook, then I whip open my watch necklace and spin the year dial. I'm not even counting the ticks. I don't care where I go. I just have to get out of here.

"Iris, no!" Alpha yells.

He leaps at me. His hand closes on my wrist. I twist away and snap the watch lid shut.

Alpha's office dissolves from view as I'm ripped away. The physical pain of projecting without the gravity chamber is intense, but the emotional pain is worse. My head stretches and pulls, and I hug the files and the notebook to my chest and scream.

I'm falling.

Still falling.

Still falling.

This won't end. I'm going to die. Inside my chest my heart is exploding, and I'm not going to make it.

And then it stops. I stop. I open my eyes, expecting to be standing in the same office, some years earlier. But I'm not. I'm in the middle of a forest.

CHAPTER 18

I whip around. Forest, as far as the eye can see. Holy shit. How far back did I go? When was Boston founded? Sixteen hundred . . . something. Oh no.

My mind flashes to what they told me before, about how the farther back you go, the more time elapses in the present. A minute four hundred years ago really passes two days in the present. Fifteen minutes is a month. What if I'm five hundred years back? Six hundred? I choke.

I open the watch face again and turn the year dial forward. I give it two full turns. That's a hundred and twenty years. I turn again when—

POP!

What was that? I drop the watch, and the pendant *thunks* to my chest. I whip around, hugging the stolen files tight.

It's Green.

I gasp. The tracker! They're tracking me!

Green holds up a taser. "Don't move!" he yells.

My hand fumbles for the chain of the necklace. I find the watch and snap it shut.

Green disappears, and I'm plunged into darkness. My body is yanked apart again as I fly up into the future. I scream. It hurts. It hurts so much.

I land again and open my eyes. Where am I?

I'm not in a forest. I'm in Boston. Colonial Boston. It has to be. It looks exactly like it did when Zeta and I went to the Boston Massacre. I'm even standing in front of Hancock Manor. I have to be sometime in the eighteenth century.

Why am I standing here? I have to move! I tear across a dirt-covered Beacon Street into Boston Common while already turning the year dial.

POP!

Here we go again!

I whip my head around as I run. It's Violet.

"Iris, stop!" she yells.

"Screw you!" I slam the watch shut.

I hear Violet's voice screaming, "You can't run forever!" as I fly through darkness. Pain rips at my entire body.

I'm in Boston Common again. It doesn't look that different. There are a few more buildings and more people around, and—oh no. People around. They're screaming. Why are they screaming? And then I realize. It's me. They're screaming at me. Because I'm wearing clothes from 1962 and have just materialized out of thin air.

I keep running with my head down. People jump out of my way. They're afraid of me.

POP!

No! Not again!

I look back as I run. Orange is on my trail, and he's fast. He's too fast. I pop open the watch face and spin the year dial. I need to get closer to the present! I don't fit in here.

"Stop or I'll shoot!" Orange yells behind me.

I snap the watch shut. I didn't turn it nearly enough. I'm only going a few years. I fly for a few seconds. My body barely has time to register the pain when it stops.

I gasp when I land. The Boston before me hasn't changed that much, but there are even more people now. They scream. A woman faints. I throw myself out of Boston Common and onto Tremont Street. There are horses clomping through the cobblestone streets.

Violet is right. I can't run forever. I have to get this tracker out of my arm. But how?

And then I see a man selling cheese and eggs from a wooden pushcart. There's a knife sitting right beside him.

Oh my God. Can I do this?

POP!

I have to. I spin the year dial a half turn, grab the knife, and shut the lid as Yellow lurches toward me.

My body explodes again. *I can't take this.*

I'm gasping for breath on the side of Tremont Street. People are still yelling. It's a never-ending symphony of screams, a cacophony of horrors, shrieks following me through time. I run down a side street. I don't know when I am. Sometime when women wore long dresses and men wore top hats. But there's no time to process. I have to do this.

I yell and plunge the knife into my forearm. Pain explodes through my entire body. I scream like I've never screamed before, and people on the street run away from me with horrified looks on their faces. I twist the knife into my arm and choke back tears.

I don't have much more time. A few seconds.

Blood spills out onto my light-pink sweater, and I drop the knife and press on the wound. I move the skin around, looking, searching. Every movement is agony. My vision is getting blurry, but I focus on something green and metallic. The size of a computer chip. I blink. That's it! I pull it out.

POP!

I hold on to the tracker with my left hand while spinning the year, month, and day dials with my right.

"Iris!"

My heart skips a beat. I don't need to look. I can tell by the voice. It's Indigo.

"Iris, stop running!" He holds up a taser as he charges toward me. His eyes are sad. Regretful. "I don't want to have to . . ."

I push myself up from the wall, cradling my blood-soaked arm. I sway to the side. I've never been this dizzy before.

"You don't have to," I tell him. "We're done here."

I throw the blood-spattered tracker at his feet and shut the watch. And I'm gone.

CHAPTER 19

I land in a crumpled heap on the street. Tears flow down my cheeks, and I don't try to stop them. Blood seeps out of my arm, and my body feels as if it's just been stretched on the rack. I take short, shallow breaths.

When am I? I need to figure this out. I need to get to a hospital. I'm losing too much blood.

I push myself up and stumble back onto Tremont Street. A horse trots past, pulling a carriage. Horses still? I didn't go very far. But then a car whizzes past. An old Ford Model T. And then another.

So I'm in the twentieth century. The early-twentieth century. The 1920s. The 1930s. I don't know. I can't breathe.

There's a man ahead wearing a white butcher's apron. He's standing outside his shop hammering a board with meat prices onto a rail. Dead, skinned animals hang in the window. I stumble over to him, and he gasps and drops his hammer.

"Miss, are you all right? Let me help you!" He grabs hold of my waist, and I have to fight every impulse in my body not to allow myself to sink into his arms and drift off to sleep. . . .

"What year is this?" I whisper.

"Ssh," the butcher says. "Don't speak. Rogers!" he yells to a man down the street. "Come help me! This girl needs help!"

"What year is this?" I repeat.

"It's 1921," he says. "What happened to you? Were you attacked? Can you describe your attacker? Where else are you hurt?"

"What's the date?" I whisper. I'm so dizzy. Faint. I'm fading.

"May the fourth," he says.

The other man rushes up, takes one look at me, and gasps. "Why, she's been stabbed!"

May 4, 1921.

"She needs the hospital!" the butcher says. "Flag down a car. We'll take her to Mass General."

The hospital. I do need the hospital. But not in 1921. I need blood. I'm losing too much. I don't know if they have blood in 1921 like they do in the present.

"Help me up," I whisper, pushing away from the butcher. The files and notebook start to slip from my hands, so I hug them closer to my chest.

"Let me take those," the other man says. He grabs at the files and tries to pull them away, but I yank back.

"No!" I croak. So dizzy. So weak. Blood is seeping from my arm. "I have to go."

"We're taking you to the hospital," the first man says. He

THE EIGHTH GUARDIAN

loops a hand under my knees and I'm in his arms, still holding the files. They're slipping.

"Let me down!" In my mind I scream it, but in reality it's barely a whisper. The cobblestone street is swirling in front of me as we walk. I have to get out of here. I don't have much longer until I pass out. If I pass out here, I'm dead.

The files are plastered to my chest, and I can feel the watch pressing into my sternum. I slide one hand under the files and grab hold of the pendant with my pinky finger, then bring it to the front. I pop open the lid and turn the dial one whole rotation. Sixty years. That will take me to 1981. When did they start screening blood? I don't know.

I keep turning, concentrating and counting as best I can. Black spots cloud my vision. I think I've turned it so that I'll go back a year before I left. But I don't know. Now I have to get free from these men so I can disappear.

"You have to let me down," I whisper.

He doesn't hear me.

"Sir, please," I whisper. "You have to let me down."

He doesn't even look at me. Am I really speaking or am I only thinking the words in my head?

But I have to go. I'm fading.

"I'm sorry." I shut the watch.

The pain is blinding. I can't take this. It's too much. I'm fading. I'm flying. I'm done.

When I come to, I'm in a sterile, pale-green room with linoleum floors. There are two IVs stuck in my arm, one pumping blood into my body, the other giving me fluids. I'm wearing a hospital gown. I gasp and bolt up. When am I? Did I make it? My eyes dart around the room. I'm in a hospital bed. I'm in a hospital. Where are my files?

A nurse rushes in.

"Honey, lie down!" she commands. "Now! You lost a lot of blood."

"The files I had with me," I gasp. "Where are they?"

"You need to lie down," the nurse says. She takes hold of my shoulders and guides me to the pillow. She's bony and thin, with flabby arms. Under normal circumstances, I could push her off me and get out of here. But today she feels like a linebacker.

"The files—"

"Are right there." The nurse points to a small wooden table a few feet away from the bed.

I blow out every ounce of air that had been housed in my lungs. They're safe. Now if this nurse will just get out of here, I can grab them and go.

"Don't you want to know how you got here?" the nurse asks, hands on her hips.

I shake my head. Not really. All that's important is that I've been stitched up and pumped full of blood, and now I'm ready to disappear again.

"An ambulance brought you." Her voice drips with no-nonsense attitude. "You were found lying in the middle of Tremont Street with a huge gash in your arm. What happened to you?"

"I don't know," I mumble. *God, just leave already!*

"What's your name?"

What is my name? That's an excellent question. It sure as hell isn't Iris. Maybe it's Amanda again, but I'm not going to tell her that.

"Jane Smith."

The nurse raises an eyebrow. "We'll chat later."

The door hasn't even fully shut when I rip the fluid IV out of my arm. I leave in the one giving me blood. There's half the bag left. I'll wait until it's drained, then I'm out.

The IV is on a wheeling cart, so I get out of bed and slide the cart over to the table. I grab all three files and the notebook and toss them onto the bed. My necklace is there, too. I slip it over my head, then tuck it inside the hospital gown.

I slide Alpha's notebook inside my grandfather's file for safekeeping and grab my dad's. I almost don't expect to find it. This all has to be a dream. A weird, very sick dream. But there it is. Mitchell Obermann. Delta from Annum Guard Two.

Born on May 1. Killed on November 2.

The word cuts me straight through.

Killed.

Every mission he's ever been on is in this file, but I flip straight to the back. To Dallas. And I gasp. There's a report on my father's death. Everything I've ever wanted to know. And the report is authored by Alpha the day after my father died.

Name of Reporter: Alpha
Summary of Events: Only a short time ago, in the late evening hours of November 2, the tracker injected in Annum Guardian

Delta went off. Delta was tracked to Dallas, Texas, on November 22, 1963. Delta did not have any missions scheduled on that date, which is immediately apparent as the date President John F. Kennedy was assassinated.

My breath catches in my throat. My dad was trying to stop the Kennedy assassination?

I immediately dispatched Guardian Beta to assess the situation and escort Delta back to Annum Guard Headquarters before he could inflict any permanent alterations on the course of American history.

Why didn't Alpha just go himself? That doesn't make sense.

At approximately 1:00 p.m., Guardian Beta arrived back with the body of Delta. Delta had been shot once in the chest at close range. I debriefed Beta immediately.

When Beta arrived in 1963, he located Delta staked out in front of the Texas School Book Depository at 12:15 p.m. He confronted Delta, who told him he was on a covert mission that came directly from President Clinton, funneled down through me, to stop the Kennedy assassination. I had already briefed Beta that no such mission was authorized, and Beta ordered Delta to surrender his weapon and return to the present.

Delta refused to do so, and Beta attempted to subdue him with force. Delta knocked Beta onto the sidewalk outside of the depository and escaped into the building. Beta pursued him on foot through the building and up the stairs. It was on the landing below the sixth floor that Beta ordered Delta to drop his weapon and surrender. Delta refused, and Beta shot him once in the torso. Delta died almost instantly.

My hands shake, and the file drops to the bed. My father was killed by a member of his fellow Guard. By Beta, who's also now dead. My mind is flying a million miles a minute, trying to process what I've just read. My dad was sent on a covert mission. Or he acted on his own. Why did they kill him? They didn't need to kill him.

I have more questions than answers. This doesn't make sense. None of it makes sense.

The door opens behind me, and I shut the file. I turn to tell the nurse to back off and let me be, but then there's this weird whirring sound that stops my heart. It's wrong. All wrong for a hospital. Someone steps into the room. It's not the nurse.

It's Yellow.

CHAPTER 20

I scramble backward on the bed and rip the IV out of my arm.

"What are you doing here?" I spring up and inch my way to the window.

"Those don't open, in case you were thinking of trying to leap out," Yellow says. Her voice is as flat as a calm sea.

"How did you find me?"

Yellow shrugs. "It was pretty easy. After you so dramatically flung your tracker at Indigo's feet, we realized you'd need medical attention and that you'd probably look for it fairly close to the present. So we've just been working backward and following up on any traumatic arm injuries reported at the major hospitals over the past few years. We've been on quite a few wild-goose chases, but now here you are." She slowly nods her head with a smug, telling look in her eyes. "And now I'm going to take you back."

"I don't think so." I just need to get out my necklace, and I'm gone.

But before I can make a move, Yellow throws herself straight at me. I grab onto her shoulders and spin her around, slamming her back into the wall. She gasps, then drops down and rolls away. I whip around, and my head explodes with light. I put my arms out to steady myself. And then Yellow kicks me—hard—with the heel of her foot, right in my solar plexus.

I double over onto the floor. The room is spinning. I don't know the ceiling from the floor. I groan and try to push myself up, and Yellow appears over me, her face only a few inches from mine.

"Submit. Submit now, and I'll take it easy on you. Continue to fight, and I'll—" She doesn't get a chance to finish, as I ram the palm of my right hand up into her nose.

Yellow screams and doubles over.

"My nose!" she screams. "I swear to God, if you broke my nose, I will kill you. I will kill you dead."

There's banging on the door.

"Open this door!" the nurse yells. "Open it now!"

I look at the door. The latch is broken. It's been dismantled. A cheap electric screwdriver lies abandoned by the door. I look back at Yellow. She smiles and nods her head. But then she flies at me again, and I don't have time to duck. She slams me onto the ground and pins my arms over my head. A flash of pain stabs at my newly stitched wound. Blood pours from Yellow's nose, ruining her ivory cashmere sweater. I try to lift my arms, but Yellow has them pinned too hard. I'm normally stronger than she is, but I'm too weak in this moment. I roll from side to side, but I'm stuck.

The nurse gives three sharp raps on the door.

"Tell her everything is fine," Yellow orders.

"Because she'll just believe me and leave?" I suck in air, and my head spins.

"Fine, whatever," Yellow says. Her hands are pressed into my wrists. "Take out your necklace. We're going home."

"I'm not going anywhere. They all lied to me. I'm one of you, Yellow. I was born into this."

Yellow's face contorts into a confused expression, and she presses my wrists even harder. It hurts. "What are you talking about?"

"My father was Delta."

"Shut up!" Yellow commands. "You're a liar!"

"I'm not! It's all there, in the files on the bed. All of it! My dad was Delta; my grandfather was Four. I have the genetics, and I always have. Alpha lied to me. Zeta lied to me. Everyone lied to me."

"I said shut up!"

"Go look at them." My head is spinning. Yellow's pressing into my arms so hard my hands are tingling. "Go and see for yourself. Everything is right there in those files."

"Nice try," Yellow says. "I let go of you to read the files, and the next thing I know, your hands are around my neck."

"I won't."

"Yeah, like I'm going to trust you. I know what happened. Alpha told us. The experiment failed because you suck at life, and you freaked out when he told you and ran."

"There was no experiment, Yellow!"

The banging on the door gets louder.

"Open this door this instant!" the nurse yells. "Open it or I'm going to have security break it down. They're already here!"

Yellow looks back at me. "Where's your necklace? I'm taking you back now. Screw the files."

I smile at her. "The necklace is under my gown. You're going to have to unhand me to get it."

Yellow's eyes travel down to my chest, and I see the exact moment appear on her face when she realizes I'm right. "Crap!"

A big *THUMP!* comes from the door. They really are breaking it down.

"Go read the file on top. The one marked Delta. Then look at mine."

THUMP!

"That door can't take too many of those," I say.

Yellow grunts and pushes off of me, then jumps up and scrambles over to the bed. I watch her from the floor and push myself up. I'm torn between attacking her and sticking my hand in my gown, grabbing the necklace, and fleeing. But I do neither.

Instead I watch Yellow. I want someone else to know the truth.

She's holding two files in her hands, and her eyes dart back and forth between them. She shakes her head, over and over and over. "This can't be right. It can't be."

THUMP!

The door splinters and breaks.

Yellow looks at the door, then whips around to look at me, her eyes wide with shock. "We have to go!"

"I'm not going back with you." I take out the necklace and pop open the lid.

Yellow holds up a hand. "Don't go! Wait for me!"

"Huh?"

Yellow scoops up all the files and the notebook in her hands, then fiddles with her own watch. "Come back one month with me."

"What?"

"I need more time to process this!" There's another *THUMP!* The door gives way, and two burly security guards barrel into the room, followed by the nurse. Her face is red with anger.

"One month!" Yellow shouts. And then she shuts the watch and disappears—taking my files with her!

The security guards and the nurse stop in their tracks. They stare at the empty space where Yellow used to be and then look back at me.

"I'm sorry." I know I'm about to give them their second shock, but I have to follow my files. There's still more I have to know. So I turn the month dial back one click and shut the lid.

Searing pain rips across my entire body, but it only lasts for a second. And then I'm standing in the same hospital room.

"Finally!" Yellow whispers. She nods her head at the bed, where a very old woman is sleeping. She holds up the files. "Tell me you didn't doctor these."

"Excuse me?"

"You didn't make these up, did you?"

"When the hell would I have found the time to do that? And why would I have done it?"

"So these are real? Your father and grandfather really were Annum Guard?"

"Looks like it." I shake my head. "Listen, I'm just as stunned by the whole thing as you are. But something is going on over at Annum Guard, something they're clearly not telling us. It's all Alpha. I think the entire thing was a ploy to get me to kill Ariel Stender."

"Who's Ariel Stender?" Yellow asks.

"He created these." I finger the watch hanging from my neck. "Alpha sent me back to try to convince him not to add the genetic link and then to kill him if he wouldn't agree. I refused to do it. I was coming back to tell him that I failed, and that's when I found the files. So Alpha set the whole thing up. But I don't know why."

Yellow's mouth pops open into a little O. "Because Alpha can't project."

My stomach lurches. "What do you mean, Alpha can't project?"

"Honestly, are you that dumb? You never wondered why he doesn't go on any of the missions?"

I don't even hear her insult. I'm too busy trying to process. "Alpha seriously can't project?"

"No," Yellow says. "He's the government suit that oversees us. He's the nongenetic link, there to keep us honest. Same thing with Red, who's going to take over."

"Wait, Red can't project either?" I feel as if I've been slapped.

"Gosh, you're slow. Red is being groomed to take over for Alpha. He's a suit-in-training."

The old lady in the bed twitches but doesn't wake. I drop to a whisper. "I bet the switch is happening soon! I bet Alpha is being forced to retire, and that's why he suddenly pulled me into all of this."

Yellow shakes her head. "That doesn't make sense. If you had the genetic makeup all along, why didn't you grow up a part of it like we did?"

I shake my head, but in an instant I *know*. It's like how your entire life is supposed to flash through your mind before you die. A bunch of images flood my memory, all of my mom.

I'm five years old. We're at the local park, and I'm swinging as high as I can on the swings, trying to touch the sky. My mom is pushing up, up, as hard as she can. It's a manic day, back when I was too young to know any better and thought the highs were fun. We've already been to the library, the ice cream shop, the toy store; and we spent more than an hour shopping for art supplies. There's a brand-new canvas for me to throw paint on, too, next to hers in the back of the Jeep. And now we're at the park.

A woman comes over and starts talking to us. I don't remember what she says. But I do remember my mom's reaction. She pushes the woman down to the ground and yanks me off the swing. She barks at the woman to never talk to me, to get the hell out of Jericho and never come back, and then she drags me home. I ask her who the woman is, and all she tells me is "She's a bad person. Very bad. You stay away from her."

I'm nine years old. I'm walking home from school when a white van pulls up next to me. It's a man driving this time.

"Your mom is sick," he tells me.

I keep walking.

"Your mom doesn't have your best interests at heart," he says. "You're not where you should be."

I run. Fast. I cut through the park, where there isn't a road. The van screeches to a halt at the entrance but doesn't try to follow me down the weathered, cracked sidewalk. I come out the other side and run straight home. At the time I thought the man was from DCF, a social worker called by one of Jericho's know-it-all citizens, come to take me away from my mom.

It wasn't.

I'm fourteen. My letter from Peel has arrived. My mom is locked in the bathroom. Her wailing moans travel down the hallway and into my bedroom. I catch bits and pieces. "They can't." "She'll die." "They'll take her."

At the time I think it's just my mom being my mom. Emotional instability at its best. But it's not. I get it now. It's not. She knew about Annum Guard. My dad probably told her what he really did for a living. She knew that he died on a mission, but I doubt she knows the whole truth about his death.

But I do. And I know that my mom has spent her life trying to protect me from the same fate. She knew that if I went to Peel, I'd wind up in Annum Guard. But I thumbed my nose in her face and went anyway. I chose my fate and abandoned a very sick woman in the process. I am a horrible person.

When this is over—all over—I'm going back to Vermont. I'm going to make things right. I'm going to get her help, and then I'm going to fix us.

Yellow is staring at me, eyes wide, still waiting for an answer to her question.

"Because of my mom." I rub my temples. I blamed her. For everything; for years and years and years I thought that she loved her precious artwork more than me, that I was a distant second. But she protected me. "My mom kept me away from the Guard. Or she tried to, at least. You all got to me eventually."

Yellow looks down at her feet and blows out a long, sad breath. "I can't believe this is happening. They lied to us, too. My freaking *father* lied to me."

I feel my face recoil in horror. "You're Alpha's kid?" My voice is loud, and the old lady stirs.

"What? No." Yellow drops her voice to a whisper. "Alpha doesn't have children. My dad is Zeta."

"Zeta!" The old lady stirs, and I drop my voice to a whisper, too. "No, that's impossible. Zeta is Indigo's dad."

"Yeah, he's called my brother."

Yellow and Indigo are brother and sister? How did I not know this?

"I want my files back." I thrust out my hand. "I need to know what else they've been hiding from me."

Yellow hands them over, and the woman lets out a loud snore and thrashes her arms.

"We have to get out of here," Yellow whispers. She rubs her hands up and down her arms. "I'm in deep trouble. I projected back in time again. I wasn't supposed to do that. Red is monitoring me. He probably thinks I followed up on another lead, but Alpha is going to know. He's just going to know. And then they're going to come after me."

"So go back." I shrug. "Let me be and go back."

Yellow shakes her head. "I want to know what you're planning on doing."

"I don't know, but Alpha needs to be stopped. He tried to get me to kill an innocent man, just like . . ." *Just like my dad.* Goose bumps line my arms. Was my dad an innocent man, too? Was he set up by Alpha? There's so much I still don't know. So much I *have* to find out.

"Just like what?" Yellow says.

"Nothing."

"Look, I'm not going back if your plan is to sneak into Annum Hall in the middle of the night and kill everyone."

"Wow," I spit. "Do you really think I'm a sociopath? Honestly. I'm not going to kill anyone. I'm going to . . . I don't know. Gather all of this evidence and take it straight to the Department of Defense?"

Yellow's eyes get wide. "You can't do that."

"Sure, I can. I just have to collect—"

"No, I mean you really *can't* do that. Alpha must have anticipated that you would try to turn him in to the authorities. We've already gone back. We've changed it. You can't . . ."

What is she talking about?

"Will you stop with the verbal diarrhea and just tell me?" I say.

"You're on the most wanted list," Yellow says, and my neck reels back like I've been slapped. "The one they don't hang in post offices. The one that only a handful of people get to see. You step foot inside DC and you're done for."

My body feels light. I made a rash decision when I ran away, and now I can't ever return. Because I'm *wanted.*

"Yellow, go back and leave me alone. I'll figure this out."

"I'm not going back. I just told you that they're going to realize I made an unauthorized projection."

"So tell them you were following a lead!"

Yellow sighs and walks over to the old woman lying in the bed. There's a plastic drawstring bag on the table next to the bed. Yellow picks it up, opens it, and tosses me a flowered muumuu and a pair of fleece-lined plastic mules. "Put these on."

I grit my teeth. "I'm not stealing an old lady's clothes."

"Put them on," she snarls. "Someone from Annum Guard is going to be here any minute. Do you want the manhunt to end before it's even started?"

I huff but realize she's right. I slip the muumuu over my head, then take off the hospital gown underneath it. I slide my feet into the shoes, and Yellow grabs my hand and leads me out the doorway.

"Yellow, what are you doing?" I hiss as we run down the hallway. But Yellow zips this way and that until we're running down the stairs and into the emergency room. People are everywhere. Doctors, nurses, patients. But Yellow charges ahead as if she belongs. She flings open the curtains to the triage beds as she goes. There's a little girl holding a broken arm. An old man whose breathing is all raspy. And then there's a doctor with a mobile suture cart rolled up next to him, working on a teenage boy with a gash on his calf.

"Who are you?" the doctor practically snarls. He's young, probably a resident, and has bloodshot eyes with defeat written all over them.

"Sorry!" Yellow says. "Wrong bed. Looking for my mom." The doctor turns back around, and Yellow swipes a scalpel from his tray. I raise my eyes at her, but she tucks the scalpel into the sleeve of her sweater and leads me out of the ER, onto the street. Only then does she drop my hand.

She hands me the scalpel and holds out her arm. "Cut it out."

"Excuse me?"

"The tracker. Cut it out of my arm." Her hand is shaking. The scalpel waves in front of me like a flag in the wind.

"I'm not cutting anything out of your arm. I want you to leave me alone. Go back to the present, Yellow."

"Like it or not, I'm your only ally now. Alpha has everyone convinced that you're trying to bring down Annum Guard."

"So go back and convince everyone otherwise!"

"You don't understand the climate there. It's freaking scary, Iris. Alpha has everyone on lockdown. There are cameras all over the place. More cameras. Everyone thinks you're dangerous. Even my dad."

I shake my head. "Why should I believe that your dad wasn't a part of this setup from the get-go? He knew my dad, too."

"I don't know what he knew." She drops down onto a bench and cradles her head in her hands. "I don't know. Maybe you're right. Maybe my dad *did* know about you all along. Maybe he's been in on the lie. I don't know who to trust anymore. And that's why I can't go back there. So I'm staying, and you're going to help me cut this damned tracker out of my arm. That'll send a message. My tracker will deactivate, and they'll know I'm not a puppet anymore either. That will rattle them."

"Or they'll think I killed you, and that will only strengthen their resolve."

Yellow holds out her arm again. "Cut it out. Now. Or I will."

"Yellow—"

"Use the scalpel, Iris!"

"You're going to need medical attention. How are you going to get it if Annum Guard is already following up on every arm injury to teenage girls recorded in the last—whatever—years? You're going to get caught."

Yellow doesn't respond, but her teeth tug on her bottom lip, so I know she didn't think about that.

"We'll go back before there were records," she says. "We won't get caught if we go back far enough."

"And you also might die of blood loss."

"1812," Yellow says. "This date, 1812. Set your watch."

"Yellow, that's ridiculous. I'm not going to—"

POP!

Yellow and I gasp and turn. Orange stands a few feet in front of us at the entrance to the hospital. His eyes narrow when he sees us.

"Yellow," he snarls. "What the hell are you doing?"

Yellow turns to me with panicked eyes. "Do it!"

My fingers fumble with my watch as I turn the year dial. The hands fly around the face, and I pray I counted right.

Yellow shuts her pendant, and there's another *POP!* as she disappears out of view.

"No!" Orange screams, then he looks right at me. "Don't you dare!"

"Don't believe everything you're told," I tell him. And then I project back to 1812.

CHAPTER 21

When I land, I'm standing on an empty tract of land where Massachusetts General Hospital will one day be.

"Sixty seconds," Yellow gasps beside me. "That's all we have. More like fifty seconds now. Cut it, and we'll project again!"

"This is crazy, Yellow, where do you expect to project to?"

"Forty-five seconds!"

I grab the scalpel from her. "Damn you!" I snarl. "Hold out your arm and grit your teeth!"

Yellow steadies her feet and turns her head to the side. "Do it."

I take a breath and dig the tip of the scalpel into Yellow's forearm. She gasps but doesn't yell. But then I cut deeper, and she does. She lets out a scream that echoes across all of Boston. I'm hurting her. I flinch, but then there it is! I dig the little green chip out with the blade of the scalpel. The cut is much cleaner than the one I made on my own arm. Having a proper medical tool sure helps.

"Five seconds." Yellow's voice is all breathy and stunted. "Done!"

I fiddle with her watch, giving it a half turn back. My hands are covered with blood, and my fingernails clatter against the face. I wipe my hands on the old lady's dress before I turn my own dial.

"Here we go. We're going to 1782. I'm sorry." And then we project.

There are even fewer buildings than there were before. 1782. I try to remember my history. Is the Revolution still being fought? Dammit, are we going to walk into a battle? I should have been more careful.

But there's no one around. I think it's really early in the morning, judging by the sun. Yellow is grumbling beside me. She's taken off her sweater and pressed it around her arm as a tourniquet, but blood still spills down her shirt and gray corduroy skirt.

"This hurts so much." She pants.

I want to tell her it's her own damned fault, but I don't. "Come on." I take hold of her shoulder and drag her across the empty plot of land, toward the Old State House. We need to find people.

Yellow stumbles, and her knee lands on the ground. I pick her up. And then in the distance I see a boy atop a horse, guiding a wagon. He can't be more than twelve or thirteen.

"Help!" I shout at him. "Help, please!"

The boy turns his head and sees us, then turns the reins so the wagon heads toward us.

"Hold on, Yellow, he's coming." My head whips over to her as she stumbles. I loop my arm under her elbow and yank her up.

The boy's face scrunches up into a confused expression the

closer he gets. It's understandable. I'm wearing an old lady's blood-stained muumuu, and Yellow's in a miniskirt. Not exactly colonial garb. But then he takes one look at Yellow's arm, and his eyes grow wide. It's clear our clothes are instantly forgotten.

"We need a doctor," I tell him.

"Who are you?" He sounds horrified.

"Does that matter?" I snap as I guide Yellow into the back of the wagon. I jump up behind her. "Please, just take us to a doctor."

The boy looks back at us, then snaps the reins, and the horse starts toward the harbor.

Yellow sits slumped over, cradling her arm.

"How are you?" I ask.

"This hurts," she whispers. But I have to say, she looks a lot more coherent than I was. Of course, I did do a better job of cutting the tracker out of her arm than I did my own. I was more careful. More precise. I didn't go digging around for the damned thing, probably nicking several arteries in the process.

A few minutes later, after we've passed the Meeting Hall, a very primitive form of Fanueil Hall—hard to believe that will be a tourist mecca someday—and a street that will one day house a line of bars, the boy stops the wagon in front of a shingled two-story house.

"Dr. Hatch lives here," the boy says.

I jump from the back of the wagon. "Thank you." As I help Yellow down, I turn back to him. "Is the doctor at home?"

The boy shrugs his shoulders. His eyes are wide, as if he's afraid of us. He looks away, flicks the reins, and the wagon takes off.

Yellow pulls away the sweater to examine her injury. "Looks like the bleeding is slowing down."

I peer in to look, too. She's right. The blood's still flowing, but it isn't pouring out of her arm like it was before. And Yellow seems fine. Well, not fine, I guess, but she's in no danger of passing out like I was. Although it probably wasn't the smartest idea to use cashmere as a tourniquet. Little ivory fuzzies are now mixed in with the blood.

"Do you think we can just leave it?" she asks.

I glance at her arm again and shake my head. "The cut is too deep." I reach up and knock on the door. "It won't heal without stitches."

Yellow nods.

A few moments later, the door swings open, and a very small man stands before us. He's practically Yellow's size. He's wearing a white shirt with wide, puffy sleeves, brown short trousers that stop at his knees, white stockings, and black shoes with a big buckle on each of them.

"Are you Dr. Hatch?" I ask.

"I am." He looks Yellow and me up and down. He has a distant, distrustful look on his face.

"We need your help, sir. My friend was . . . was stabbed. With a knife. In the arm. Can you stitch it for her?"

The doctor takes another look at Yellow, and his eyes fall on her supershort skirt. "No." Then he takes a step back and slams the door in our face.

I recoil. I can't believe that just happened. What about the Hippocratic oath? Is that just a load of crap? I look at Yellow, expecting her to mirror my shock and disgust, but she just shakes her head with a sad expression on her face.

"Dr. Hatch!" I shout as I bang on the door with my fist. "Dr. Hatch, you open this door this instant! You are doing harm by refusing to help us."

A few seconds later the door swings open again, and Dr. Hatch is back. He's staring at me with squinted, angry eyes that I can look right into, seeing as he's about an inch shorter than I am.

"I know what you are," he spits. "The both of you. I don't help common whores. I am a God-fearing man."

My eyes get really big as the door slams in my face again. Did I just hear that right? Whores. This asshole just called me a whore.

I whip around to look at Yellow. "It's because of how we're dressed," she says.

I know, and I don't care. I reach for the doorknob and turn it. The door swings open into a living room. It practically bangs into the staircase. There's a fire going in a fireplace across the room. Only a few wooden chairs and a dining table stand between me and Dr. Hatch. He jumps.

"What are you doing? Get out of my house!"

"We need your help," I repeat, enunciating every word. "I know what you think of us, but you're mistaken. We're not . . . what you said we are. We're just two lost girls from . . . from Philadelphia."

I shouldn't have said that. Philadelphia is a long way from Boston. How the hell would two young girls have made their way from Philly to Boston alone in the middle of the Revolutionary War? I've always been bad at lying on the fly. Those were my lowest Practical Studies grades.

"Philadelphia?" the doctor repeats with raised eyebrows.

"Yes, our fathers are in Boston . . . doing business . . . with . . ." I'm making this ten times worse. I should just shut up. But instead I try to rack my brain to think of anyone I can remember from history class who lived in Revolutionary Boston. "With Paul Revere!"

Yellow's face scrunches up into a disgusted expression. *Paul Revere?* she mouths. And then she turns to the doctor. "Please, sir, I'm a good Christian girl myself." She reaches into the neck of her shirt and pulls out a small gold cross. It's dwarfed by the owl pendant lying on her chest.

"What's that?" The doctor points to the Annum watch.

"A gift from my father." She pops open the lid to reveal the watch face. The doctor's eyes light up.

"I'll stitch you up, but that's my price. I want *that* as payment."

"No way," I scoff. "Give me a needle and thread, and I'll do it myself." This isn't true. I would have no idea where to start. But I could try.

"Okay," Yellow says. "I agree to your terms."

I grab onto Yellow's other arm. "Are you insane?"

But Yellow just slips the necklace over her head and hands it over. The doctor takes it in his hands, examines it, and closes his fist around it. "I'll be right back." Then he disappears through a door into a back room.

"What is wrong with you?" I ask Yellow.

She shrugs. "I'm done with this. Chronometric Augmentation. Annum Guard. I'm so sick of it. I've always thought I belonged in another time period, so why not here?"

I blink. And then I blink again. "You're going to *stay* here? Permanently?"

"Why not?" Yellow says. "It's . . . what is it, 1782? Maybe I'll hop a boat over to England. The Regency period is going to start in a few years. I've always loved Jane Austen. Maybe I'll live in a manor house and fall in love with an earl or something. It'll be nice."

My mouth drops open. I close it, but it drops open again. "Are you out of your goddamned mind? I should have known you were one of *those* girls who's all into Jane Austen just because she read *Pride and Prejudice* in an English class, but ugh."

And then Yellow's face betrays her. She cracks a smile and laughs. "I'm joking, genius. Handing over the necklace was the quickest way to get him to stitch me up so we don't waste any more time. Every hour we spend here is like four days. We need to get out, and soon. So while I'm getting stitched up, you go outside, sneak around back, break in, grab the necklace, and we're gone. Got it?"

The door swings open, and Dr. Hatch is back. I stand there, shaking my head. I have to admit it. She got me good. Well played, Yellow. Well played. If I didn't hate her so much, I think she and I might actually get along.

The doctor pulls out a flat tray that holds a needle as big as one you'd use for quilting and some stuff that looks like twine; and even though I'm not squeamish, looking at these downright primitive medical tools twists my stomach. I turn to Yellow, and she's as white as a ghost. But then she makes eye contact with me and jerks her head toward the back door.

"I'm going to wait outside," I say as the doctor picks up the needle. Yellow settles into one of the dining chairs and grits her teeth.

"Can't stand the sight of blood, eh?" the doctor asks. He uncaps a plain glass bottle filled with amber liquid and hands it to Yellow.

"Something like that," I mumble. I set the files and notebook on the table next to Yellow.

"Take a drink of that," the doctor orders.

Yellow lifts it and eyes it. "What is it?"

"Whiskey. Strongest stuff I got. You're going to need it."

Yellow sets the bottle down on the table, untouched. "I'll be fine. Just fix my arm, please."

The doctor presses the needle to Yellow's arm, and I fly out the door. I shut it behind me, but the heavy wood does nothing to hide the scream that Yellow lets out. It starts small, as if she's trying to hold back but builds into an "Ah-ah-aah-aah-AAH!" My heart sinks for her. This is not going to be pretty.

I rest my back against the brick exterior for just a second to collect my thoughts. Yellow lets out another scream from inside the house. I'm wasting time. I take off around the corner to the back of the house. There's a window and a door. I try the door first, but it's locked. Dammit. This is colonial America. Aren't people supposed to be trusting?

Window it is. I try lifting the glass, but it doesn't budge. And then I let out a disgusted grunt. God, I'm stupid. It's 1782. Windows don't slide open in 1782. I'm going to have to break it. But first I press my face to the glass and look in. I hear Yellow scream again as I stare into a small kitchen. There's a fireplace that doubles as a stove, and several pewter spoons and brass pots hang on the wall. And that's about it. Tiny. There's also the narrowest staircase I've ever seen in the corner, leading up to the second floor.

I need to find something to wrap around my elbow to muffle the sound when I break the window. I look around, but there's nothing. A few other houses line this cobblestone street, but no one's left out a spare sheet of fabric so I can break into their neighbor's house. Shocking. I wish I'd had the foresight to grab Yellow's cashmere sweater, but I guess my old-lady house dress will have to do. I lift it over my head and immediately wrap it around my elbow.

Come on, Yellow, scream again. I'm standing here in a bra and nasty, old underwear. I'm sure they lock you up for stuff like this in colonial times.

"Ah-ah-aah-aah-AAH!"

I don't hesitate. I slam my elbow into the glass, and it shatters. I do it again, clearing away an area where I can climb through without worrying about impaling myself on broken shards of glass. The last thing I need is to injure myself even worse.

I jump back and throw the dress over my head. One of the arms gets snagged on my elbow, and I yank so hard I'm surprised I don't rip it. I stare at the window, then through it at the closed door leading into the front room. And then I hoist myself up and in through the window.

There's glass all over the floor, so I can't jump down. Instead I stay crouched in the window frame, my arms outstretched and plastered to the wall to keep my balance. I have to jump. I'm waiting for Yellow to scream again, hoping it'll muffle whatever noise I'll make. How long does it take to stitch up an arm?

But Yellow stays silent. *I'm wasting time!* I take a deep breath and go for it. I push off the balls of my feet and sail over the glass. I land on the balls of my feet, too, and sink my knees into a squat when I land; soft but not completely silent. There was a thump. I hold my breath and stare at the door. Was I too loud?

"Ah-ah-aah-aah-AAH!"

I jump. Straight up in the air. My heart hammers in my chest, and I reach up a hand and shove it against my breast, as if trying to keep it from escaping. I whip around and scan the small kitchen. I don't see the necklace, and there aren't a lot of hiding spots for Dr. Hatch to stash it. It's not as if this is a fully stocked modern kitchen with twenty feet of cabinets. It's barely bigger than a closet. The doctor must have taken the necklace upstairs.

The house is quiet as I put one toe on the corner of the first step. It doesn't make a sound. So I lift off and put the toes of my other foot on the corner of the next step. Silence. I do this again, then again, going as slowly as I can. I only have a few steps to go when—

CREAK!

I shut my eyes. There's always a creaky stair. Why is there always a creaky stair? I turn my head and stare down into the kitchen. That was *loud*. There's no way the doctor didn't hear that. He's going to burst through that door any second now, and he's going to catch me.

"Sarah!" the doctor's voice calls out from the other room. "You get back in bed this instant!"

Sarah? Who the hell is Sarah? I whip my head back around and nearly fall. There's a child standing at the top of the steps, staring at me. She can't be more than four, and she's as thin as a rail. A damp cloth nightgown clings to her skeletal frame, and stringy brown hair is plastered to her bright-red cheeks. A rash covers nearly every inch of skin that's not hidden by the nightgown.

"Who are you?" she asks, her voice soft and weak. She's sick, clearly. Sick with some kind of fever. I try to remember history. Scarlet fever? Yellow fever? Some other colored fever?

"Sarah!" the doctor's voice booms.

"Answer your father," I whisper to her. "I'm here to help you." A pang of guilt surges through my heart as I lie to her.

"Yes, sir," Sarah calls down the steps. Her voice is so weak, I'm not sure if Dr. Hatch even heard her. Then she turns and plods down the hallway. I follow after her.

Upstairs is a hallway with two doors on the right and another staircase at the end. And that's it. Sarah walks into the first room. Her bedroom. It's tiny, only slightly larger than the kitchen. There's a little Sarah-size bed, and next to it is a wobbly, wooden table barely bigger than a stool. The table is filled with herbs and potions and all sorts of metal instruments that look even worse than the ones Dr. Hatch is now using on Yellow.

Sarah climbs into the bed, and I peer into one of the clay pots on the table. I pick it up, give it a whiff, and gag. It's awful. It smells like rotting eggs.

"Who are you?" Sarah asks me again.

"I'm a nurse," I lie as I set down the pot.

"What's a nurse?" Death is on the tip of her tongue. The back is speckled with tiny white bumps resembling a strawberry.

"I'm here to help," I repeat, and it's in that moment that I realize it's true. I have to help Sarah. This child is dying. But first I have to find Yellow's necklace.

The necklace isn't on the bedside table, and the only other piece of furniture is a small, closed armoire. If I had to guess, I'm going to say the doctor stashed it in his own room.

"I'll be right back," I whisper to Sarah. "Lie down and be a good girl."

She has no reason to obey me, but she does. She closes her eyes, and I realize that even holding them open was a chore for her. My heart does a flip. I wonder how long she's been sick. I wonder how much longer she has. But then I shake my head. Necklace first.

"Ah-ah-aah-aah-AAH!"

I want to clamp my hands over my ears so I don't have to hear Yellow. But I can't. I creep back into the hallway and tiptoe to the second room. The door is shut, so I turn the knob slowly and carefully. What if someone else is in the room? What if the doctor has a wife?

When the door is cracked, I peek in. There's a slightly bigger bed, and it's made and empty. A small wooden cradle sits beside it. Also empty. I breathe a sigh of relief and swing it open a little wider. A dresser lines the wall with the door, and the necklace sits right there on the corner. I pick it up and slip it into the pocket of my dress. Well, that was easy. Although, really, how hard is it to find something in a sparsely furnished house that's like five hundred square feet max?

I shut the door to the doctor's bedroom and tiptoe back to Sarah's room. She hears me enter and opens her eyes. They're a mixture of sadness and fear and resignation. Sarah knows she's dying, and my heart shatters. I need to help her, but I don't know what I can do here in 1782.

"Am I going to die?" Sarah asks. She coughs, and her entire body shakes.

I don't say anything.

"My mama died," she whispers. "And so did Ben. My papa won't say it, but I think I'm going to die."

"No, you're not."

"I'm done," the doctor's voice says from the floor below.

Oh, not good.

"I'm going to get you medicine," I whisper to Sarah as I glance into the bowl of herbs next to her bed. "Real medicine. It's going to make you better."

I hear the door to the kitchen open downstairs.

"What is this?" the doctor's voice yells as he spots the broken window. "Sarah!" His feet land on the first step, and I fly out of the room, down the hallway, and into the other stairwell. I thump down the stairs.

"Who's in here?" The doctor's voice is now coming from the second floor.

Yellow is still sitting in the same chair, slumped back. Her face is white, and her breath reeks of whiskey. There's a bucket on the floor that's half full of vomit. I try not to gag as I pull Yellow's necklace out of my pocket and spin the year dial two full turns. I toss it to Yellow, and she catches it.

"I set it," I bark. "Go! Grab the files!"

I'm spinning my own dial as Yellow slips the necklace over her head and tucks the files into her waistband. She tries to stand but staggers backward and falls to the floor.

"The necklace!" the doctor roars from the second floor. "She stole it!"

His footsteps thunder down the stairs. I throw myself over Yellow, grab her pendant, and shut its lid a second before I shut mine.

Yellow and I are ripped through time. I hear Yellow scream. We land, and she stumbles back onto the street. She looks around, and familiarity crosses her face.

"When are we?"

"1894." I drop my head, grab Yellow's hand, and pull her into an alley as a policeman rounds the corner, swinging a nightclub.

Yellow looks up at a redbrick building that casts a shadow over us, then leans her back into it and sinks onto the ground. "This is my time."

"Excuse me?"

"My time," she says. "My time period. We're all assigned different eras that we specialize in. I'm the late-nineteenth century. I feel at home here."

"Except that we're not staying." I hold down my hand to help Yellow to her feet, but she doesn't take it. "Every hour we stay here is like, what?"

"Twelve hours in the present, more or less."

"So if we stay two hours, we lose an entire day. We can't do that."

"Well, I don't want to project again." Yellow sighs. "Look at this. Look at what he did to me." She holds out her arm, and I recoil. Her stitches are crude, thick black strings snaking up half her forearm. "I can't project again. Physically. I need to recover, at least for a night. I don't care if I lose a day or a week or even a month. If I project again, I might die."

I rest my head in my hands. My life is literally racing past me. When I left the present yesterday, it was November. I'm not sure exactly how much time has passed, but it has to be weeks later, maybe even a month or so. And I've only passed a few hours.

I could leave Yellow here. I never wanted her tagging along in the first place.

I look down at her, sitting in the street with her legs straight out in front of her. Her patterned tights are ripped, her once crisp dress shirt is ruined, and her skirt is dotted with blood. Because of me. Yellow chose to leave Annum Guard and help *me*. I can't abandon her. It would be like leaving an injured man behind on the battlefield. There are some things you just don't do.

I hold up my index finger. "One night. We'll develop a game plan and figure out how we're going to bring down Alpha. So tell me, Miss Nineteenth Century, is there a hotel we could check into or something?"

"The Parker House," Yellow says. "It's the best hotel in Boston. I've eaten in the restaurant a bunch of times, but I've never stayed there. I've always wanted to."

I scrunch my nose. "And how exactly are we going to pay for that?" It dawns on me that when I ran away, I didn't count on having to pay for things. Ever. I have exactly zero dollars on me. I haven't eaten in a day. As the thought crosses my mind, I realize that I'm hungry. Starving. And thirsty. It's as if I was blocking out all the discomfort because I was so high on adrenaline, but now that I can finally breathe, I've come crashing back to Earth.

I place my hand on my stomach. "We need to eat. Do you have any money on you?"

She pushes up, pulls a twenty out of her pocket, and looks at it. "This would more than cover a room and dinner, except that we might run into a problem right here." She holds it in front of my face and taps on the lower-right corner, where the words *2008 SERIES* are printed.

I sigh. "So we have no money."

"And you're in a muumuu, and I'm in a corduroy miniskirt."

"You sure you can't project again?"

"Positive."

I nod my head. "Okay." I look down at the charm bracelet dangling from my wrist. My Hanukkah gift from Abe's family. I hate to part with it, but sometimes you have to make hard choices. "We can sell this." I shake my wrist.

Yellow shakes her head. "No, you're not selling that. It was a gift from your boyfriend, right?"

"How did you know that?"

"You told me it was a gift when you first started at Annum Guard. I just guessed it was from a boyfriend."

I can't believe Yellow remembers something I told her in passing about my bracelet.

"We'll sell these," she says. "Or one of them, at least." She unscrews one of her diamond stud earrings and holds it up, then she drops it into my hand. "You have to do it, though. Those suckers were five thousand dollars apiece, and I think I might pass out when they give me, like, a hundred and fifty for it."

Yellow leads me down Washington Street and stops in front of a door. SHREVE, CRUMP & LOW is written on a sign out front.

"Tuck your hair up and pretend you're a man," Yellow tells me before I go inside. "They'll give you a better price."

"I'm in a flowered muumuu. They're going to think I'm an asylum patient."

"Oh. True. Well, then, just do your best."

The man standing inside the jewelry store gives me a very blatant once-over, but all appearances are overlooked when I pull out that diamond stud. He tries to lowball me, but I talk him up to $175. I honestly have no idea if that's a fair price or if I'm getting ripped off, but, oh well.

Next, Yellow and I duck into a small clothing shop down the street and buy dresses and shoes that are good quality but at least ten years out of fashion. At least that's what Yellow says. But we can afford them; that's the important part. Then it's on to the Parker House.

The lobby of the hotel takes my breath away, even in 1894. Massive Corinthian columns line the room, stretching all the way from the marble floors to the coffered ceilings. Dozens of dome chandeliers dangle above our heads. We go to the desk, money in hand, ready with our cover stories. Yellow and I are the daughters of a foreign dignitary here in town on business. Our father sent us to check into the best hotel in Boston. But the man behind the counter doesn't even blink. He gives us a metal key to room 303 and that's that.

Finally. Something is simple for once.

The room is small, with two beds, a dresser, and a night table. Yellow collapses onto one of the beds, but I refuse.

"Uh-uh. Get up. I'm starving, and we have to figure out a plan. We can rest later."

Yellow grumbles but pushes herself up off the bed. I grab the files and Alpha's notebook, and we head downstairs into the restaurant, which is already filling up, even though it's just five o'clock.

When we sit, I glance around, sort of to make sure no one is eavesdropping on us but mostly to see where the damned waiter is with the dinner rolls. I toss Alpha's notebook onto the table, and Yellow scoops it up at once.

"Is this Alpha's?" she asks.

"Yeah." I drum my fingers on the table and look around again. "I took it from his office. I haven't gotten a chance to look at it yet." Yellow's already flipping through it. "There's so much to process here. What I don't get is why Alpha wants Ariel Stender dead."

"Who's Ariel Stender?" Yellow asks, flipping a page. She doesn't look up at me.

"He invented these," I say, fingering the watch hanging from my neck. "I already told you that."

I look around. Seriously, where the hell is the waiter?

Yellow flips another page. "But who's Ariel Stender? Was he part of the original Annum Guard?"

"No, he's still alive in the present. He's . . . he's my boyfriend's grandfather."

At that Yellow looks up at me over the top of the notebook. Her eyes are wide with surprise.

"Alpha told you to kill your boyfriend's grandfather?"

I nod.

"And you considered it?"

"No!" I hiss. "I didn't. I wouldn't ever—"

And then the waiter sidles up to our table. *Finally.* Yellow ducks her head back to the notebook.

"Good evening, ladies." He sets a small basket of bread on the table. I have to restrain myself from jumping on it. "Have you had a chance to look over the menu?"

I haven't even opened it. Yellow's sits untouched, too.

"I'll have the green turtle soup and the filet of beef," Yellow says, her head still down. "Rare, please. Oh, and a side of the truffled duck in jelly."

I blink. Most of that sounds absolutely disgusting. I quickly glance at the menu and want to gag. Larded sweetbreads, kidney, mutton, tongue. I could never live in 1894.

The waiter clears his throat.

"The filet of beef, too," I tell him. It's like the only edible thing on the whole menu. "But medium, please." On the outside, I might seem like a rare-meat kind of girl, too; but really, meat that is too pink and bloody and, well, *raw* makes me want to hurl.

The waiter raises an eyebrow. "Medium? I don't understand."

My head whips over to Yellow, and she quickly shakes her own. People haven't heard of medium in 1894? I look back to the waiter. "Um, just not rare. A little more cooked."

This doesn't seem to clear much up, but the waiter takes our menus and leaves. I pounce on the bread basket and rip open a half moon–shaped roll with my teeth. I don't pause to bother with the butter, and I sure as hell forget my manners. The roll is warm and buttery, and I could eat seventy of them.

"Anyway," I say. "It's clear that Alpha's up to something, so we need to figure out what it is and then come up with a way to stop him, which is going to be difficult, considering I'm apparently a wanted felon these days. Any ideas?"

Yellow doesn't even acknowledge that I asked her a question. She still has her nose buried in that damned notebook.

I clear my throat and grab another roll. "Ahem, I asked if you had any ideas."

Finally she looks up. She has a bewildered expression on her face. "You haven't read this?"

"No," I mumble with a mouth full of bread. I should have ordered an appetizer. "When would I have had a chance to do that? When I was running from you guys? When I woke up in a hospital room, and you showed up like a minute later? While I was breaking into a colonial house to get back your necklace? Huh? When in all of that free time was I supposed to sit down and do some pleasure reading?"

Yellow shakes her head. "You don't have to be so snippy about it." She tilts the notebook at me. "It's our missions. Every single one of them. I think Alpha was selling them on the side."

I reach over and snatch the notebook out of her hands. It's open to an entry marked June 5 from last year. It reads:

JL
7.5

I scrunch up my nose. "And how exactly did you come to the conclusion that this is a mission?"

"Because of the date. June 5. I remember that mission. Green and I tampered with a Supreme Court decision on some transportation statute, then he tried to cop a feel before we projected back. I kneed him right where it hurts. I'll never forget that day."

"What's seven point five?" I say. "This doesn't strike me as having anything to do with money."

Yellow grabs back the notebook and flips it to the beginning. "Look, here." She holds it up and points to a page of entries. My eyes scan them.

RF
$5.75

BB
$2.8

KP
$3.0

"He stopped using the dollar sign almost right away, probably because it was too obvious," Yellow says.

I take the notebook from her and flip forward a few pages. She's right. The dollar sign is on that first page and then it disappears. I thumb through and find the JL entry. "So what's seven point five? Seven and a half million?"

"No way," Yellow says as she shakes her head. "There are hundreds, thousands of entries in there. Alpha isn't making several million dollars off each of them. He'd be a billionaire or something. Alpha doesn't have billions of dollars, I can tell you that much. Seven and a half thousand, maybe? Or seven hundred and fifty bucks?"

"Who's JL?" I ask.

Yellow shrugs. "Code for one particular person, I'd imagine. And I'd really doubt that those are initials. Alpha's smarter than that."

She drops her napkin into her lap and reaches for the bread basket.

"You ate all the rolls?" she asks in horror.

I barely hear her. I've already flipped the notebook to the last few pages and am staring at the dates. The Boston Massacre mission is there. KA bought it for 50.0. Well, tried to buy it, at least. I failed that mission, as evidenced by the angry blue scratch mark through the number.

Fifty thousand dollars. Yellow's right. It has to be thousands. Alpha would have made fifty grand off that.

The mission in DC with Senator McCarthy is there, too. OO bought it for only 3.0. Small potatoes. The Gardner mission's there, too. That one went for a million dollars. Holy shit.

I flip to the very front of the notebook. Looks as if Alpha started selling the missions in the early 1990s. Which means . . .

I flip forward a few pages and feel the rolls I just pounded start to rise in my throat.

It's there. It has an entry. Alpha *knew* about the JFK mission. It wasn't unauthorized at all. Alpha might have set up my dad.

I stare at the entry. Alpha was set to make *ten million* off stopping the JFK assassination.

Instead there were two assassinations that day.

CHAPTER 22

"We're going to Dallas," I say as the waiter sets down two plates, a low bowl of soup, and a rectangular serving platter on the table. My mind is racing.

Yellow picks up her spoon and swirls it around in her reddish-brown soup. "Excuse me?"

I toss the notebook across the table at her. "Someone code named CE bought the Kennedy assassination for *ten million dollars*."

Yellow swallows and sets down her spoon. Her face turns sour. "Look, I don't know if that's the best idea."

"And why not? It's the only idea we have, and I don't see you throwing out any suggestions."

"You're saying we should go back to the mission where your dad died." She says it like a statement, not a question.

"Yeah. So?" I shove my knife through my steak and saw back and forth. It's well-done.

"So what do you want to do, stop your dad's death? We can't do that."

I set down my fork a little more forcefully than I mean to. The couple at the next table looks at us. The man is wearing a white dress shirt with a high collar and a gray-striped frock coat. His wife has on a long, corseted gown with ruffles. She raises her hand to her face as if she's shocked by the way I'm acting.

"What are you looking at?" I snap at her. Her face grows red, and she drops her gaze.

"Iris, stop it," Yellow says through gritted teeth.

"No!"

She kicks me. Hard. Right in the shin. "Stop making a scene," she mutters under her breath. "You are the most selfish person I've ever met; you know that?"

My eyes fly open. "I . . . what?"

"It's always you you you. What's best for Iris? That's the only thing you think about. And then you lash out at people who don't immediately see things your way."

"You don't know me at all, Yellow."

"Really? I think I do. You haven't stopped talking about yourself since you joined Annum Guard. You were born in Vermont. You thought your dad was a Navy SEAL. Your mom is bipolar. You had to leave your boyfriend behind. No one likes you. Boo freaking hoo. Iris Iris Iris. All the time."

"That's not true," I whisper.

"Really? So tell me something about myself then. I mean, other than the fact that you finally figured out who my dad and brother are, which, for the record, it kind of hurts my feelings that you haven't mentioned it since I told you."

"I . . ." I open my mouth and then shut it. Because she's right. I don't know anything about Yellow.

"Do you have any idea how much I sacrificed to be here for you? I left the only life I've ever known. I abandoned my family. And let's not forget about this." She thrusts her arm across the table.

"I didn't ask you to . . ."

"You didn't have to." She pulls back her arm. "I like doing the right thing. And believe it or not, I think you're doing the right thing. I want to help, but you're not making it very easy. And now you're talking about going back in time and stopping your dad's death. That's not what I signed up for."

I shake my head. But she's right. *God, she's so right.* I've been nothing but selfish since I joined the Guard. The only person I've thought about is me. How can I advance? How can I get the next level of clearance? You get what you give, and all I gave was negativity. It's no wonder the others never really liked me. Well, besides Indigo.

Yellow's brother.

"I'm sorry," I tell her. "I . . ." Everything running through my head about being out of my element sounds like an excuse, and I don't do excuses. "You're right. You're exactly right. I've been really unfair to you. I judged you the first second I saw you, and I haven't let that go. I'm sorry."

Yellow lets out a breath, and her shoulders relax. "Well, if I'm being perfectly honest, I totally judged you, too. And I resented your presence. Most of us didn't like the idea of outsiders coming in and taking over the Guard. We probably weren't as welcoming as we should have been. But everyone does think pretty highly of you. You're smart. You're resourceful. And you have some balls, woman. I mean, the Gardner. That was intense, and you didn't even break a sweat."

"No, I pretty much wanted to piss myself the entire time."

Yellow's face widens into a smile, and I reach across and grab the notebook. I flip it back open to the page of the Dallas mission.

"Look, all I want to do is to go back to Dallas and figure out who CE is. This thing is like a spiderweb. We tear at one corner of it, and the rest will collapse. We identify CE, and that's all the proof we'll need that Alpha is corrupt."

"But why CE? And why Dallas?"

"We're not going to get any bigger than CE and this mission. Ten *million* dollars." I toss the notebook back to her. "Flip through there and try to find another. But considering all we have are dates, it's kind of hard to figure out what the missions are. Dallas is pretty much the only lead we have right now. Stopping the JFK assassination? That's huge. We uncover CE, we rip away half that spiderweb."

Yellow flips through the pages. "But doesn't that mean CE is going to have his tracks pretty well covered?"

"Probably." I pick my fork back up. My well-done steak is kind of cold now, but I'm so hungry it doesn't matter. "We'll have to work extra hard."

"And your dad?"

I swallow a bite. "We'll see what happens."

Yellow sets down the notebook and picks up her fork. She pushes her beans around on her plate. They pool in the blood-red juice seeping from her steak. I can tell she's still hesitant about this plan.

"Okay," she finally says. "We'll go to Dallas. First thing in the morning."

My stomach is in knots when I wake up the next morning. I ignore it and pack up the three files and the notebook, and we leave the Parker House. The streets are filthy, lined with animal waste and trampled food. Horse-drawn wagons clomp down the cobblestones. We pass a butcher stall right there on the street. A dead pig hangs from a wooden rail. I fiddle with my watch, and Yellow looks visibly nervous. Like maybe she doesn't know if she's strong enough to project again.

"Do you think we can get away with using the gravity chamber?" I ask. "It's only a few blocks from here."

Yellow shakes her head. "I wouldn't risk it. They probably have it rigged so they'd know when we used it."

I nod in relief. Because *obviously* they have it rigged. I only offered to be polite. I suggest we head into an alley to get some privacy before we project.

"Hang on," Yellow says. "I want to duck back into Shreve, Crump & Low first."

"The jewelry store? What, do you have your eye on a necklace or something?"

She shoots me a dirty look and walks into the store. A few minutes later, she's back, holding a small velvet satchel.

She shakes it as she walks up to me and smiles. "Gold. I bought two ounces of it with the rest of our money. It's going to be worth significantly more in 1963. Instant money in our pockets."

I open my mouth to say something, then close it. Because that was a genius idea. I wish I'd been the one to think of it.

We duck into an alleyway where there's not a soul around.

Yellow tucks the satchel inside her dress and turns to me. "Is your watch set?"

"Yep."

"November 21, 1963?"

"I said yes, Yellow."

She huffs. "I was just checking. There's no need to get pissy." She grabs both of my hands and takes them in hers. "Let's do this together."

"That's a charming sentiment and all, but I can't close my watch face if you're holding both of my hands."

Yellow lets out a giggle and releases my right hand. I reach up and grab the pendant hanging from my neck, and Yellow does the same, then squeezes my hand.

My dad. We're going to see my dad. I have the image of him from his Annum Guard file in my head as I click the lid shut.

We're shot up into darkness, and I instantly know something is really, really wrong. A loud screeching sound erupts in my head, and light explodes in front of me. My body is pulled and stretched, and the screeching is getting louder. It's going to rip open my eardrums. It tears down my body and penetrates my heart. I feel the screeching echo in all four chambers, and it's going to kill me. I try to clutch at my chest, but we're going too fast.

Yellow and I land in the same alley, sixty-nine years later. I drop onto my knees and grab at my chest with my hands. I feel as if I'm having a heart attack. Deep pains throb inside my chest and shoot down the left side of my body. I'm dying. My heart is going to give out, and I'm going to die.

"That was kind of awesome," I hear Yellow say above me. "That wasn't bad at— Iris?" Her voice is panicked now, and she drops down next to me. "What happened? Are you all right?"

I keep breathing, forcing the pain away. I try not to inhale too deeply.

"Iris!" Yellow shrieks.

I just keep focusing on my breath. *Inhale the pain. Exhale it all away. Inhale the pain. Exhale it all away.*

"Iris, say something!"

"I'm okay," I whisper, keeping my eyes closed. "It's getting better."

"What's getting better? What are you talking about?"

I open my eyes. Everything seems to be fading now. "That wasn't the worst projection you've ever made?"

Yellow scrunches her nose. "No. That was the *best* projection I've ever made. Well, apart from the chamber ones. I barely felt a thing."

My head starts to shake, back and forth, though I have no idea I'm doing it. "No. That was terrible. That was like every projection I've done over the past couple days added together and multiplied by ten."

Yellow presses her lips together. "That doesn't make sense. Why would I feel nothing and you feel—" And then she gasps. "It's not just a rumor!"

I sit up and lean my back against a brick wall. I still can only manage the short breaths. "What's not a rumor?"

She drops down next to me. "Dual projection! It's real."

"English, Yellow. Speak English."

"Dual projection. It means force another Guardian to project with you. I could have my watch set to some completely different date, but if you were to grab on to me, you'd force me to come on your projection."

"I don't understand." I take another slow breath and lean my head back.

"The rumor was that if one of us was really strong and really focused, we could dual project. I mean, we've all tried it, but it's never worked. But you just did it."

"But we just traveled to the same date," I point out. And then I bend forward. Breathing still hurts.

"No, don't you see? I must have transferred all my energy to you, so you took the full force of both of our projections, while I felt nothing."

I take a slow breath. "All I know is, you're staying far the hell away from me the next time we project."

"Deal." Yellow stands and takes the satchel out of her skirt pocket. "I'm going to go sell this, and then I'll get us clothes. You stay here."

I don't argue. I close my eyes and keep breathing. It takes a few minutes, but finally the pain subsides and I feel like myself again. And then Yellow's back. Her face is contorted into a frown. "Problem. Turns out gold really wasn't worth that much more in 1963 than it was in 1894."

"What?" I push up off the wall to stand. It takes me longer than it should. "How is that possible?"

Yellow shrugs. "I don't know. But I bought this for thirty-seven dollars, and that guy in there is telling me it's only worth seventy dollars. That's not going to get us to Dallas. I asked the guy. He said a round-trip plane ticket should set us back about seventy-five dollars."

"So we're close."

"Seventy-five dollars apiece."

"Shit."

She cocks an eyebrow at me but doesn't say anything, and I think of Abe. How many times he's teased me about the "small-vocabulary" thing. Oh, Abe. Where are you right now? Do you still think of me?

"Um, hello." Yellow waves a hand in front of my face.

I snap out of it. "Sorry. Okay, so we need to come up with another hundred dollars or so." I can't help but stare at the remaining diamond stud hanging in her left ear.

Yellow catches me staring and reaches up to finger it. She sighs and starts unscrewing the back. "I know; it's our only option. My dad is going to kill me. He gave me these when I joined the Guard."

An image pops into my head. Zeta handing over a small box. In my mind, it's Tiffany blue with a white ribbon on top. Indigo stands beside them, beaming. A perfect little family.

"Where's your mother?" I ask her.

Yellow's head snaps back. "What?"

"Your mom. It's something that Blue said to me. He said Indigo had a perfect little family with two functioning parents."

A snort escapes Yellow's lips. "Well, that couldn't be further from the truth. My parents are both still alive, but they've been divorced forever. My mom lives in Manhattan with her new husband and family." There's more than a hint of hurt in her voice.

"She knows about us. Of course. What we do. But she never mentions it. We don't even talk unless I call."

"Wait, you talk to your mom?" Alpha made it sound like we would never have contact with our friends and family members again. Was this a lie, too?

Yellow scrunches up her nose like I just asked the dumbest question in the world. "Um, yeah."

Suddenly the smallest weight is lifted from my chest. Abe. My mom. They might not be gone from my life forever. If I make it through this—no, *when* I make it through this—I can see them. I can be with Abe. I can get my mom help.

I smile for the first time in a while. "That's . . . really great. I just assumed—"

"Look, do you want to stand here and have a joint therapy session, or do you want to go to Dallas?" She raises an eyebrow at me and closes her fist around the earring. "I'll be right back."

She shakes her head as she walks out of the jewelry store a few minutes later, and I force myself to stop thinking about Abe. Stop imagining how our potential reunion would play out.

"Come on." Her voice is heavy and sad, and she's making me feel incredibly guilty. She leads me to a big brownstone on Washington Street, right where Macy's is today. Iron letters float on a ledge welcoming us to Jordan Marsh & Company. Once inside, we wave off a petite sales clerk who attacks us with a perfume bottle that reeks like little old ladies. I leave the shopping to Yellow, and she buys us two very plain, pencil-thin dresses, one in a dark gray and one in a brown tweed, both of which look seriously itchy. Also, pencil skirts and I don't exactly get along. But I squeeze myself into the gray dress, and we head to Logan.

Even at the ticket counter, I realize that air travel is completely different in 1963 from what it is today. Everyone in line is dressed in their Sunday best. Suits and ties for the men. Dresses, hose, hats, and gloves for the women. We buy our tickets from a young, chirpy blond who takes our money and hands us tickets. Just like that. She doesn't even ask for ID. Security is nonexistent. We just walk up to the gate, and no one seems to care that we're traveling without bags. I mean, come on; Yellow and I are hitting just about every suspicious-traveler check mark that exists in the present, but no one bats an eyelash.

"This is weird, right?" I ask Yellow.

"Totally weird." She points to the window and squints. "Are those . . . passengers out there? Having a picnic on the tarmac?"

The flight is even weirder. We go outside and climb a metal staircase to board. Everyone makes a huge deal that we're on the plane. A perky young flight attendant who can't be much older than I am asks me if it's my first time flying as we board. I mutter that it's not and push my way to my seat as I try to ignore the fact that the whole plane smells like a stale ashtray in a dingy New England crab shack.

I give Yellow the window seat and take the middle. A businessman in a suit and tie slides in next to us and immediately lights up a cigarette. Well, that explains the smell. I cough and pivot in my seat so that my knees are practically on top of Yellow's, but either the man doesn't notice or he doesn't care. Probably the latter. Yellow and I spend the entire flight trying to make a plan by writing notes on cocktail napkins. There are some things you just can't say out loud, and the fact that President Kennedy is less than twenty-four hours away from being dead is one of them.

We touch down in Dallas, and the flight attendant wishes everyone a great day as they start down the staircase. Except for me. She purses her lips shut and glares at me. I think it might be because I politely shook her off when she tried to serve me a hot meal that smelled like plastic and preservatives. There was no way I was eating it.

We hop in a cab and tell the driver to take us to Dealey Plaza.

"Dealey, eh?" the driver says in a slow voice. "You girls know the president is going to be riding through that plaza tomorrow, don't you?"

"Mmm," I say. "Yes." I look at Yellow, and I see it written all over her face that the enormity of the situation has just hit her. The Kennedy assassination. We're going to witness the Kennedy assassination. It's one of those things that happened so long ago—I mean, before my mom was even born—but I've seen the video. I've read about it in the history books.

And all I can think about is my dad. He's going to be there. Trying to stop it. And he's going to die.

The driver drops us off in front of the Dallas County Records Building, a white, window-filled building that rises several stories in the air. The weather is crisp—almost cold. Across the street, kitty-corner to where we're standing, is the seven-story, redbrick Texas School Book Depository.

"That's it," Yellow whispers.

I nod my head and look to a window on the corner of the sixth floor. That's where Lee Harvey Oswald is going to be when he shoots and kills President Kennedy tomorrow. And where Alpha is going to try to earn a boatload of money off of stopping it.

I feel sick.

If this was a normal mission, I would be all over that building, all over this plaza. I'd scour every inch of the place and come up with a plan of attack. But it's not a normal mission. I don't even know what we're doing here. How on earth are we supposed to figure out who CE is?

Yellow and I check into the cheapest motel we can find. There are two double beds covered in thread-bare dark-green comforters, a wobbly night table between them, a beat-up old dresser, and carpeting that I assume used to be beige at one time.

"I can't believe we wasted all that money on the Parker House," Yellow says as she drops down onto one of the beds.

"Mmm-hmm." I stare at the dresser. There are scratches on the top of it, dozens of them. I trace my finger along the deepest ridge and wonder how it got there. Hotel key? That's a scratch of anger. Of contempt. That scratch makes me think of Alpha.

"Iris," Yellow says.

I turn.

"You need to be honest with me right now." She drops her voice to a whisper. "Are you planning on stopping the assassination tomorrow?"

"No." I drum my fingers across the dresser, then wipe them on my dress. Dusty. "Why would I stop it? If I do, Alpha gets ten million dollars, and who knows how we'd affect the world. I'm not going to risk it."

Yellow nods her head, moving barely more than an inch in either direction. "And what about the other assassination?" She holds up a hand. "I'm not judging, but I need to be prepared."

"I don't know what I'm going to do." Yellow raises an eyebrow.

"Honestly, I don't. I just . . . want to be there . . . when it happens. It's the only lead we have right now."

Yellow doesn't say anything for a while. Then she simply says, "Okay."

I don't sleep very well. I toss. I turn. I imagine my dad's face. I wonder if I'll recognize him. There are only two pictures of my dad in my house. One sits on a side table in the living room. It's a picture of my dad holding me as a baby, staring down into my eyes. My mom stands above him, watching us. My dad's face is hidden, partially obscured behind a mop of floppy hair that covers his eyes. That picture is part of the reason I have such a complicated relationship with my mom, because you can see it written all over her face in the photo: She only has eyes for him. She tolerates me, but she *loves* my dad.

Except that now I know she *did* love me. She tried so hard to protect me. I shake my head; but the guilt remains, firmly nuzzled, no intention of budging.

The second picture sits on my mom's dresser in her bedroom. It was taken on their wedding day. They're looking right at the camera. I spent hours staring at that picture as a child. I used to talk to it. Talk to my dad.

In my head, my dad is going to look exactly like that picture tomorrow. Young. Handsome. Wearing a tuxedo and a bow tie.

Okay, that's probably not going to happen. But it might.

I wake up Yellow at six the next morning, mainly because I'm jumpy, and I can't sit there and watch her sleep anymore.

"Plan," Yellow says as she flops our cocktail napkins full of poorly thought-out gibberish onto the bed. "We need to have a better idea what we're doing."

I nod. She's right. I pull out my dad's file and flip to the very end. I read over the details I only skimmed before.

"According to this, the main confrontation with Beta happens on the landing in between the fifth and sixth floors."

"And Lee Harvey Oswald is on the sixth?" Yellow says. "How close to the stairs is he stationed?"

I realize I have no idea what the layout of the building is. That's such a simple, basic detail, and I don't have a freaking clue.

"He can't be too close to the stairs," Yellow says, "or else he would have heard the argument; and as far as I know, the assassination happens just like it always has."

"Or he does hear it and carries on anyway."

"Either way, we need to figure out where we're going to be. How many floors does the building have?"

"Seven," I tell her. At least I know that.

"Okay, so we could set ourselves up on the sixth floor where Oswald is"—Yellow cocks her head to the side—"which just seems like a recipe for disaster, or we could be on the stairs too, on the landing above."

"Yes, the landing above," I say. "That way we can be there the whole time and just wait for it to happen."

It's seven in the morning by the time we cross Dealey Plaza and head over to the book depository. The president isn't due to arrive for more than five hours, but already the crowds are gathering, setting up to get the best look.

"These poor people," Yellow whispers. "They have no idea what's going to happen."

A pit forms in my stomach. They don't know. The president doesn't know. No one knows except for me and Yellow and Lee

Harvey. For a second I wonder if maybe we *should* stop the assassination. Reading about something in a history book is so much different than actually being there.

Kind of like the time my mom took me to Disney World when I was seven. She'd been on a high for a week already. My mom is almost always a happy manic. Anything is possible during that time. It's when she gets all her painting done. Passionate swirls of color thrown onto canvas that sell for enough money throughout New England to ensure that the rent gets paid. She always paints first whenever mania hits—exhausts the muse, as she calls it—and then it's onto whatever else she feels like in the moment. This time it was Orlando.

We started driving in the middle of the night, and I was so excited I barely slept. Before the trip, I could have cared less about all that Disney princess crap, but there was something about being inside the park. Seeing the characters right there. Getting my picture taken with Cinderella. I had to have the merchandise. Dress-up clothes and wands and dolls. Plates and cups and straws. My mom bought it all.

I'm feeling the same urge today. I'm in Dallas. On the day of one of the biggest tragedies in American history. And I can stop it. Alpha will get a windfall, yes, but I could save my dad, too.

Yellow looks at me. "Are you thinking what I think you're thinking?"

Am I being that obvious? I shake my head. "No," I lie. "Of course not."

"Don't get caught up in this." Yellow gets right in my face and stares me down. "It's so hard to do, but you have to distance yourself. You *have to*, Iris."

"Mmm-hmm." I brush past her and open the door to the depository and hold it for Yellow. I pass through and then Yellow's in my face again.

"Seriously," she says. "Get yourself out of the moment. Think with your head, not with your heart. You're a trained government operative."

Of all the things she could have said, this is the worst. Because she's right. She's so right. This excitement is a feeling—nothing more. It will wear off. Just like my mom's high suddenly stopped in Virginia on the car ride back from Disney World. It was the first time she rapid cycled, so there was no normal phase. She sank straight to the bottom. We spent three awful nights in a motel that rented out rooms by the hour, as my mom cried and wailed and drank an entire bottle of Jack Daniels. I pitched all the princess crap into the parking lot Dumpster and never thought of it again.

Think with your head, not your heart. That's been the moral of my story since birth. I know better.

I nod my head once to show Yellow I'm serious, and we start climbing the stairs. They're located in the back left corner of the building, as far as you can get from the front right window where Oswald is going to start shooting in a few short hours.

Yellow and I camp out on the landing between the sixth and seventh floors. If I peer over the railing, I can see two landings below me. The landing where my dad is going to die. I pull my head back.

We pass the time by flipping through Alpha's notebook and making notes of all the entries where CE appears. That sucker is everywhere. All over this notebook, going back more than twenty-five years. Most payouts are small, insignificant even. Other than the Kennedy assassination, there are four big ones.

One commissioned before I was even born, before the Kennedy mission. That one earned Alpha $300,000. Another commissioned eight years ago for $250,000. Another one from four years ago, for a half million. And then one more, for an even million. The ink is barely dry on that one. I recognize the date. Yellow does, too.

"The Gardner," I say.

Yellow nods. "The Gardner."

Just then there's noise. Below us. A hammering of footsteps up the stairs. Yellow and I scramble up, and she tucks the notebook inside the belt of her dress. I look at my watch. It's 12:20. That has to be my dad on the stairs.

And then there's a voice. A loud voice. It's shouting things. I catch "sniper" and "gun," and I have no idea what's going on; but my heart starts thumping away in my chest with the realization that this isn't right. It's not right at all. I look at Yellow, and she has terror written all over her face.

She leans over the railing for a half second before yanking her head away. Her eyes get wide as she mouths, *A cop.*

My mouth drops open as the two of us plaster ourselves against the back wall. A cop. A cop who knows about the assassination attempt? None of this is in the history books. What the hell is going on?

I guess we're about to find out.

THE EIGHTH GUARDIAN

CHAPTER 23

The footsteps pound against the stairs, almost making a sort of rhythm. I close my eyes and try to make out individual patterns, to count how many men there are. It's one. Only one.

I open my eyes, and Yellow grabs my hand. She tilts her eyes up and mouths, *The roof?*

I shake my head and wave her off. I'm not running away from this. I need to know what's going to happen.

The footsteps are louder. The man is on the landing right under us. But then a door opens with such a bang that I jump.

"Back off!" a voice shouts. It's a male voice, smooth and authoritative. "I have him."

There's a scuffling and a grumbling.

"I saw a man with a gun!" someone else shouts. The cop?

"I said back off!" the first man shouts. "Dallas PD has no jurisdiction here anymore." There's another rustling. "FBI. We have the situation under control."

Yellow and I exchange a glance. Her eyes are wide, and I'm sure mine are wider. The FBI is here? They've captured Oswald before the shooting even begins?

"You're in Dallas!" the other shouts. "My jurisdiction." The cop.

"And you're trampling all over my crime scene. The situation is under control. Go back down and don't speak a word of this to anyone." The first man's voice is calm, collected.

"But—"

"Don't give me a *but*. There's a crowd down there, and the less they know, the better. You want mass pandemonium with the president's motorcade in sight?"

"No, but—"

"The situation is under control." There's a shuffling of footsteps and a muttering of angry words, and I close my eyes but can't tell what's happening. "Don't breathe a word of this. Not now. Not yet. Not until the parade is over. I have backup on the way, and then I'll be down to your squad car to take your statement."

Then the voices speak over each other, and there's more grumbling and scuffling, and I look at Yellow again. She shakes her head at me with uneasy eyes. She's as clueless as I am.

The footsteps on the stairs start again, but this time they get fainter and fainter as the Dallas cop races down them. I try not to breathe. The FBI is on the landing below me as we speak. They've already captured Oswald. I have no idea what the hell is going on and how we're going to get out of here.

But then. A whisper. Barely audible.

"Delta, you're cutting off the circulation in my arm."

Delta. My dad.

A laugh. "Sorry." It's the first man. The first man is Delta. The first man is my dad. He's not FBI. He's . . . pretending to be FBI.

"That was too close," the other man says.

I shake my head, over and over, as if I can shake out the truth and understand what's going on. This is nothing like Alpha's report. Nothing at all. I keep waiting. Waiting for some sign that my dad thinks this is an authorized mission. That President Clinton okayed it and that he's there to stop the assassination. Any second now the truth will come out.

It does.

"You hear that?" my dad says. "The motorcade must be approaching Dealey."

A crowd cheers in the background.

"Is Oswald in position?" the other man says.

Wait. No. I—this isn't right—

"Should be," my dad says.

Next to me, Yellow grabs my hand and squeezes. I'm stunned into silence. I can't move. My feet are granite slabs cemented to the floor.

A shot rings out in the distance, and my neck snaps back. What is this? Why isn't my dad trying to stop this?

"Hear that?" my dad shouts. "That's the sound of Old Cresty coughing up ten million dollars!"

I can't breathe. I bend over and wrap my arms around my body as I shake and convulse and— WHAT THE FUCK IS THIS?

A second shot in the distance, out over Dealey Plaza. And then silence.

"I ought to say that did it," my dad says. "Dallas PD will be swarming these steps again any second now. Time to go, Beta. We gotta take care of that real cop."

Beta. The other man is Beta. That doesn't make any sense. Beta and my dad are in on it.

"You're right. Time to go," Beta says. He clears his throat. "I'm sorry about this, Mitch. I always liked you."

And then I bolt up. Because I know what's about to happen. There's a gasp on the floor below that echoes up to my stairwell. And then. A blast of gunfire. It pierces my eardrums as fireworks explode in my mind.

I stumble to the wall. Yellow grabs my shoulder, but I shake her off. I fumble with my necklace, and my legs buckle and my knees slam to the ground. My hands are shaking. I need to get away away away. I turn a dial. I don't know which one. And then I start to close the watch.

"Iris!" Yellow hisses. She lunges at me, but I've already shut the watch.

I'm yanked up for a quick few seconds, and I don't feel the pain this time. Not the physical pain at least. I drop on to the landing, and Yellow pops next to me a few seconds later.

"No!" Yellow screams. "No! You do not project without me, do you understand? You never, ever project without me. Thank God I saw your dial."

I drop to my knees and grab at my chest with my hands. I feel as if I'm having a heart attack. Deep, shooting pains throb inside my chest and fly down the left side of my body. But this has nothing to do with projecting. My heart has broken into a million pieces, and I'm going to die.

My dad wasn't a Navy SEAL. He wasn't a war hero. He was a traitor. Alpha didn't set him up.

He assassinated a president.

I don't understand. My father is a cold-blooded killer, and I don't understand anything anymore.

I inhale the pain and refuse to blow it out. I let it fill me, consume me, crush me. My hands find the floor, and I sink into it. It's a lie. Everything I've ever known has been one massive lie.

"Get up," Yellow says.

I ignore her.

"I said get up."

"Go away, Yellow."

"I'm only going to tell you to get up one more time before I bend down and pull you up myself."

We studied the physical effects of trauma aftermath at Peel. Rationally, I know I'm in shock. I tell myself I am. But I can't snap out of it. I'm classic: numb dizzy weak nauseated confused. I can't process my thoughts. Too fast. They're coming too fast.

Yellow bends over, loops her elbows under my armpits, and yanks me up. "You are going to look me in the eye right now and swear to me that you will never project without me again."

What is she talking about? The scene replays in my mind. My father prevented that cop from stopping the assassination. That cop knew about the sniper, and my father deflected him and made sure Kennedy was shot.

"Iris!"

My father changed history so that Kennedy was assassinated? Kennedy made it through Dealey unscathed before my dad interfered?

"Iris!" Yellow grabs my shoulder and shakes me.

"What?" My voice is a whisper.

"Promise me you will not project without me."

I push her away. "Are you kidding right now? What difference does it make? Nothing matters anymore."

Yellow's eyes bulge open. "Nothing matters? So your whole big plan about bringing down CE, who we now know is named Cresty Something-or-other, doesn't matter?"

"What happened back there, Yellow? My dad is a—" I choke. I can't finish it.

"An assassin."

The words hang in the air and refuse to dissipate. He is. My father is a killer. He didn't pull the trigger, but he might as well have. Before he interfered, that cop must have caught Oswald and stopped the assassination. My father changed all that.

I don't want that to be the truth. This can't be the truth. I need to know. I pull out my watch.

"We have to go back," I tell Yellow.

"Go back where?"

"Go back to before this mission. Before my dad died. To read what the history books say. To figure out whether President Kennedy was assassinated before my dad interfered or not."

"That's not how it works," Yellow says.

"When do you want to project to?" I turn the year dial forward.

"Iris," Yellow hisses. "I said that's not how it works. No one explained Chronometric Augmentation to you, did they? How it fundamentally works?"

That sounds ominous. "No."

Yellow sighs. "We're in a parallel future right now. A new future. That's what happens when we change the past. We create a parallel universe that we all shift up to. You can't go back to the old one to see what history books said before we changed the past, because those history books don't exist anymore in our future. There are new books, and those books reflect the changes we made. Period."

Her words bounce around in my head. My brain processes them, but my heart won't believe it.

"Are you telling me I don't get to know what happened here?"

Yellow takes a slow breath, as if she's not sure what to say. "But you do know what happened here."

I do.

I do.

I do.

I lean over and rest my forehead on the cool, metal railing. "He killed Kennedy. My father killed a president. This changes everything."

"Yeah, he was in on it. But how does that change you wanting to bring down Alpha?"

I jump back. "My father was a bad person! I can't just get over that!"

There's shouting right below us, and footsteps pound up the stairs. Before I can even think, three men tear up the stairs to our landing. They're all wearing suits with skinny black ties and horn-rimmed glasses and have FBI written all over them. Yellow and I exchange one panicked glance, and then we're surrounded.

"Who are you?" one demands.

"How did you get in here?"

Shit. When are we? When did I project to?

Yellow drops to her knees and holds up her hands. "I'm sorry, sirs," she says with a convincing mock sob. "I just . . . I'm such a fan of the president's . . . I had to see. I dragged my friend."

"Get up!" the man in the middle says. "You both should be arrested. This is an active crime scene."

"I'm sorry," Yellow wails.

The man on the left grabs her and spins her against the wall, then pats her down. The man on the right comes over to me, and I hold up my hands in submission. He pats me down.

"Clear," he says.

"I've got this," the man holding Yellow says. He tosses Alpha's notebook to the third man. Yellow looks at me with terrified eyes.

The man flips through it. "What's this?"

"My notes from a home economics class at school," Yellow says without missing a beat.

The man raises an eyebrow. "There's an entry right here for June 17, 1998. HY. Eight point five. What's that got to do with home economics, missy?"

Yellow clears her throat. "It's an advanced sewing class. We're trying to predict what fashion is going to look like in the future based on past trends. HY stands for Hiro Yu. He's a Japanese fashion designer who's currently creating some very avant garde pieces. I'm going to base my design on his. Eight point five is what I need to set the bobbin to. It's just a note."

I blink. I'm speechless. She just completely pulled that from her ass and passed it off like it makes all the sense in the world. Yellow is hands-down the best liar I've ever met.

"Sounds like a waste of class time to me," the man says. "You girls need to be learning cooking and cleaning and maybe some typing."

Yellow bows her head. "I'm sorry, sir."

"What you girls did was very foolish." He juts his chin toward the men holding Yellow and me. "Escort them out." Then he looks right at Yellow and hands her back the notebook. "Don't you ever enter this building again."

It's a long, tense walk down six flights of stairs. We're given another warning to stay away from the building and pitched out onto the street. Piles of flowers, some long dead, some fresh, litter the front of the book depository. There are at least a dozen people out front, some crying, some praying, some standing and staring.

"Holy crap," Yellow breathes after the door slams shut in our faces. "That was way too close."

There is nothing like nearly getting arrested to snap you back to reality. Was it really only a few minutes ago I was curled up in a ball in the stairwell?

"Eight point five is what you set the bobbin to?" I ask. "What does that even mean?"

Yellow shrugs. "No clue."

"When are we?"

She looks at the people in front of the building, then grabs my arm and marches me away. "December 23, 1963. You turned the month dial forward once. Thank God I saw you do it. Now promise me you will never project without me."

"Yellow, I—"

"Promise me!"

"I won't project without you," I say through gritted teeth.

"Tell me how things have changed."

"What?" I push off her.

"Murder, Iris. Assassination. This thing with Alpha is worse than we thought. And did you ever stop to think that maybe this means the entire organization is corrupt? Including my dad?"

I—no. I didn't.

She huffs. "I'm sorry you had to find out about your dad that way. Really, I am. But that just means we have to work even harder to stop it. Do you get that? We *have* to stop it. And I have no idea where to go from here. None. It's you and me, floundering around in 1963. We need help, and I don't know how to get it."

I close my eyes. I have to focus. I don't want to focus. I'm sick of putting on a strong face. I've been doing it my entire life. For once it would be nice if I could just lie down, curl into a ball, and cry. But the only way I'm ever going to be able to do that is if I end this. If we end this.

"I do," I whisper.

Yellow's head whips around. "Huh?"

"I know where we can get help. We need to go back to Massachusetts. Cambridge. MIT."

CHAPTER 24

Neither Yellow nor I say much on the plane. I take the window seat and stare out of it the entire flight. I don't want to think about my dad. It hurts too much. But my mind won't stop replaying the moment when my dad mentioned the ten million dollars. When I discovered he orchestrated an assassination, only to be betrayed and murdered himself.

How many other kickbacks had he taken before that—gotten away with?

I know the truth, but I don't want to believe it. It's Alpha. It's all Alpha. He corrupted my dad. Blackmailed him, maybe. My dad would not have done this on his own. Please let that be the truth.

I puke in a tiny, cramped airplane bathroom.

We're climbing down the metal stairs onto the tarmac at Logan when I lean over to Yellow. "What happened to Beta?"

Yellow cranes her head around, and her face turns pained. "I don't think you really want to know the answer to that, do you?"

"Tell me."

Yellow sighs. "He committed suicide. Years ago. Probably not too long after . . . uh . . ."

"Committed suicide or got taken out just like my father did?"

Yellow presses her lips together.

"Whose father was Beta?"

She hesitates for a moment. "Green's."

I nod once. I never got a warm and fuzzy feeling from Green; but here we are, locked together in a mess of corruption and murder. He and I will be forever linked. And I'm kind of glad Beta got his due, all things told. He murdered my father.

Even if my father deserved it.

Maybe.

Probably.

I don't know.

It's a short cab ride from Logan to MIT, and I know exactly where I'm going now. Yellow pays the driver while I start walking, head down, toward the building in front of me. I hear Yellow take quick steps to catch up. We are the only two souls wandering the campus right now.

"Are you sure he's going to be here?" Yellow looks down at her Annum watch. "It's eight o'clock the day before Christmas Eve."

"The man practically lives here," I say. "Besides, Ariel's Jewish, so it's not like he'll be rushing off to trim a tree or anything. He'll be here."

"But if he's not?"

I sigh. "Then I know where he lives." Although I'd like to avoid going to his house. I don't know if I'd have the strength not to collapse into a puddle of tears and mourning in the living room.

We round the corner. The sky is dark, and a window on the fifth floor is illuminated. I point.

"Bet you anything that's Ariel's office."

The front door is locked. I jiggle the handle a few times to make sure, but it doesn't budge. Christmas holidays. Of course the door is locked. I don't know what I was thinking. We're going to have to break in.

I turn to tell Yellow, but she's already standing in front of a first-floor window with a fallen tree branch. "Is there an alarm?"

I shrug. I have no idea. But I guess we'll find out.

Yellow heaves the limb through the window, but apart from the sound of the glass shattering, it's quiet. We clear out the glass, then I hoist Yellow up through the window. She scoots a chair over, and I jump to grab her hand.

We're in.

The hallway on the fifth floor is dark, but light spills from Ariel's open door.

"Told you," I whisper to Yellow.

Ariel sits in the corner of his cluttered office with his back to the door. He's hunched over a stool, tinkering with a small metal object. Papers are piled up and pushed to either side of the desk. I clear my throat, and Ariel turns at once. He somehow looks older than the last time I saw him, which seems weird. That was in 1962. Just over a year ago. Yet the Ariel who's looking at me now has a harder face, more lines. There are bags under both of his eyes.

"Ah," he says when he sees me, "Miss Hart, was it? I was wondering when I'd see you again."

There's a coyness in his voice. I look over to Yellow to see if she's caught it, but Yellow's just standing there staring at Ariel with her mouth open.

Chills dance up and down my arms. "My name isn't Miss Hart."

"I am very well aware of that," Ariel says. "When are you from?"

"I—" Wait. Did he say *when* am I from?

"You—you know who I am?" My head snaps over to Yellow again. But she has the same shocked expression on her face.

"Not specifically, but when you showed up out of nowhere, begging me to change the design of my machine, I was willing to bet that you were, in fact, already using it at some point in the future. So now I'm asking you when you came from."

Yellow's fingers grab my bicep. "Don't tell him," she whispers.

I turn to face her. "What?"

Yellow starts backing out of the room, one foot at a time. "We need to go. Now."

"Yellow, what are—"

"That's Seven," she whispers.

My mouth turns bone-dry as my mind races back to my Annum Guard orientation. The first generation Guardians were code named numbers. Only one of that generation is still alive.

Seven.

Ariel.

Which means . . . *Abe.*

I gasp. No. NO! Not Abe. Not Abe. NOT ABE! I whip my head back to Ariel in a flash. I'm not going anywhere.

"You're a liar!" I say. "I know you. I've known you for years, which means you knew exactly who I was all those times. All those dinners. All those holiday celebrations. And you never said a goddamned word!"

Ariel holds up his hands and rises from his stool. "You need to stop talking right now."

"Do you know what Annum Guard is?" I ask.

"Of course I do." He waves his arm in the air. "It's been in place for over a year. We've experimented, and we're still at least another year away from consistently traveling, but we're getting there. I'm Seven." He looks right at Yellow. "I think you already know that, don't you?"

Yellow doesn't say anything, and Ariel looks back at me.

"Now will you please tell me who you are, when you are from, and what you want?"

"Iris, don't," Yellow says.

I look right at Ariel. "I know your grandson."

"No." Ariel holds up a hand with a very stern look on his face. "I don't want you to tell me anything specific. Nothing at all. Anything you tell me has the potential to completely alter my life's course, and I'm not interested. I'm on a path for a reason, and I will follow it to the end. So just keep it all to yourself."

"I only want to know who you are, when you come from, and what you want."

Why should I? Why shouldn't I tell him every tiny detail of his life to come?

But I know, deep down. Abe. Anything I tell Ariel could affect Abe's future.

Me being here right now could affect Abe's future. My first visit, too, when I pointed out Mona. What if I planted that idea too early, and she and Ariel have already dated and broken up? What if Ariel marries someone else, which means no Abe? Ever?

I open my mouth, but my tongue can't find the words. I don't know if I can do this. I *have* to do this. We're at a dead end. Without help, we're going to fail. *Breathe.*

I tell Ariel that I'm Annum Guard, too, and give him the date I ran away. My voice cracks as I do.

"And what do you want?"

I open the notebook and tear out the back page, the page on which Yellow and I had scribbled the information on the four other big CE missions. I hand it over.

"These are four missions that . . ." I stop myself before I tell him about CE. "I just want to know what they are. The dates and locations. Someday in the future, you're going to have access to this information. All I'm asking is that you share it with me."

Ariel sighs but holds out his hand for the paper. I hesitate before I give it to him. There are so many other things I could ask for instead. I could ask Ariel to get rid of Alpha the second he's put in charge. I could ask him to kick my grandfather off Annum Guard One. I could ask him to lock me away so that the Guard would never find me in the first place, but I don't. I don't say anything. I'm too close to my future, and I could wreck it all with one innocent comment.

"Why should I do this?" Ariel asks.

I hesitate. I don't know how to answer that without giving too much away. "Because one day I like to think I'm going to mean a great deal to you, and you're going to know that I will always do the right thing." Ariel's face tightens. "You don't have to decide now. But if that day comes, and I'm right, then help me. Please."

Ariel lowers onto his stool. He props his elbow on the desk, closes his eyes, and cradles his head in his hand. He's quiet for a while.

"I can't make you any promises," he finally says.

"Okay. But I hope you will." It's all I can say.

Yellow and I leave the building the same way we came in. The broken window on the first floor.

"So now what?" she says.

"Now we project."

Yellow raises an eyebrow. "Where? You know, I'm starting to lose patience with you."

"I don't know where, and it really doesn't matter. Our present won't be affected until we project again, right? So if Ariel is going to help us, we have to leave today before we can find out. Isn't that how it works?"

Yellow nods.

"So pick a date, and let's go there."

"I don't know," she says with a sigh. "Tomorrow. Christmas Eve 1963."

I set my watch. One bump of the day knob. "Fair enough." I watch Yellow do it, too, and then we shut our watches at the same time.

The projection lasts a fraction of a second. I don't even feel it.

"Well?" Yellow asks, looking at me with wide eyes that blink rapidly with impatience. "Do you magically know the answer now?"

I stop. I think. I don't feel any different, not that I was expecting to. It wasn't like Ariel was going to pull me aside when I was fourteen and tell me the truth about everything. No, if he's going to help us, it's going to be by giving us the information subtly. But how?

I reach up and run my hands through my hair, tugging on the ends. It pulls on my scalp and it hurts. "Maybe we should project again. Maybe we're supposed to go see Ariel again in the present?"

"The present?" Yellow repeats. "You want to go to the house of an Annum Guard member in the present? Are you that insane? Maybe Ariel—*Seven*—isn't going to sabotage us, but I can tell you that his house is sure as hell being monitored, especially because of your connection."

She's right. Of course she's right. I shake my head. "Then maybe we go to my mom's house? Maybe Ariel sent me something."

"You don't think your mom's house is triggered with all sorts of alarms, too? Iris, you're falling apart on me."

"Well, then I don't know what to do!" I raise my hands and press the heels of my palms into my forehead. Something jingles.

"Oh my God," I say. "That's it."

"What's it?" Yellow asks, but I'm already clawing away under the sleeve of the itchy gray dress. My fingers loop around my bracelet, and I shinny it to my wrist and undo the clasp. I hold it up for Yellow.

"Ariel gave me this," I tell her. "The first Hanukkah I spent with Abe's family."

"And there's a clue hidden in your bracelet?"

"There is." As soon as the words escape my lips, I know it's true. Ariel hid the information we need to know in this bracelet. My Ariel. My Abe's grandfather. The man who opened his arms and his heart to me when he knew who I was but also knew that I had no idea. He would help me. And the answer is in this bracelet.

I hold it up to my eyes and squint. It's a silver bracelet with a number of charms dangling from it. There's a mini Eiffel Tower—not that I've ever been to Paris—next to a mini poodle—not that I've ever owned a dog that wasn't a mutt—then a silver key, a birdcage, and a—

Hang on. I squint my eyes even more so that they're almost closed. And then they pop open, and I gasp.

"It's here!" I tell Yellow. "Right here!"

"What's here?"

I hold up the birdcage, which can't be more than half an inch tall. "Look!" Inside of the tiny cage, behind the thin metal bars, is a small scroll of yellowed paper.

Yellow's eyes cross as she peers in. "You're sure that wasn't there all along?"

"If it was, I never noticed it. I have to get this open." The charm is purely decorative. There's no door on the birdcage, and the bars are only a few millimeters apart. I'm going to have to break it. "I need your bag!" I tell Yellow. "Do you still have that scalpel you swiped?"

"The one you used to butcher my arm?"

"Hey, you told me to—"

"Dude. Joking." Yellow roots around in her bag and pulls out the scalpel. She hands it over, and I slide it through the bars and twist. Two of them pop right off. It's a pretty bracelet, but not very well made. In a matter of seconds, all the bars litter the ground, and I'm holding the tiny scroll of paper in my hands. And I mean tiny. I unroll it, then unfold it, and it's like two inches by two inches.

There are four things written on the paper. Four things. Four CE missions.

"He did it," I whisper. "Ariel came through."

Yellow peers over my shoulder at the paper. I hold it close so we can both make out the tiny writing.

280 Fenway, Boston, MA, March 18, 1990, 1:24 a.m.

Palais des Tuileries, Paris, France, April 30, 1803, 4:21 p.m.

100 Bureau Drive, Gaithersburg, MD, October 21, 1939, 8:00 a.m.

1100 Western Avenue, Lynn, MA, June 2, 1890, 9:12 a.m.

Yellow takes a breath. "What is this?"

"I think it's the exact locations and times of the other four big CE missions."

"So what are we supposed to do?" Yellow leans in closer to the paper. "Catch the next flight to Paris and head to the—" She grabs the paper. "*Palais?* That means 'palace.' We don't have the money for that, and I'm fresh out of things to sell. Not to mention, how are we going to get inside a palace?"

"Look," I say as I point to the first entry. "That's the Gardner. We know that one. It's a nonstarter. There was nothing about a CE or a Cresty. We can count it out, as well as Paris, because . . . well, yeah. But"—I point to the last one—"Lynn is, like, not even ten miles from here. Maryland is farther but still doable. We'll take those two and see what we can figure out."

Yellow shakes her head. "But I don't understand what we're supposed to be doing."

"Yeah, me either." Which is the truth. I have no idea what we're supposed to be looking for. But in this moment, I'm going to trust Ariel. I should have trusted him from the beginning. "That's what we're going to find out. I think we should split up this time. Do you want Lynn or Maryland?"

"Neither," Yellow says.

I raise an eyebrow at her.

"Look," Yellow says with a huff in her voice. "What if . . ." She takes a breath. "What if the entire organization is corrupt? Every single member? What if my dad is working with Alpha? I don't know if I can face the fact that my father might be a . . ." Her eyes get big as she realizes what she's about to say.

"A traitor?" I finish. "Like my father was?"

"I didn't mean—"

"It's fine," I interrupt. It's not fine. Nothing my dad did will ever be fine. "For what it's worth, I don't think your dad knows. I mean, Alpha had my dad and then Beta, and then when they were . . . taken out . . . he had to move on to someone else for these two." I tap the last two locations on the list. "I don't know what happened to that person, but now, all of a sudden, Alpha is trying to get the ability to project himself. That's why he sent me back to get Ariel to change his design. The whole entire thing was one big setup to give Alpha the ability. If someone else was in on this CE thing, Alpha wouldn't be so desperate."

"That's Eta or Gamma," Yellow says.

"Huh?" I know she has to be talking about two members of Annum Guard Two, but I have no idea who they are.

"Eta and Gamma. They both died only a few years ago. Gamma's—well, she was Blue's mother. I'm going to doubt it's her. She did a lot of the early lifting on missions, before the gravity chamber was invented. Lots of repeated projecting."

"You mean like we're doing?"

She ignores me. "Her body gave out on her. Just stopped. She lost the ability to walk, then even to stand. Her muscles atrophied. She—"

I hold up my hand to stop her. I don't want to hear any more. I'm picturing Epsilon as she was in my orientation, her body twisted and broken by years of unprotected projections. How much damage am I doing to my own body trying to bring down Alpha? I'm young and healthy now, but how many years do I have left before I suffer the same fate? I don't want to think about it.

"Eta?" I prod.

Yellow nods. "Eta seems most likely. I—I hate saying this because she is—was—Violet's mom, and Violet's been my friend like forever; but I can see Eta being swayed by the idea of money and power."

"What happened to Eta?"

"She died," Yellow says, looking down at the ground. "On a mission."

"Or do you mean Alpha had her taken out during a mission because she knew too much?"

Yellow's head snaps up, and her mouth falls open. "Do you think? I mean—oh my God—he really could have, couldn't he?"

I shrug. Because now that the words have come out of my mouth, all I can think about is my dad. That maybe Alpha set it up so that Beta would kill my dad on the mission. So that he wouldn't have to split the money with him. Maybe my dad was just a pawn. He got caught up in something he didn't understand and got too far in. Or maybe he was just pretending on the Kennedy mission. It was a sting operation to bring down Alpha and Beta, and Beta got him first.

Or maybe that's just the wishful thinking of a girl who doesn't want to know the truth about the man who'd fathered her.

I look down at the piece of paper Ariel smuggled into my bracelet. "Okay, so we go back and look for Eta," I mumble. "Lynn or Maryland?"

"I'll take Maryland," she says.

I nod. I'm relieved. Getting to Lynn is going to be so much easier. And faster.

We agree to meet up when we're done, at the Christian Science reflecting pool in Boston on Christmas Day 1963. We already have the clothes, and it's safer to stay away from the present, especially in Boston. Who knows what the manhunt looks like now.

Yellow and I walk to the bus station together. There's a bus leaving for Lynn in twenty minutes and one leaving for the capital in three hours.

"Good luck," I tell her as I climb the steps of a silver bus with a rounded top. She reaches out and squeezes my hand.

"You, too."

The doors close behind me, and I take a seat. Here goes nothing.

CHAPTER 25

I spend the entire bus ride with my head leaned against the window. When I get out of this—*if* I get out of this—I'm going to get my mom help. I won't take no for an answer this time. I need her. I need normalcy. I'm going to haul her to the doctor, then the pharmacy; and I will shove those pills down her throat every damn day if I have to. I won't let her stop taking them after two weeks—not this time.

I will be enough for her, goddammit. She will get better for me. I'm only a year away from eighteen. One year before I'm officially an adult. She owes me one last year of a normal childhood.

Normal.

I laugh. My father was a time-traveling assassin, and I'm a minor employed by a secret wing of the United States government. That's as far from normal as you can get.

The bus drops me off at Market Square, which is somewhere in Lynn. I don't know. I've passed the stops for Lynn on the highway before, but I've never been here. I find someone manning the ticket counter. He's short and squat and wears a greasy blue shirt and an expression that shows he's none too pleased about working on Christmas Eve.

"Pardon me," I say. "I need to get to 1100 Western Avenue. Could you point me in the right direction?"

The man squints behind his glasses. "What did you say the address was?"

"1100 Western Avenue."

The man's brow furrows. "The GE plant?"

"The . . . the what?"

"GE," the man says. "General Electric."

I'm not sure why, but a funny feeling tickles the middle of my stomach. "Oh, right, yes." I say it as if all along I was headed to a huge power plant.

The man points. "That crossroad there is Western. Hang a left and start walking. It'll be on your left in a mile or so. Can't miss it."

I'm walking toward the water. An inlet of the bay. The wind is kicking up, and a light snow falls from the sky. I hunch my shoulders and keep walking. What I wouldn't give for a coat right now. Or even a jacket. Anything to block out the cold that's blowing right through the arms of my dress and piercing my skin. I can see my breath.

The streets are nearly empty as the sun sets on the horizon. Church bells ring in the distance, which reminds me that it's Christmas Eve. I have no idea what day it is in the present. Definitely past Christmas, I would imagine.

There's not a soul near the GE plant. I walk up to the front doors of the main building and peer inside the glass. It's dark. Then I look up to the corner of the doorway. No camera. I have no idea when cameras became standard fare, but I was sort of expecting one here. You know, this being a power plant and all.

I unravel the black dress Yellow bought me in 1894. It's so wrinkled that the few shakes in the air I give it do absolutely nothing. I glance down the street once more to make sure it's safe. Deserted. I slip out of my 1963 dress and into my 1890s one, then stash the sixties dress behind a trash can. I'll be back soon enough to pick it up.

I turn the dials on the Annum watch back to June 2, 1890. And then I laugh. I'm standing in front of a massively huge power plant, and I'm about to go back in time to try to track someone I don't know and have never seen a picture of as she does something (I have no idea what) somewhere inside this building.

Easy.

I snap the lid of the watch face shut and am immediately ripped back through time. I land on the sidewalk in the early-morning light and gasp for breath. I close my eyes to block the vision of Epsilon's broken body mangled before me during orientation, but it comes anyway.

That won't be me. It won't. As soon as we stop Alpha, I'm never projecting again. Ever.

Time check. 5:30 in the morning. I shake my head and turn around, then I gasp. I should be used to this by now, but I'm not. The plant that stands before me is probably half the size of the plant I left behind. Well, that should make finding Eta marginally less difficult. A sign outside the door welcomes me, not to General Electric but to Thomson-Houston Electric.

Just as I suspected, the plant is pretty empty at this time. I wander around the perimeter to get my bearings and try to come up with a plan. There's an entrance marked WORKMEN ONLY around the side of the building, and I figure that's going to be my best bet. I'll pretend to be an employee.

But when workers start showing up a few hours later, I realize the fatal flaw in my plan.

They weren't kidding when they said work*men*. They're all men. Men dressed in pants and shirts and work boots. And I am very obviously a female wearing a wrinkled black dress.

I put my head down and duck behind a group of men anyway. They're carrying silver-colored lunch pails and talking about the census. It dawns on me that I don't even know what day of the week it is. A workday, obviously, but Friday? Monday? Who knows?

Vulnerability creeps into my skin. I feel so unprepared. I hate this feeling more than anything.

I duck my head even lower as I follow the workers through the doorway. My eyes are trained on my feet, and I'm not really watching where I'm going.

Which explains why I run right smack into a tall man with enough girth to put a sumo wrestler to shame.

"What are you doing in my plant?" the man growls.

I meet his gaze. One eyebrow is cocked to the sky, and he's peering down at me from a very red face.

"I work here." I straighten myself. It's something they taught us at Peel. Standing up straight asserts authority even when you have none. Which is what I have in this situation. None. Less than none.

The man's eyebrow raises even more. "Since when?"

"Today." My voice is loud.

"You one of Bessie's girls?" he asks.

"Yes." I have no idea who Bessie is. Hell, she could be running a prostitution ring for all I know. But if telling him I'm a part of it means I can stay in the plant, then I'll pretend to be a hooker. Emphasis on the word *pretend*, of course.

The man's left eyebrow lowers to meet his right. "Bessie's girls don't enter through this door. They go in through the front. Turn around and go back to the main door."

My mind races. What if I go back to the main door and they won't let me through? That will make two entrances that are blocked for me. There can't be that many more doors in and out of this place.

"I'm already late." I give a sheepish smile. "Is there a way through from here?" And then I blink my eyes a few times because it strikes me as something Yellow would do, and Yellow seems to have no problem getting what she wants.

The man grunts but jerks his head toward a hallway to my left. "That's the main hallway. It'll take you to the entrance. You know where to find Bessie from there."

I fly down the hallway and pick up the hem of my dress to prevent from tripping. The hallway ends in a lobby of some sort. There are a number of men standing around, so I slow myself and wait. I close my eyes and try to listen to their voices.

Male voices run together in my mind. Deep. Some of them have the distinctive North Shore accent, and some of them don't. I squeeze my eyes and concentrate.

One voice floats above the crowd. It's lighter than the others.

Not as masculine. The voice stops speaking, then starts again. I peer into the lobby and look at everyone. There are a lot of conversations going on, but I zero right in on the one I'm listening for.

The speaker is a short, thin man wearing a three-piece suit. His wildly curly hair peeks out from under a top hat, and . . . hang on a second. I stare at the man's hands. They're small. Delicate. I look at his feet. Same thing. That's not a man at all.

That's Eta. Pretending to be a man.

I squint. Eta is white. Violet is not. I guess I never really stopped to think about this before. Just then, a man with white hair and a white beard strolls into the lobby and extends his hand to Eta. She takes it, shakes it firmly, and then she follows him down another hallway.

I need to see where they're going.

I take a deep breath and step out into the lobby, then walk across it like I own the place. Confidence can get you anywhere.

Except when it can't.

A big arm reaches out to stop me halfway, and a man in a gray, three-piece suit with a gold pocket watch chain pinned to his vest stops me. I have no idea who he is, but from the way he's looking at me, I think it might be a good guess that he does actually own this place.

"Who are you, and where are you going?"

I bow my head at him. "I'm one of Bessie's girls, sir."

"Are you now?" He draws himself up tall.

I do the same. Two can play at that game. "I am."

"Then you wouldn't mind if I escorted you to Bessie right now so she can confirm your employment."

Shit.

"Actually, I'm supposed to be with them." I nod my head down the hallway as Eta and the group of men get farther and farther away from me. But then they stop at what looks like the last door before the hallway curves to the right. They all file into a room.

"That," the man says, causing my head to snap back to him, "is a financial meeting that I'm certain doesn't concern you."

"I'm . . ." I'm what? *Think!* I say the first thing that pops into my head. "I'm to make sure your guests are well accommodated, Mr. Thomson." The name is a complete guess. I'm at the Thomson-Houston Electric Company, so I just threw it out there. But from the way the man's lips press together and his chin tilts down, I instantly know I've guessed wrong.

"My name is Bauer," he says with a telling look. "Now, since you've clearly been here before and are in my employ, I'd like for you to lead the way to Bessie."

And I'm done for.

But then a girl right about my age strolls into the lobby. A floor-length black dress hangs off her skeletal frame, and she's wearing a long apron and a lacy cap that looks like something I wore with a Halloween costume when I was five. She meets my eye, and I instantly read her. She has meek, little mouse written all over her, from her timid expression to her hunched shoulders; and I pounce like the lion I need to be.

"She knows me!" I cry, pointing to my mouse. "She can confirm I work here."

Bauer turns to the girl, and his face dawns with recognition. "Annie, know this young lady?" His arm flies in my direction.

I stare at Annie and raise my eyebrows at her, hoping I'm being both persuading and intimidating.

"I do, sir," Annie says. "She's new."

Bauer brings his hand to his chin and takes a long breath. I can see he's mulling over the whole thing—deciding whether he wants to be a hard-ass and press me on this or just let it go—and I bow my head to him like Annie did. Sometimes winning means knowing when to submit.

Then Bauer pulls out his pocket watch and takes a quick glance before tucking it away. "Very well then." He turns and starts down the hallway after Eta and the other man.

I wait until he's out of range before turning to Annie. "Hey look, I really appreciate what you—"

And then I stop. Because I have completely neglected to realize how the parable of the lion and the mouse ends. But it's clear Annie hasn't. My meek, little mouse has fire in her eyes.

"That's going to cost you," she says. "I don't know who you are or what you want, but unless you want the coppers hunting you down, I suggest you pay up."

"I don't have any money," I say. It's partly the truth. I don't have any *1890s* money.

Annie clicks her tongue and takes a step back, eyeing me from head to toe. And then she zeroes in on my wrist. On my bracelet.

"No," I say. *No.* She can't have it. It's the only thing I have left connecting me to Abe, to my past.

"My brother's a cop," she says. Brother sounds like *bruddah.* "In Boston. He'll hunt you down."

He won't, actually. I'll be long gone by the time he gets word.

But that doesn't change the fact that Eta is right down the hallway and I'm wasting time.

My hands are tied. I slip the bracelet off my wrist and squeeze it tight in my palm before I hand it over. Annie smirks, and I want to punch her. But I don't. I take off down the hallway.

Annie follows me. I hear the triumphant *pat pat pat* of her buckled shoes on the wooden floor behind me.

There's a rolling cart with a sterling pot, several teacups, and a platter of pastries and rolls outside a door. Male voices echo into the hall.

Jackpot.

I pull the car closer and place my hand on the doorknob, but Annie steps in front of me and grabs the cart handle. My charm bracelet slides down her wrist, and I tense my shoulders.

"I'm supposed to service the meeting," Annie says.

"Yeah, well, now you're not. So let go of the handle or I'll break your wrist." I'd like to say it's an idle threat, but I'm not so sure.

"My *bruddah*—"

"Is a cop. Yeah, I know. Screw your brother." I'm sure she's probably never heard my modern-day insult before, but her narrowed eyes tell me she's caught the gist. "Now *step aside*."

She stares at me for a few seconds before raising her wrist and flicking it back and forth to make my bracelet jingle. Then she gives me a smirk and backs up to let me pass.

I take a breath. *Focus on what's important,* I remind myself. I swing open the door and take hold of the cart. "I suggest you make yourself scarce," I hiss to Annie.

I duck my head as I roll in the cart. I don't think Eta will know who I am, but you never know. Alpha sure knew everything about me from childhood. Maybe Eta will, too. I keep my head down and peer up out of the tops of my eyes. Bauer sits at the head of the table, and a number of men line each side. Eta sits in the middle, on the right side, in front of the window. I can feel Bauer glare at me as I push the cart past.

"I suppose my main question," Bauer says, "is why you're interested in investing in the company now. Why not seven years ago when we first started?"

I settle into the corner of the room and turn my back to everyone as I pour tea into the cups. That's a really good question. I want to hear Eta's answer.

Eta smiles politely. "I'm sorry, I was under the impression I was to meet with the president of the company."

Bauer's lips press together. "Mr. Coffin is unavailable today. I assure you I am well prepared to hear your proposal. Now why are you just offering it today?"

Eta pauses for several seconds, then her shoulders relax and she leans forward and rests her forearms on the table. "My company has not been around for seven years," she says. "We only started last year, making investments in those companies we feel have real potential but could use a greater financial backing. Thomson-Houston Electric is such a company."

She's lying. But why? Thomson-Houston Electric doesn't even stay Thomson-Houston Electric. At one point it becomes General Electric, and . . . oh. There it is. It all comes back to money, doesn't it? Invest now and reap a huge reward when GE really starts booming.

I set down the teapot and steady myself. Corruption wafts

through the air and threatens to choke me. I feel dirty right now, and no amount of scrubbing will wash away the truth.

Someone clears a throat. "Tea?" Bauer asks his guests in a tone that makes it clear I need to serve it already.

My head snaps up, but I don't turn to look at him. I nod with my back to him and lift two teacups. My hands are shaking as I carry the saucers and set them on the table before Bauer and the man to his right.

Bauer drums his fingers on the table and cocks an eyebrow. "And what sort of investment are you proposing?"

I grab two more cups and set them on the table, then start back for the last two.

Eta clears her throat and folds her hands on the table. She's trying to act confident, but from here I can see her foot tapping rapidly under the table. "It's all outlined in our proposal," she says. "We provide you with one hundred thousand dollars in capital, and in return we get a minority-ownership interest."

Which she can then sell for a ton of money someday in the future, no doubt.

I set a teacup in front of Eta, and she doesn't even glance in my direction. And so I stand over her and stare. Some crack operative she is. Disgust creeps up in my throat like bile. She took an oath. To her country. Did it mean nothing?

Did it mean nothing to my dad?

I want to kick over the cart and run from this room, but so far I haven't learned anything that will help me identify CE. And I'll be damned if I gave away my bracelet for nothing.

Bauer clears his throat again. "Does anyone take their tea with milk and sugar?" He's staring right at me with a pointed look.

I snap out of it and scoot around the edge of my cart to get back to my tray.

"I'm terribly sorry," Bauer says to his guests. "She's new. It's as if she's never served tea a day in her life."

Out of the corner of my eye, I see Eta's head snap up and over to me. I turn my back to her and pretend to busy myself with the milk and sugar. I can feel Eta's eyes boring holes into my back. Does she suspect anything?

"Well," Bauer continues, "I am a man in a rather enviable position. My initial investors were good to the company, so good that I don't have to say yes to your proposal by any stretch of the imagination. So tell me"—I hear him flip over a stack of papers—"what other investments has Eagle Industries made recently? Why should I trust you?"

Eagle Industries. Who is running Eagle Industries? Come on, Eta, tell me.

"Well—" Eta begins.

"Milk and sugar," Bauer says.

I grab the creamer and the sugar dish and set it on the table in front of Bauer, then I return for the plate of pastries. I use the silver tongs to place one on the edge of everyone's saucer.

Eta clears her throat. "I am uncomfortable naming the other business deals in which we've recently taken part. You would grant my company some level of privacy, would you not?"

Bauer waves his hand in the air. "And I've seen nothing in your proposal that details exactly who makes up . . . what was it?" He flips the paper again. "Eagle Industries?"

I hold my breath.

"Nor will I tell you," Eta says, sending my hopes crashing

down to the ground. "For it is unimportant. What is important here today is that I have a great sum of money that I wish to invest in your company. If you tell me no, as is perfectly within your right, then I can certainly take my money elsewhere. Perhaps to Edison."

Bauer juts his chin in the air and stands. He extends his hand across the table to Eta, who rises to take it. "I will take your proposal under advisement and get back to you within the week."

Eta nods. "Thank you, sir. It was a pleasure meeting you."

"Likewise."

And with that Bauer spins and marches out of the room. The rest of the men follow, save for Eta. So much for tea service. I bend my knees and pretend to fiddle with a stack of plates on the bottom shelf. Disappointment washes over me. I don't know anything about the men who make up Eagle Industries. Nothing. I pray Yellow finds out more, because Paris just isn't an option unless we steal some money, which is way too risky. Not to mention illegal.

I hear Eta's footsteps at the door. She hesitates for a second, and I wonder if she's looking at me. Hoping I'll raise my head. I pick up the six plates on top of the pile and move them to the bottom, then I stand and brush a few crumbs off the top shelf into my hand. She's still standing there. She has to be looking at me.

And so I turn, though I keep my head bowed. "Is there anything I can get for you, m—sir?"

My stomach lurches. I almost called her ma'am.

Eta looks at me, and I keep my eyes trained on the floor like a timid baby bunny. But I do glance toward the table. Bauer took those papers with him. Of course he did.

"No," she finally says. She tips her hat at me. "Have a good day."

I nod to her and turn back around. I don't take a breath until the door has shut firmly behind her. I don't bother clearing the table. Instead I wait. I want to give Eta enough time to get out of the building. I could follow her, but I don't see the point. It's not like she's going to head back to Annum Hall while mumbling under her breath the names of all the people who make up Eagle Industries.

But then I hear voices. Two of them, both female, getting louder. I freeze.

"She threatened me, ma'am!" an hysterical voice wails. "I think she means to harm Mr. Bauer!"

Annie.

Bitch.

I whip out my watch, set it to Christmas Day 1963, and disappear. I land in the same empty meeting room, but it's changed. A lot. Gone is the massive wooden conference table and velvet-backed armchairs. In their place are a shiny white table with metal legs and beige leather chairs. The wood floor has been covered with a pea-green carpet.

For a second I wonder whether Annie is still alive. Whether she still has my bracelet. Then I shake my head. *Let it go.* I have more important things to do.

There weren't cameras outside, but I'm not going to gamble that there aren't any in the hallway. I hurl a chair through the window, drop a twenty on the table to cover some of the damage, then think better of it and pocket the cash. I feel bad, but I don't want to hitchhike back to Boston.

Yellow is already there, pacing back and forth in front of the reflecting pool. A few people amble around, but for the most part the plaza is empty. It's Christmas morning, after all.

"It's about time," Yellow says. Her hair is stringy and greasy. There are big black bags hanging underneath her eyes. And she smells like a public bathroom. I raise an eyebrow at her.

"What?" she says. "It took me two days to get to DC and back. Have you ever tried sleeping on a bus?" She cracks her neck left and right. "But that's not important. What did you find out?"

I sigh. "Not much. You first."

"I didn't do any better." Yellow hesitates for a moment. "It was your dad," she finally says, confirming what I already knew deep down. "He went to a secret congressional meeting about the Manhattan Project."

"The development of the atomic bomb?"

"Yep. Early stages. Your dad said he was from some company and wanted to invest in the development."

Every hair on my arm stands on end. "Eagle Industries," I whisper.

Yellow opens her eyes wide.

"Same thing with my mission. It was Eta, like you thought, wanting Eagle Industries to invest in a power plant that eventually gets bought out by General Electric."

"Did Eta say anything about who was behind Eagle Industries?"

"Nope." I blow out my breath. "Did . . . my dad?"

She shakes her head. But then a thought hits me.

"CE," I say. "What if the *E* stands for *eagle*?"

A lightbulb goes off on Yellow's face. "And the *C* stands for *Cresty*," she practically shouts. "Cresty Eagle! Do you think that's someone's name?"

"It's a really awful thing for a parent to do to a child if it is a name," I say. "Maybe it's a kind of eagle?"

"Only one way to find out." She trots away from the reflecting pool and looks over her shoulder. "Come on, the library is only a few blocks from here."

"And it's Christmas Day," I say.

Yellow skids to a stop. "Crap. We have to project."

I tense my shoulders, then release. Pain still lingers in all my joints and muscles. I would kill for a hot bath and two ibuprofens. But she's right. We have to follow this lead, and there's no following it here.

"Let's go forward," I tell her. "I'm done with 1963."

We go forward two weeks, to January 8, 1964. It feels at least twenty degrees colder. A bitter wind whips off the bay and through the city, and my teeth chatter as we run down Huntington Avenue toward Copley Square. The streets are crowded this morning with men and women bundled in wool coats and scarves and hats, staring in disbelief at two teenage girls running down the street without any protection from the cold.

Yellow makes a left onto Dartmouth Street, and I follow. We race up the steps to the library, zipping past the statutes representing Art and Science, and run through the open metal gates. My shoulders are pressed up into my ears, but I release them as the heat of the building crawls under my skin and starts to warm me.

I look up, and time stands still. Apart from the woman next to me wearing a swing coat and cat's-eye glasses, this building looks exactly as it did the last time I was here. It never ceases to take my breath away. Yellow and I are silent as we climb the great marble steps that lead to Bates Hall. Two massive marble lions leer at us on the landing, and Yellow and I exchange a glance.

And then we're in Bates Hall. A barrel-vaulted ceiling runs the length of the room, which is at least two hundred feet long, and the ceiling itself has to be fifty feet high. Long tables with wooden spindled chairs fill the center of the room, and green banker's lamps set on each of the tables wash the room in a rich, elegant glow.

Yellow is unfazed. She leaves me standing there, gaping at the ceiling, and walks up to a man sitting behind a desk. I watch out of the corner of my eye as he stands and leads her to a shelf. He points at it, then returns to his desk. I look over at her, and she jerks her head toward the shelf.

The man has led her to a section all about birds. She's scanning the titles at the top, so I kneel on the marble floor and scan the titles at the bottom. My eyes stop on two red books on the second-lowest shelf.

I pull volume one of *Eagles, Hawks and Falcons of the World* off the shelf and hold it up. Yellow nods and sits in the end chair at the nearest table. I take the seat next to her and hold my breath. She really does smell of something rank. At least her arm wound appears to be healing all right.

The book has eagles in the front, and it's alphabetical. I flip past a number of pictures and statistics on my way to the Cs. Both Yellow and I draw in our breath on page thirty-seven. Because there's an entry for the crested eagle.

My eyes fly to the picture, and my breath catches in my throat. The bird that stares back at me is small, and a mop of what looks like tangled curls sits atop its head. Like a hawk with a bad perm.

My mind flashes back to Testing Day. To graduation. To the pin that Headmaster Vaughn wore on his lapel. It's the same bird.

CHAPTER 26

"Wait," Yellow whispers. "Your former headmaster is behind Eagle Industries?"

"He's definitely involved somehow. Whether or not he's behind it I really don't know."

"How old is he?"

"Huh?" I say it louder than I'm intending. A man looks up at us from the next table and glares.

"Your dad," Yellow whispers. "He called him 'Old Cresty.' How old is old?"

"Oh," I whisper back. "I don't know how old he is. Pretty old. Grandfather old? In his seventies?" That's a total guess. "He was a CIA operative for a really long time, then a division chief before he came to Peel. And he's been headmaster for a while. At least two generations."

"Two generations to gain influence in all the government organizations. CIA, FBI, NSA . . ."

"And all the other ones we don't know about."

"Annum Guard," Yellow whispers.

"Annum Guard," I repeat.

Neither of us says anything for a while. Yellow stares down at the picture of the crested eagle, and I look out the window as the snow falls on Copley Square. I know Yellow is trying to figure out what to do now, and I should probably do the same. But all I can think about is my dad. Maybe this really wasn't his fault. Maybe Headmaster Vaughn corrupted him early on. And maybe—just maybe—if we go back and stop the headmaster before he has a chance to worm his way into Annum Guard, we can prevent my dad's death.

"We have to go to Peel," I whisper.

Yellow shuts the book then looks up at me with a blank stare.

"We have to stop this at ground level, just like with the Gardner." I put my hands on my hips and stand up straight. "We can't bring this information to the authorities. Both of us are on the most wanted list in the present."

Yellow leans back in her chair and continues to stare at me. Her gaze is intense. I'm sure it would unnerve most people, but I'm focused right now.

"We're going back to 1982," I say. "We're going to stop Vaughn before he has a chance to start."

Yellow has a confused expression. "What?" And then her face settles into understanding. "Your dad was at Peel then, wasn't he?"

I push back the chair and stand. It makes a scraping sound on the marble floor, and every head in the room looks at me. I walk toward the door, and I hear Yellow follow behind me.

"Iris!" she hisses when we're on the stairs.

I stop on the landing and turn. The marble lion looms overhead.

"What about Alpha?" Yellow says. "Are you just going to keep making up new enemies in your head until we figure out a way for your dad to live? You can try to deny it all you want, but I know that's what you're doing."

I don't deny it. I deflect it. "You don't think Vaughn is an enemy?"

"I don't think he should be our top priority right now, no. We need to bring all the information we've discovered to Alpha's boss."

"Yeah, that's a genius plan. Alpha's boss is the *secretary of defense*."

Yellow crosses her hands over her chest and glares at me.

I narrow my eyes. "Fine. You do it your way, I'll do it mine. Project to the present and march yourself through the Pentagon demanding to see the defense secretary. Have fun with that. I hope you enjoy prison. I'm going to stop Vaughn, which is going to stop Alpha, which, yes, just might save my dad."

Yellow narrows her eyes right back at me. "You are the most frustrating person I've ever met. Will you just listen to me?" Her voice echoes through the entire library, and the woman in the swing coat tears up the stairs toward us. Yellow holds up her hand to her. "I'm sorry!" She flashes her most innocent smile. She does have that virtuous-naivete thing down pat.

The woman adjusts her glasses and gives us an icy glare as she holds her finger to her lips, but then she turns and leaves. Her kitten heels click down the steps.

"Look," Yellow whispers. "I'm not opposed to going to Peel. It's the only lead we have right now, and we need to follow it through. But I'm not going to follow you blindly without any sort of plan just so you can resolve your daddy issues."

I take a breath. I want to lash out, tell her I don't have any unresolved issues, but that would be the biggest lie told since I was drugged and blindfolded on Testing Day. My head is swimming. Bits and pieces of information are flying through it, and I'm trying to grab on to anything that might make sense.

I take another breath. "There's a chance that Vaughn recruited my dad when he was still in school, right?"

"I guess."

"My dad graduated in 1982. If we go back to right before he graduated, then that's our best shot of figuring out whether Vaughn was already using him. We need to find some sort of physical evidence if we want any chance of being believed. I don't think our word is going to go very far."

"It's not," Yellow agreed. "Not with all the damage control Alpha is doing in the present. He's completely discrediting us."

"So we go back, find something concrete, and we'll figure out how to get it to the proper authorities. That's the best plan I can come up with right now."

Yellow takes a minute. I can see her processing what I said. Her eyes flick back and forth as she thinks. Finally she nods her head. "Okay. We go back right before graduation, 1982."

I nod back. I don't tell her the obvious wrinkle, that I have no idea when Peel's graduation was in 1982. It could have been an early graduation, like mine was, or it could have been a later one, like in May. Or anytime in between, really. It's a total crap shoot. We just have to pick a date and hope for the best.

"How's February 25 sound?" I say.

"Cold," Yellow says.

We project to 1982 inside the library's basement bathrooms. Warmer that way.

"How much money do we have left?" I ask Yellow.

She counts it. "Enough for two bus tickets and some really, really cheap clothes. And after that we're totally screwed unless we start stealing. I can't believe we stayed at the Parker House. What was I thinking?"

"Let it go, Yellow." I shrug. "We can always bet on football games we already know the outcomes of."

"Which is what I like to call stealing."

We take the T from Copley to Park Street, then hit up Filene's Basement. Yellow hands me twenty bucks and tells me it's all I'm getting. I find a pair of light-wash, tapered jeans and a really ugly lavender sweater on the clearance rack. But the sweater is thick and oversize and will keep me warm, along with the puffy blue jacket I also manage to find squeezed in between two shirts. The total comes to $19.82, which wakes me right up. It's like a sign or something.

The bus leaves out of South Station. I slide into the window seat and lean my head up against it. It's a cold, gray day in Massachusetts. Snow has turned to slush, which crunches beneath the big bus tires. I stare at the dead trees whipping past us, and I can't help but think of my dad.

I'm going to see my dad. A seventeen-year-old version of my

dad. A dad who's my age. A dad who may or may not have already started down the road of selfishness and corruption. Butterflies flit around in my stomach. I wish there was some way I could convince him not to even join Annum Guard in the first place. Or I could—

I sit up straight as the thought hits me. Oh my God. Yes. I could do that.

I look over at Yellow. She's slouched down in the seat and has her head resting on the seat back. Her eyes are closed. My teeth find my bottom lip, and I decide to let her be. I still need to think things through. My head isn't exactly clear right now.

The bus stops in front of the old corner store a quarter mile from Peel's campus. My heart is still bouncing around in my stomach as we walk through the woods.

"I'm nervous," I say. "I'm trying to hide it from you, but my hands are trembling; and do you see that tree over there? That's where Abe kissed me for the first time ever. I'm about to walk into a fountain of memories, then add my dead dad to the mix, and I'm scared shitless that I'll blow the whole thing."

Yellow squeezes my shoulder, which makes me jump. She pulls her hand away. "Sorry," she mutters. "But you're not going to blow this. I think you're like physically incapable of blowing anything."

"Oh, so should I not tell you about what happened at that tree over there?" I point.

Yellow looks at me with shock.

"That was a joke!"

But she's already grinning so hard that she can't contain it, and then she collapses into a fit of giggles. I tuck my head down and laugh, too. Just a little at first, but then so hard that it hurts to breathe. It hits me that I've forgotten how good it feels to laugh. To completely let go. I look at Yellow and see a similar realization on her weary face. She's really come through for me. I misjudged her big-time.

Peel comes into view. There's a guard at the gate, and I pull Yellow out of view.

"Can't we just slip the guard a twenty to get us in?" she asks. "It will pretty much wipe out the rest of our funds, but if it's going to get us in, I'll part with it."

"Only if you want to pay twenty bucks for the pleasure of getting arrested. Come on, there's a way in around back." Or, rather, a way for students to sneak out, frolic in the forest, and buy beer at the corner store. It's supposedly been there for years. I'm pretty sure the administration knows about it, but no Peel kids have ever gotten into serious trouble on any excursions, so they allow it.

There's an eight-foot evergreen hedge that runs the entire perimeter of the campus and an iron gate on the other side, but I know where to go. Right to where there's a small hole in the hedge and the iron bars are bent enough that most kids can fit through them.

I go first, and Yellow follows behind me. We're way back in the corner of campus. Right in front of us is where the maze was set up on Testing Day. Well, *will be* set up. Many years from now.

We stick to the perimeter rather than cut across the wide, open field. There's no one around, so I guess classes must still be in session. I look down at my watch. Nearly eleven thirty. Assuming they haven't changed the schedule, we have about twenty minutes to kill until the lunch bell rings and everyone fills the quad on the way to the dining hall. Headmaster Vaughn will be among them. He always eats with students, sitting up there on his dais looking down at us. I think it was supposed to make us feel nervous. It did.

We reach the quad, and my heart lifts for just a moment before crashing into my toes. Peel looks the same. The exact same. A wall of ivy snakes up Archer Hall, the dorm where I spent two years and a couple months of my life. The looming oak trees are bare now but come summer will provide a canopy of shade. Sidewalks crisscross in perfect order. It's almost as if I never left. I half expect the bell to ring and Abe to trot down the steps. We'll eat lunch together and swap physics homework.

Stop.

I force Abe out of my mind. This isn't a homecoming, it's a mission. Maybe the most important mission ever in the history of Annum Guard.

The bell rings and echoes across campus. I stand up straight and look all around as kids wearing the same Peel uniform as mine pour onto the quad. My eyes dart from the science building to the math building, over to the humanities building. I look for Vaughn. Not my dad. I really don't even know what my dad looks like. My only memories come from the two pictures at home and the one in Alpha's file. No, I train my eyes on the administration building. Any second now Vaughn will come waltzing down the steps and walk toward the dining hall.

A lock of hair falls in my face, and I flick my neck to bat it away. And then—shit. I see my dad.

He's coming out of the government building. He's holding hands with a girl who is very clearly not my mom, and he's smiling and laughing. My heart stops. Stops beating in my chest. Because there he is, clear as day. He has the same crooked nose as in the picture in his file. The same floppy haircut. But mostly I know it's him because of my heart. The heart knows.

"Have you seen Vaughn yet?" Yellow whispers beside me, then she turns. Out of the corner of my eye, I see her head whip from me to my dad. "Iris. Is that your dad?"

I choke out a breath and nod.

"Iris." Her voice is soft, sad.

My legs start walking. I don't mean for them to. They just do. "I just . . . I have to . . ." I don't finish the thought. I don't know what the end of the thought is.

Yellow doesn't follow. At least I don't hear her behind me. I'm looking straight ahead, watching my dad run two fingers under his collar, unbutton his top button, and loosen his tie. He drops the girl's hand, and she plants a kiss on his cheek and takes off for the dining hall. My dad watches her go.

I can't take my eyes off him. He's so young. He looks like he belongs here. A student. My body doesn't know how to feel. My stomach is nervous, but my heart is lifted. I'm light-headed, but I'm thinking clearly. My legs are tingly, but my feet are strong.

My dad is right there, two feet away from me. A real, living human being. I clear my throat, and he turns around. His eyes grow wide with surprise, as if he can't believe a nonstudent managed to break into one of the country's most secure government training schools.

"Who are you?" he asks.

His voice. It's different than it was at the Kennedy assassination. The day he died. His voice isn't rushed or frantic. It's as smooth as silk, yet warm and inviting.

"My name is . . ." Amanda. My name is Amanda. I'm your daughter. "Iris."

"How'd you get in here, Iris?" He looks beyond me, toward the dining hall. I turn my head and peer over my shoulder. Most of the kids are filing inside, but there are a few stragglers, mostly guys, standing around watching us.

"I know about the hole in the hedge and the bent bars," I say.

My dad makes this face that I only assume is his stern face. The stern face I never got a chance to see. But I can change that. I can change that right now by telling my dad what I know. So why am I hesitating?

"It's not important," I say.

My dad's eyes flick over to the dining hall, then back at me. "Look, do you need me for something?"

I take a breath, ready to open my mouth and spill out everything. How I know that he is going to leave Peel and someday join Annum Guard. How Headmaster Vaughn is going to pay him to go on certain missions. How he's going to die on one of them. How it is absolutely critical that my dad plays it straight and clean.

And then my dad's face changes. He looks right into my eyes— the same shape and color as his own—and recognition dawns on his face. I see him struggling to put two and two together.

THE EIGHTH GUARDIAN

"Do I know you?" he asks.

I'm going to lose it. I'm not this strong. I want to leap into my father's arms and have him hold me, to make up for all those scraped knees and wounded souls he wasn't there for.

Yes! my mind screams. *Yes, you know me! You made me. You left me. Please don't leave me. My mother is sick, and I can't take care of her. You're the only one who can. She needs you. I need you.*

But the words stay firmly entrenched in my mind, never making it to my lips. Because deep down, this is wrong. It feels all wrong. I can try to pass off my motives as being for the good of the world, but they're not. They're purely selfish. I'm doing this because I want my dad back. I want to grow up with a father. And a mother who's not sick. I want a normal life.

But no matter how much I may want and wish for that, I can't have it.

"There's been a mistake." It comes out barely louder than a whisper. "You're not who I'm looking for."

But my dad doesn't turn away. "I'm sorry, but you look really familiar. You sure I don't know you?"

I'm about ten seconds away from losing it. "I—" My voice cracks. "I don't know you." I whip around and fly down the stairs toward Yellow, and there is the absence of everything. No sound. The scene before me goes fuzzy. I can't even remember why I'm here.

Then a door slams, and I'm brought back.

"Julian!" my dad calls in a loud, happy voice.

"Hey, Mitch, who was that?" another male voice says from behind me.

"I don't know," my dad says. "Some girl named Iris."

Yellow's eyes get big, and I look over my shoulder. She gasps. I gasp. Because my dad is standing there talking to a teenage Alpha. An Alpha who apparently went to Peel. And an Alpha whose memories now include a weird teenage girl named Iris showing up at school one day with something important to say to my dad.

"Iris!" Yellow yells, and my head snaps to her.

I race toward her. "Project!" I yell. "Now! This is going to be an ambush!"

CHAPTER 27

We don't even get the chance to pull out the watches.

POP!

POP!

POP!

"No!" Yellow screams. We bump into each other as we run. Run away from Orange and Green and Violet.

POP!

POP!

POP!

Three more forms appear in front of us. Blue. Indigo. And who's that? A male form is crouched on the ground, his hands over his ears and his head ducked. It's someone new? They added a new member? And then I stop running.

I know who it is. My heart leaps up into the clouds and dances on air because I didn't destroy his future. He's here. Alive. But then it falls crashing back to earth because now I know they've got him.

Before I can make a move, we're surrounded.

Click! Click! Click! Click! Click! Click!

Six gun barrels being locked. Not tasers. Not paintball guns. Real guns.

"Oh, what, you're going to shoot us?" Yellow screams as she throws her hands in the air. "You're all being lied to! Every one of you!"

I'm looking at Orange, but I pivot around on my heel to find Abe. His eyes are waiting for mine; and the moment they meet, he lowers his weapon, and my heart soars.

"Abe!" My feet leap forward, and before I know it, I'm running to him.

Abe raises the gun again. "Iris, stop!"

I skid to a halt. He called me *Iris*. And his eyes are distant. As if they see *through* me, not at me. Alpha's got him. I blow out a breath, blow out my shock. Somehow Alpha got to Abe. Did he threaten him? With what?

"Abe, talk to me! Say something!"

He doesn't look at me. He's still looking through me.

"Abraham!" I yell. "I know you. I know about Ariel."

I start toward him again, but he raises the gun higher with his right hand, so I stop.

"I didn't," he says in barely more than a whisper. There's hurt and bitterness emanating from those two simple, hushed words, and my heart aches. I want to hold him, kiss him, tell him that we'll figure it out together. But then Abe's face changes. It contorts into anger. "Why didn't you tell me?"

"Because I didn't know either!" I yell. "Abe, why are you here?" I hold up my hands and take short, easy steps toward him.

"Iris, what are you doing?" Yellow shouts. "You're going to blow this."

I turn around. Yellow's panting and sweating and staring at me with big, scared eyes. She runs toward me, and then a million little things happen at once, and I don't know how to process it all. Yellow opens her watch face as she runs. She turns the dials. Orange leaps at her. Everyone else runs. Green grabs my arm and yanks it back. But then.

But then.

A deafening blast fills the air. A gunshot. Just one.

And a scream.

"Yellow!" I shout. Green lets go of my arm and gasps. There's chaos. Everywhere. I can disappear now. I can close the watch face lid and disappear.

Except Yellow is lying on the ground, bleeding from her abdomen, and my boyfriend is standing there watching it all.

I'm not going anywhere.

Indigo pushes past me. "Oh my God!" He drops to her side. "Elizabeth! Oh my God! No! Who did this?"

For a second we all forget that we're no longer allies. We glance around. And all our eyes lock on Blue—on Tyler Fertig—who still has the gun raised and both hands gripping the handle.

But then he drops his hands. Only for a second. He lifts his right again and brings the gun to his temple.

"No!" I shout. I don't think. I leap at him and pull the gun down and away before he can do it. But he squeezes the trigger as we fall, and another shot rings out over the trees.

Blue and I thud to the ground. He looks at me, and I look at him, and then his head ducks into his chin and rises and falls as he lets it out. All of it. His failed hopes of escaping his fate. His mother. I reach and touch his shoulder, but he bats my hand away and sinks lower into the ground as if he's willing it to open up and swallow him whole.

"Elizabeth!" Indigo screams again. "We need to help her."

No one moves. "The mission was to kill or capture," Orange says. His voice is empty, methodical. What the hell did Alpha do to everyone?

"She's my sister," Indigo yells. "*Our* teammate. She needs help!"

Two shots have gone off on Peel's campus now, and the doors to the dining hall swing open. Teachers run out first, but students are right behind. I don't try to look for my dad.

Chaos erupts again. I jump up and back as Violet scrambles toward Blue and everyone else rushes to Yellow. Abe doesn't move. His eyes lock on mine.

"Back to the present!" Orange yells. "Everyone!"

But I've already set my watch. And I have no intention of going back to the present. I know what I have to do. I doubt anyone is manning the trackers back at Annum Hall right now. I take a running start and slam my watch face shut. But as I do, I jump at Abe and grab his wrist.

And then the two of us are torn through space and time, and I'm taking the pain for both of us. High-pitched shrieking invades my ears and burns my head. I scream as I'm shot up. All of my weight pushes to my heart. The pressure. I can't take the—

I land on the ground in a heap. I'm shaking and crying, and I think I might be dead.

"What the hell?" Abe yells. "How did I get here?"

I open my eyes and make myself breathe.

"You brought me here?" There's astonished awe in his voice as he whips around, looking everywhere. "How did you do that?"

I push up and suck in my breath. This isn't the present. This is the date I set on my watch. There's a rickety wooden tower in the corner of campus, overlooking a plywood maze that was slapped together just last night. I can't see it, but I know there's a dropping device set up over the pool. And inside the government building there's a fake detention room with a faulty sprinkler system.

"This is Testing Day," Abe says. "You brought me to our Testing Day."

"I know." I stare at the gun still in his hand.

"My watch is set to present day."

"Abe, I brought you with me for a reason."

"My name isn't Abe anymore, *Iris*." He emphasizes the last word, making his point.

"My name is Amanda," I spit. "Look around. My name is Amanda. Your name is Abe. Right now, you and I are lying with our arms wrapped around each other in a corner of the dining hall. I'm telling you that I have an awful, sinking feeling about tonight. You're telling me not to sweat it. But I'm freaking out because deep down I know that this might be the last time I lie in your arms for a while. Maybe even forever. Because I know. *I know*. I'm being drafted tonight."

Abe doesn't say anything. He looks straight ahead, and in this moment he's a stranger to me.

"Abe, talk to me. Tell me why you're here."

He keeps his head trained on the maze, but his mouth opens.

"To get you back."

"Why? Why you? Why are *you* here, Abe? Why aren't you—" I wave my hand in the direction of the dorms—"*there*? Sleeping. Right now in the present."

"They took me." He wrings his hands in front of his body. "They showed up at Peel and took me. They told me you were committing treason and were hatching a plan to bring down the entire government. They knocked me out, then told me a bunch of crap about how my grandfather—Ariel—could time travel, which meant my dad could do it, which means I can do it, too, and then they threw me back here and told me to go get you."

I shake my head. *No.* There's more. There has to be more. "Have you talked to Ariel?"

"I haven't seen anyone! I haven't talked to anyone! I just have to bring you back. I have to bring you back, Iris. I have to."

I think Abe might cry. His voice is shaking, and his hands are trembling. What did they do to him?

"My name is Amanda," I tell him. "Stop calling me Iris."

"Please, it makes it easier." He squeezes his eyes shut for one brief second, but it's enough to tell me that he's completely lost focus.

"I don't know what they told you, but they're lying to you, Abey Baby," I whisper.

Abe lets out a little choke and raises the gun. His face is

twisted. Pained. "Please don't call me that. I have to take you back. Iris."

They've gotten to him. I know they have now. Alpha must have something in his back pocket, but what?

"Please talk to me," I say. Behind us, a gong sounds. Someone has just finished the maze. "What did they do to make you hold a gun in my face? The Abe I knew would never do that. The Abe I knew would throw *himself* in front of a gun barrel if he knew I was in danger."

"I've changed." His voice wavers, just a bit, but enough.

"Bullshit! What did they tell you, Abe? What did they do to you?"

"They took her, okay?" he yells. The gun falls to his side. "They took her, and she's sick, and she needs to be at home, and they won't give her back until you're caught."

I shake my head. "Took who?" I have no idea what Abe's talking about. The only female in his family is his mother, and she's fine. Perfect health. Unless something changed while I was gone. "Are you talking about your mom?"

"Not my mother, my grandmother!"

I shake my head again. "What? Your mom's mom? But you barely know her. She lives in Israel. How would Alpha have gotten—"

"No!" Abe shouts. "Mona! They took Mona!"

I feel as if I've been punched in the gut again. Mona's dead. She died from lung cancer several years ago, before Abe and I met. But—I suck in my breath—

And then I blink.

I blink again.

I grabbed a cigarette out of Mona's hand in 1962. Me. I did it. I threw it on the ground. I told her Ariel would never go for her if she smoked. Did she stop after that day? Because of me?

"Abe, does Mona smoke?" I ask.

"What?" His body shakes. "Why are you asking me this? Of course she doesn't. You know she doesn't."

"Did she ever?"

"No! I don't know! As long as I've been alive, I've never once seen her with a cigarette."

I changed the past. I went back and saved Mona's life. The weight of this realization sinks in, and I feel dizzy.

"She's sick now?" I ask.

Abe gets a disgusted look on his face. "Really? What, you conveniently forgot that she was diagnosed with Stage IV lymphoma a week before Testing Day? A week before this?" He waves his hand at the maze.

I crane my neck toward the buildings on the other side of campus. Somewhere over there, there's another version of me. A version of me who knows Mona. Who was heartbroken by the diagnosis. Who's loving and comforting Abe as best she can.

And somewhere, Alpha is walking around this campus, pretending to evaluate all the students while really just foaming at the mouth because he's so close to taking me. To using me.

"Abe, we have to talk," I say. "They're lying to you." I look around for Alpha. I don't see him.

"How do you know?"

"Because they lied to me, too!"

"Why would they lie about my grandmother? That doesn't make any sense!"

"Because they're using you! Will you shut up and listen to me? Tell me, who told you about your grandmother?"

"Alpha."

"Only Alpha? Did anyone else actually confirm that she was taken? Ariel? Your dad? Your mom? Anyone?"

Abe's face betrays the answer. No. No one. He violated one of the cardinal rules of information, which is to always confirm when the source is shady. He knows better. Dammit, he knows better!

"Abe, Alpha's corrupt, and he's using the entire organization to make a quick fortune; and you know who his biggest investor is? Headmaster Vaughn. They're both the reason my father is dead. I ran because I found out the truth, and the truth is that—"

But then a tree branch cracks behind us. I whip around. Oh God! Please don't let it be Alpha!

It's not. It's Katia Britanova. The sophomore who lives in my dorm. The girl who escorted me to the dining hall after all my testing was completed and who overheard Alpha talking about me.

Katia's eyes shoot up, then she looks me up and down. "Amanda! What the hell are you wearing? And what are you doing here? I just dropped you off at the dining hall like ten minutes ago." And then her eyes zero in on the gun Abe's holding. Abe sees her staring and tucks the gun behind his back. "Why do you have a gun?"

"We were just practicing," he says. "In case there's another secret test. They didn't really emphasize gun work in this one—"

"So you're cheating." Katia jerks her neck back and juts her chin in the air.

I raise my hands and take a step forward. "I know this probably looks bad, but I promise you we're not cheating. At anything. And right now, I need you to turn around and walk back to campus. I need you to pretend you never saw Abe and me here. You don't understand."

"You're cheating," Katia says. "And you know the honor code. Both of you do. I have to turn you in for this. I have to take you to the headmaster."

Shit!

Abe whips the gun up and points it at Katia.

Double shit! What is he doing?

And then Katia swoops down and grabs a knife from the holster she always has strapped to her ankle.

Triple shit! Oh, this is not good. This is not good at all.

Katia stares Abe right in the eye. "Go ahead and try." She tips the knife at him. "I guarantee you I'm faster."

I step in between Abe and Katia and hold out my hands, one at each of them. "Okay, here's what we're going to do." I turn my head to Katia. "You're going to drop that knife"—then I look at Abe and give him my best pleading stare—"and you're going to drop that gun. Now, on the count of three. One. Two. Three."

No one moves. No one drops anything.

"I told you," Katia said. "I'm bound by the honor code to take you to the headmaster. And I'm going to do that."

"Abe, drop the gun," I say. "Katia, the knife. Come on, guys; it doesn't have to come to this."

Katia jumps. She kicks the gun out of Abe's hand. He screams and clenches his fingers, but she's already grabbed it.

"Headmaster," she growls. "Walk."

I have a choice. I could fiddle with my watch and get out of here. I'm no one's captive. But where am I going to go? How long am I going to run? I don't have a plan, and Abe has no idea what's going on, and dammit all, I start walking.

"I never knew you were such a bitch, Katia," I mumble. It's a cheap shot, but I'm pissed. Mostly at myself. Katia's doing the right thing. The thing she *has* to do. Peel's honor code is strict. If you catch someone cheating, you turn them in. If you don't and it's discovered later, you're out on your ass, too. No second chances.

Katia ignores me. She marches Abe and me toward the administration building.

"You know we're screwed, right?" I whisper to Abe. "Completely and totally screwed. Even more so if Alpha sees us right now."

"Stop talking," Katia says.

"Oh, shut up, Katia," Abe tosses over his shoulder. "It's not like you're going to bury that knife in my back if I don't."

"Abey, you have to listen to me," I whisper. "You really, *really* didn't know Ariel had anything to do with Annum Guard?"

Abe looks at me and shakes his head.

I crane my neck around toward Katia. She's staring me down, so I turn back around. "I didn't know about Ariel either. Or my own family. Was your dad a part of it?"

"My dad's a corporate attorney. You know that."

"But is he really?"

"Yes," Abe practically growls. "Unless the boxes of contracts and licensing agreements he pours over each night are a part of the world's most document-intensive cover."

Suddenly it all makes sense to me. Ariel broke the chain. He didn't want his son—his only son—to join Annum Guard. He must have known the havoc Chronometric Augmentation would wreak on his body, which is why he almost never projected himself. That's why he's the only survivor, and that's why Abe's dad never joined. And why Abe never knew about it. I gasp. And why Alpha was brought on during the second generation. The numbers were down to six.

I whisper my theory to Abe, leaning in close to make sure Katia doesn't hear.

"No whispering!" Katia says.

Abe ignores her. "How do I know you aren't lying?"

I feel as if I've been slapped. "When have I ever lied to you?"

Abe sighs. It's long and sad, the kind of sigh I've heard from him before. "I'm sorry. I'm just . . . I'm so confused. I don't know who to trust. Who to believe."

"Yes, you do." I reach over and squeeze his hand.

"No touching!" Katia snaps.

Abe drops my hand. "Hey, remember that Practical Studies class with Missy Garvin?" he whispers.

I nod my head. Of course I do. Freshman year. Missy Garvin was assigned to tail me. And when I say she tailed me, I mean she *tailed* me. She never got more than three feet from me. It was annoying as hell. So I took care of it. It's one of those moments I'll never forget. One of those moments I'm going to relive now.

I whip around and fly at Katia. My elbow connects with her ear, and my other hand grabs her wrist. I twist the knife out of her hand, and it falls to the ground.

"I'm sorry!" I yell as she groans.

Katia jumps up and raises her fist to punch me, but Abe grabs it, then grabs her other one and holds her hands over her head.

I fiddle with my watch. "Where do we go?"

"The present," Abe says. "We end this right now."

I nod my head. I don't like projecting without a plan, but this is the best chance we've got. We're two now. We're two again. We can do this.

Abe spins Katia around and pushes her away, then grabs my arm. I close the watch face, and Abe and I tear through time.

We land back in the present day. I gasp and open my eyes. And then I gasp again. Alpha is standing right there in front of me, dressed in a tailored suit that must have cost thousands. Wonder where he got the money. Red is behind him, wearing a button-down with the sleeves rolled up. I take a second to note the large tattoo on his forearm. The good old stars and stripes intertwined with another flag, this one made up of three blue stripes, two white stripes, and a white star centered in a red triangle at the hoist.

I look beyond Red, but no one else is here.

And then Abe grabs both of my wrists. I let him.

"I got her!" he yells. "I did what you asked. Now let my grandmother go."

Alpha laughs. "Not quite yet." He nods his head at Abe. "Let go of her and step away."

I feel Abe squeeze my wrists. And then he lets them free.

"The traitor returns," Alpha says. His hard face is relaxed and even. Real. It's as if he's convinced himself that I really am a traitor. Maybe he's a psychopath.

"I figured out your little notebook," I tell him.

"Did you now?" His voice is calm, but I see a flash of panic in his eyes.

"Yep. I know the truth. I know who CE is." I jerk my head to the administration building, then I turn my attention to Red. "My father was Delta, you know. I'm one of you. I was born into this. There is no experiment. Or did you know that already, too?"

"Lies!" Alpha seethes. But his hands tremble. I catch sight of them before he shoves them behind his back.

"Did you also know that Alpha is taking kickbacks on every mission he can sell?" I ask Red.

And then for a second—one short but important split second—Red's training fails him, and his eyebrows creep up a few hairs. That tells me everything. Red doesn't know.

And then I look at Alpha. I trusted him. I thought he was on my side. But he never was. Ever. He lied to me; he lied to Abe; he lies every time he opens his mouth.

"You're going to prison," I tell him. "And I can't wait until I get to testify against you."

Alpha laughs, and I can hear his nervousness, can see him struggle to compose himself. "Oh, Iris. My dear, sweet, *powerless* little Iris. You know why I gave you that name, don't you? Iris, the mythical goddess of the rainbow. I saw in you the potential to be a leader, to take charge of all of Annum Guard." Red stiffens. "But now I see that you take after another Iris. A dainty, delicate flower that can be crushed in the palm of my hand."

"You don't give me enough credit."

"No, I give you too much credit. I thought you were strong. I thought you were like your father." Red stiffens again. "I was mistaken. You're not your father's daughter. You're your mother's daughter. Weak. Unstable. Completely detached from reality."

His words are worse than a slap to the face. My head reels back, and I want to pounce. I don't. But Abe does. He lunges at Alpha. But Alpha grabs something from his waist and points it at Abe. I scream as Alpha's wrist flicks, and Abe crumples to the ground. *NO!*

I drop beside him and grab his hand. My head spins, and I look for his wound. I need to stop it. I pat my hands all up and down his chest. Abe groans. I need to find it. I need to apply pressure. I need . . . wires. There are wires. There wasn't a shot. Alpha didn't shoot him. He stunned him.

"Red," Alpha says, "take her."

Red doesn't move.

"I said take her!"

"Was her father a part of the Guard?" Red demands. "I need to know if there's any truth in what she's saying."

"No, what you need to do is to follow orders when I give them. Now take her."

"He was!" I shriek as Abe writhes on the ground next to me. "My father was Delta. He met Alpha here at Peel, and together the two of them hatched a plan to start making money off all the missions. It's been going on since before I was born. Probably since before you were born, Red."

"Where's your proof?" Red shouts, his chin jerking up in the air.

"She doesn't have any," Alpha says. He takes a step over to me, then yanks me up and pushes me toward Red. His hands tremble. "Because there isn't any."

"I've seen it. Yellow has, too." Oh God, Yellow. Please let Yellow be okay.

Red draws in a breath through his nose. He's trying to take it all in; I can see it. He looks from me to Alpha, then back to me. And then he reaches a hand to his earpiece and mutters, "Whiskey Oscar Lima Foxtrot."

I don't know what that means, but judging from Alpha's reaction, Red believes me.

"No!" Alpha shouts. He lunges forward, and Red pushes me behind his shoulder. Alpha raises the taser again, and Red brings up his hand to block it. But the sputtering sound rings out again, and Red screams as he drops to the ground.

I jump back. My heart thumps in my chest. And then Alpha turns to me.

He's straining to keep it together. His eyes dart from Red to Abe to me. He drops the taser to the ground, and for one brief second my heart leaps as I think Alpha's going to surrender to me.

The second is short-lived.

Alpha unhooks a gun from his holster and raises it. I don't flinch.

But Alpha does. Because just then there's a distant sound in the air. *Whup whup whup whup.* I know that sound. I don't have to look up. It's a helicopter.

Alpha's head snaps up toward the sky, then down and over at Abe. "Red!" he yells.

The Black Hawk is getting closer. I can see men dressed in

black hanging out of the doors. And they can see me. And Alpha. And the gun he's pointing at me.

Alpha lowers the gun and takes off running across campus. I scream and stare up at the helicopter. It's still too far away. They won't be on the ground for at least a minute. That's giving Alpha too much of a head start, so I take off running. It's stupid. He's armed; I'm not. But I can't let him get away.

Alpha darts through the quad just as class is letting out. Kids spill out onto the sidewalks. I don't look at them as I run past.

"What the—?" someone shouts. "Is that Amanda Obermann?"

I ignore it. Alpha zips into the science building. I'm only a few steps behind. I rip open the metal door with such force that it bangs against the brick exterior. I don't see Alpha. I stop. Listen. Footsteps above me. Hard, heavy footsteps clomping up the stairs.

"Stop running!" I race up the stairs. In the landing, I see him. He's thundering down the hall, heading toward one of the chem labs. He ducks in and slams the door, and I go barreling in after him.

"When are you going to give up?" I shout as I fling open the door. "You're—" I stop. He's standing right in front of me, and there's a gun pressed into my forehead. I blow out the rest of my breath.

"Hands up, please," he says. "And don't try to grab the gun. I'm anticipating it."

I raise both hands slowly. The gun in Alpha's hand doesn't waver as he stares at me, and my mouth goes bone-dry. People have pressed guns into my head before, but always in training. Never for real. I swallow.

"Don't do anything stupid," I whisper.

"I'd give you the same warning," he says, "but it seems we're a bit late for that. Take off the watch."

Not good. That watch is my only means of escape.

"Now." He punctuates the word. I keep one hand raised as I lower the other one and slip the chain over my head to hand the watch to him. "Thank you," Alpha says, then he waves the gun back, ordering me into the room.

Alpha shuts the door and points the gun toward the nearest stool. I keep my hands up as I lower myself onto it. I scan the room even though I know it. I had a class in here. There are three rows of long tables, each with six stools behind them. There's a whiteboard at the front of the room and cabinets at the back.

"Where's the notebook?" Alpha demands.

"In a safe place." I try to keep my voice as calm and flat as I can. Because the truth of the matter is that I have that notebook tucked into the back of my jeans, and I can't believe in this moment that I have it with me. So stupid.

"You're going to need to get it."

"No problem." I smile. "Just let me go, and I'll fetch it for you right away."

Alpha doesn't blink. "Nice try," he says, but I know that he's at a crossroads, same as I am. He needs that notebook back so he can destroy it. And I need to keep holding on to it.

Alpha walks over to a Bunsen burner set on the first row of tables. He switches it on, and it sputters a second before the smell of propane wafts toward me and a blue flame flickers up and sends my stomach plunging into a frigid ocean of fear.

"Do you want to do this the easy way or the hard way?" Alpha asks. His voice is changing. There's desperation in it.

I don't answer. I stare at the flame.

"Where is the notebook?" Alpha barks.

"I don't have it!"

And then before I know what's happening, Alpha grabs me and yanks me to the first row. His fist clenches around my wrist, and I turn and scream and kick; but he has me pressed against the table, and I can't move. My hand lowers toward the flame, and the heat pricks my palm. Tears roll down my face and I choke.

"Why?" I sputter. "Why are you doing this to me?"

And then the flame goes out, and the Bunsen burner goes crashing to the floor. It clatters against the linoleum. He unhands me, and I stumble back, gasping and panting and shaking.

Alpha raises the gun and points it at me, and I flinch. But only for a second. Because then I look at his eyes. Something's changed. They're still dangerous, but now there's fear and resignation lurking behind them. I need to act.

I raise my hands so that they're chin level and slowly extend my right. "Give me the gun."

Alpha doesn't lower the gun, but he also doesn't put his finger on the trigger.

"Please give me the gun," I say. "My dad wouldn't want this."

Alpha blinks but doesn't say anything.

"You and my dad were friends," I say. *Right up until the point you had him killed.*

I stare at Alpha's hand. The one holding the gun. Waiting for any sign, any moment of hesitation or relaxation.

"I never meant . . ." Alpha's eyes shift from me to the side, and I take my chance. I leap at the gun. I grab on to it and try to force it down, but then Alpha snaps back to attention and twists away from me. He raises it to my forehead, and I suck in my breath.

"Stop it!" he yells. "I told you I was anticipating that!"

"You don't want to hurt me," I whisper. "I know you don't."

He doesn't respond, but I know I'm right.

I think of the hostage negotiation training I had right here on this campus and choose my words carefully. "Tell me what happened. Why you got mixed up with this in the first place. I'm sure it's not your fault." It's a lie. He's totally to blame. But I need him on my side.

"I can't fight them," Alpha says. "They're too dangerous."

Yes!

"*Who?* Who's too dangerous?"

"XP."

Chills race up my arms. "Who is XP?"

Alpha shakes his head, as if he's trying to snap himself back to being the collected, professional, authoritative figure I've always known, not this man who's on the verge of breaking.

"I'm not dragging you into it."

"I'm already in it!"

"Not like this." And then he lowers the gun. He's still staring at me, and for once I see the glimpse of a different man. A man who's regretful. A man who knows he's defeated. I hold out my hand for the gun. He waits—staring, reflecting—and then he starts to hand it to me.

"What the hell are you doing, Julian?"

The door opens behind me, and Alpha retracts his hand and

jumps back. I whip my head around to see Headmaster Vaughn walk in. His silver eyebrows rise when he sees me. "Hello, Amanda."

He's a man I used to admire, someone I used to want to emulate. He fought in Korea. He was a spy during the Cold War (well, this is unconfirmed but highly rumored). He was a close adviser to two presidents. He treated his students with dignity and respect. He listened to us. Counseled us.

But all along he was buying the past, and now he's standing here before me, not even trying to deny it.

"Hello, Cresty," I say.

Vaughn's mouth creeps up into an amused smile. "Amanda, dear, I know we've trained you better than that. I've seen your transcript."

"What, don't antagonize the enemy?"

"No, don't be stupid in captivity. It could get you killed."

With those words, everything fades away. The truth floats through the air and settles in my lungs. Vaughn is a bad man. A very bad man, and this situation is very real and very dangerous.

"Sit down," Vaughn tells me.

"Don't sit down," Alpha says, the gun hanging to his side. He turns to Vaughn. "It's over. Can't you see that?"

"Nothing is over," Vaughn says coolly. "You're in this until the end. You knew the terms when you took the deal."

"I want out," Alpha says.

"Do you now?"

The two men stare at each other with such ferocity that I forget to breathe. This is a standoff to see who's going to blink first. Vaughn does.

"Very well. Have it your way."

And then I know what's going to happen. I open my mouth to scream, but before a sound can form on my lips, Vaughn has reached into his shoulder holster, and there's a Glock and a shot and Alpha crumples to the floor. Vaughn kicks Alpha's gun out of his hand and sends it spiraling across the floor. It bangs against a trash can.

A scream is out of my lips before I can think. He was going to surrender; I know he was! I sway to the side and slam into the table. Vaughn grips his gun with his right hand and yanks my shoulder with his left.

"Shut up!" he says as he pushes me into a stool. "I told you to sit down."

I lower onto the seat and look at the table. Not at the floor. But I can still see Alpha lying there in a puddle of red out of the corner of my eyes, so I close them.

"Start talking," Vaughn orders. "I want to know everything you know. And please don't insult me by lying. I spent thirty years training intelligence officers and then students to lie. I'm going to know."

He's right. I'm so dead.

Vaughn gives me a pointed look. "Talk!"

"I found Alpha's mission ledger. I figured out how to decode it."

He nods. "Mmm-hmm, very good. Now where is it?"

"It's in a safe place." That's not exactly a lie.

"We're not playing games right now," Vaughn says. "You are going to tell me where that ledger is, and I am going to go get it."

"And then what?"

"One step at a time." Vaughn sets down the gun and places both hands flat on the table.

I slide my hands into my lap and then up on the underside of the table. I'm feeling for anything I can use as a weapon. A metal joint. A loose screw. Hell, even a sharpened pencil would be better than nothing. My hands feel something. A valve. And a tube. This is the advanced chemistry lab. And I mean *advanced*. So that means—

"Hands on the table," Vaughn says. Dammit. Of course he would notice. I yank out the tube without moving more than a millimeter, then I place my hands flat on the table and touch the valve with my knee. I shift in my seat a tiny bit to see if it will turn. It does.

"Where is the ledger?" Vaughn repeats. "You have thirty seconds to tell me."

I don't ask "or what?"; I shift again and turn the valve on full blast. This is either the most genius idea I've ever had or the decision that is sure to send me to an early grave.

"I'll tell you where the ledger is if you tell me one thing." My voice shakes. Dammit. I take a quick breath.

Vaughn raises an eyebrow but doesn't respond.

"Why did you have Kennedy killed?"

Vaughn's mouth creeps into a smile. "Not the question I thought you were going to ask. I thought you were going to ask if I ordered that your dad be killed on the mission, and for the record, the answer to that question is yes." I don't blink. He's trying to throw me off guard. He is. My insides collapse into a puddle of anguish, and I feel vomit rise in my throat.

"Answer the question!"

Vaughn clucks. "You're in no position to be making demands, Amanda."

"I think I am. You want to know where the ledger is, and I'm willing to tell you. You just need to—"

"Because!" Vaughn yells. "Because Kennedy needed to be taken out if we were going to go into Vietnam. Kennedy negotiated a withdrawal in 1964. We needed Johnson to rush us into the Gulf of Tonkin and escalate the conflict. I knew Eagle could make a fortune off a war, so I studied the conflict, read the necessary classified documents, and made an educated guess."

I blow out a breath. "You killed a president on a guess?"

"An educated guess," Vaughn says. "Which turned out to be correct."

I'm dizzy. I sway to the side and fall off the stool. My hands are on the floor, just inches from where a pool of blood begins. Vaughn just told me everything. He has no intention of letting me escape here alive.

But then a loud roar of voices erupts in the courtyard below. Vaughn is over at the window in a flash. I know that he sees them. The backups. The men from the helicopter. They must be storming the building as we speak. But I don't have time to wait for them. Vaughn aims his gun at me and cocks the trigger.

"I wouldn't do that if I was you," I say as I push up. "You see, I turned on the hydrogen valve, so the gas is slowly seeping into the room. You do remember what happens if you mix hydrogen, oxygen, and fire, right?"

Vaughn looks at me with disbelieving eyes, and he's at my side in a second. He bends under the desk to check, and I don't think. I raise my elbow and bring it back down onto his neck.

Vaughn falls to the floor, and my training tells me to make sure he stays down, but my instinct has me scrambling to the door. Vaughn hops up and yanks me back. I swing. I connect with flesh. My hands and knees hit the ground. The ledger falls out of my back pocket. I gasp. Vaughn gasps. He pushes me out of the way and lunges for it. I grab on to his head and push him back. But his arms are longer. His fingers close around it. And then he pushes me to the ground as he rises.

I fly across the room to the trash can. Alpha's gun is sitting on the floor next to it. I grab it, cock it, and aim it at the hydrogen valve.

"Drop it!" I order.

"You shoot that, you kill us both."

"Don't think I won't do it."

"That's exactly what I think."

A door bangs open down the hall. The backups! Vaughn rushes to the window. He's going to jump! He's going to escape.

I don't think. I squeeze the trigger, and the room erupts in a burst of flames. My body is picked up and hurled back. I slam into the door, which opens, and I drop to the ground in the hallway. Black boots rush toward me. The world spins overhead. A voice I recognize. Abe. Abe is here. He's over me, screaming and touching my face, and that's the last thing I remember.

CHAPTER 28

I come to in the back of an ambulance. It feels as if someone took a hammer to both of my temples. The door to the ambulance is open, so I see it's parked in the middle of Peel's quad.

"Hey," a voice breathes next to me. I don't have to look to know who it is.

"Abe," I whisper. "What happened?"

Abe's face appears over mine. He looks older to me. There are dark-blue bags under both of his eyes and dirt caked on his face. No. Not dirt—smoke. The explosion. I suck in my breath as it all comes back to me.

"Alpha?" I ask.

Abe presses his lips together. "Dead."

I close my eyes and squeeze them as hard as I can. "He tried to surrender to me. He . . . he seemed truly sorry." Life's not black-and-white. Nothing ever is. There are very many shades of gray that litter the spectrum. Alpha wasn't on the white side, but he wasn't on the black side either, I'm starting to realize. Somewhere in there was a man who got caught up in something he couldn't control. And while what he did is unforgivable, I did see glimpses of the man he could have been had he made better choices. I open my eyes and look at Abe.

He's quiet for a few seconds. "If it's any consolation, Vaughn survived. He's pretty banged up, but he'll live to answer for his crimes." Then Abe's face changes. "Close your eyes!"

I obey without question, and several moments pass before Abe finally says, "Clear."

I open my eyes and raise an eyebrow.

"Investigators. Dozens of them. State and federal and higher-ups that you would not believe. They all want to talk to you. I figure you want to be left alone for a little while."

"Talk to me?" I ask. "You mean interrogate me?"

"Probably."

"It's still my word against Vaughn's, isn't it?" I squeeze my eyes shut. "Nothing's changed."

Abe's fingers interlace with mine, and he brings one of my hands to his mouth and kisses it. "Everything's changed. They found a notebook by Vaughn. Half of it had been burned but the other half had a bunch of numbers and dates in it, and they're trying to figure out what it all means. Plus, Annum Hall is probably being torn apart as we speak. Vaughn's the one under investigation now, not you."

I think of what Alpha said before he . . . before he died. One of his ramblings. *XP knows*. XP. I wonder if that's related to Vaughn and Eagle Industries. It has to be. Why else would Alpha mention it? I wonder if XP is anywhere in that notebook.

Suddenly there's a voice outside the ambulance. A crotchety, no-nonsense voice.

"I don't care that you don't want me in there; I'm going in there. Now stand aside."

Ariel appears in the back of the ambulance.

"Abraham, help me up," he says. Abe extends his hand to his grandfather and pulls him up into the ambulance. And then Ariel's warm, familiar arms are around me. He's holding me so close it's like he's my own family. And I realize that he is. He is my family. He always has been and always will be. I wrap my arms around him.

"You came through for me," I say.

"I did." Ariel sits up. "And I also failed you. I knew who you were the second Abraham called and said he'd met a girl. I knew and never told you. You were right. I knew the Guard was going to take you, although I had no idea they'd take you so soon." He looks at Abe now. "I knew where she was, and I didn't tell you." His old eyes are sad, regretful.

"You didn't know what Alpha was up to." Abe says it like a fact, not like a guess.

"I did not."

"Maybe I should have told you in 1963." My voice is weak. My mouth is dry. I swallow. "Maybe you could have stopped Alpha from the start. Maybe then my dad—"

"Let your father go," Ariel says. "I didn't want you to tell me about the past, because I didn't want it to influence my future behavior. And I'm glad you didn't tell me, because now I've been able to watch the organization unfold over three generations; and there is no doubt in my mind that I no longer believe in it and will fight to shut it down."

"But you founded it!"

"When I was very young and very naive. Back when I thought changing the past was the right thing. I no longer think it is. There's a reason I never let my son join, as well as a reason the president himself received a phone call when I found out they'd taken Abraham."

Abe takes my hand. "But I'm in the Guard now. If Amanda is in, I'm in."

"No, you're not," Ariel says. "You're done, and you're going back to school, and you're moving on with your life."

"Grandpa!" Abe protests.

Ariel squeezes my hand again. "I can't make that call for you. But I hope you'll make the right decision." Then he stands up as much as he can in an ambulance and backs his way to the door.

"We're not done talking about this!" Abe throws at his grandfather.

"Yes," Ariel says as he climbs down, "we are."

Abe's head whips back to me, and he leans down close. "I meant what I said. If you're staying, I'm staying."

"I don't know what I'm doing," I whisper. It's the truth. My head is spinning in a million different directions. Between Alpha and Yellow and now Ariel and Abe, and I just want it to stop. I want it all to stop.

"Abe, I don't know if I can do this."

He takes my hand. "If it's what you want, I'll help you. We'll both be Annum Guard together. And if it's not what you want, we'll both be CIA together. And if you're sick and tired of everything, then we'll just go be normal together. Go to college. Get a place together someday. You and me."

Once upon a time that idea would have filled me with excitement. But now I don't know. I don't understand anything anymore.

"Abraham!" Ariel's voice booms from outside the ambulance. "Now!"

Abe squeezes my hand. His eyes are moist. "I'll find a way for us to be together. It will happen, Amanda. It will."

I nod my head. Tears are forming in my eyes, and I don't know how to hold them back. Abe lets go of my hand, breathes a good-bye, and disappears from the ambulance.

And then the tears fall. I don't try to stop them. I cry for my dad, for my mom, for Yellow, myself, even Alpha. And especially for Abe. It's as if the universe doesn't want us together, and I don't know how long I can keep fighting it.

Abe's gone. He's gone. And I don't know when I'll see him again. Whether I'll ever see him again. I choke.

"Abe!" I yell after him.

He doesn't respond. But someone does. Many someones. And then the secretary of defense, the director of National Intelligence, the National Security adviser, the FBI director, and the vice president all squeeze into the back of the ambulance and shut the door.

CHAPTER 29

I don't go back to Annum Hall. I don't want to. I'm so tired. I lost my leader, then my boyfriend, and maybe even my friend. I went through a whole night's worth of questioning. It's seven in the morning, I haven't slept since Dallas, and I don't want to contemplate anything: Vaughn, CE, XP, the charred notebook. I just want to go to Mass General. So I do. To the reception area.

"My friend was shot," I tell the very no-nonsense woman with frizzy hair sitting behind a computer. "I need to find her."

"What's her name?" the woman asks as she places her fingers over the keyboard.

I open my mouth, then close it. Because I don't know. Somehow I'm going to doubt she's here under "Yellow." But then I remember Indigo's anguished screams piercing the sky. The name he called her. The name he yelled over and over again.

"Elizabeth," I say. "Her name is Elizabeth."

"Elizabeth what?" the woman asks in this totally annoyed voice.

"I don't know her last name."

The woman takes her hands off the keys. "I guess you guys aren't very good friends then, are you? I can't help you without a last name."

And now I really have to restrain myself. I'm tired. I'm sore. I've lost almost three months of my life. I've lost my boyfriend. My father. My father's friend. Everyone. Everything. I have no idea if Yellow is all right. I'm ready for a release. I clench my fists.

"Iris!"

My head pops up.

"Indigo!"

I push off the desk and run over to him. I run right into his arms, and he wraps them around me and holds me tight.

"How is she?" I ask, my mouth pressed into his shoulder.

"She's okay." Indigo's voice is hurried, scared, exhausted, all in one. "They had to rush her into surgery to repair the damage, but she made it through."

"I'm so sorry," I say. "This is all my fault. Yellow getting shot. I should have stayed when I found out the truth. Then no one would have chased after me and no one—"

Indigo holds a finger to my mouth. "Stop. None of this is your fault."

"But—"

"None of it." He steps back and looks me in the eyes. "Your dad really was Annum Guard?"

"Yes," I say.

"I always wanted to believe you were right. I think deep down I knew it. You're a good person. You wouldn't do all those things Alpha accused you of doing. All those months we were tracking you, I was actually hoping we wouldn't find you. That you'd just disappear and go be free and happy somewhere."

"There was never freedom and happiness. Not until I ended this."

Indigo nods. "Everything's changing. I don't know where Annum Guard is going to go from here. If we'll even exist anymore. We don't have a leader. I mean, maybe my dad will take over when everything gets cleared up, but I don't know. I don't know if he wants to. Seems we're dropping like flies these days. Blue's gone."

I should be shocked. But I'm not. Blue has always been gone. Ever since he was betrayed on Testing Day his junior year.

"Tyler," I say. "His name is Tyler. And my name is Amanda. Not Iris."

Indigo waits a second and then holds out his hand. "Nice to meet you, Amanda. I'm Nick."

Nick. I repeat the name in my head a few times. *Nick. Nick.* It sounds so weird.

Beside us, someone clears a throat. Indigo—Nick—and I both turn. Zeta is standing there. He looks as if he's aged twenty years since I last saw him. His blue eyes are weary and weathered, and his hair seems less brown and more gray today. Wrinkles snake across his face. "They just moved her out of Recovery. She's awake and asking for you."

Indigo drops my hand. "I have to go." I nod at him, and he starts down the hall. But Zeta holds out his arm to stop him.

"I meant you," he says, looking directly at me. "She's asking for you."

"Me?" I repeat.

Zeta nods. "I'll show you the way."

We trudge down the hall in silence, but then a thought occurs to me. I make a dead stop, and Zeta and Indigo do the same. They turn to look at me.

"Where were you?" I demand of Zeta.

He grimaces. "1942. Sent on a last-minute mission by a very frantic Alpha that turned out to be nothing." His face contorts into a look of physical pain, and he walks away, as if standing here talking about it is too much to bear. He stops in front of the elevator, the doors open, and we file in. Zeta pushes the button for the fourth floor. "I should have known something was wrong based on his demeanor. I never should have gone. Then I would have been there and—"

He doesn't finish the thought. I look away. I'm sorry I asked. As it is, I'm sure he's going to beat himself up for years over being on a bogus mission when his daughter was shot.

We get off the elevator and are greeted by a glass door with a buzzer on the wall. Zeta scans a card that opens the door for us. And then we're in the ICU. All the doors are glass, and the rooms are tiny. I see Yellow right away. She's in the third room, lying in bed, staring at the ceiling. She looks like hell. There are dark-purple circles under her eyes, and she's whiter than the sheets she's lying. She looks up and sees me staring at her from the other side of the glass, so I slide open the door and walk in. As I do, I notice her name has been written on a dry-erase strip outside the door.

ELIZABETH MASTERS

She'll always be Yellow to me. And Indigo is always going to be Indigo, now that I think about it. I'll probably be Iris to them. It's who we are.

"Hey," I whisper.

"Please tell me it's all over. Please tell me I didn't take a bullet for no reason."

"It's all over."

Yeah, it's nowhere close to being over. The investigation hasn't even begun. But there's no need to trouble Yellow with the details now.

Yellow nods. "Good." She closes her eyes, then opens them a few seconds later. "Getting shot hurts like a bitch, in case you were wondering."

"I would have guessed as much."

"So that was your boyfriend, huh?"

"*Was* my boyfriend is right." It sounds so wrong when I say it.

"You broke up?"

"No." I think about it. "Maybe." I think some more. "No. I don't know what happened."

"Are you going to start dating my brother now?"

I turn my head to look out the windowed doors, where Zeta and Indigo are standing with arms crossed looking in. Indigo gives me a little smile, and I return it. Then I look back at Yellow. "Not a chance. Your brother's a great guy, but no. We're friends. Besides, he uses finger quotes. I could never be with a guy who uses finger quotes."

And Abe and I aren't over. Screw the universe. Screw the house. We'll find our way back together.

"Okay, good," Yellow says. "Because that would be totally weird if my friend was dating my little brother."

"So we're friends then?"

"Um, duh," Yellow says. "I took a bullet for you."

"Technically you didn't," I point out. "Blue just got a little jumpy."

She smiles. It's a weak smile, and I can tell her eyes are struggling to stay open.

"I'm going to let you rest," I say. "I'm really glad you didn't die today, Yellow."

"That makes two of us." And then she closes her eyes.

I slide the door closed behind me as softly as I can. Zeta reaches out and squeezes me on the shoulder.

"So where do we go from here?" I ask.

Zeta swallows. Then he shrugs. "You go back to Annum Hall. I go . . . somewhere for now. I'm out."

I gasp. "What? Why?"

"I'm being investigated, too. We all are, but my generation is being more heavily scrutinized than yours is." He gives a weak laugh. "My generation. I'm pretty much the only one left from my generation."

His eyes are sad, and I look away. I can't take one more sad, defeated person today.

"I'm not allowed within fifty feet of the hall until the investigation is complete," Zeta says.

I don't say anything. I look down at my feet.

"And for the record," Zeta continues, "the investigation is going to show that I knew nothing about what Alpha was doing."

I look at Zeta. He's staring at me with those scary, intense eyes. But behind them is a softness, a look of concern.

"You knew my dad," I say. It's one hell of a subject change, but I don't care.

"I did know your dad. I knew him well. Since childhood."

"And?" I say, looking from Zeta to Indigo and then back to Zeta.

"And let me make it clear to you that I didn't know you were Delta's daughter until today. I want you to know that. I'd never met you or seen a picture of you or anything like that until the day Alpha brought you to us. Your mom was fiercely protective of you, Iris. She completely cut you off from our world, and for good reason, I now see."

I swallow the lump in my throat.

"And what if I decide that I'm done with Annum Guard? That I don't want to be a part of it anymore?"

"Well, that's your choice. But I know that I'd be disappointed. You're a good addition to the Guard. We're a broken, bleeding Guard, but we'll continue."

I nod. "I want to come back." I do. I don't think I realized it until this exact moment, but I do. I'm going to go to Vermont, make things right with my mom, and then I'll be back. Annum Guard feels like a part of me. It's in my blood. It's who I am. And I feel like I owe it to the Obermann name to prove that we can do it right, without the corruption. "But what if they don't want me back?"

"Of course we do!" Indigo says.

"I broke just about every rule we have. I projected in front of people. A lot of people. I changed the past."

"Oh, of course you changed the past!" Zeta says. "That's what we do. We give you the 'enhancing, not altering' lingo in the beginning; but when it comes down to it, a change is a change.

A minor tweak has the potential to change the past just as much as a material alteration. We just try to do our homework ahead of time and make sure we're not in danger of changing the world for the worse."

"So changing the past is okay?"

"It can be."

"In that case, I need to talk to you about something. Alone. It's important."

Zeta takes a breath, then turns to Indigo. "Go see your sister."

"What?" Indigo's head whips to the glass door. "She's asleep."

"I don't care," Zeta says. "Go see her. Now."

We wait until Indigo has shut the sliding glass door behind him. Then I turn back to Zeta. "What's your security clearance like?"

Zeta raises an eyebrow. "What did it used to be like, or what is it like now? If you need sensitive information this minute, you're out of luck."

"I'm not talking about log-ins and passwords," I say. "What's your building clearance? Like, for instance, in this hospital?"

"Ah." Zeta slowly nods his head and unclips the plain white pass key from his belt that got us into the ICU. "They forgot to take this from me. I'm sure they'll figure it out any second now, but in the meantime you saw the doors it can open. I'm sure I could go observe a brain surgery if I wanted to."

I hold out my hand. "Can I borrow that for a few hours? I have some unfinished business I need to take care of."

Zeta hesitates for a second but then hands me the key. "I trust you."

I close my hands around it. "Thank you," I whisper. And then I walk out of the ICU.

CHAPTER 30

I dress a little more appropriately this time. I'm in the dress I wore for the Boston Massacre, corset and all. The corset was not by choice. I tried to lace up the dress without it, but hell if it isn't tighter than it was a few days ago. I mean, a few months ago.

Damn.

I'm going to have to get used to the fact that it's February. Not November. I slide my brand-new charm bracelet onto my wrist. My mom bought it for me. She's here. In Boston. Staying at the Omni Parker House, of all places, until a spot opens up at McLean, which has the best damned bipolar treatment program in the country. And it's only eight miles west of here.

She cried when I called her from the hospital. She's sorry, I'm sorry, and while we have miles still to go toward fixing our relationship, McLean is a start. A twice-daily dose of lithium is a start. My sincerest apology is a start. The joint therapy and PTSD counseling our government is springing for is a start. And the one charm hanging from the bracelet is the biggest start of all. It's a bird. Not in a cage. Free from the weight of its past and soaring into the future.

I've been down this road before with my mom, but this time it feels different. This time I think she has a shot. I have a shot.

I grab the edge of the dress and puff it out before slipping down the stairs as quietly as I can. Two female investigators are in the library on the computer, but they don't even glance up at me as I walk by. Perfect. It's as good as empty.

Except that it's not empty. I take a few steps, my heels *click-clack* against the hardwood floor by the stairs, and Abe sits up from behind the back of the couch.

My feet grind to a halt, and I gasp as he makes eye contact.

"What are you doing here?" I ask.

"Um, I live here," he says.

My mouth drops open. "You mean you're staying? You're going to be in Annum Guard from now on?"

"I think that's what I just said."

"But what about Ariel?" I didn't dream that, did I?

"Ariel said one thing," Abe says with a smile, "but my dad said another. My dad knows about the Guard. Always has. I guess he's a little resentful that Ariel refused to let him join. My dad thinks it's a great honor, and the physical risks aren't nearly as bad as they were a generation ago. I have my dad's blessing."

"And you live here now." I repeat the words, but my brain is having a hard time processing them.

"Seriously, were you always this bad at listening?"

I run. I pick up the edge of my damn dress and I run. Straight to Abe. I fling myself into his arms and throw my hands around his neck.

"You're here," I whisper. "You're really here. To stay."

Abe slips his arms around my waist and touches his forehead to mine.

"I thought you were going to break up with me," I say.

"Never."

I press my mouth into his. I've missed the soft feel of his mouth, the tenderness of his kiss. I don't know how long I stay there, entwined with him. For once I don't care how much time passes.

Soon enough, Abe pulls away. "What's with the costume?"

"Oh." I look down at the dress and all of its restricting layers and bones. "I have one last mission before I can put this whole experience behind me." I hold up the plain brown bag I've been clutching.

"What's that?" Abe asks.

"Penicillin I swiped from the hospital."

"Isn't that a felony?"

"Possibly," I say. "But it's for a good reason. There's a little girl in 1782 who needs this. And I promised her I'd help her. I won't be long. Wait for me?"

Abe smiles. "Always."

He slips his hand through mine and walks me to the gravity chamber. I enter the code they gave me that morning—seriously, they change the codes around here every twelve hours now, and let's not talk about how many forms I had to fill out to get this mission authorized—and the room opens to blackness.

I give Abe's hand a squeeze because I know he'll be right here when I get back. Like he promised. Like he always will. And then I leap.

Author's Note

I'm not sure how old I was when I first started figuring out that some of the history that filled my schoolbooks was a partial, if not total, fabrication; but this discovery stayed with me for a while. It even inspired many of the events in this book. I tried to stay as close to true historical accuracy as I could, but there were a few instances where I fudged the truth for the sake of narration.

In the Boston Massacre scene, I have James Caldwell and Samuel Maverick running to the location together, under the impression there was a fire. There's no indication in history that Caldwell and Maverick knew each other, much less that they ever spoke during the massacre. And while it's true that both boys probably would have assumed there was a fire when they first heard the church bells ringing throughout Boston, by the time they reached the Old State House—the location of the Boston Massacre—they had already realized what was going on and joined the mob.

But my biggest fabrication in the Boston Massacre scene lies with Patrick Carr. Not much is known of Carr's history. There's no indication that he was married with a family, so it's certainly not true that he was there with his young son. But it is true that Carr, being from Ireland, was used to political mobs and would have known instantly the danger of the situation. It's also true that Carr's deathbed account of the massacre was perhaps the most important piece of evidence in the subsequent trial (and acquittal) of the British soldiers. (Legal trivia: Carr's testimony is one of the first recorded instances of the dying declaration hearsay exception used in an American courtroom.)

Also, I tried to keep the events and timeline of the notorious Isabella Stewart Gardner Museum heist as close to accurate as I could, but I have to admit to embellishing the security system in place at the time. The museum did use electric eyes that were hooked up to alarms, but they were not audible alarms that would have rung throughout the museum. This detail was added to the book just for dramatic effect. None of the artwork stolen that night has been recovered, although the FBI recently came out and said they know who was behind the heist. As of my writing this, however, no suspects have been identified.

Next, the scene where Iris causes Senator McCarthy to miss a cab is a complete fabrication. Senator Eugene McCarthy was a real person with a long, winding (and pretty fascinating) political career, but the vote he was late for and his exact residence were fictions of my mind.

Finally, there is no indication that any member of the Dallas police force was in the school book depository at the time of the Kennedy assassination. What is true is that Lee Harvey Oswald, after killing the president and fleeing the building, encountered Dallas officer J.D. Tippitt on the street. By that time, police were already on the lookout for someone matching Oswald's description, and when Tippitt confronted Oswald, Oswald shot him four times, killing him. The police officer portrayed in this book is not meant to be Tippitt, however. This is just a bit of trivia.

Any other historical inaccuracies that might be revealed are, unfortunately, simply errors on my part.

Acknowledgments

I have just now realized that writing an acknowledgments section is harder than writing a book. So many people contributed to this story in so many ways, and I worry that I won't be able to sufficiently express my gratitude.

But I'll try.

First, thank you to my agent, Rubin Pfeffer, for taking a chance on a wide-eyed newbie, for whipping this book into shape, and for finding the perfect home for it. And to my editor extraordinaire, Marilyn Brigham, thank you for loving these characters as much I did and for polishing their story until it shone. And to this book's copyeditor, Andrea Curley: you did a tremendous job, and I can't thank you enough.

Thank you to my mom, for making me a reader, which then made me a writer, and to my dad, who made sure my early cultural education included a dash of James Bond and Jack Ryan. That shaped me more than you know. To my sister, Hilary, for being my own personal PR rep and for patiently answering bizarre medical questions without batting an eyelash. To my brother, Patrick, for sharing a love of books and writing and for helping me cultivate a thick skin with regard to the latter.

Thank you to two individuals who gave me the early encouragement I needed to try my hand at writing. My aunt, Kathy Goût, whose interest in my early childhood writings led me on this path. And my high school English teacher, Mr. Charles

Balkcom, who was the first teacher I had who recognized that, for me, books were more than words on paper and who gave me the confidence I needed to write some words of my own.

A huge debt of gratitude to my fearless critique group— Kerry Cerra, Michelle Delisle, Jill Mackenzie, Kristina Miranda, and Nicole Cabrera. You taught me so much about writing, about publishing, about *life*. And you read the very early (very rough) chapters of this story, encouraged me, and gave me a push to get it moving in the right direction. I would not be here without you.

Thank you to Susan Dennard, Jenni Valentino, Katy Upperman, and Corinne Duyvis, who read this story at various points. Your insight made it so much stronger and saved me from several embarrassing mistakes. I still cringe when I think about them.

Thank you to Greg Bollrud, who answered countless questions about MIT and who introduced me to the lore of Building Twenty.

Thank you to my FK girls, for being the world's best cheerleaders.

And finally, I could not have done this without my family. Vivian and Audrey, thank you for being the world's most patient three-year-old and newborn, respectively. And to Scott, for being my rock, my support, my plot whisperer. This book would not exist without you, and for that I will be forever grateful.

MEREDITH McCARDLE attended the University of Florida and received degrees in magazine journalism and theater. She later studied law, graduating from Boston University School of Law. Meredith spent seven years working as a commercial litigator by day and writing by night before committing to writing full-time. This is her first novel. She lives in South Florida with her family, where she is now working on the next book in the Annum Guard series.

Learn more: **www.meredithmccardle.com**.